AN
WAITING
TO HAPPEN

AN ACCIDENT WAITING TO HAPPEN

DONNA LATTANZIO

Columbus, Ohio

This book is a work of fiction. The names, characters and events in this book are the products of the author's imagination or are used fictitiously. Any similarity to real persons living or dead is coincidental and not intended by the author.

The views and opinions expressed in this book are solely those of the author and do not reflect the views or opinions of Gatekeeper Press. Gatekeeper Press is not to be held responsible for and expressly disclaims responsibility of the content herein.

AN ACCIDENT WAITING TO HAPPEN

Published by **Gatekeeper Press**
2167 Stringtown Rd, Suite 109
Columbus, OH 43123-2989
www.GatekeeperPress.com

The editorial work for this book is entirely the product of the author. Gatekeeper Press did not participate in and is not responsible for any aspect of this element.

Library of Congress Control Number: 2021949826

ISBN (paperback): 9781662921773
eISBN: 9781662921780

For Ellen, my love of thirty-four years,
who makes even the dreariest of days so much brighter.
For my parents, Terry & Dan and my brother, Danny, thank you
for your unwavering love and support.

CONTENTS

AN ACCIDENT WAITING TO HAPPEN

Published by **Gatekeeper Press**
2167 Stringtown Rd, Suite 109
Columbus, OH 43123-2989
www.GatekeeperPress.com

Library of Congress Control Number: 2021949826

ISBN (paperback): 9781662921773
eISBN: 9781662921780

AN ACCIDENT WAITING TO HAPPEN

DONNA LATTANZIO

Columbus, Ohio

OBSERVATION

Accidental death must be the worst kind of death.

Totally unexpected.

Irrational and unreasonable.

Occurring at a time and a place when people have no control of their future or their predicament.

Victims die at the hands of heart-crushed lovers or in hunting mishaps, bank heists, or as the result of terrorist actions.

There is no easy explanation for loss of life due to accidental circumstances.

All we know is that it happens.

And it happens far more often than we realize.

OBSERVATION

Accidental death must be the worst kind of death.

Totally unexpected.

Irrational and unreasonable.

Occurring at a time and a place when people have no control of their future or their predicament.

Victims die at the hands of heart-crushed lovers or in hunting mishaps, bank heists, or as the result of terrorist actions.

There is no easy explanation for loss of life due to accidental circumstances.

All we know is that it happens.

And it happens far more often than we realize.

FOREWORD

No one could have foreseen the horrific collision to come. No, neither the pilots nor the co-pilots would have been forewarned, not the air traffic controllers or the flight attendants or the ground crew. Emergency responders would be in the dark until the alarm sounded; sounded way too late for there to be an effective measure of response.

On that day, I was known as Margaret Lido, the air traffic controller partially responsible for the mid-air collision—a dreadful catastrophe reflected not of malice or forethought nor of intricate scheming. Nothing of the cloak and dagger charade that the media attempted to foster upon a very susceptible public.

I often wished for a do-over of that day. Perhaps a do-over of the lives I have lived.

Or maybe that is for you to decide.

For you to separate fact from fiction.

Right from wrong.

THE DAY TO COME

June 26, 1977

The day of the accident began like any other ordinary morning in most people's lives. An extra minute of sleep as the clock radio blared its insistent prod, the slow drip of the Mr. Coffee machine as it doled out the day's first cup. A quick shower, a fluffing of hair, a stroke of blush to pale cheeks, a dab of gloss to lips.

And then, like clockwork, came the trilling blast of music from next door. My young neighbor who deliberately cranked the music to its highest volume and caused my windows to vibrate a bungalow-distance away.

As I scurried for my purse, keys, and cigarettes, I yelled aloud, "I'm going to kill that kid!"

Outside, I jogged to my beat-up Volvo, which languished in the narrow driveway adjacent to my home. The bungalow was a rental and was perfectly located in a quiet suburb of Atlanta, not too far from the airport and directly across the street from a local train station. The hypnotic chug of the trains at night gently lulled me to sleep, and I joked to friends that it was my own personal nonprescription sleeping aid.

The day was grizzly, with mist like smoke from a witch's brew swirling through the trees and lampposts and garbage cans. On the drive to Hewitt-Jackson Airport, I managed a one-handed rummage through my purse for a small bottle of aspirin. Waiting at a red light, I dry swallowed three and hoped for the best.

Nursing an angry headache and a roiling stomach, I was furious with myself. It had been a mistake, a breach of my resolve for overindulging on a night prior to the next day's work shift. Unfortunately, I sometimes lost my resolve, and that morning, I felt the effects.

Behind me, a car horn screeched.

My normal response would have been to stare at the rear-view mirror and lift my middle finger. But because people were so crazy these days, I was not prepared to take up the fight. Not today, not in a week or even a month. Not so soon after having lost Savannah. And certainly not while the hurt remained so brazenly raw.

Savannah is—was—my best friend since we were kids. I would bicycle to her house every day after school and very early on Saturday mornings, my skinny little legs pedaling like a cyclist trying out for the Tour de France.

Savannah was a true beauty, pageant-worthy beautiful, and it was her dream to one day be crowned Miss America. But her daddy put an end to that dream early on, insisting it was "a terrible waste of a perfectly good mind."

Compared to Savannah, I was a drab-looking girl. Forgettable with my cardboard-colored hair, a gap between my front teeth, and dull eyes hidden behind ugly glasses.

Now, a dozen blasting car horns shook the memory of Savannah from my mind, and I sped the car forward.

Minutes later, I pulled into the employees' parking garage inside the air traffic control tower, followed the curve up to the third tier, parked in my designated spot, and walked to the elevator.

The headache had not abated, and my stomach flip-flopped like a dolphin performing a trick. Still, I maintained my poise and forced a smile as I strolled into the tower.

"Morning," I called to everyone in the room as I avoided the powdered donuts on the coffee cart.

I needled the shoulder of Michael Pointer, the controller who would pass me the responsibilities of Olympian Airways Flight 177, along with five additional midair flights. After a quick briefing of current altitudes and coordinates, I attached my headset, settled into the seat, and followed the blips on my screen. Absently, I waved goodbye to my tired-looking counterpart and settled in for my shift.

NOW BOARDING

June 26, 1977

JEFFREY

"Olympian Airways Flight 177 nonstop to Atlanta, Georgia, with a connecting flight to Newark Airport, is now boarding at Gate 12," came the announcement.

It is inexplicable how or why a tiny slip of time—a changed rendezvous location or a meaningless hiccup in one's schedule—might alter another's life in a catastrophic manner.

Seated at Gate 12 was Jeffrey Kaye, a quiet, unassuming twenty-five-year-old man of the garden variety type who had not budged from the hard plastic seat he had occupied for the past nine hours and forty-one minutes. Although he heard his flight's boarding announcement, he refused to spend one moment longer than necessary strapped into a too-narrow airline seat for the next six-plus hours.

Jeffrey's original flight would have placed him on a chartered flight the day earlier, the day he had deboarded the cruise ship. However, the charter's last-minute cancelation had forced him to make alternate arrangements. Unbeknown to Jeffrey, another young man had extended his own trip, which in turn had freed up a seat on the Olympian Airways Flight.

Solemnly, Jeffrey watched as a slow-moving line of weary travelers crawled past him. He scratched at his newly grown beard, a moratorium against everything that had held his life together like a dollop of Elmer's glue.

His eyes ricocheted from the line of passengers, then down to the boarding pass in his hand: a long, nonstop haul to Atlanta, which would connect to a shorter flight to Jersey, followed by a local train to Manhattan, where his mother would open their apartment door and smother him with kisses as if he were a newborn just arrived home from the hospital. A question-and-answer grilling would follow as he dozed on the sofa.

However, nothing remotely similar would happen on the 26th day of June.

Because it could not happen. Not with his changed travel plan due to the whim of a stranger.

So, Jeffrey Kaye sat there. Tired, thirsty, and still wearing his sweaty Grateful Dead tank top from the previous day. He sat there and waited until the last possible moment to board.

It was an unfortunate ending to a blissful vacation aboard a cruise ship touring the Greek Islands. Mykonos and Santorini had captured his heart. Already, he sorely missed the pretty white adobe homes backdropped by postcard-perfect blue skies and the long stretches of turquoise beach.

If only I had been able to extend the magical trip, he thought. Not that he could have afforded the trip, period. Not on his crummy salary. No way. Instead, he had been the lucky raffle ticket winner of a grand prize cruise to the islands of Greece. A raffle ticket he had purchased two months earlier at his mother's church bazaar.

"This will be the last call for passengers for Olympian Airways Flight 177," came the final announcement.

Rising, Jeffrey grabbed his heavy backpack and joined the last of the stragglers as they boarded the plane. He cautiously sidestepped his way along the narrow aisle to his seat, coming up short when he stumbled upon it at the very back of the aircraft, nudged tightly against a thin wall shared with a restroom.

Shit, he thought. His seat had him trapped between a heavily perfumed woman and an incredibly old man slouched low in the aisle seat. The old guy was asleep before take off.

From his knapsack, Jeffrey pulled out a newly purchased Dean Koontz paperback to stave off any conversation with the perfumed lady.

Besides, he was totally exhausted.

When the beverage cart finally wheeled its way to Jeffrey Kaye in Seat 32B, he guzzled a beer, then immediately fell asleep.

RUNNING

June 26, 1977

VIOLA

In everyone's life there are ups and downs. Bliss and cause for great celebration. Distress and unbearable heartache. And then there is everything else in between.

Interstate 95 North was an easy travel route during midday—that slice of time between noon and the five o'clock rush. The woman had left Naples, Florida, twelve hours earlier, had sped through Orlando and Jacksonville. Chugged past Charleston and Myrtle Beach. She was surprised that her '63 Chevy Malibu—with its nearly bald tires and wiper blades permanently stuck in the "ON" position—hadn't already coughed up its engine and died at least a hundred miles back.

All four windows of the Chevy were lowered, tumbling her hair about like a haystack caught up in a tornado. After a very long day of driving, she needed food and rest, with food winning out.

She was Viola Cordova, smuggled from Russia to the United States as an infant and deposited at a church in rural Illinois. She never knew her birth parents, only that they had perished in a Siberian work camp during the late 1940s. But she did possess a photograph of them—so young, so impressionably in love. Whenever Viola peeked at the black and white photo, she recognized her mother's high cheekbones and fair skin and her father's merry eyes in her own dazzling face.

Her papers claimed she was Varvara Pavlishchev, but her foster parents felt the name was too difficult for a child to manage. Eventually, they called her Viola, then attached their own surname to it, and there she was, reborn as Viola Cordova. She was one of the luckier foster kids, having lived with her foster family for seventeen years and properly cared for right up until the night she ran away with Bobby Lee Riggle. Back then, she hungered for independence and an escape from the drudgery and boredom of her sheltered existence.

But she and Bobby Lee had not worked out well, and neither had the other two men that followed.

She had watched the last one shrink in her rear-view mirror as she left him behind, standing dumb founded at a rest stop in Charleston.

The look on his face was priceless.

And well deserved.

CAPTAIN SPEAKING

June 26, 1977

JEFFREY

Asleep in Seat 32B aboard Olympian Airways Flight 177, Jeffrey Kaye snored gently, his Dean Koontz paperback forgotten on his lap. Four rows in front of him, a woman tried to soothe her young son, who had fidgeted and cried since takeoff. The boy's mother was completely zapped of energy.

Jeffrey remained unaware of the turbulence that wobbled the plane. His sleep was deep and warranted. The trip to Greece had been anticipated, a much-needed reprieve from the cocooned life he shared with his mother. As a single parent, she had smothered her only child with an overabundance of love, and coupled with her hovering presence, had molded him into a quiet, unassuming mama's boy.

It was because of his deep sleep that he did not hear the pilot's staccato message as it squeaked through the speakers a few moments later.

"This is your captain speaking. Please remain seated with your seat belt firmly fastened. Looks like this rough turbulence will last for the remainder of our trip. Nothing to worry about."

ABORT

June 26, 1977

As two planes taxied past, I watched as the thick mist that surrounded the airfields turned into an ugly black fog that forced the closure of several runways, which, in turn, caused serious delays. We were all mentally exhausted and stretched thin on patience.

From the windows of the tower, I watched as a flotilla of angry dark clouds sailed past like battleships headed to war. Numb and anxious, I briefly removed my headset and tried to rub life back into my stiff neck. For hours, we had not budged from our stations. I inhaled deeply, replaced my headset, and studied the console. Four departing flights and another aircraft, which was already in its descent pattern, remained my responsibility.

At 2:22, I cleared an Olympian Airways aircraft to land on runway L-23. Outside, the fog shimmied, a lone dancer on an empty stage.

The Olympian Airways jet descended, and I was certain that the captain would find it impossible to see anything beyond the brutal mass of clouds swirling around the aircraft. I dared not waiver from the blips on my screen. Moments later, I cleared a full-flight Air Com 747 to taxi into position and to hold. The pilot responded affirmatively.

When the clouds finally parted, my heart raced like a train rounding a bend at breakneck speed.

I saw exactly what the Olympian Airways pilot saw: the taxiing Air Com jumbo jet was approaching on the same L-23 runway that I had cleared for the Olympian Airways aircraft to land.

I jumped to my feet, the headset nearly strangling me. "ABORT! ABORT!" I screamed.

It was immediately clear: there was not time to abort. The Olympian Airways pilot tried valiantly to accelerate back into an ascent, but the big jet continued to careen downward and forward. The plane's left wing tilted toward the tarmac. I shrieked.

My body shook and my eyes teared as I thought of Captain Bouchard, the pilot of the Air Com aircraft, who had just become a grandfather for the first time. How he must have recoiled when he spotted the huge Olympian Airways jet bearing down on them like a ghost from the sky. He could not have had even a moment to recite a prayer as the jet sheared off the top of his taxiing plane and spiraled it into a Fourth of July fireworks extravaganza.

Inside the tower, we all felt the reverberation of the explosion from runway L-23. A fireball the size of a small skyscraper penetrated the fog as a cacophony of sounds and screams echoed throughout the tower's room.

"OH NO! NO!" voices moaned. There were screams of hysteria; someone vomited noisily.

I slumped back into my seat, sweaty and fuzzy, as if I might faint or have a heart attack.

Suddenly, every instruction, every communication I had given during my shift, zigzagged in my head. Where had I messed up? How could this have happened on my watch?

I lurched forward over my console, hands splayed on the windows. "OH MY GOD!" I screamed. "OH MY GOD!"

It was a mantra I could not stop chanting. All sense of professionalism evaporated. I was not prepared for this . . . this . . . catastrophe of my own making. How had I let this happen?

Time moved forward in slow motion as I floated on a cloud of disbelief. Suddenly, strong arms eased me from the console, circled my shoulders, and walked me away.

"It's okay, Margaret," the voice crooned. "It's not your fault. Not your fault, Margaret."

When I looked up toward the voice, I saw Jake, the senior traffic controller—a big, burly guy with a shiny bald head—sway before my eyes. He helped me to a wooden bench at the back of the room, far removed from the consoles and headsets and the dead-on view of the carnage.

Fainting or vomiting seemed inevitable. Through my sobs, I felt Jake cradle me in his big arms. He soothed me with hushed, quiet tones, much the way a father might soothe an infant.

A silence louder than any pounding drum filled the room. With my head lodged against Jake's chest, I managed to hear a great deal of foot shuffling and whispering, and I sensed discreet finger-pointing in my direction.

Finally, the fear of fainting became a reality, and I sank from the bench, grateful for the darkness, grateful to be snatched from the horrific nightmare.

CRASH LANDING

June 26, 1977

JEFFREY

Jeffrey Kaye remained asleep until the roar of the plane's brakes screamed him awake. A tremendous jolt followed, as if a monstrous bomb had exploded.

Later, much later, Jeffrey would learn that an Air Com 747 had taxied head-on to the same runway on which his plane was preparing to land; would learn that the Air Com plane had exploded on impact and had taken with it the souls of all one hundred and eighty-nine passengers and its crew.

On Jeffrey's plane, he heard the crunch of metal, the sound much like aluminum foil being removed from a hot oven. A second later there was a fireball explosion, and Jeffrey watched, dumbfounded, as the entire front section of the plane was sheared away.

The rear of the plane spun wildly, like a carnival ride gone crazy. Terrified screams pierced the air as flames flicked through shattered windows and barreled up what remained of the carpeted aisles. Immediately, the stench of burning fuel and scorched upholstery and sizzling human flesh made him gag.

Faintly, he heard a muffled moan, wondered if it was the perfumed lady next to him in the window seat. He turned to look and saw that her head was crushed like a small melon.

A curtain of dark smoke whirled before his eyes and nearly blinded him. As he choked on the fumes, the acrid taste in his mouth multiplied tenfold. Time became a slowly ticking clock—the type of slow tick usually reserved for those condemned to death.

He was afraid, deathly afraid, and the fear undulated in his belly. There was no movement in front of him. The old man seated next to him remained either asleep or he was dead.

Jeffrey's seat remained wedged up tight against the restroom wall. His basic instinct was to flee. But to where?

Inertia paralyzed him, stole his lucidness. Ahead, he saw that three, maybe four rows of fuselage remained in tact, but the seat occupants were not.

Then, from the thick cloud of smoke, as if she were an anomaly from an old *Twilight Zone* episode, the pretty twenty-something stewardess—the same girl who had welcomed him on board and had handed him an ice-cold beer—crawled along the tilted aisle, her hair ablaze like an out-of-control bonfire. Horrified, Jeffrey watched as she collapsed against a crushed passenger seat.

Jeffrey was cemented to his seat. He could not move, could not cry or pray. He was frozen. Immobile. A tow truck would not have been able to budge him.

Nearby, he heard a bellowing sound. A sound like animals about to mate; a sound which caused his bowels to clamp and to wreak havoc on his senses.

BREAKING NEWS

June 26, 1977

VIOLA

The long drive had begun to threaten Viola Cordova's stamina, and if she had to sit through one more achy-breaky-heart song, her patience would soon fray. She played with the radio knob, settled on an all-news station.

"Breaking news from Atlanta, Georgia: an Olympian Airways plane has collided with an Air Com jumbo jet at Hewitt-Jackson Airport. According to airline personnel, the aircraft collided on a runway amid heavy, dense fog. Eyewitnesses report a horrific scene of carnage and little hope of survivors. Please stay tuned for further updates."

Solemnly, Viola shook her head. This was the very reason she refused to board a plane. Never had and never would.

A few miles shy of the North Carolina border, she pulled off an exit that promised a McDonald's and a Howard Johnson Motor Lodge. She found them both a mile later. At the McDonald's, she parked, entered the fast-food eatery, ordered two cheeseburgers and a large Coke. She slid into a booth facing the front door.

Two tables away sat a man wearing a camouflage T-shirt and khakis. He shook a finger close to the face of his companion, a skinny woman with limp hair and slumped shoulders. Obviously, they were arguing, but from the look of things, the man was in serious control of the verbal exchange.

Viola watched them. Munched her burgers, sipped her Coke. As the little scene played out, she wished the woman would flee the man, run for her life just as Viola had done. After slurping the rest of the Coke, she bunched the food wrappers and tossed them into the garbage bin.

Twenty-three minutes later, she had checked into a room at the Howard Johnson Motor Lodge and, freshly showered, climbed into the not-so-soft bed.

And, as she usually did at bedtime, she wondered about her birthmother. It seemed too incredible a journey—being born to a person on one side of the world, only to be passed along to someone else, half a world away. She wondered why her parents had been imprisoned, but there was not anyone to answer the question for her.

Viola guessed that she would never know. And maybe that was a good thing.

ESCAPE HATCH

June 26, 1977

JEFFREY

Abject fear has a way of tumbling one's soul into a dungeon of despair. Just as it can collapse a willful mind and body to pure jelly. Logic melts into disbelief, rage screams in discordant volume, and the terrified mind finds it a lesson in futility to reconcile that which can and cannot be undone.

Jeffrey Kaye tried to reel in his fatalistic thoughts. As he fought to focus, he counted off the time that had elapsed since the crash; he believed it to be not more than two, three minutes at most. His seat belt had him harnessed tightly, and plumes of smoke made it impossible for him to see his fingers in front of him. Breathing became a frightening chore. He pinched his nose with his fingers to stave off the noxious fumes as he struggled to release himself from the snug belt.

Through the din, he heard sirens, loud and urgent. He refocused his attention. The heat was unbearably oppressive, tight, and brutal; the grueling smoke stung his eyes and lungs. He labored mightily to gulp a bit of fresh air.

Frantically, he struggled with the seat belt, finally gripped the locking mechanism with all his strength and wrenched the clasp free. As he coughed and sputtered, he climbed over the old man reclined in the seat next to him. *Poor guy has already succumbed,* Jeffrey thought. Or was he dead before takeoff?

Using his arms to shield his eyes and nose, he blindly inched himself forward. The tilted angle of the fuselage made it difficult to maneuver. His heart thrummed painfully. Using his hands to guide him, he touched something directly before him. Peeked through splayed fingers. A hazy shape. A woman? Not young, not old, not a teenager, his mind volleyed. She appeared shell-shocked. Blood cascaded from an ugly wound near her eye.

"MOVE AHEAD, LADY!" he screamed hoarsely. "MOVE, DAMMIT!"

She refused to budge, remained stuck in the aisle among the crushed seats and charred bodies and seared fuselage. A toddler, a little boy barely older than two, lay limply on her shoulder. Jeffrey was not sure if the child was still breathing, but truthfully, he did not care. His only desire was to escape the inevitable deathtrap the three of them shared.

Jeffrey squeezed his body past her and the child, stepped atop a body, soft and malleable underfoot. The woman with the child remained rooted in place. Jeffrey reached his hand behind him, searched madly for her arm, her hand, anything to get her to move. For a split second she responded, then tripped over a crumpled seat. As she collapsed atop the seat, she shielded the child with her arms and chest.

The kid moaned. *At least he's alive,* Jeffrey thought. "MISS, COME ON!" he screeched. "FOLLOW ME!"

Again, he reached his arm to her and again, the woman remained immobile, as if she were mired in quicksand. Her eyes were big orbs of fear and darted wildly in all directions.

Jeffrey Kaye knew he had only a few more precious seconds to react. *I don't want to die here,* his brain screamed. *Not like this.*

Finally, he dipped his shoulder and struggled forward. But he knew, knew deep within his soul, that he should turn around—to lift, or shove, or heave—the woman and her kid upright. Steer them to safety. He knew it was the decent thing to do, knew it as easily as he knew his own name and address.

But his desire to escape overwhelmed any further sense of honor or civility.

Panic seized him in a bear hug. He swung himself left, right, blindly searching for an escape. Tiny shards of light and deep darkness coalesced into an unimaginable nightmare. He struggled past twisted debris and bodies, heard tiny mewing sounds. Flames licked through the sheared fuselage that had once been the forward portion of the cabin. Time continued to tick by in a slow-motion, tap-tap-tap tempo.

Close behind him, or beside him, he heard the bleating sound of the toddler, the desperate whimpers of the child's mother. But Jeffrey no longer worried of their distress; his momentum was focused strictly on survival.

His feet hiccupped on soft objects that barred his path. He sidestepped over them—reverently, but quickly. Ahead, he spotted a tiny blot of sky, not blue or sunny or filled with white, puffy clouds. No, the blot he glimpsed was gray, a mesh of swirling, angry clouds. As he neared the blot of light, it grew bigger—bigger and wider.

He guessed that they were imprisoned in the midsection of the plane. All that remained was a gaping, jagged hole. He felt for the opening with outstretched hands. Jeffrey's lungs begged for fresh air; he feared he might faint before he could reach safety.

As he stumbled toward the ripped fuselage, brutally hot flames licked at the back of his tank top, nipped at his exposed neck and shoulders. He yelped like a wounded puppy.

Finally, he grabbed at the jagged edges of the hole, and as he did, the flesh on his fingers tore painfully. He bled, covered in sweat and soot, and stared down at the abyss beneath him. As his life hung in the balance, he wondered if he should make a last-minute confession to a god he did not believe in.

He stared at the asphalt so far below. It was a long drop, for sure. But time had indeed run out. *Live or die?* he thought frantically as his T-shirt melted directly into his skin.

Jeffrey inhaled deeply. A millisecond later, flames taunted his face as he flung himself as far out and away from the plane as possible—as if he were diving into a swimming pool.

He flailed his arms in a windmill rotation as he belly-flopped toward the ground.

QUESTION MARKS

June 26, 1977

Life's travesties always seem to have a hand in swaying a person's soul in infinite directions, just as a breeze will help a kite to ascend or pollen to float through the air. It is the same as believing you are guilty of something but hoping you are not.

I would be remiss, a liar, a coward if I did not admit that the long hours that followed the crash were insufferable. An unbearable weight settled on me. *Devastated* was too tiny a word to explain my grief.

After collapsing at the air traffic control tower, I was taken to an area marked RESTRICTED. The room was small, suffocating, full of lurking gray shadows. Even the square metal table and chairs were an ugly shade of gray. Jake, the senior supervisor, helped me to a chair and sat beside me, his foot tapping restlessly against the dingy floor. The tapping sound resonated like a ticking bomb about to explode.

My hands shook as I sipped water from a paper cup, leaving behind a faded pink lipstick stain. My eyes were ringed with caked mascara and, oddly, I wondered if I looked more like a racoon than a seasoned air traffic controller. My nose dripped mucus until finally, Jake found a tissue and handed it to me. "It wasn't your fault, Margaret," he whispered. "I promise, it wasn't your fault."

I so wanted to believe him, but as I sat in that gray windowless room, waiting for the investigators to arrive to interrogate me, it was impossible not to replay the scene of the Olympian Airways jet as it barreled down from the sky and onto the taxiing jet. Impossible not to cringe, recalling how the top of the jet had been sheared off. How it had erupted like a volcano.

My hands shook badly, mimicking the shaking of salt and pepper shakers over a plate of food. Maybe my stepfather had been right all along. He had always said I had no business becoming an air traffic controller. "Women don't have the comprehension or the aptitude for such stressful and demanding work," he would goad. Now, my tongue felt too big for my mouth and I worried I wouldn't be able to answer the questions to come.

It felt like three days had passed since Air Traffic Command had remanded me to the restricted area, but it was only a few hours until personnel from the National Transportation Safety Board and the Federal Aviation Administration arrived. There were no pleasantries exchanged, just a swift unpacking of notepads and pens and an immediate start to the interrogation. I wondered if they saw me as I saw myself in that instant: a pathetic, sniveling person who had lost her sense of being.

Yet, with acute detail, I relayed every nuance of what had transpired prior to the disaster. Recounted every verbal communication and every instruction I had given as if my mind had recorded and stored the words and syllables to later be offered verbatim, in defense of my actions.

Still, a volley of questions was hurled at me:

"Had Olympian Airways received any threats connected to these flights . . . ?"

"Did you or your coworkers notice anything unusual . . . ?"

"Is there a possibility that the air traffic controllers were pre-warned?" This question was hurled by a stout blonde woman who seemed far better suited for a prison matron's role than this special squad of aviation experts.

"Of course not!" I cried. "It was an accident, and I've asked myself again and again if there is anything I could have done differently. There wasn't!"

Hours passed; tepid coffee was poured into Styrofoam cups and passed around the table. The faces of the experts changed, but the insanely repetitive questions continued. In a separate room, my colleagues were being equally interrogated, although "badgered" seemed a more appropriate consensus.

My friend and coworker, LaTonya Edwards, had worked the shift with me. She was tall and regal, with ebony hair and a golden body. She later shared the details of her own questioning:

"What was Miss Lido's reaction immediately following the collision?"

"If I tell you she was horrified, it would be redundant to what you have already heard, Inspector," she replied. "How would you feel if your worst damn nightmare came true?"

Another man from the team asked, "Had she recently ended a relationship? Had someone close to her died? Was she depressed? Angry? Suicidal?"

"No. Her mama died, but that was a couple years ago."

"How did she take it?" asked the stout blonde woman.

"How do you think she took it?"

"No need to get cute, Miss Edwards. Do you recall how her mother died?"

LaTonya shrugged her shoulders. "An accident. That's all she said."

"What type of accident?"

"I didn't ask. What difference does it make?"

Shortly after dawn, I was escorted home by Jake and LaTonya. They both offered to stay the day with me, but by then, I craved privacy. I showered, changed into a pair of shorts and a T-shirt. Listlessly, I prepared a cup of tea. Two sips later, I vomited it back up.

I was mentally, physically, and emotionally exhausted. A wreck of a human being. For a while, I avoided turning on the television, knowing the accident would receive rabid news coverage by all three networks. But I had to watch, had to know what was being done, what was being said.

Television news crews remained at the crash site. Viewers had a front-row seat to the images of the smoldering planes, the fuselage scattered like litter on the runway, the horrible cloud of dust that hovered above the airfield.

Reporters spoke to eyewitnesses, fire personnel, first responders. They repeatedly asked the same questions: Who was responsible for the disaster? What caused the crash? Were there any survivors?

I feared that someone would leak my name, point a finger at me. It was standard procedure that personal information regarding any air traffic controller involved in a deadly crash was to be kept strictly private.

Specifically for the individual's safety.

Yet the following morning, a dozen reporters and camera crews were camped outside on my small patch of lawn. They waited there like hungry wolves, anxious for me to show my face. To tell my story.

So, which of my coworkers had played Judas and leaked my name to the press?

MOTHER & CHILD

June 26, 1977

JEFFREY

Jeffrey Kaye might have yelled or screamed. He might have begged for his mother or for the god he did not believe existed. But he would not remember because when he hit the ground after jumping from the burning plane, all he heard was the sickening sound of bones snapping and tearing through his flesh.

From his daze, he felt strong arms grab and yank him hard, away from the burning wreckage. He was barely conscious; his watery eyes lolled about like marbles being played in a child's game. He would not recall if he had seen the fire rescue personnel, the paramedics, police, airport security, and morbid on-lookers, or if he had imagined them. He thought he had watched as heavy rubber hoses doused the flames with airy foam and great gushes of water, but he would never be certain.

He felt himself heaved onto a gurney and quickly rolled toward one of a dozen waiting ambulances. Another set of hands jammed an oxygen mask over his face. Beneath the mask, Jeffrey faded into a slippery void, but the paramedic continually shook him awake.

"Stay with me buddy!" the voice shouted. "Stay with me."

Time swayed, a Ferris wheel of rocking motion that cradled his tired brain.

As he lay there helplessly, an image floated behind his eyes: two people. Who were they? he wondered.

Then, as if she were standing right beside him, he heard his mother's sing-song voice remind him, "It's never wrong to do the right thing, Jefferey."

As his eyes struggled to remain open, a loud eruption jarred him. His eyes fluttered open, and they tracked the loud shouts. "Up there! Look!"

Jeffrey looked, then wished he had not. Up in the remaining shell of Olympian Airways Flight 177 was the horrific silhouette of a dazed woman and her child. She stood in the chasm of the burning fuselage, back lit by roaring flames and billowing smoke as the rag-doll toddler dangled loosely from one arm.

A horde of firefighters held a jumping sheet to help cushion her fall. They screamed to her, "JUMP! COME ON! JUMP!"

Beneath his oxygen mask, Jeffrey, too, begged her to jump.

A nanosecond of time elapsed—a mere pinprick of an instant—until flames as huge as tidal waves engulfed the two in its fiery fold.

Whimpering and gurgling, Jeffrey stretched upward from the gurney. He feared he might drown in his own saliva. It was excruciating to witness the incineration of two human beings.

Then, as if a relief pitcher had been sent to save him, Jeffrey Kaye descended into the blackness of his own personal hell.

BYE-BYE, LEROY

June 27, 1977

VIOLA

A roar of heavy diesel trucks pounded the road just beyond the window of Viola's room and rifled her awake. Her neck and legs felt stiff beneath the papery thin sheets.

She hauled herself from the bed, brushed her teeth, and jammed yesterday's clothing into her black satchel. She eyed the room for errant possessions, then closed the door behind her. Although she was eager to leave North Carolina behind in a plume of exhaust fumes, her stomach rebelled and instead, she marched into the little café adjacent to the motor lodge's lobby.

She chose a table that faced the door, eyed the other diners. Leroy was not tucked in beside the family of five to her right, nor was he with the two elderly couples seated to her left. With the remaining tables unoccupied, she exhaled an audible sigh of relief.

The guy she had left behind at the rest stop in Jacksonville was Leroy Stills—the type of guy who could talk a good game but who could not follow through on anything. The type of guy with a short fuse, quick hands, and a nasty mouth.

That Leroy Stills remained a huge malignancy in her life.

The first time he raised his hands to her had also been the last time. He had bruised her cheekbone and left ugly welts on her arms. Had blackened an eye that swelled itself shut. But later that night, as he lay in a stupor, breathing out the stink of rancid whiskey, Viola had whacked him hard with a frying pan.

Whacked him two times.

Leroy had wound up in the emergency room, and Viola had wound up satisfied. In her mind, they were even.

And, as far as she was concerned, they were finished.

But she had nowhere to go and even less money to get there. Until her friend Lucy offered a solution. She and Lucy worked together at Scooters—an upscale bar and grill whose clientele were wealthy patrons and generous with their tips.

"You've got to leave him," Lucy insisted. Her voice was as tiny as her compact body, the body of a waif, if one could still politely use the term. "He's a loser and if he hit you once, he'll do it again. Guaranteed."

Viola cringed. "Lucy, I have nowhere to go."

"Maybe I can help," she whispered. "My uncle Sammy is very sick, and he probably won't make it through the weekend. He lives in a rent-controlled apartment in New York and for some crazy reason, I'm listed as an occupant on the lease."

"Why?" Viola asked.

"I don't know," Lucy said with exasperation. "Maybe he thought I would move there someday and live with him. You know, take care of him as he got older. But it doesn't matter why, Viola. The apartment will be available, and the rent is cheaper than anywhere else in the city."

She took a deep breath and whispered, "You can pretend to be me. Live in the apartment."

Twelve days later—and eight days after Lucy's Uncle Sammy died—Viola filled an oversized duffel bag with jeans, T-shirts, a few sweaters. Necessary toiletries. Her tip money—which she had squirreled away and hidden from Leroy—was shoved to the bottom of her duffel. While Leroy was at work, she stashed the bag deep inside the Malibu's trunk.

On the morning of her departure, she tiptoed from the mobile home they had shared for the past thirty-two months. Tiptoed out as Leroy slept. Was halfway inside her car before the passenger door was forcibly yanked open.

Leroy stood there, tall as a basketball player, hair tousled, and wearing a white T-shirt and cut-off denim shorts. He leaned into the car and asked, "Going somewhere?"

In a flash he was inside the car, throwing his backpack into the rear seats. Gleefully, he rubbed his hands together and shouted, "H-e-l-l-o, New York City!"

Ten miles into the trip, Viola bluntly asked, "How did you know?"

He stretched his arms above his head, yawned, and said, "I heard you and Lucy talking about it at Scooters. And when I saw your tip jar was missing, it was obvious you were ready to bolt."

He smiled wickedly. "It was kind of silly of you to hide the tip jar behind your Tampax box. First place I thought to look. Guess I'm not as dumb as you thought, babe."

She fumed and cursed herself as she sped along the interstate, juggling ideas to rid herself of Leroy Stills. A future saddled with him was not an acceptable future.

Luckily, Leroy slept through the entire ride through Tampa, did not stir until they were close to Jacksonville. "I got to pee," he grumbled.

Viola pulled off the interstate, chugged along until she happened on a small decrepit rest stop nestled between a junkyard and a sad-looking bait and tackle shop. The bumpy road was littered with discarded beer cans and overflowing garbage bins. The place looked like it had not been updated since the early thirties.

A handful of vehicles were parked in front, all of them badly battered pickup trucks. Leroy tugged his wallet from his denim shorts and tossed it onto the dashboard. "I don't want to get rolled by some hick in there," he snarled as he stepped from the car.

Steadily, Viola eyeballed him. Watched every step he took as he shuffled into the shack-like structure. As soon as his retreating back disappeared, Viola yanked the gearshift into drive and floored the gas.

The Malibu fishtailed, and the tires screeched as she spun the car back in the direction of the interstate. Leroy, having heard the loud rev of the engine, backstepped out of the shack, screaming and flailing his arms.

He remained close enough for Viola to witness the look of incredulity that was pasted on his milky white face.

As she had said earlier, the look was priceless.

Seated in the Howard Johnson café, Viola snapped back to attention. She repeated her order to a young waitress, a girl surely too young to possess legitimate working papers. She wore a uniform two sizes too large and way too much makeup. Viola ordered three scrambled eggs with crispy bacon, toast, and a carafe of coffee.

Looking up, she noticed a small television screen suspended from the ceiling, the type often found in a patient's hospital room. The man on the screen was handsome, neither young nor old but hovering somewhere in between.

She looked away as the waitress placed a plastic, tan-colored coffee carafe in front of her. As she toyed with adding milk and sugar to her mug, the newscaster's velvety voice drew her attention.

". . . And reported just moments ago: Olympian Airways has now confirmed there is a sole survivor from the deadly crash that occurred yesterday afternoon at the Hewitt-Jackson Airport in Atlanta, Georgia. The survivor, who has not yet been identified, remains in severely critical condition. This is Jordan Meeks, KLNC-Channel 3."

Viola dug into her breakfast. *Never getting on a plane,* she promised herself. *Never.*

FOOLS & CHILDREN

June 30, 1977

Inside the busy Atlanta Trauma Center, Jeffrey Kaye was quickly wheeled from the ICU unit to an operating room on the fourth floor. He had arrived at the trauma center four days earlier, presenting with myriad injuries: second-degree burns, fractured and crushed bones, a collapsed lung. He underwent surgery to repair a shattered hip and fractured femur—the bone protruding grotesquely and painfully through his skin.

He had arrived as a John Doe, without identification. Hundreds of hopeful people had telephoned the hospital, hoping it was their loved one who had survived the plane crash. The trauma center's administrator, Leslie Carrington, had set up a makeshift call center to sort through the calls.

On the day following the survivor's arrival, a call came in from a woman in Manhattan, New York, inquiring if the survivor might be her son. A checklist of questions was asked and answered: age, height, weight, facial hair, hair color.

"Any scars, tattoos, birthmarks?" the rep asked.

"Yes," the woman's voice responded. "He has a tattoo on his left forearm. A heart with a ribbon around it."

"Is there anything written inside the heart?"

"Yes!" the woman cried excitedly. "It says 'Mother.'"

On the evening of June 30, a dangerous brain bleed forced doctors to return Jeffrey to the OR. Decompression of his brain was required to release pooled blood and to relieve pressure. Following the procedure, his surgeon placed him into a medically induced coma.

The surgeon monitoring his care was Dr. Scott Sinclair—fortyish, with a marathon runner's body and small feminine hands, and with a viral disregard for fools and children.

Dr. Sinclair spoke to Jeffrey's mother by telephone, requested permission to perform the critically necessary surgeries, and afterward, to explain to her the nuances of the medically induced coma.

His first impression of the woman: she was a flat-out idiot who was more concerned with her anticipated travel expenses to Atlanta than about her son's very serious medical condition.

Dr. Sinclair was not at all looking forward to meeting Jeffrey Kaye's mother.

YOUNG AT HEART

June 30, 1977

FITZ

Windows on the World—an elegant restaurant on the one-hundred-and-seventh floor of the World Trade Center—offered a remarkable view of the Manhattan skyline after dusk. Somehow, the city managed to shed its boisterous daytime clamor and evolve into a sexy portrait of tall buildings and distant bridges aglow in a wash of light.

On that evening—just as Jeffrey Kaye was gently being floated into a medically induced coma—Larry Fitzgerald Jr., known to most as "Fitz," sat at a table in the swanky restaurant, awaiting his guest. He sipped a tall gin and tonic, admiring the view.

The restaurant was crowded with guests, most of whom believed themselves to be Very Important People, and those who were indeed Very Important People. His eyes danced around the room, caught a glimpse of Mayor Abe Beame huddled with a group of old cronies.

His eyes skipped along, stopped on two CEOs of major investment banking firms. They sat with their wives—two dowdy, run-of-the-mill-looking women—who could not compare with the raven-haired beauty who was making googly eyes at real estate up-and-comer Donald Trump.

A white-gloved waiter with a waxy complexion asked to refill his drink. Fitz nodded, lit a cigarette, then turned his attention back to the window's view.

Four nights earlier, he had entertained a young girl at his firm's corporate apartment on Central Park South. At the time, his brain had complained that he was taking a huge, unnecessary risk. His body, however, did everything in its power to fight his brain.

The girl was young, fifteen, sixteen at most. He knew painfully well that if discovered, he would become a pariah, shunned by family and colleagues, the brunt of brutal jokes and ridicule by his father's clients.

It worried him, this incessant desire to have sex with underaged girls. It was their innocence, their willingness to please, that worked as such a powerful aphrodisiac for him. He believed his nobility lay in guiding those girls who teetered on the precipice of adolescence and womanhood through their transition. Or so he hoped.

To Fitz, young girls were all the same: easily flattered by the tiniest spark of male interest and thoroughly infatuated with luxurious lifestyles that might eventually benefit them, as well. They were still young and immature and not aware of the invisible powers they wielded over such men.

Of course, there were plenty of women of Fitz's age who vied for his attentions. It was no wonder—he was tall, with muscular arms and shoulders, a narrow waist. His skin was clear, bone structure solid. From his mother, he had inherited his dark, inky black hair and boyish dimples. From his father, he had inherited his name. And, at twenty-seven, he had more money than most guys his age.

Yet, he found women of his own age to be as annoying as summer gnats. Most spent their days and nights eagerly searching for a husband, preferably a wealthy one.

The waxy-faced waiter reappeared, placed a fresh drink on his table, removed the empty glass. Fitz thanked him, crushed his cigarette into a clunky ashtray.

He thought back to the girl he had met at the corporate apartment that night. Her lips were thick, glossy with bright pink lipstick. She wore baby blue gym pants and a matching shorty top, which revealed a flat, taut stomach.

She had looked nervous, as if it were her first time. Not wanting to frighten her, he sat across from her, legs casually crossed as he sipped his drink. He inquired of her life, the school she attended.

When he had finally made love to her, he was gentle, sweet. She had indeed been a virgin. When they finished and she shimmied back into her clothing, he handed her two crisp fifty-dollar bills. Watched as her eyes widened in disbelief, how she quickly shoved the money into her shoulder bag, afraid he might ask for it back.

Shyly, she smiled at him. "Is it okay if I leave now?"

"Of course," he replied. "Thank you."

Once she had gone, he stripped the bloodied sheet from the bed, balled it up. Found a notepad and pen on the desk. Scribbled a quick note to the housekeeper. "Lindy, sorry, stomach virus had me puking all over the sheets. Please replace them for me. Thanks, F."

He left the apartment, took the stairs down three flights to the seventh floor, pushed the balled-up dirty sheets into the incinerator bin. And then he had gone home.

He smiled at the memory, lit another cigarette. Glanced at his Rolex watch.

His pal Gregory Maison had arranged the date with the girl. By night, Maison ran a sophisticated, professional operation, which hosted private, by-invitation-only parties that matched and arranged dates for plenty of men with desires like Fitz's. An expensive proposition for those who attended such parties.

Fitz snapped to attention as the maître-d' touched his shoulder. "Mr. Fitzgerald, your guest is here. Shall I bring her?"

"Yes, Paul. Thank you."

He smiled, contemplated the night ahead, possibly the weekend ahead. The maître-d' believed it was Fitz's niece joining him for dinner.

She arrived at the table, gorgeous and big breasted, looking more like a woman than had been promised. Politely, he rose. Looked into her eyes. Gently took her hand in his. Gestured for her to sit.

He knew he would enjoy a pleasant dinner with her.

And nothing more.

HOUNDED

July 5, 1977

The release of my high school yearbook photo to the media altered my life in ways I could not have imagined. I lived with a daily barrage of death threats. Lunatics who insisted they should burn my home—right to its foundation—with me in it. Dead rats and dog feces regularly showed up on my doorstep. Someone painted KILLER in red paint on my front door and mailbox. Beer bottles were flung at my back porch. An effigy with my face pasted on it was burned from a tree across from my bungalow.

I do not believe I have ever been as frightened in my life, forced to recalibrate my trust of everyone. So, I hibernated, insulated myself from the outside world. The media was unkind, downright brutal in its portrayal of me.

Fired-up journalists from around the country reported on my story nonstop, including CBS Evening News with Walter Cronkite and *Sixty Minutes*. My photo, along with images of the smoldering planes, was splashed across every major newspaper. I was thrust into the spotlight as an unwilling cast member. The evil villain of a terrible story. Spoken about in pubs and coffee shops from Seattle to Singapore.

But I was not the icy-veined woman they portrayed me to be. I was not a shark that rattled cages.

Still, the small patch of lawn beyond my front door remained littered with journalists and lookie-loos who had neither the decency nor the desire to clean up after themselves. The tired grass suffered the refuse of empty Coca-Cola bottles and scrunched up sandwich wrappers, cigarette butts, soiled tissues, and yesterday's wrinkled newspapers.

Soon, my homey bungalow with its pretty yellow curtains and comfortable lounger felt tiny and suffocating. I couldn't bear my reflection in the mirror; hated the sight of my wild eyes, smudged and puffy and fearful. Hated seeing the person I now was: a mass murderer who had snatched away mothers and children, lovers and spouses, friends and coworkers. People who had been going about their daily lives much as I had been doing that day. But here I was and there they were: ashes and dust and a lingering memory.

It was on that Tuesday morning that the call from the FAA came, mandating immediate counseling. Counseling that was very cleverly dubbed "Critical Incident Stress Management." They should have called it what it really was: "Post-Traumatic Stress Disorder."

It meant I would be under the care of a therapist, counselors, and possibly a shrink. For my protection, the FAA—keenly aware of my notoriety since the accident—had arranged for me a car and an escort so I could safely atttend the sessions. My stress management counselor was Bridget, a pretty girl not much older than me. She promised that my reactions to the disaster were normal, that my level of guilt and paranoia would eventually subside. But I found it difficult to believe. Because each time I tried to reconcile the events that led up to the disaster, the answer always rubbed me like a canker sore that refused to heal. The truth was, on the night prior, I had been to a club, had enjoyed a bourbon or two after a long stretch at the controls.

"Were you drunk?" Bridget asked.

"No, I swear," I replied.

"What about the following morning? Were you okay?"

I didn't know how to answer. I had nursed a crushing headache. Should I tell her that? Would it make me seem guilty of something? Some might insist it was a hangover. I did not.

Finally, I answered. "I was fine the following morning." But had I, on that day, dozed at the controls—even momentarily? Had I blinked too slowly? Too quickly? Distracted, had I glanced from the control screen? Perhaps I misread the coordinates? Had the fog skewed my decisions? How could I have instructed both planes to use runway L-23?

It seemed terribly easy to second-guess myself. But by then, it was too late. I had already fallen to pieces.

Bridget studied me, then her notes. "The FAA report indicates that your mother died a few years back," she said gently. "An accident. Can you tell me about it?"

What was there to tell? My mother had slipped on toys left behind on the stairway by my half brothers Mickey and Roger—named for the famous baseball duo. She was DOA when the ambulance arrived.

So really, what could Bridget say or do to help me?

HOME SWEET HOME

July 5, 1977

VIOLA

Viola Cordova arrived in Manhattan on a Tuesday afternoon at the end of a long Fourth of July weekend. The rush of traffic felt to her like a stampede of jungle animals running from danger.

She was astonished by the sounds and the bevy of activity that zipped around her: cars, taxis, and trucks, all authoritatively blaring their horns. Big unsightly buses that belched smelly exhaust fumes into the already stagnant air.

From loud boom boxes she heard music: reggae, blues, jazz, and disco. She watched as a chubby teenager simultaneously walked ten dogs, spotted an elderly man as he waved a rolled-up newspaper above his head and shouted to no one in particular. A woman removed her shoe after stepping on a dead pigeon.

How can a person's senses not be on high alert amidst all this commotion? she wondered.

Exhausted from the long trip, she circled several blocks before she found a place to park the Malibu. Carefully, she hugged her duffel bag to her chest and trudged up the four wide steps that led into Uncle Sammy's apartment building.

Inside, she stood within a small rotunda with stairwells that branched into four directions. Slotted metal mailboxes lined one wall with a resident directory mounted nearby. She quickly located the superintendent's apartment, rang the doorbell. It sounded harsh and stubborn.

The man who opened the door was Raphael Lopez, a short man with a lazy eye. He looked to be in his early thirties.

"Yeah?" he said.

"Hi," Viola stammered. "I'm Sammy Carrano's niece."

"Yeah? So what?"

"Well, I'm supposed to..."

"Carrano?" he snorted. "The old guy in 5D? What, he lost his key again?"

Nervously, she nodded.

"Damn," he said. "Okay, wait here." His accent was pure New York, and Viola was certain she sounded like a country hick to him.

A minute, then three, then six passed. Finally, Raphael Lopez returned, handed her a key, and said, "If he loses this again, I got to charge ya two bucks. Got it?"

"Of course," Viola said. Smiled and turned away. Was it possible, she wondered, that Raphael Lopez was ignorant of the old man's death?

With her duffel bag slumped over her shoulder, she slowly climbed the five flights of stairs to the fifth floor. When she reached her level, she stepped into a small communal hallway, saw that each of the five apartments on the level were clustered closely together—only two or three arm lengths apart.

Luckily, Uncle Sammy's apartment was the furthest from the others, twenty or so steps past the communal hallway. At Apartment 5D, with its front door peeling long strips of red paint, she stepped into the tiny foyer of a compact, three-room apartment. It smelled artificially clean.

Tentatively, she shuffled inside. To her right she saw a tight little kitchen with a grimy window that overlooked a back alley. Outside of the window, dozens of clothes lines crisscrossed each other, with pajamas and T-shirts and bras and bed sheets drying in the faint breeze.

To her left was a bedroom, equally small. Rounding out the space was a living room, square and unimpressive. Uncle Sammy sure hadn't done much to spruce up the place.

The living room boasted a wooden rocking chair and an ugly green sofa. The floor was covered in a yellowish linoleum, putridly ugly, which had obviously seen better days.

In the tiny bathroom was a pedestal sink not large enough to rinse a pair of nylons and a bathtub, which looked like it had been there since World War I.

For a scant moment, Viola worried if an about-face might be appropriate. There were at least ten good solid reasons to flee.

Instead, she remained, unpacked her duffel. Neatly folded and placed her clothing inside an antique bureau. Pulled out Leroy's cracked vinyl wallet and flipped through the billfold. She counted forty-one dollars. Combined with her own ninety-seven dollars, she had enough money to last a few weeks.

She had a place to live, a place to call home. Now, all she needed was a job.

VISITING HOURS

July 10, 1977

The woman who stepped from the elevator onto the ICU ward at the Atlanta Trauma Center was short and squat, with a Humpty-Dumpty-like body: round upper torso, broomstick-thin legs. She wore red Bermuda shorts—which unveiled a host of bulging varicose veins—and an oversized T-shirt with "Jesus Loves Me" stenciled across her chest. Behind her, she dragged a beat-up green suitcase.

When Dr. Sinclair spotted her, he pegged her as Jeffrey Kaye's mother. He did not know why he thought it. He just did.

As she approached the nurses' station, he intercepted her. "Mrs. Kaye?"

Startled, she said, "Yes?"

"I'm Dr. Sinclair. Jeffrey's doctor."

"Oh." Perplexed, she stared at him, perhaps expecting someone older. Or younger.

"Why don't we chat before you visit Jeffrey?" he asked.

Deftly, he guided her to a small room with two straight-backed chairs and a tiny glass coffee table. A colorful paneled quilt was pinned to the wall: a testament of thankfulness to the doctors and nurses and technicians employed at the trauma center.

Once seated, Dr. Sinclair explained Jeffrey's injuries, the procedures performed, and the medications administered to alleviate his pain.

"He's undergone a great deal of trauma," he said. "So far, he has responded well, and we are keeping him as comfortable as possible. Still, the swelling of his brain remains a concern, but I hope to bring him out of the coma soon."

Jeffrey's mother sniffled as her eyes spilled fat tears. Speaking to the woman face to face, Dr. Sinclair found her to be a far more responsive parent than the woman he had spoken to on the telephone a few days earlier.

Uncharacteristically, he reached across the small divide to squeeze her hand. "I don't want you to be alarmed when you see him. There are a lot of machines in his room, and he remains on a respirator."

"Why?" she asked.

"The induced coma keeps his organs from working too hard. The respirator helps him to breathe. But I promise you, he is doing quite well despite his injuries.

"Is he going to live?"

"Yes, I'm confident he will recover. But it will take time."

She nodded her head. "Can I see him?"

"Yes. Yes, of course."

As Dr. Sinclair steered her to Jeffrey's room, he said, "He's receiving nourishment via a feeding tube, but he has lost a bit of weight."

As Jeffrey Kaye's mother entered her son's room, the doctor heard her deep intake of breath. "Oh my God," she moaned softly.

Dr. Sinclair gently placed his hand on her shoulder. "I'll leave you now. If you need anything, the nurses are right outside."

Jeffrey's mother nodded, walked slowly to her son's bed. The hiss of the machines was surprisingly soothing. A quiet cadence of noise: in and out. She peeked down at Jeffrey, barely recognized him beneath his beard, a beard she was seeing for the first time.

She leaned in close to him. "Be strong, Jeffrey," she whispered. "God will heal you."

DISMISSED

July 15, 1977

FITZ

He knew it was going to be a dreadful day from the moment he woke that morning. Larry "Fitz" Fitzgerald sat at the edge of his bed, scuffed his fingers through his hair. He felt agitated, restless. Several times during the night he had woken—abruptly and uncomfortably—with a keen sense of someone hovering over him. *That's absurd,* he chastised himself. Bogeymen were a thing of his past.

He showered, shaved, nicked himself twice. Quickly swallowed a cup of coffee and headed to the train station. Ralph, who usually escorted him in the company car, was ill, and Fitz was forced to use the public subway system.

Outside, a pounding rain drummed against his umbrella. He wore a new, expensive Italian-tailored suit, cursed as the cuffs and his socks became soaked.

As he waited on the platform for the train to take him to his father's firm, Fitzgerald Alloy Corporation, he was jostled and nudged by crowds of commuters traveling to and from work—all eager to get where they were going. The *New York Post* was clutched in his right hand, heavy and damp, the headlines smudging ink onto his fingers.

The circumstances which had brought him to become employed at the firm—a company his father had started years earlier—were not unique. Not a soap opera saga of family infidelity, nor of gossip.

His father, Larry Fitzgerald Sr., had wanted Fitz to join the firm immediately after he graduated college. But it was not the future Fitz had envisioned for himself. Nuts and bolts, screws and planks did not excite him. Nor did the idea of being under his father's watchful eye.

He knew it would spell trouble for him and for their relationship. Besides, employment in a musty factory in Brooklyn and having to learn the business from the ground up was not an appealing notion.

The M train pulled into the station, and Fitz shouldered his way onto the already crowded subway car. He stood, held onto the tall chrome pole to steady himself, his head nearly wedged beneath the underarm of a ridiculously tall man. Beside him, a woman with garlicky breath was unable to keep her balance and every few moments, she teetered and bobbled against him.

But here I am, he thought.

After graduating from college—not an Ivy League school, impossible with his poor grades and preoccupation with marijuana—he had passed on the opportunity to join the family business. Instead, he had opted for an entry level position at Dawson-Brown Investment Banking, a very conservative and well-respected firm. His friend Damon Ross was already employed there and had put in a good word for Fitz.

It had gone very well for the first nine months. He was a good salesperson, brought several huge accounts to the company. Money was rolling in.

Until it all fell apart on the morning that Joe Walsh of Human Resources ushered Fitz into his office.

"Have a seat," Walsh said. He was a huge man with a droopy white handlebar mustache that reminded Fitz of a walrus.

"We have a problem, Mr. Fitzgerald." Walsh's voice was soft, almost velvety. "Jenna Gold. Name sound familiar?"

Fitz shook his head. "No. Should it?"

"She was a young woman who interned here this summer."

Fitz hunched his shoulders in an I-don't-know shrug.

"Well," Joe Walsh said, "she says you groped her. Pressed her up against the copy room wall and fondled her. Touched her breasts. Sound familiar now?"

Fitz did not flinch or blink. "I have no idea what you're referring to, Mr. Walsh. Besides, that's just her word against mine."

Joe Walsh folded his massive arms, shook his head. "I don't think your denial will hold water here, Mr. Fitzgerald. You see, Jenna Gold is the daughter of board member Richard Gold."

Fitz felt as if his blue-striped tie might squeeze the very breath from him. Behind him, he heard the gentle swoosh of a door as it opened and closed.

"I'm sorry, Mr. Fitzgerald, but Dawson-Brown will no longer require your services. Security Officer Peterson will escort you from the building."

The subway car screeched to a halt, and the lady with the garlicky breath finally exited the train, replaced with a man with colorfully beaded dreads. The subway car was stuffy, everyone's wet and damp clothing making the crowded space even more uncomfortable.

Fitz had wandered the city streets for hours. Crowds of people jostled him with their briefcases and shopping bags. The humility, the utter disgrace of his dismissal from Dawson-Brown, spiraled him into a near catatonic state.

Finally, he ducked into a side street tavern, sat at the bar, and ordered a whiskey neat. It was not yet noon. He gulped it quickly, felt the fire of the whiskey dump into his empty stomach.

The next two, he sipped.

What the hell am I going to do? he agonized. *What am I going to tell Dad? I can't tell him the truth, he'll kill me.*

By the fourth whiskey, he rehearsed the only speech he knew his father would accept. Aloud he said, "Dad, I've left Dawson-Brown. You were right—I should join the family business. Follow in your footsteps."

Two men at the end of the bar clapped loudly.

Fitz exited the subway station, walked two short blocks to the factory on Kent Avenue. A massive blue sign welcomed him to Fitzgerald Alloy Corporation.

At first, he had loathed coming to the factory, loathed the loud, clanging noise of the machinery, the dust that settled everywhere. Surprisingly, he quickly learned the nuances, the little ins-and-outs of the industry, and realized he could become a powerhouse of a salesman for his father's business.

In short order, Fitz designed a fresh marketing campaign for the company. He insisted his father toss the old-fashioned catalogs they had been using for decades. New, glossy catalogues were printed; special incentives were offered to first-time buyers. Fitz perfected the art of entertaining clients and prospective new accounts. He found their weak spots and their sweet spots.

He became the fresh, youthful face of the company, a bright young man filled with innovative ideas. He submitted requests to bid on major government, school, automotive, and aeronautic contracts. With his easy-going personality and good looks, he helped to propel sales tenfold.

It was the first time in Fitz's life that he had ever seen his father so happy.

In less than a year, Fitz became vice president of sales and marketing and reaped the rewards that came with the title: a hefty salary and bonus, use of the company's car and driver, and, most importantly, occasional use of the corporate apartment on Central Park South. His was an enviable lifestyle, one he relished.

Inside the factory, it was business as usual. Fitz hurried to his office, shook water from his umbrella, rested it in a wastepaper basket. Removed his shoes to dry and sat at his desk in his stocking feet. Milly, the plant's office manager, stood in his doorway, rapped her knuckles on the frame.

Fitz looked up, smiled. Milly had been with the plant for decades. She wore orthopedic black shoes and a stuffy gray dress. But she was still as sharp as any tack Fitzgerald Alloy manufactured.

"Sorry to bother you, Fitz," she said. Her raspy voice bore the result of a forty-year, two-pack-a-day cigarette habit. "There's a gal out here insisting to see you."

"What does she want?"

Milly shook her head. "Won't say. Only that she needs to speak to you now and that it's important.

"Okay," Fitz shrugged. "Send her in."

Milly escorted the girl into Fitz's office, then closed the door behind her.

Fitz looked up. Did a quick double take. It was the girl he had been with at the corporate apartment last month.

"What are you doing here?" he mumbled. He wasn't sure he remembered her name.

She smiled sweetly. "I just thought that maybe we could get together again. Like last time, you know?"

Fitz stared at her. "So, you came to my place of employment? How the hell did you find me?"

The girl became unhinged. Whispered, "Uh, I saw your business card on the desk. When you went to the bathroom that night."

Fitz rose, panicked as he stood on his shoeless feet. "Sshh!" he whispered urgently. "You're a nice girl, but you are not to come here again. Ever! Is that clear?"

The girl remained rooted in place, her face a road map of insecurity.

"Do you understand me?" Fitz growled.

"Yes," she replied meekly.

"Good. Then leave. Right now."

The girl opened the door and stepped outside. A moment later, Milly appeared. "Everything okay?" she asked.

"Yes. That was a friend's daughter asking for a job."

"Kind of young to be working here," Milly grunted.

"Yes. That's exactly what I told her."

THE QUEEN BEE

July 16, 1977

VIOLA

McNulty's Bar & Grill on East 57th Street in Manhattan hired Viola Cordova on the spot—smack in the middle of the interview—and it happened the way she suspected it might.

One glance at her, and Chubs McNulty was floored—thought he had hit the lottery after grilling her for a full four minutes. *Not unusual,* she thought as Chubs eyed her appreciatively. *Men are drawn to me like bumble bees are drawn to the queen bee.*

It was true because Viola Cordova had been blessed with incredibly good looks. The type of good looks that had helped catapult Marilyn Monroe and Raquel Welch to fame. Lush, wavy blonde hair and bedroom eyes. A knockout body. Yet, it was a small dark mole at the top of her lip that created for her a persona of titillation and defiance. Her foster mother once scolded her for referring to it as a mole. "For God's sake, Viola! It's a beauty mark," she said. "A mole is simply ugly."

As a young teen, Viola had harbored a secret wish for a career in modeling or acting.

She possessed neither talent.

But as her teenage appearance morphed into an adult version of herself, it had frightened her parents, much as it should have frightened them. Most parents would prefer not to hear the word "voluptuous" mentioned in the same sentence with their daughter's name. Such a big word, synonymous with sex and sexual innuendo.

During the interview at McNulty's, Viola remained poised, courteous. She took stock of the environment: upscale clientele, oversized circular bar with plenty of customers sipping exotic cocktails. The restaurant portion of the tavern was in full view from the bar.

Viola visualized a ticker-tape parade of thoughts marching across McNulty's mind when he asked if she was interested in the job.

She nodded her head vigorously. "Yes, sir. I am very interested."

"Happy to have you aboard," he said. "But please, call me Chubs." He smiled at her and reached for her hand. She took his, big and bear-like, into her own and marveled at its softness. She could almost hear her stepmother's words: *never judge a book by its cover, Viola. The story inside may be incredible.*

Viola walked to the subway station in a daze. In less than two weeks she had fled Florida, set up home in Manhattan, and had landed a decent job. It felt as if the gods were finally smiling in her direction.

She skipped down the concrete stairs that led to the subway system, paid her fare, and waited on the platform for her train. She tried to avoid the stench of urine and sweaty bodies, discarded newspapers left behind to float onto the train tracks.

For an uncomfortable moment, she felt transported back to her life with Bobby Lee. She had run away with him in the dark of night, leaving a stark note for her foster parents. *Thanks for taking care of me.* That was it, plain and simple. She did not have a way with words.

The train pulled into the station, and she hurried through the doors, found a seat, and sank into it. Thought about her crummy first job as a bartender.

Two days after settling in Florida with Bobby Lee, she turned eighteen. She was a kid, really. Didn't know the first thing about earning money or paying taxes. Never had a checking or savings account. Had never paid a bill.

THE QUEEN BEE

July 16, 1977

VIOLA

McNulty's Bar & Grill on East 57th Street in Manhattan hired Viola Cordova on the spot—smack in the middle of the interview—and it happened the way she suspected it might.

One glance at her, and Chubs McNulty was floored—thought he had hit the lottery after grilling her for a full four minutes. *Not unusual,* she thought as Chubs eyed her appreciatively. *Men are drawn to me like bumble bees are drawn to the queen bee.*

It was true because Viola Cordova had been blessed with incredibly good looks. The type of good looks that had helped catapult Marilyn Monroe and Raquel Welch to fame. Lush, wavy blonde hair and bedroom eyes. A knockout body. Yet, it was a small dark mole at the top of her lip that created for her a persona of titillation and defiance. Her foster mother once scolded her for referring to it as a mole. "For God's sake, Viola! It's a beauty mark," she said. "A mole is simply ugly."

As a young teen, Viola had harbored a secret wish for a career in modeling or acting.

She possessed neither talent.

But as her teenage appearance morphed into an adult version of herself, it had frightened her parents, much as it should have frightened

She was hired as seasonal holiday help at a dump called the Port 'O Call. A titty bar with a crooked stage and four poles bolted into it. A red curtain taped to the back wall of the stage was supposed to make it look classy. The place was always dark and the bar always sticky, no matter how often she dragged a wet towel across it.

Everyone wore cheap Santa hats and she made more money in the three weeks leading up to Christmas than she had made in the previous two months combined.

At the time, she knew little about tending bar. Just that tonic water was mixed with gin or vodka, and Coca-Cola with rum. Everything else was poured from the bottle, straight up. Fancy umbrella drinks did not exist at the Port 'O Call.

They handled a rough crowd: construction workers, bikers, a general assortment of riff-raff. Every forty-five minutes the girls would come out with their titties swaying—little red holiday bows pasted on their nipples—and pretended to pole dance.

More than a fair share of customer attention was thrown her way, but she avoided trouble by lying about being pregnant. That backed them off faster than a mouthful of chewed garlic.

When the seasonal stint ended, Bobby Lee needed less than a week to skip out on her.

The train coughed itself to a hard stop, and Viola jumped up and exited the train. She flew up the stairs and walked the three blocks to her . . . Uncle Sammy's . . . apartment.

Three weeks after Bobby Lee bolted, she lucked into a full-time gig at Scooters, an upscale bar that catered to rich folks who adored fancy umbrella drinks; the place where Lucy had befriended her.

The sad part was, it was also the place where she met Leroy Stills.

WAKE UP

July 20, 1977

JEFFREY

In Jeffrey's muddled dream, he was seated in the basement of Our Lady of Sorrows, his mother's church. *Why am I here?* he wondered. He did not like the church. Did not like to pray. He did not believe in prayer, so what was this about?

Sobering thoughts swirled behind his eyelids like marshmallow fluff. *What's going on?*

Then, poof, the dream evaporated. He was relieved to see it go.

Jeffrey heard voices. Voices which sounded as if they were floating through the air, floating like musical notes in a child's cartoon show. *Am I still dreaming?*

A commotion of activity erupted, and Jeffrey's eyes shot open. He blinked rapidly to stave off the harsh glare of the fluorescent lighting. *Am I inside a bubble?*

Bursts of noise whizzed past his ears like rapid-fire bullets. His heart accelerated in a rapid rat-tat-tat rhythm.

An echo of heavy footsteps followed. He heard a discord of hissing and beeping sounds—a strange assortment of blended noises. He tried to swallow, but his throat felt clogged, as if he had swallowed a wad of tissues. He wanted to talk, to shout out to the people he sensed nearby. *Save me,* he begged silently. *I'm suffocating.*

Then, a sharp pin prick of light lasered into his pupils. He blinked hard. Blinked again.

A muffled voice said, "He's coming around."

Jeffrey felt a searing pain accelerate its way up from his ankle and into his calf, until finally, it rooted itself into the center of his leg, a leg suspended upright in an arcane pulley contraption.

He gagged on his scream. With every blink of his eyes, the sounds in the room were amplified a hundred times louder. He shifted slightly, felt a new burst of pain wrap itself around his neck, his shoulders, the burn of a thousand wicked suns. The pain was hardcore, a twisted pain one might feel if wounded on a battlefield.

"Is he all right?" he heard a woman ask. "He's not suffering, is he?" The words were followed by a choke of tears.

Have I died? He thought. *Is this my funeral? Are these shadows here to mourn me?*

Slowly, his eyes adjusted to the overhead lights and settled on a silhouette standing at the foot of his bed. Squinting, he saw it was a man wearing loosely fitted green scrubs. The man juggled a bedpan.

The beeping sound near Jeffrey's head grew louder and more insistent. He felt someone lean into him, the weight like cement against his shallow chest. "Jeffrey, can you hear me?"

With significant effort, Jeffrey nodded.

"Okay now, Jeffrey," Dr. Sinclair said. "We're going to remove the tube from your throat. It will feel weird, but I promise you, it will be over quickly."

As the tube was removed, Jeffrey coughed and sputtered. In a child like whisper, he croaked, "*Water.*"

The next morning, with Jeffrey's mother seated near his bed, Dr. Sinclair pulled a chair close and spoke to him.

"You were in a very bad plane crash, Jeffrey," he said softly. "You suffered extensive injuries: cracked ribs, a collapsed lung, damaged spleen. Most serious of your injuries were an open femoral fracture and a shattered hip. Both required surgeries. You have second-degree burns on your neck and shoulders. A swelling of your brain forced us to place you into a medically induced coma." He paused. "You're remarkably lucky to be alive."

Jeffrey shook his head. A dull ache had begun to gnaw at the base of his neck. "Why can't I remember anything about an accident?" he groaned.

Dr. Sinclair pursed his lips. "Sometimes when the brain registers an overwhelming trauma, it can block that memory. It's a process called disassociation or detachment from reality. It's the way the brain tries to protect itself."

"Will I ever be able to remember?"

"In time, perhaps. Sometimes a person can become disassociated from the exact moment of the trauma, yet the brain will allow the memory to be released in short flashbacks."

Dr. Sinclair reached out, gently touched Jeffrey's arm. "I realize that dealing with this trauma—present or disassociated—can be a very overwhelming and frightening experience. I urge you to seek therapy once you're physically able to do so."

Jeffrey squirmed uncomfortably. "How long will it take to recover from all of this?"

Dr. Sinclair stood, folded his arms in front of him. "Your longest recovery will be for the femoral fracture. Four to five months to heal. Long term, you will experience muscular weakness, limited standing, or walking. You may heal with a slight abnormality to your gait."

"A limp?"

"Yes. But with proper rehabilitation, it shouldn't be pronounced." Dr. Sinclair pushed the chair back beneath the window. "I'll be in to check on you a little later."

Jeffrey Kaye did not respond. He stared straight ahead, a vortex of information whirling about his unsteady mind.

"It's okay, Jeffrey," his mother cooed. She stood and kissed his forehead and cheek. Jeffrey felt the heavy crucifix she wore as it swiped against his chin.

"God will help you through this difficult period. After all, He did allow you to survive the crash. And, as Dr. Sinclair said, you're incredibly lucky to be alive."

As his pain medications began to wear off, Jeffrey wondered how luck could possibly be associated with him or with his situation.

THE KID

July 21, 1977

Surely, I do not need to tell you that as the traffic controller involved in the Hewitt-Jackson Airport disasters, I was pulled from my controlling duties. A union rep informed me that I qualified for remedial training, but if I could not successfully recertify as a controller, I could be reassigned to a new position within the FAA.

That was out of the question for me. I refused to ever again return to the controls. The mental impact of having been involved in such a major incident affected me deeply, and I knew I would always second-guess myself, would always doubt my actions and inactions.

Instead, I remained on paid leave. When it ended, I would tap into an accumulation of paid time off—personal and sick days, unused vacation hours. My bank account was sufficient to see me through the next few months, but after that, I simply did not know what I would do. But I knew that I would never return to the FAA.

Foolishly, I hung on to the notion that the police or the FBI or agents of the FAA would one day be at my door with cuffs and shackles to arrest me. Logically, I knew that here in the United States, there is a law which protects air traffic controllers. A law which prevents us from being held personally liable for an accident or incident, provided we were not intentionally or recklessly doing something wrong. Still, I worried.

The bungalow remained my safe nest, and I feared stepping too f from my comfort zone. After losing Savannah, friendships had not com easily. I had no one to depend on for help. A handful of acquaintances, yes. People likely to share a beer after work, an occasional movie. Certainly not anyone I could depend on to buoy my spirits or whom I could phone at three in the morning during a crisis.

I had not found a compatible partner either, not anyone suited for a long-term relationship. I did not have a revolving door of men in and out of my life as Savannah had. No, the only solid and steady partner in my life was my career. Now that, too, was in shambles.

Surprisingly, unforeseen dynamics pulled me into a quasi-friendship with the kid next door. We met one dark night while most people remained asleep. My rear porch faced a marsh that was abundant with wild tiger lilies and nocturnal little creatures. The night was pleasantly warm, the sky spilling over with stars as I sat there and chain-smoked my second cigarette.

I heard the creak of a porch door as it squeaked open. Looked over and saw the kid. Quiet as a mouse, he hitched up his jeans and lit a cigarette. A cigarette that did not smell at all like tobacco. It was the smell of marijuana, sweet and fragrant as it wafted its way to my porch. The kid looked over at me, and like conspirators, we nodded to each other. Beneath the dim porch lights, I saw that he was a replica of what I had imagined he might look like: fifteen or sixteen, tall and bony, with long, unkempt hair. I could see pimples on his chin, a layer of fuzz above his lip.

We both finished our smokes, lifted our hands in a silent goodbye.

Every night for a week, the kid returned to his porch, smoked his funny cigarette, waved good night. He was as punctual as a school marm.

Our bungalows were crowded together with only a thin strip of grass separating us. On the eighth night of our unrehearsed rendezvous, the kid looked over at me and said, "Your Volvo hasn't moved from your driveway in weeks. If you don't run the engine, it's going to cut out on you."

I nodded. "Yeah, well, that's the least of my problems."

The kid blew a stream of smoke toward the cloudless sky. "I can start it for you if you want."

When I turned to fully face him, I realized he was older than I had previously thought, closer to eighteen than sixteen. "Thank you. That's very nice. I may take you up on the offer."

The kid nodded. His hair was pulled back into a ponytail, and I clearly saw his elongated face and a harsh topography of acne that swallowed most of it.

"Been tough on you since the accident, huh?" he said. "All those reporters hounding you. Giving you no peace, no chance to recoup."

I lit another cigarette. The kid was sharp, had assessed my situation without my ever having to say a word. "Yeah," I mumbled. "Very tough."

"It would have to be," he replied softly. "With your face all over TV, that can't have helped either. Is that why you never leave your house?"

"Yes," I said tightly. "I've had death threats and awful, vile phone calls. It's gotten to me in a bad way."

For a few minutes, we were silent.

Then the kid said, "I hate the injustice of it. Hate for anyone to be treated unfairly."

"Have you been treated unfairly?"

The kid laughed harshly. "Are you kidding? Look at me. I'm the poster boy for pimple creams."

"Don't say that about yourself."

"Why not?" he said sarcastically. "Girls won't look at me, and guys have contests to come up with the worst nicknames for me."

My face softened as I looked at him. "I'm sorry to know that. It's awful."

He stood up, unwound his hair from the ponytail. "Tomorrow I got to go to the supermarket for my mom. If you need some stuff, I can get it for you."

The next day, I found a note slipped beneath my door: FOOD ON DOORSTEP. When I cracked the door, four brown A&P bags stared up at me. They were filled with canned goods, some fruit, milk, bread, and eggs. A six-pack of beer.

It was the kindest gesture I had been afforded in a long time.

JET KING

August 2, 1977

FITZ

"Fitz" and his father, Larry Fitzgerald Sr., sat in the rear of a chauffeur-driven Cadillac Seville en route to a business meeting in New Jersey. The car and the driver were owned by Fitzgerald Alloy Corporation. Fitz wished they could drive themselves to the meeting, but his father would not allow it. "Image is everything," he often reminded Fitz.

Father and son were dressed identically: gray and white pin-striped suits, crisply starched shirts, muted blue ties, freshly buffed shoes. Both wore cufflinks and carried pricey briefcases.

Fitz had submitted a proposal for a huge contract with Jet King Executive Airlines, one of the fastest growing private air transport companies in the industry. Catering to wealthy businessmen, movie stars, sports figures, and prominent politicians, they exacted exorbitant prices, but their level of luxury, discretion, and privacy was well worth the price.

Jet King had been impressed with Fitz's proposal and wanted to iron out final details. Fitz was convinced they would be awarded the contract.

His father leaned forward in his seat, tapped the driver's shoulder. "What's our estimated time of arrival, Karl?" he asked.

"Less than ten minutes, Mr. Fitzgerald."

"Thank you."

Fitz glanced sideways at his father. The man was always polite and respectful to his employees, far more polite than he was to his family.

It was blatantly clear that his father remained miserably married to Fitz's mother, Theresa Anne. They had married too young, right after high school. She was pregnant, and with her father involved with people who would gladly cut out a tongue with a rusty razor, Larry had been easily swayed to marry her.

Their relationship had struggled through thirty turbulent years. Years filled with arguments and bitter confrontations, dinner plates tossed at innocent walls. But during those rough years, Fitzgerald Alloy had prospered and expanded; money had streamed in like trout to a healthy pond. And all of it happening while Fitz's father habitually screwed anything that walked in high-heeled shoes.

But his mother would not concede their marriage. As a devout Catholic, she refused to divorce his father, and it simply made things worse.

A few years earlier, Fitz had confronted his father about the situation. "Okay, so she won't divorce you. Why not just pack a bag and leave? Move out of the house, get an apartment somewhere," he had said.

"I can't, Fitz," his father said solemnly. "Your grandfather may have returned to Sicily, but he still has powerful connections here. If I were to leave your mother, he might blow up the factory. Or something worse."

Fitz was pulled from his reverie as they pulled up to Jet King's main terminal at Teterboro Airport.

"Here we go, Dad," Fitz said. "Let's knock this one out of the park."

Later that night, at a moderately upscale hotel near Broadway, a black Lincoln Town Car pulled up to the busy entrance. A young woman who looked barely past her sixteenth birthday exited the car and with her chin held high walked into the busy lobby.

To some, she might appear a teenager. If, of course, one overlooked the heavy blue eyeshadow on her lids and the velvety red lipstick and the too-tight blouse that accentuated nicely tanned skin. She was thin as a model, with long golden hair. Purposefully, she walked to the east elevator bank, rode up to the sixth floor. Long strides took her along the hallway to room 606. She knocked discreetly.

When Fitz opened the door, he sensed relief sag from the girl's body. *Maybe she was expecting a fat old guy with a cigar hanging from his lip*, he thought. Instead, she saw a man with a clear, handsome face, a strong body.

He waved her inside, poked his head out into the corridor. Saw no one lingering along the carpeted hallway. Smiled to himself and gently closed the door.

Fitz smiled as he eyed the girl. *Perfect,* he thought. This one was a dream. Blonde, pretty, and young. Just the way he liked them.

"Champagne?" he asked.

The girl smiled shyly, nodded yes.

At the end of the night, Fitz rated the experience a perfect ten.

A MADMAN IS CAUGHT

August 10, 1977

VIOLA

Viola Cordova was resourceful, had been since childhood. It was an attribute most helpful when sharing a farm home with six other foster kids. She had been one of the lucky ones. Placed with a family of good, decent people who graciously offered her and the other kids a safe home, three solid meals a day. There was a variant of love, too, compassion. But expecting her foster parents to dole out a whole lot of love to seven emotionally needy children was, in Viola's young mind, far and above what they might have signed on for.

When Bobby Lee had come along to offer Viola an escape to a different life, a life that promised her relief from the monotony of farm life in rural Indiana, she had leaped at the opportunity. Yes, she had felt a sting of remorse when she slithered from the farmhouse during the early morning hours, way before the cocks crowed or the cows mooed.

She hadn't looked back, and she assumed that her foster parents hadn't either.

During her first six weeks in New York, Viola quickly adapted to the pace and vibrancy of the city. She discovered an abundance of small bars and cheap cabarets tucked away in dark alleyways. She memorized bus schedules and subway routes and knew which kiosks sold cigarettes at the cheapest price.

Uncle Sammy's apartment was a lifesaver. Immediately, she repurposed the staid apartment into a warm, cozy home, filled the small space with colorful pillows and throw rugs and curtains, added an assortment of green potted plants, a small wooden wine rack.

She was happy and content, enjoyed her job at McNulty's, earned enough money in wages and tips to maintain the rent-controlled apartment and her daily living expenses. But there was not much left for discretionary spending. Living in New York City was frightfully expensive.

A week earlier, she had sold the old Malibu, though it broke her heart to do so. The car had been a lifeline to freedom and allowed her the ease of coming and going as she pleased. Realistically, though, the city was not conducive to automobiles, especially with its wicked law of alternate side of the street parking to allow monster-sized street cleaning trucks to rumble along the roads before sunrise.

In addition to the street cleaning obstacles, the city coughed up its fair share of unique problems, one of which was a city-wide energy blackout that left her cowering in her bathroom for hours.

But the most critical problem plaguing the city that sweltering summer was Son of Sam, the monster who, for a year, prowled the city and its nearby boroughs, indiscriminately shooting young victims. Women, men, gay, straight—everyone was fair game; everyone was walking about with a giant bull's-eye on their back.

During that muggy night of August tenth, everyone at McNulty's was jubilant—screaming with glee, dancing among the tables and chairs, toasting each other with bottles of beer and glasses filled with liquor. All of them heaving a big sigh of relief because Son of Sam had been caught!

People waited at the bar three and four deep, with the list for dining tables two pages long. It was as if a moratorium had been lifted. Euphoria engulfed the room, energetic and palpable. McNulty's was finally exhaling, a release from being wound way too tightly for way too long.

Viola scrambled behind the bar, poured drinks, rinsed glasses, filled the cash register, which kept dinging and dinging as her tip jar filled to overflowing. At one point, she shoved the jar beneath the bar and replaced it with an empty one. That, too, quickly filled.

And it was that night she began to skim money from the register. Leroy Stills had taught her how to do it quite efficiently.

"Two ways to do it without getting caught," he explained. "First, when the place is super busy, you ring up only half the price of the drink. That half goes into the register. The other half goes in your tip jar. No one's the wiser, babe."

Viola remembered how he had laughed when he saw the look of surprise on her face. "Another thing," he said. "When someone wants to buy you a drink, you pour water instead of vodka into a glass. Toss in a lime to make it look real. Alcohol wasn't involved, right? You drank water, so consider the money as a tip."

Viola's feet and back ached; twice her knees threatened to give out. Splashes of juice and red wine and beer foam soiled her white shirt; perspiration dampened her hair and clung to her face.

Nearing midnight, the bar crowd thinned. The earlier jubilation had succumbed to the late hour as excutives and secretaries and doctors and lawyers and construction workers all realized that the next day's workload was only a few short hours away.

It was then that Viola finally noticed Larry "Fitz" Fitzgerald. He was seated at the bar, squeezed between an obese man and a woman who looked as if she had just lost her best friend. She stopped in her tracks, halfway to delivering margaritas to a trio of young women.

She allowed herself a good long look.

He was blue-ribbon perfect: shiny dark hair, blazing black eyes, dimples that added boyish charm. He looked nothing like the bad boys she often preferred. He wore a pale blue shirt, which looked expensive, open collared, sleeves rolled to his elbows.

"Gin and tonic, please," he asked pleasantly. Viola mixed the drink, placed it in front of him. He sipped it, placed a twenty-dollar bill on the counter.

"You're new here," he said. It was stated, not a question.

"My third week," she smiled at him.

"Well, it's a wonderful place to work."

For a moment, Viola was tongue-tied. "Guess you come here often?"

"Since I've been in diapers," he laughed.

Viola laughed too. Reached across the bar top, offered to shake his hand. "I'm Viola."

He held her hand as gently as if she were a wounded bird. "I'm Larry Fitzgerald Jr. My friends call me Fitz."

"Nice to meet you," she said. "Excuse me. Those two at the end of the bar look thirsty."

When she popped back to him a few minutes later, he said, "You're a very beautiful woman, Viola." Then he quickly sucked in his breath. "Sorry," he apologized, "you must hear that a hundred times a day."

"No," she lied. "It's sweet of you to say."

Viola felt a familiar ache, one that had been on hiatus for way too long. She was accustomed to boys and men with cocky, superior attitudes. Men who treated women as playthings until life became too real for them. When their fists became their main weapons against their insecurities.

But this man was different. She guessed he did not drive a Harley or sell drugs, would not rob her purse while she was asleep.

Still, looks were deceiving, and she could not be 100 percent certain he was not that type of man. But the stirring inside her, well, she was 100 percent certain it was entirely because of him.

She smiled at him, her eyes dancing with interest, but she was quickly whisked away by shouts coming from a group of rowdy businessmen who had taken up a huge chunk of real estate at the end of her station.

When she next looked up, Fitz was gone.

MELEE

August 11, 1977

FITZ

Fitz lay on his queen-sized bed with his hands linked behind his head. The sheets were clean and crisp beneath his naked torso. He thought about Viola—the bombshell barkeep at McNulty's. He knew she had been attracted to him, recognized him as a mover and a shaker. A man capable of snapping his fingers and getting whatever the hell he wanted. A man with deep pockets and sexual prowess. He saw it in her eyes. In the way she had devoured his face.

But Fitz was not interested in Viola Cordova. She was a beauty, yes, but too old for his tastes. There were plenty of men for her to choose from; most had been sitting right there inside McNulty's earlier that night. Men who had eyed her openly, some surreptitiously, but all of them wanting the same thing: the gorgeous blonde behind the bar.

He promised himself he would be careful around her. She had a tough, gritty edge that let people know she meant business. Her eyes, too, were veiled, surely hiding secrets. Perhaps hiding fear.

Earlier, he had slipped unnoticed from McNulty's just as things were getting out of control. The night had begun perfectly, due to the capture of Son of Sam. But it had turned into an ugly finish when a brawl broke out between a group of smartly dressed businessmen in a heated argument about an unpaid gambling debt.

He had watched as a short fellow clocked a taller one with his briefcase. Watched as the briefcase caught the poor guy hard against his forehead. The snap of the lock had dislodged and snagged the guy's eyebrow, tearing a large zigzag gash down to his eyelid. Sliced it open like a watermelon. Blood splattered everywhere, women screamed, fists were raised, punches were thrown, glassware shattered, barstools toppled. McNulty's looked as if an earthquake had struck.

Immediately, Fitz scrambled past the melee and slipped away as quietly as a mouse with a hunk of cheese in its cheeks. There was not a reason he could think of to place himself in a situation that might turn sticky at any moment. He had jogged two blocks east of McNulty's before hailing a taxi. The trip home to Forest Hills in neighboring Queens County took a quick nineteen and a half minutes, to where he lived comfortably in a fourth-floor apartment tucked inside an elegant pre-war building.

There, Fitz maintained a low profile. Never brought girls home. Had not attempted friendships with his neighbors, though he did have a fondness for Mrs. Weiss, an ancient woman who had survived Auschwitz. On occasion, he trotted to the local grocer to buy her cigarettes and cat food for her kitten, Marvelous.

Only once had his mother visited him at the apartment. "You know how much I hate leaving Long Island, Fitz," she had said stiffly. "It's too urban here."

That was his mother to the core. Interested only in what benefitted her own needs.

With his head resting against the bed's headboard, he thought about how horribly his mother treated his father.

Thought about how lucky he was to live far enough away from them to conduct his personal life in private, without anyone snooping around or asking questions.

CHOCOLATE ICE CREAM THOUGHTS

August 18, 1977

JEFFREY

Jeffrey Kaye's room at the Atlanta Trauma Center resembled every other hospital room in the country: drab and devoid of any distinctive touch. For weeks he had been sequestered in the small room, relegated to staring at the scum-colored walls and consuming meals which should have been labeled "WARNING!" His only respite was watching hours and hours of old movies and local news on the small TV that hung from the ceiling. Jeffrey was willing to sky dive from his room's window to escape the boredom.

On his dinner tray he stared down at something square and brown floating in a blob of congealed sauce. The only edible thing on the tray was a small cup of chocolate ice cream—the kind you would get as a kid with a little wooden spoon attached.

Thankfully, his mother, Nancy, had finally returned to her motel room, and frankly, he was relieved. All afternoon he had listened to her read aloud verse after verse from the Bible. He felt as trapped as a rabbit in a metal claw.

Sure, he loved his mother, respected her, was grateful that she was here in Atlanta to supervise his recovery. But that respect was dwarfed by his resentment of her. She was a good person, but her presence was overwhelming whether at home or at work or at church.

He lifted the lid off the ice cream cup, dug the little wooden spoon in and popped a bit into his mouth. *The trip to Greece was supposed to be a breather for me. Seven glorious days without her constant hovering, without her endless preaching.*

As he finished the last swipe of chocolate ice cream, Dr. Sinclair entered his room. Jeffrey was always surprised by the doctor's height, the way he slightly ducked his head under the doorframe, a man well suited for an NBA team. That night he wore a rumpled white lab coat and scuffed sneakers. Behind him was a petite nurse who wheeled a steel cart crowded with blood pressure cuffs, syringes, and a small mountain of patient charts.

"So, how are we this evening, Jeffrey?" asked Dr. Sinclair. His voice was melodic, as if he were about to sing a ballad.

"I'm doing okay, Doc. Can't wait to get out of here though."

"Don't blame you a bit." He flipped open a chart, skimmed through a few pages. "Looks like some improvement with the physical therapy. Heard you refused to use the cane, huh?"

Jeffrey cringed with embarrassment. He had insisted to the nurses that he could manage on his own without the cane. In fact, he had been ridiculously adamant about it. Three steps in and he was sprawled on his face, kissing the ugly linoleum floor, and was mortified when the orderlies were summoned to help him upright. After that, his machismo vanished, and he used the awful cane for all future attempts.

Dr. Sinclair's voice interrupted Jeffrey's thoughts. "...and your last brain scan showed no swelling at all. I am optimistically encouraged that you will be ready for discharge, perhaps as soon as next week."

After the doctor and nurse had left the room and the horrible dinner tray was removed, Jeffrey's emotions see-sawed dramatically. Of course, he wanted to go home, to sleep in his own bed, on his own pillow. He could not wait to sink his teeth into a juicy burger with a cold bottle of beer.

He exhaled deeply at the reality of what going home really meant. *My job is gone, and I don't have a girlfriend waiting for me. There are months of physical therapy ahead, and I'll be forced to use the stupid cane wherever I go. How will I climb the five flights of stairs to the apartment?*

His eyes began to fill. *It will be just me and Mom. Like always.*

Finally, the tears erupted.

Why did this happen to me? Why?

DISAPPEARING ACT

August 18, 1977

The consequences of self-isolation quickly became apparent, for it allowed me too much time to think and fret and despair.

Twenty-one days had passed since the neighbor kid had left groceries at my front door, and I had not seen him since. I thought perhaps his mother wasn't too keen with him chatting up a woman clearly a decade or so older than her teenage son. I wondered if she, too, despised me.

It was late afternoon as the sun spat a tiny ray of thin sunlight into the room. A glass of cheap scotch dangled from my hand. Three Billie Holiday albums were stacked on the stereo, and Billie's thin, airy voice washed over me as easily as bubbles in a warm bath.

Three songs into the first album—a hard knock on my front door.

I jumped up, splashed a good amount of liquid onto the carpeting. Who the hell could this be? With all the death threats I had received, I worried it might be a lunatic hoping to leave a bullet hole in the middle of my forehead. Frantically I spiraled in a semicircle, searched for a weapon.

Another round of hard knocks, and I yanked open the door. Behind my back I clutched the base of a small lamp. On the front steps waited the kid, his hands scrunched low inside his jean pockets. "Hey," he said. "Feel like company?"

Relieved, I let out a long sigh. The words blurted from my mouth before I could stop them.

"Where have you been?"

Surprised, he stepped back, lifted his hands in a whoa-calm-down sort of way. "Can I come in?" he asked.

Slowly, my racing heart settled. I motioned the kid inside, then closed the door. "Sorry," I murmured. "I'm a little on edge."

"Sure. I get it."

He plopped into a chair near the stereo. "Guess I should've told you. Every couple of weeks I got to stay with my dad. A joint custody thing."

I smiled at him. "Sorry, didn't mean to sound so..."

"Hey, it's okay. Been a tough couple of days for all of us."

He reached into his shirt pocket, pulled out a fat joint. "Do you mind?" he asked.

"No, it's okay."

He lit the joint, inhaled deeply. Handed it to me with a questioning look.

I shook my head, lifted my glass. "This will do just fine."

As I looked at the kid, it dawned on me that he had never told me his name, though I had heard his mother sometimes yell out to him, "Daniel, dinner's ready!" I wondered if he had siblings. If his mother was kind or mean and for how long she had been divorced from his father.

Billie Holiday's voice began singing "God Bless The Child."

"Tell me about your family," the kid asked gently. "Where are they? And why aren't you staying with them until this whole thing blows over?"

"My family's gone," I whispered.

Astonished, he said, "Oh wow, that's heavy. Is it okay to talk about it?"

I scrunched my shoulders up into my neck, but then the words came in a rush. "My mother had an accident three and a half years ago. My stepfather claimed she fell down the stairs."

My hand shook ever so slightly as I reached for my cigarettes, lit one. Offered one to the kid. "I don't smoke," he joked.

We both chuckled, then I continued. "He told me she tripped on the twins' toys while carrying laundry down the stairs."

"Twins?" the kid interrupted.

"Yes. My three-year-old half brothers—Mickey and Roger—named for Mantle and Maris, the famous Yankees duo. Their toys."

I tapped a long cigarette ash into a lopsided ashtray I had made back in junior high. "It was hard to believe she was gone. I had spoken to her just that morning." An avalanche of emotion tumbled and whirled in my gut.

"You had doubts about it being an accident?" the kid asked.

"Yes. There was no way my mother was carrying laundry down the stairs late at night. And she would never have allowed toys to be left on the stairs. She was obsessively careful with the twins. They were a handful and so speedy for two little kids."

A long silence sat with us. The kid got up, walked to me, squeezed my shoulder. "Refill?" he asked, pointing to my empty glass. I nodded, swiped at my nose as he walked into the little kitchen. I heard him pull ice cubes from the metal tray, plunk them into my glass. Heard liquid splash against the cubes. Then the refrigerator door opened, followed by the click of a beer cap being flicked off.

He returned to the living room, gently placed my glass on the ancient coffee table that was already covered with plenty of old stains. "What kind of man was your stepfather?" he asked as he sat and took a long pull of the cold beer.

"Howard? He was horrible. A callous, dictatorial man. An out-and-out bigot."

"Did he ever raise his hands to you? To your mother?"

"No. Never. But I suspected he wasn't very nice to her emotionally."

The kid looked down at the floor. "Do you . . . do you think he pushed her down those stairs?"

I shifted up, leaned forward to make my point. "It's what I believed at the time and what I still believe. But I had no proof. When I confronted the sheriff about it, he said, 'There was no wrongdoing here, Margaret. You read the report and it's clear. It was a terrible, terrible accident. Try to let it go and get on with your life.'"

Tears brimmed and finally flowed. "Can you imagine?" I said faintly. "He told me to let it go, as if I were holding a kite string. He said it so matter-of-factly." I swiped at the wetness on my face. "Sheriff Maynard was a close friend of Howard's, and I wondered if he was covering for him."

"God, I'm so sorry," the kid said. "I wish I could say something helpful, but whatever comes out of my mouth will sound dorky and lame."

"You're not dorky," I sniffed. "And you're not lame. You're very kind."

For a while we sat quietly, listened to Billie Holiday, sipped our drinks.

Finally, the kid asked, "What happened to Howard and the twins?"

I stared up at the ceiling.

"Three weeks after the service, I phoned Howard to check on Mickey and Roger and wanted to look through my mother's jewelry. She was quite fond of a tennis bracelet my father had given to her before they were married."

"Did you speak to him?"

"No. He didn't return my calls. The last time I tried to phone, the number was no longer in service."

"Damn," the kid growled.

"Yeah. Finally, I tried to call him at his office and learned he had resigned weeks earlier."

The next album on the stereo dropped into place; it sounded so loud in the quiet of the room. When I looked at the kid, his face was etched with concern. "What did you do?" he asked.

"I grabbed my keys. Drove out to the home where I had grown up. There was a realtor's sign on the front lawn with a big SOLD poster plastered over the FOR SALE words. I ran around the house like a burglar, searching for entry. The windows were dark; it was obvious the house was vacant."

I stopped talking, blew my nose. Took two gulps of the scotch. Bleary-eyed, the kid watched me anxiously, half folded into the chair, his elbows resting on his knees, fists supporting his face.

"I ran back to my car," I continued. "Found a pen, scribbled the phone number of the realtor onto my palm. Then I spotted their mailbox with the little carved woodpecker atop it. I rummaged inside of it, found a bunch of junk mail and an envelope from First Bank of Atlanta. My hands were shaking badly as I tore into that envelope. It was the month's bank statement, and it showed a zero balance. ACCOUNT CLOSED was stamped in big red letters across the top of the page."

Standing, I paced the room, my brain whirring like a fan as I finished the story.

"When I returned home, I called Liz Larson, the realtor's name on the FOR SALE sign. I asked about the house at 787 Forsythe Drive. She told me the property had already been sold. That it went to market on February seventeenth and that it had sold the very next day. An all-cash sale and at full price."

"Did you ask her where they had moved to?"

"Yeah. She didn't know. Only that they were leaving Georgia."

I slumped to the sofa, my breath sucked out of me.

The kid seemed incredulous. "So, he just took off? No warning? No explanation? No fucking goodbye?"

"Yup. My mother died on the tenth of February; services were held on the twelfth. Which meant that Howard put the house for sale just five days after burying her. Probably the same day he resigned from his job, emptied their bank account."

Now, the kid was crying. Big fat tears that cascaded around the bumps on his face. "You didn't deserve that," he sniffled. "No one deserves to be treated like that."

We sat in silence for a while, the stereo needle stuck on the last groove of the last album, a scratchy sound that droned on until I rose to replace the needle in its cradle.

Of course, Howard had pushed my mother down the stairs.

Why else would he have pulled his disappearing act so swiftly after her death?

FLIRTING

August 19, 1977

FITZ

The phone call to Fitzgerald Alloy Corp in Brooklyn came after all the staff had gone and only the janitorial crew remained. It whistled through the telephone lines as it shot past the factory floor and the employee break room and finally settled at Fitz's office on the seventh floor.

Fitz was giddy with delight when he learned they had won the Jet King contract, a potentially huge revenue-generating account. In his mind he calculated how big a boost it might mean to his compensation.

His car and driver waited at the front of the building. Too excited to face an empty apartment, he instructed the driver to head into Manhattan, and when they reached Madison and Forty-Ninth, Fitz exited the car and began to walk.

It's too nice a night to ride, he thought, stopping occasionally to peek into shop windows. He inhaled the mingling scents of hot dogs and pretzels and bus fumes, all coalescing into one steamy aroma.

The air was warm, with a shiny quarter moon dangling in the sky. He was buoyed by the faint tendrils of night rolling toward him like a red carpet ready to whisk him away on a magical journey ride.

His slow-paced walk brought him to Fifty-Seventh Street, where he ducked into McNulty's Bar & Grill.

Happy hour had wound down, and the place was not as crowded as it had been during his previous visit. He found a seat at the end of the glossy-topped bar and settled in, eager for a drink, eager to rip off his tie, to unclasp the top button of his shirt.

He shrugged out of his suit jacket, rolled up his white shirt sleeves. Waved to the pretty bartender.

"Hi," he said. "A gin and tonic would be great."

She smiled at him, nodded.

He admired her firm body as she glided along the bar, fixed his drink, served it to him in a fat club glass.

"Thank you. I needed this."

"Don't we all?" she joked back.

He pushed a crisp twenty-dollar bill to the edge of the counter. "For you," he said.

"Thank you, but that's way too generous."

"Nothing's too generous for a beautiful woman," he said warmly. Silently, he scolded himself. *Why am I flirting with this girl if I'm not interested in her?*

But flirting came as naturally to Fitz as blinking his eyes.

He grinned. "You're Viola, right?"

"Yes. And . . . you're Fitz."

He was wearing his phony wedding ring. The one he wore when he went to bars and clubs. When he wanted to make it perfectly clear that he was already spoken for. When he noticed Viola noticing his phony wedding ring, he saw the unmistakable look of disappointment in her eyes.

She excused herself to refill the beer mugs of two lumberjack-sized men, and Fitz watched as the men gently teased her, how good-naturedly she played along.

Later, when she returned with a freshly made drink for him, she commented on the tattoo on his forearm. A name inked in red and green and surrounded by angels.

"Is that your wife's name?" she asked, pointing to the tattoo.

"No," he said sadly. "My sister, Rose."

Viola's brows arched.

"She was a nurse in Vietnam. Killed while helping to unload wounded soldiers from a helicopter."

"Oh geez. I'm so sorry."

"Yeah, me too." He did not like to talk about Rose; it tore wide a wound in him that had never properly healed. Thankfully, he had been spared the horrors of Vietnam—the first time while in college, the second time after being classified 4-F due to a pattern of sleepwalking.

"So," he said, changing the subject. "For someone who's only been working here for what...three weeks now...you seem to have found a good rhythm with the customers."

She laughed. "That's not hard to do. This is a nice place. Nothing like the place I worked at in Florida."

My God, Fitz thought as he looked at her. *She's dazzling. And she's looking at me like a lioness stalking prey.* He wondered if he should quickly finish his drink and leave. Lingering might give her the wrong impression.

But he was enjoying their conversation, enjoying the ease of being in her space. And she certainly was easy on the eyes.

"So, Florida, huh? What brought you to New York?" he asked.

She stared straight into his eyes. "A jerk who didn't appreciate what he had."

SECOND BANANA

August 19, 1977

VIOLA

When she spotted Fitz walking through the door of McNulty's, a flare of desire assaulted her. The need was so intense it became a physical hurt. Since her arrival in New York, there was no denying that her love life had hit a dry spell.

She had not stopped thinking about Fitz since their first meeting. His intrusion into her dreams and fantasies was embarrassing. She was totally bewitched.

Her sexual encounters with boyfriends and casual one-night stands had been hugely disappointing. Guys the likes of Bobby Lee, with his strutting posture and poor sexual skills. With Leroy, usually stinking of whiskey, attacking her mouth with slobbery wet kisses, and who still managed to make her feel uneasy from a thousand miles away.

But this feeling, this was new to her. Here was a real man, a beautiful man of privilege as evidenced by his expensive clothing and the large tips he left for her. He had a gentle manner, and she liked the way his lips twitched when he smiled at her.

Clearly, he was hands-off, evidenced by the wedding ring. Viola did not date or bed married men. It was not her style to be the second banana, because nothing good ever came from being the second banana.

Still, she enjoyed conversing with him but was sad to hear the story of his sister Rose's death in Vietnam. She knew of friends from high school who had returned home in wheelchairs, missing arms or legs or eyes, or who shook violently at the sound of a dog's bark.

She shook the memory away. Refocused on Fitz. A friendship with him would be quite easy.

Keeping him out of her dreams, well, that would be infinitely more difficult.

HOMEWARD BOUND

August 26, 1977

JEFFREY

Jeffrey Kaye's discharge from the Atlanta Trauma Center on the morning of Friday, August 26, happened without fanfare, quietly and unobtrusively, as if his hellish days and nights there had been a mere blip of time. There were no balloons, no flowers. No stuffed animals. Just a hearty handshake from Dr. Scott Sinclair and wishes for a good life.

His mother's plan to extricate him from the trauma center was smart, concise and brilliantly executed.

When his mother arrived for her daily visit, another woman breezed in behind her. She was all legs, with a pasty white face and thin, tight lips—pressed together as if she had recently eaten something vile and was trying not to puke it out. But it was her mop of red curls that caught Jeffrey's immediate attention.

From her shoulder hung a huge carry case. She walked directly to Jeffrey, stuck out her hand, and in a heavily accented Irish brogue said, "Hello, Jeffrey. I'm Shannon Laura O'Reilly, and I will be representing you in your civil lawsuit against Olympian Airways."

"You're going home, Jeffrey," his mother said.

"What?" Jeffrey's head spun toward his mother's voice.

"No time to get into it now," his lawyer demanded. "Dr. Sinclair will be here in . . . let's see . . . about five minutes. Do you have anything to pack?"

Jeffrey stuttered, "To pack? No. What the hell is going on?"

Shannon Laura O'Reilly ignored the question. Instead, she asked, "ID? Do you have any ID?"

"No, I have nothing."

"Good," the lawyer muttered.

From a Walmart bag, his mother unpacked newly purchased jeans and a long-sleeved blue pullover. A moment later she was helping him out of his hospital gown and into the clothing.

"What the hell is going on?" he whispered harshly.

His mother simply shook her head and shushed him with a finger to her lips.

The two women helped him into a wheelchair, and then Dr. Sinclair was there, taking control and wheeling him from the room with his mother and lawyer in tow. They hurried down a short corridor where all the hospital room doors were closed.

As they hurried around a corner, the wheelchair turned sharply, and Jeffrey felt a searing pain shoot through his legs. A quick moment later the four of them were inside a huge service elevator, clunking downward. When he looked at his mother, Jeffrey saw she was beaming. Who could blame her? Her son was finally going home.

When the elevator doors opened, he saw they were in the bowels of the hospital, near to the stinking rot of garbage that spewed from several industrial-sized dumpsters. A small black car waited nearby, its engine humming, his mother's two suitcases already packed into the trunk.

Dr. Sinclair offered his hand to Jeffrey. They shook and the doctor said, "Take care of yourself, Jeffrey." Then he disappeared back into the elevator.

His mother sat in front with the driver as Jeffrey and his lawyer crammed themselves into the back seat. The wheelchair was abandoned where it sat.

"Will you please tell me what is going on?" Jeffrey asked in a faint voice.

"Yes, of course, you deserve a reasonable explanation," said the lawyer. "I am an aviation accident attorney and an ex-pilot. Your mother hired me to represent you because of my substantial settlement and trial experience. I am the best there is, Jeffrey. And I will win you a large settlement. I promise, you are in good hands with me."

"Okay," Jeffrey said slowly. "But why was I rushed out of the hospital like an undercover spy?"

The lawyer turned to look at him fully. "You were scheduled for discharge the day after tomorrow. Your mother feared if the information were leaked, it would be a disaster for us. You see, reporters have been crawling around the hospital for weeks, trying to learn of your identity. The crash was a major news story, and as the sole survivor, it's only natural that the world is eager to know who you are."

She cleared her throat and continued, "Once your mother learned you were the lone survivor, she feared journalists would tear your life apart, they would dip into every little hiccup of your personality, your private life." Shannon Laura O'Reilly stared into Jeffrey's bewildered eyes. "And I agreed. Your mother explained that a few years back, you experienced panic attacks, bouts of anxiety."

She gently reached down and patted Jeffrey's hand. "Nothing to be ashamed of. But we could not risk a future jury being prejudiced against you in any way. Striving for a large settlement can be quite tricky."

It was Jeffrey's turn to stare at Shannon Laura O'Reilly. "How did you manage to pull it off?"

"Patient confidentiality," she chirped. "A breach of it would have the trauma center facing a critical lawsuit with very stiff penalties. You, Jeffrey, have a privacy interest that trumps the public's interest in your name. To the trauma center's credit, they took it all very seriously; hired security guards, put up metal barriers. It was a successful threat."

"So, what you're saying is, nobody out there knows I'm the survivor?"

"Correct. We've done an excellent job of containing it." Then, softly, she said, "Your mother hoped to protect you and insisted on your privacy and we prefer to keep it that way."

"So, the airline hasn't released my name either?"

"No. They followed protocol. Contacted all of the victims' families to advise them of the accident. You arrived at the trauma center as a John Doe. When your mother learned of a survivor, she contacted the trauma center's hot line. And here we are."

She gave Jeffrey a tight little smile. Patted his hand again. "Your mother brought your birth certificate, so you'll have no trouble boarding the plane."

The taxi headed toward the Hewitt-Jackson Airport. Jeffrey felt himself tense as they neared the airport exit. He hoped he would not lose his cool—not experience a panic attack or anything resembling a panic attack—when they lifted off.

Mostly, he hoped they would not crash.

The car pulled up to the Olympian Airways terminal and as soon as they had exited the car and retrieved his mother's luggage, the little black car zoomed away. A wheelchair had been pre-arranged, and his mother chatted nonstop with the attendant who wheeled him. They were headed toward the baggage check area.

"It's so exciting, isn't it, Jeffrey?" his mother squealed. "First class! I've never traveled anywhere first class!"

That's because you have never traveled anywhere, he thought. Quickly, he scolded himself for being so petty. She had remained with him at the hospital for weeks without complaint. Stoically endured the crummy motel room she had been offered by the airline. Why hadn't they placed her in a nicer, larger hotel? Why hadn't they flown her out sooner?

The attendant slowed as they approached the baggage counter. Beside him, Jeffrey heard his mother root through her purse for a tip for the attendant. "God bless you," she said as she squeezed two one-dollar bills into his hand.

Once they were on the plane and were belted in and had taken off safely, Jeffrey requested a beer from the pretty stewardess. His mother asked for tea. Together they looked out of the small window, watched as Georgia disappeared beneath them.

Jeffrey sighed. His mother touched his hand. "Are you okay?" she whispered.

"Yeah, I'm okay."

She turned halfway in her seat to face him. The snug seat belt strained against her large breasts. "Jeffrey, I have a few things to tell you."

Jeffrey nodded. "Okay."

"Well, I hope you're not angry that I went ahead and hired Ms. O'Reilly without your permission. But she really is the best attorney for your type of case."

"No. I'm glad you did. I'm going to sue every goddamn person who was involved with what happened to me."

"Yes, of course."

His mother sipped her tea, made a face, placed it back on the little white lap tray.

Sternly, his mother said, "It's important that you continue to protect your identity, Jeffrey. Loose lips sink ships, you know. And after your settlement, we wouldn't want people we've never known to come knocking on our door, looking for a handout, now would we?"

He shook his head. *Why does she keep saying we?*

"And that goes for girlfriends, too, Jeffrey. Girls who latch onto you might think they've hit the lottery, so you must be extremely careful. Okay?"

Solemnly, he shook his head. *Does she really think any girl will give me a second look with these horrible scars? How will I ever again lie naked next to someone?*

His mother's voice continued, just slightly above a whisper. "Even if your friends or coworkers question your injuries, we'll need to have concocted a story. Something believable." She hesitated for a second. "You can say that you extended your vacation and were trapped in a house fire or a car fire, or some such freakish accident."

Jeffrey nodded, finished his beer in one long swallow. Mulled over their conversation. *Maybe she's right. Any girl I meet may be hiding an ulterior motive. Maybe I do have to keep my mouth shut.*

As the plane steadily made its way to New York, Jeffrey spent the remainder of the flight toying with different scenarios he might offer to explain how he had become gimpy and scarred.

It was a mind game he found mildly entertaining and which helped to make the flight pass quickly.

EYE OPENER

August 27, 1977

An invader visited my dreams. Someone dark and evil. Someone who wished me great harm.

I woke abruptly, rose straight up in the bed just like it was in the movies. I panted and shook like a junkie waiting for her next fix. My fear was too real, even in the light of day.

The clock radio showed 10:42, the latest I had slept in months. My breathing slowed as I forced in great gulps of air. Sweat clung to my body like a spent lover.

Slowly, I inched from the bed, walked tentatively into the small kitchen. Filled the Mr. Coffee machine with water, plunked in a thin filter, and filled it with Maxwell House coffee.

As I stood in the kitchen wearing only my bikini panties and a halter top, I waited for the coffee to brew. Tried to recreate the dream that had so frightened me, but nothing came. When the coffee was ready, I poured a mugful and carried it into the living room. Turned on the television and caught the last of *Live! With Regis and Cathy Lee.*

Something felt off as I watched the two graciously spar.

And then it hit me.

I knew who had leaked my yearbook photo to the press. Knew who it was that hated me enough to do so. Knew it as well as I knew the lines that crisscrossed on the palms of my hands.

My stepfather, Howard Ford. A bland-looking man with a military style haircut and too-short trousers that exposed his socks and the milky white skin of his calves. A man deeply rooted in his belief that America belonged strictly to the Caucasian race; to financially secure and politically motivated men of the law, and of the courts.

How stupid I had been! Finally, he was punishing me for the night I had dared to bring my boyfriend, Vern Taylor, home for Christmas Eve dinner.

That night, all hell had broken loose.

Vern and I had been dating during our final year of high school. He was handsome, kind. The sweetest boy I had met in my short life. We were wildly in love. Nothing like the immature passions of most teens our age.

We hoped to marry once we turned eighteen. Our only obstacle: Vern Taylor was a Black boy.

I guess we were doomed from the very beginning. There I was, as white as Pillsbury flour, and Vern the color of a chocolatey Yoo-Hoo drink. During that era in Georgia, mixed relationships manifested their own bridges of racial divide. And despite the small strides made during the civil rights movement, racial inequality remained alive and well in the South, regardless of how sublimely it was veiled behind a cloak of denial.

Vern's friends, too, taunted him about our relationship. Said he was an Oreo cookie: Black on the outside and white on the inside. I heard plenty of nasty words too. Despicable, incendiary words far more hurtful to Vern than to me. Why were people so blindsided by color? The only rightful place for color was in a crayon box.

That year, it was a chilly Christmas Eve night. The fireplace was lit, red stockings embroidered with the twins' names dangled from the mantle. The Christmas tree was big, a real pine tree, not the usual artificial tree my mother preferred. "Less chance of a fire starting," she insisted. "And less mess to deal with."

As my mother filled our big dining room table with heaping platters of ham and sweet potatoes, collard greens, and freshly preserved apple sauce, Howard cornered me in the kitchen.

"Now you listen to me, girl," he growled. "We do not accept people of color at our table. We stay with our own kind. And he should too. You two do not belong together, do you understand?"

"No, I don't understand, Howard," I replied stiffly. "Why don't you spell it out for me?"

"I just did."

"No, you didn't. You simply regurgitated the same hateful rhetoric you've been spewing for years."

Howard's face turned a shade of purple, all puffed out with rage and indignation. "Don't give me your sassy lip, Margaret. This is my house. My rules."

Unfortunately, Vern had been in the doorway. Heard every word. Stomped out of our house and faded from my life faster than warm breath on an icy window.

INFATUATION

August 29, 1977

Sometimes it felt as if my life were being orchestrated as a symphony, minus the entire string section.

It was an unbearably hot Monday, with the coolness of the shower evaporating from my body the moment I stepped from it.

As if on cue, the heavy pulse of a Pink Floyd tune sailed through the open windows, but I no longer became angry when the kid next door blasted his music. How could I become angry after we had formed a bond, a companionable, yet unbalanced relationship—for I was the adult, and he was the kid—though our roles often seemed to be reversed. Surely, ours was a codependent friendship, but for me, talking honestly with the kid had been more cathartic than being forced to expose myself to my FAA counselor, Bridget.

Friday had been the last day of my post-traumatic counseling and though Bridget was a nice girl, there was little she had offered in the way of closure. She suggested I join a post-traumatic stress support group. Practice relaxation techniques. Spend time with positive people. Avoid drugs and alcohol.

As I toweled off, I heard the newspaper thump against the front door. I hesitated to retrieve it, always apprehensive of what I might read of myself. But my pink slippers shuffled to the door as if with a mind of their own. It was a sheer pleasure to open the front door to an empty lawn, save for the weeds that grew near the mailbox.

With a mug of coffee in one hand and a cigarette in the other, I stooped to retrieve the paper and glanced at the headline. Sucked in my breath as the words jumped out at me like a jack-in-the-box popping from its container:

SURVIVOR OF DEADLY CRASH A NO-SHOW ON DISCHARGE DATE
By Valerie Starke

Late Saturday afternoon, rumors began to circulate of the possible discharge of the sole survivor of the June 26 deadly crash of Olympian Airways Flight 177 from the Atlanta Trauma Center.
Those rumors appear to have been false.
The survivor's identity continues to remain under wraps as per the family's request. Dr. Scott Sinclair, Chief of Surgery at the Atlanta Trauma Center, spoke on behalf of the family, stating, "We have suffered a lifetime of grief. Thank you for continuing to respect our privacy."
Repeated requests for information regarding the survivor have been denied by administrators of the trauma center, citing patient confidentiality.
The collision of the Olympian Airways aircraft with an Air Com jumbo jet was reported to have involved air traffic controller Margaret Lido of Atlanta, Georgia. Ms. Lido has since been placed on administrative leave.
The Federal Aviation Administration has not yet released a definitive cause of the crash but suggests that a final determination may follow before year's end. The crash...

I sat dumbfounded, stared at the newspaper until the words crisscrossed before my eyes. For the second time in as many months, the media had thrown me under the bus.

Still, to know unequivocally that the survivor of the crash had indeed pulled through made my heart swell with joy. To know that someone's life had been spared from the unforeseen tragedy was a blessing, and I wondered the person's life, their background. They must be a good, decent human being to have been spared. A person who loved and was loved in return.

An hour passed, then two. I do not remember what I thought or what I did during those two hours. When I finally rose, I went into the kitchen, inspired to clean the mess of pizza boxes still stacked atop the small kitchen table. I scooped empty beer bottles, emptied overflowing ashtrays. My poor mother would turn in her grave if she could see the mess my life had become.

In a fit of determination, I mopped and swept floors, vacuumed rugs, tossed garbage. Vigorously, I polished furniture and scrubbed the bathroom. It was a valiant attempt to assuage the negative aura that had lingered throughout my home.

Afterward, I took another shower to wash away the grime. As I towel dried my hair, I heard the kid's signature rap on my door—tap, tap easy, tap, tap hard.

"Be right there!" I yelled as I shrugged into fresh clothes. When I opened the door, the kid was standing there, his hair loose about his shoulders, his face semi-obscured by the wispy strands. He held the day's newspaper in his hand.

"Have you seen this?" he asked gently.

"I've seen it," I said dully. "Nothing I can do about it."

As I closed the door behind him, he stepped close to me. Placed his hand on my waist and gently pulled me into him. It took me a moment to acknowledge the feel of his lips on mine, how they gently pressed against my own—not a sloppy or inexperienced kiss, not the kiss of a boy but the kiss of a man. For a second, I was caught up in the intensity, the heat of his kiss, but I forced myself to gently pull away, hoping not to cause him the emotional stress of rejection.

I removed his hands from my body, turned away from him. "We can't do this, Daniel," I said firmly. It was the first time I had ever uttered his name aloud.

Embarrassed, he turned, dropped into the nearest chair, his long hair flying behind him.

"Let's take a breath here, okay?" I said softly. "Would you like some coffee?"

"Yeah, I would." He stared down at his high-top sneakers. "So, how are you getting food and cigarettes?" he mumbled, obviously anxious to change the subject. "Your car is still stuck in that same spot."

I walked toward the kitchen, spoke over my shoulder, "Found a gal from the Penny Saver. She does the shopping and I pay her."

As I brewed fresh coffee, I shuddered, wondered if I had subconsciously recognized the attraction the kid felt for me, wondered if I had welcomed it. Had I been so lonely to appreciate the infatuation of a teenager? Had I fallen that far down the rabbit hole?

Carrying us each a mug of coffee, I returned to the living room. Handed him one, watched as he stared into the cup. I sat on the sofa, lit a cigarette.

"I'm worried for you," the kid finally said. "You can't spend the rest of your life like this, holed up in your home, people shopping for you. It's not a life, Margaret."

"I know, and I'll figure it out."

The truth was, I had not at all figured it out. My paid administrative leave was due to end in four weeks, along with a final check for my unused paid time off. Lacking any other marketable skills to fall back on, it was impossible to gauge how I would survive.

Gently, the kid said, “Maybe you should start looking for a job.”

I laughed aloud. “That doesn’t seem to be in the cards for me right now.”

The kid crossed his legs, said, “You’re a smart lady, Margaret. You’ll find a way to bounce back soon. I just know it.”

Yes, I thought, *I will get back on my feet someday. Just not today.*

SCHEMING

October 1, 1977

FITZ

The diner in Hackensack, New Jersey, was tucked far from Route 3, far from Fitz's home and office, where the walls and hallways had ears. Outside, autumn whispered of cooler times to come.

It was a chilly Saturday, overcast. Fitz sat opposite his friend Damon Ross, whom he had worked with at Dawson-Brown Investment Banking. Both had discarded their expensive weekday suits and ties, sat comfortably in baggy sweatsuits.

Sally's Diner was a throwback from the late forties with wall-mounted jukeboxes that spewed two songs for a quarter a pop. The line cooks, the waitresses, even the bus boys were anciently old, thrust into the present decade against their will. Lydia, the waitress, was a monument at the diner, and Fitz's father had known her for more than a quarter century.

She walked to their table, tugging and pulling at her uniform to un-wrinkle the permanent creases in her skirt and apron. She was pleasant though battle-weary from too many years on her feet. She smiled at Fitz, asked, "Where's your father? Haven't seen him in a while?"

Fitz chuckled. "He's been pretty busy these days."

"Well, that's good. Would you like your usual?"

He smiled. "Yes, thank you. Same for my friend, please."

Fitz and Damon sipped coffee, discussed the stats of the Yankees and the Mets. Wondered aloud if the Jets had a chance that season.

Finally, Fitz leaned across the table, his dark eyes sparkling. "We're way out in the boonies, Damon. What's so important?"

Damon, too, leaned in closer. He was only a year older than Fitz, but already gray strands of hair had weaved through his dark curls. Eyes as black as a wet seal's coat blazed at Fitz, eager and lively.

"We have an opportunity to cash in on a unique situation," he said.

"I'm listening," Fitz responded.

Damon glanced over his shoulder, saw that the booth behind them was empty. "Dawson-Brown is taking Raintree Cosmetics public. Opening price will be about thirteen dollars and change. We're expecting it to hit twenty-six at the closing bell. We could jump all over it, Fitz, if we wanted to."

Fitz stared hard at his friend, whispered, "You're talking about insider trading here, Damon."

Damon nodded, whispered back, "But if we did it right, if we kept it more than an arm's length away from us, we could make a killing."

Fitz appeared skeptical, but Damon pushed on. "That's not all. Do you remember Paul Munson from Acquisitions? Chubby guy, pushing fifty, wears his hair in a comb over?"

Damon did not wait for an answer. "Guy cannot keep his mouth shut. He let it slip that a group of solid accounts are lining up at Dawson-Brown to go public."

Fitz remained silent. Finished his coffee.

Damon began ticking off names on his fingers: "Royal Vodka, Mercer Luxury Homes, Kingston Medical Equipment." And with a flourish, he added, "And Jet King, your big new account."

"You're kidding?" Fitz sputtered.

"Not kidding, pal. If you and I got on the bandwagon before everyone else, we'd make a fortune."

Fitz sat back as Lydia sauntered to their booth. She placed big plates loaded with pancakes, eggs, bacon, and sausages in front of them. A basket of buttered toast was centered on the middle of the table. She refreshed their coffee cups. "Anything else, boys?"

"No thanks," they said in unison. They were silent as they ate, each sparring with the tumble of thoughts swirling in their minds.

Once they had finished eating and Lydia had cleared away their plates, Fitz asked, "Do you have a plan to pull this off? Without us going to prison?"

Damon cocked his head and laughed. "Fitz, I'm never going to prison. And neither will you if we do this the right way."

Fitz crossed his legs beneath the tight space, rested his arm on the back of the booth. "What's the plan?" he asked.

Damon's eyes seemed to dance as he explained, "First, we need a third party, someone sharp who knows how to keep things close to the vest. Someone who cannot be traced back to me or to Dawson-Brown. We'll offer a fair cut of the profits. We'll create a dummy corporation—that keeps us more than an arm's length away. All purchases will be transacted through the dummy company and, when we feel satisfied with our profits, we'll sell. And start all over again."

Satisfied with his pitch, Damon sat back in his seat.

Fitz mulled the specifics, felt the plan had merit. It would be nice to have his own stream of unlimited income. Of course, he could never share this plan with his father; his old man would be furious.

"Do you have someone in mind as the third party?" Fitz asked.

Damon clenched his jaw. "No, I'm struggling with that. Everyone that I would trust is too intricately connected to me. Too risky."

"Well, I might know someone who could be a good fit. Someone I think is solid. If you're willing to meet her, get a feel for her, then we can decide if she's the one."

The two men finished their coffee, paid the bill, left a sizeable tip for Lydia. Damon left the restaurant first, drove his chocolate-colored Mercedes Benz toward Route 3.

Fitz used the restroom, washed his hands, and looked at himself in the mirror.

Smiled.

He hoped Viola Cordova would think this as good an idea as he did.

True, I haven't known her for long, but I'm a damn good judge of character, and I can spot a phony two miles away, he thought. *She might find this to be a damn good opportunity. And she certainly does not have a connection to Damon or Dawson-Brown.*

He smoothed an errant strand of hair. *Another plus: she's so new to the city, she hasn't any friends to speak of. Doesn't have a boyfriend or family nearby. If I remember correctly, she told me she was adopted, lived on a farm in a godforsaken rural town in the Midwest, then wound up in Florida. So yeah, I think she just might fit the bill.*

He left the restroom, waved goodbye to Lydia. Hummed happily as he strolled to the black Cadillac. Got in the car, checked his watch. Grinning broadly, he headed back to New York, back to the corporate apartment on Central Park West.

He hoped the girl he was to meet there tomorrow would be a blonde.

BRIEF ENCOUNTERS

October 5, 1977

VIOLA

Viola had slept the sleep of the dead. When the phone shrieked, she was shocked awake by its horrible clatter and cursed aloud. The phone was a sleek pink Princess model, the type of phone a teenage girl might desire, not what Viola would have imagined Sal Carrano to have in his apartment. It blared like a five alarmer in the solace of the quiet morning.

She answered quickly, wasted no time with pleasantries.

"Who the hell is this?" she muttered.

"It's me, Chubs."

Viola sat up. "Sorry, boss. I was out cold."

"It's okay, Vi." Her boss shortened everyone's name to the least number of syllables as possible. "Listen, I'm really short-shifted today. I know it's your day off, but I really need you to come in."

He coughed discreetly. "And I need you to pull a double."

He sounded wearier than a traveler who had missed a connecting flight. Viola hesitated.

"Please, Vi. I'm desperate."

"Okay, okay. Stop begging. I'll do it."

"You're a doll. I won't forget this."

Viola hung up the phone, rumpled her fingers through her hair and reached for the half-empty pack of Marlboros on the nightstand. She pulled one out, swung her legs from the bed, and wondered if Fitz would pop into McNulty's today. *Probably not. He knows my work schedule better than I do.*

A nice camaraderie had developed between them, and though Viola knew their friendship would not turn into a romance, she harbored a secret wish that it might.

She finished the cigarette, left the bed unmade.

After a quick shower and a tepid cup of instant coffee, she grabbed her purse and hurried to leave the apartment. *Crap,* she thought, *where the hell are my keys?* She held the door open with her foot as she searched through her purse, found them lodged at the bottom of the bag, yanked them out. And that was when she saw the guy from across the hall.

The guy with the cane.

He stared at her as if she had just stepped stark naked from the apartment. To his credit, he recovered quickly, puffed on his cigarette, allowed his eyes to look down at his feet.

He's embarrassed that I caught him staring. She locked the door, turned, and tried to appear unfazed and neighborly as she forced a smile. "Good morning," she said.

"Morning," he replied. It sounded like a mumble, a stutter.

As she swished past him, she wished him a good day, then caught an eyeful of the puffy pink and white puckered flesh that hugged his neck like a scarf.

Viola quickly skipped down the stairs.

Sixteen hours later, after Viola had served more margaritas and bloody Marys and martinis than she could count, she took a short break. In the kitchen, Manny, the chef was still going on and on about the work schedule. He slapped together a hefty meatloaf sandwich for her, though she was too tired to chew.

After she had finished eating and had walked from the kitchen, she spotted Fitz in a far booth on the restaurant side of the tavern.

A pretty girl sat next to him. She looked too young to be his wife, but it was hard to tell from so far away. Viola eyed them, watched as their shoulders touched, watched as he undressed her with his eyes. There was a near-empty martini glass near his elbow; the woman had a fruity umbrella drink poised at her lips.

There was no denying how sexy she was.

Viola could not pull her eyes away when she saw Fitz snuggle his lips to the woman's arched neck, the way his hand snaked over her throat then inched behind her neck to pull her closer.

Finally, she forced herself to look away.

Her stomach felt as if it had landed way south of her knees.

NIGHTMARES

October 5, 1977

JEFFREY

He had been home from the hospital for almost six weeks. Home again in the dingy apartment he shared with his mother. It had been an uncomfortable readjustment for Jeffrey Kaye, certainly not the transition he had anticipated.

Leaving Kennedy Airport in Queens, a yellow cab had appeared almost immediately to drive them home to Manhattan. It was a speedy zigzag ride on the Belt Parkway, then a slow crawl through streets that were completely unfamiliar to them.

When the taxi finally turned the corner onto the street where they lived, Jeffrey felt a hailstorm of relief shutter through him. Seeing the familiar red bricks, the building's gold awning, and the boys in the street playing stickball and shouting for the taxi to hurry, to move on, so they might continue their game, well, it had reduced him to a puddle of tears.

The cab driver, a sweet Indian man who wore a turban and had wound his beard tightly to his chin, helped Jeffrey from the car and assisted his mother with the suitcases. Inside the building, Jeffrey stared at the stairway, which appeared to him as insurmountable as a mountain. It was five long flights up to their apartment, a climb which required

Jeffrey to halt at each level to catch his breath, to grip the cane in one hand, the banister in the other.

When, finally, they reached the fifth floor, sweat poured from Jeffrey's face, and he could smell the rank odor of perspiration as it seeped from his armpits. His head spun like a wayward top. He grabbed his mother's arm to steady himself, the exertion nearly folding him in half.

As they shuffled to their apartment, Jeffrey noticed that the door to 5D had opened, and from the corner of his eye, he saw the silhouette of a woman rooted within the doorway. She wore a short flowered dress, and for a brief, inescapable moment, their eyes met. Then, like a ghost, she disappeared, hurried down the stairs with definitive purpose.

Jeffrey remembered that 5D was Sam Carrano's apartment, the kind old man who had been seriously ill for such a long time. Cancer, Jeffrey knew. The woman was probably the niece Mr. Carrano insisted would be coming to live with him, to care for him in his final days.

"Is Mr. Carrano still alive?" he asked in a low voice.

"No, he's not. He died a few days after your accident."

Already his mother had whipped her key from her purse, unlocked the door, and assisted Jeffrey inside. She slammed the door hard behind her, wheeled her suitcases into the living room, and tossed her purse onto the sofa. She looked at Jeffrey in awe, as if they had just raised the flag at Iwo Jima.

That first night, back home in the privacy of his own room, and without doctors and nurses prodding him awake in the middle of the night to perform routine tests—as if he were a goddamn car in the shop for needed repairs—he slipped into his bed, felt the familiar give of the mattress beneath him. The room remained as it had since his teenage years: lava lamp poised on his unsteady desk, an Abbey Road Beatles poster scotch-taped to the wall above the bed.

The sheets were crisp, clean, tucked meticulously beneath the mattress, pillows plumped and inviting. When had his mother had time to do this? Or had she done it all before coming to the trauma center, with hopes and prayers that one day, Jeffrey would return home with her?

His nightmares had begun almost immediately, vague and disjointed thoughts that stuck to him like gobs of gooey glue. With gruesome fascination, he allowed the dream to lead him head-first to a group of shadowy figures with morbidly blank faces, which would melt into long strands of putty.

His bedsheets would then tangle and knot about his knees as he screeched aloud, "MOVE, DAMMIT, MOVE!" In the nightmare, his words were screamed in long, slurred, exaggerated vowels and consonants, as if hurled from a dark, hollow cave.

He would bolt awake, upright and breathless, frightened, praying his heart would not explode. His face would be puffy and wet, as if he had been crying, and his sheets, too, would be damp where he had peed himself.

Each time, it felt as if the night had sucked him into a black hole, where horror and revulsion intertwined as tightly as knit stitches on a baby's blanket.

After the first nightmare, he doubled up on his anxiety meds.

It did not stop the nightmares.

During the weeks after his return, his mother doted and hovered—a devoted attempt to nurse him back to health—but her attentiveness was suffocating. He was grateful for her support and her courage, but still, she weighed like an anvil around his neck.

Years ago, he had assumed that her unnatural attachment to him and their life together had surfaced as an atonement for her having gotten pregnant by an already-married Tire World mechanic who left her holding the diaper bag when he disappeared. Jeffrey had never blamed or hated her for her mistake.

Quite the contrary. He cared deeply for her. Wondered if he would have been as loving and caring if their roles had been reversed.

But he wanted only to move on with his life—without her breathing down his neck.

On that morning, his mother placed a platter of pancakes and bacon strips and sliced peaches before him. "Eat up, Jeffrey," she said. "We've got to put some meat back on your skinny bones."

She was not wrong, for since the accident, he had lost more than forty pounds, which made him look like a shriveled old man. And for that very reason, she prepared elaborate meals: lasagna and fried sausages smothered in onions and peppers, thick pork chops with rings of grilled pineapple, and fluffy dinner rolls. She had not realized that his deflated belly required adequate time to adjust.

She implored him to join her at church services, but he had no desire to avail himself of strange priests and pastors or the odd faces of congregants that might stare at him with pity and consternation.

After breakfast and while his mother showered, Jeffrey grabbed a loose cigarette from his desk—a handful of cigarettes and a disposable lighter that he had only recently discovered there—and stepped into the hallway. Using the cane, he shuffled to the end of the corridor, leaned against the stairwell's banister for support, and lit the cigarette. Greedily, he inhaled, then exhaled twin blasts of smoke from his nostrils just as the door to 5D opened.

At first, the woman in the doorway did not see him. She was preoccupied, searching her pocketbook for something, her keys or a forgotten lipstick tube. He stared at her, could not believe that old man Carrano's niece was such a beauty. She looked up then, caught him assessing her like a prized cow. Briefly, their eyes locked. She hesitated, locked the door, and turned to him. Smiled, said, "Good morning."

"Morning," he replied. It was a garbled sound, as if he had been chewing on a crust of bread or an apple. His eyes trailed her as she walked to the stairwell, stepped past him.

"Have a nice day," she said.

He watched as her blonde hair whipped behind her as she skipped down the stairs, leaving a clean, fresh scent in her wake.

Despondently, Jeffrey wondered if a woman like her would ever give a man like him a second glance.

Or a second thought.

At 2:59 that afternoon, Shannon Laura O'Reilly rang the Kayes' doorbell. Jeffrey had forgotten just how much it sounded like a coyote caught in a trap. His lawyer breezed into their apartment, her red hair sticking out in all directions, as if she had placed her finger in a light socket.

She smiled at them, plopped her big shoulder case onto a kitchen chair.

"Well, Jeffrey, you're looking much better than the last time we met," she said in her lilting Irish voice.

He nodded. Wished he could smoke a cigarette.

With her no-nonsense attitude, she got right to the point. "We're here today to review your case and how we shall proceed."

"Of course," said Jeffrey's mother as she eyed the bundle of folders the attorney pulled from her case.

Shannon Laura O'Reilly smiled at Jeffrey, gently touched his hand. "You survived a horrific airline disaster, which, unfortunately, took many, many lives. Your case will be predicated on your overwhelming emotional distress and your debilitating injuries."

"You almost died, Jeffrey," his mother interrupted. "Twice they had to use the paddles on you."

"I wonder," said the attorney. "Would you mind sharing anything at all that you might remember about the accident?"

Jeffrey squeezed his eyes shut, tried to bring forth a recollection. Shook his head miserably. "I boarded the plane; my seat was in the very back, near the restrooms. I stepped over an old man who was asleep in the aisle seat next to me. The lady in the window seat smelled like lavender. I had a beer, then I must have dozed."

He opened his eyes and shrugged his shoulders. "That's it. Nothing else."

"It's okay, Jeffrey."

"No, it's not okay," he said loudly. "Why can't I remember? And how was I able to survive while everyone else perished?"

"The therapist will help you to figure it out, Jeffrey," his mother said firmly. "Can we move on, Ms. O'Reilly?"

"Of course. Our plan is to file an administrative claim under the Federal Tort Claims Act, provided there was pilot or air traffic control error. If, however, the aircraft or any of its parts malfunctioned, we will then sue not only the airline involved, but the manufacturer of the aircraft and the aircraft maintenance provider. All standard procedure."

She smiled gently. "We have a rock-solid case here. Any questions to this point?"

The attorney focused on Jeffrey's face, tried diligently to avoid staring at the freshly puckered scars on his neck.

Jeffrey shook his head. When it came to important matters like these, he recognized that he was not the sharpest knife in the drawer. But if spoken to in simple A-B-C sequences, he got it.

Flipping through notes scribbled on a yellow legal pad, his lawyer asked, "You're following regularly scheduled sessions of physical therapy?"

"Yes."

"Very good, especially important. And you've begun your post-disaster psychotherapy sessions?"

"Yeah. The docs think I'm suffering from some form of post-traumatic stress disorder, just like war veterans experience, but I think they're nuts."

Embarrassed about the recent nightmares, he glossed over them.

"What you think about their diagnosis is irrelevant," the lawyer said firmly. "But it is critical to continue the sessions because they bode well for your case."

Jeffrey shrugged his shoulders, stared down at his hands. "So, what happens next?"

The lawyer shifted in her seat. "We wait for the National Transportation Safety Board to confirm the cause of the accident. If it is determined there was pilot or air traffic control error, we will file an Administrative Claim against the FAA with the dollar amount of monetary damages to be claimed. They will have six months to rule."

Jeffrey's eyes darted back to Shannon Laura O'Reilly. "How much?"

"We'll ask for $6 million, but be open to negotiation. If the FAA fails to rule within six months, or if mechanical failure was involved, we can move forward with a full lawsuit."

Jeffrey's eyes lit up, and as he glanced at his mother, he saw that her eyes, too, were glowing.

This is my case, Mom, he thought. *My case, not yours.*

CONVERSATION AT A CEMETERY

October 24, 1977

For most of my life, I had felt invincible, protected by an invisible shell that shielded me from all the villainous happenings that lived and breathed in the real world. But after the accident, I went soft, soft like a fluffy pillow. I feared everyone and everything around me. I had become a frightened, nervous Nelly.

This change in my life, in my personality, it was unacceptable to me. I was loath to stay in Atlanta and thought often of escaping. Running far away, not just from Atlanta, but from my life in general.

Wouldn't you if your life had turned into a blur of white noise?

My visit to the cemetery had been a spur of the moment decision, decided upon during a dewy morning seventeen weeks after the accident. Seated on my back porch, I crushed out my third cigarette of the day and sipped a second mug of coffee. Nearing seven o'clock, the kid had stepped through his creaky back door, his hair resembling a bird's nest, his eyes still full of unfinished sleep.

The moment I heard his door open, I jumped up, beckoned wildly to him. Immediately, he was at my porch.

"What's wrong?" he asked.

"I need to go to the cemetery. And I want you to take me there."

He nodded vigorously. No questions asked. "Okay, okay. Give me ten minutes."

I ran inside, plopped a Braves baseball cap onto my head, and shoved a pair of old-fashioned granny sunglasses onto my nose. Yanked open my bottom dresser drawer and stared at the little yellow envelope tucked into the corner.

"Thank you, Savannah." It was all I could think to mumble.

The front gates of All Souls Cemetery were smaller than I had remembered. I stared at them, the intricate design of angels and cherubs sculpted into the heavy metal. The Volvo hummed as the kid idled the engine, not sure if he should move forward or turn back and head home.

"Go on," I said. "It's okay."

The kid drove the Volvo through the heavy gates, followed my directions—left, right, left, up a gravelly road, down a quiet path. In my lap lay two bunches of tiger lilies, pinched from the marsh where they grew wild and unattended.

When we arrived at the spot, I motioned for the kid to shut the engine. I knew he sensed my tension, felt it himself like an earthquake underfoot. He rolled the car window down, turned to look at me.

Softly he said, "Tell me about her."

I stared up at the sky, so blue and idyllically perfect. "She was my best friend for what seemed like forever. Sweet, kind, full of life, full of fun. A daredevil." I chuckled. "She taught me to drink bourbon neat and how to blow the perfect smoke ring."

"She sounds remarkable," the kid said.

"She was."

I stamped out my cigarette, grasped the tiger lilies. The kid began to step from the car, but I gently touched his arm. "Do you mind staying here? I need to do this alone."

The Cranston family plot was large, a well-tended area surrounded by lush landscape, with Savannah's elaborate headstone befitting of her family's wealth.

With shaking hands, I placed the sad bouquet of tiger lilies at the foot of her grave. "I miss you so much," I whispered.

I knelt beside the headstone, reached out to touch the marble carvings in the stone. The sun felt warm and pleasant, and above me, I heard the sweet chatter of birds chirping in harmony. I leaned in close to the headstone, as if by being closer, Savannah would hear me more clearly.

"Do you remember the last time we met, Savannah? I was home on a week's recess from my FAA training in Oklahoma. We were at Carousel's. You strutted through the door as if you were attending your own gala. We sat at our favorite booth and spent hours drinking and chatting, and catching up on each other's lives."

Suddenly, I felt foolish talking aloud to the air. I glanced over my shoulder. Not a soul was in sight.

"I asked you about work and you said, 'What could be new? I'm stuck in a tits-and-ass-world, in a dingy office of my father's new publishing company.' Then you laughed and said that his new magazine might put a real hurt on *Playboy*."

Another glance around assured me I was alone. My knees were sore, so I moved into a seated position and continued my one-way conversation.

"Then, Savannah, you asked me if I was dating anyone. When I said not really, you said, 'Well, maybe it's time to move on. You know, dip your toe into somebody else's pool.' Boy, did we have a good laugh over that. But then you got serious. Very serious. You asked me for a favor."

My breath hitched. "You asked me to keep something safe for you. When I looked at you in surprise, you said, 'Nothing bad. Not drugs or anything like that.'"

Tears trickled down my cheeks. I searched a tissue from my purse, blew my nose loudly. The noise startled a flock of pecking birds, and they immediately took flight.

"Do you remember, Savannah, how you pulled open that sack-like handbag you so loved? Do you remember removing that small yellow envelope? You handed it to me across the table. Told me it was the key to a safe deposit box. You swore you did not want to keep it at the house because the cleaning staff was nosy sometimes."

I had taken the envelope, put it into my own purse, and had not given it a second thought.

Until today.

"You said, 'One other thing. If anything happens to me, I want you to promise to take whatever is in the box for yourself.' I objected, remember, Savannah? But you raised your hand to shush me. 'The box number is written on the inside of the envelope,' you said. 'It's the First Bank of Georgia. The downtown branch.'"

No longer able to control myself, I stood, sobbed aloud. I didn't care if anyone saw or heard me. I kissed my fingertips to the headstone, let my hand idle on the cool marble.

"Goodbye, Savannah. I'll never forget you."

Two hours and three bourbons later, I was numb. The kid and I sat at an outdoor Mexican restaurant that served splendidly spicy food and icy margaritas. The kid leaned in close, his pimply face inches from mine.

"How did she die?" he asked gently.

"They say she committed suicide."

"Whoa. Oh man, Margaret, I am so sorry." He reached out, covered my hand with his own. Hesitated before asking, "Did she leave a note?"

The heat of the day, the memories and the bourbon all galloped toward me at full speed.

I exhaled deeply. "Her family said no; she did not leave a note. But that was not the type of person Savannah was. She wouldn't have left things up in the air like that. She would have left a note for her mother. Or for me. I'm sure of it."

My throat felt squeezed by a lump the size of a small tangerine.

"But Savannah's brother called me that night. Told me that serious money was missing from their business accounts and that their daddy was convinced Savannah was stealing from him and from the family. He said their daddy had threatened her, had promised her he would notify the FBI. Tell them that she had embezzled funds from the company and that she'd rot in prison for years."

Suddenly, it felt as if Johnston Cranston was standing behind me, breathing down my neck like a huge dragon.

Warning me.

STUDIO 54

October 28, 1977

VIOLA

Viola Cordova had settled into her life in New York as if she had lived there since birth. Though the days had shortened, and tree limbs were exposed, and airy wind crept inside her apartment to settle itself in the walls, the floorboards, the cracked tiles in the decrepit bathroom, she felt vibrantly alive—a new and unexpected sensation.

Her shift at McNulty's began at 5:00 p.m. When she arrived that night, she shrugged out of a baggy sweater and noticed that Fitz was seated at her station, sipping a tall drink. She allowed herself a moment to stare at him. If he were a single man, Viola was certain their friendship would have by now developed into a heated, passionate love affair.

But he was married. And he would stay married.

She slunk behind the bar, gathered empty beer mugs and dirty napkins, wiped away spilled fruit juice, and trashed errant limes. The bar remained quiet, with less than an hour until the happy hour crowd arrived, less than an hour until shouting would pass for normal conversation.

"Hey, Fitz. You're here early," she said. He looked handsome in a white shirt beneath a richly tailored navy-blue suit.

His face broke into a huge grin. "Yes, I am. Meeting up with my dad for dinner later tonight. A prospective client he wants to woo."

"Where are you headed?"

"That new place, Michael Angelo's in the Village. It's all the rage these days."

Fitz glanced around, saw that no one was within earshot. Quietly, he said, "Have you been to Studio 54?"

She shot him a look that said, *Are you nuts?*

"Would you like to join me there tomorrow night?"

Viola smirked as if he had just told her a crude joke.

"No, I'm serious. No funny business, I swear. My wife usually accompanies me when I entertain clients, but she's out of town and I would be more comfortable if someone were with me."

Viola latched onto his eyes, looked to see if he was hiding a great big lie in there. "You're serious, aren't you?"

"Very serious."

"Okay, then."

Viola waited in front of her building, watched as heads turned to gawk at her as she stood there, stunning in a red dress that hugged her tighter than rubber on tires. She clutched a thin red shawl around her shoulders.

The night was chilly, with stars peeking from between the rooftops. Viola's tummy did a little twist as a sleek limousine pulled up to her. A uniformed chauffeur jumped out, helped her into the back seat where Fitz sat, already sipping champagne.

"Wow," he said. "You look gorgeous."

"You clean up pretty well yourself."

Viola thought he could pass as a movie star—his black turtleneck sweater accentuated his coal-black eyes and hair. He offered her champagne; she eagerly accepted.

She was nervous. This was a big deal for her—people like her did not just waltz into Studio 54. Her nerves ricocheted up another notch as they pulled in front of the building. Her eyes opened wide as she spotted the legendary red velvet ropes, the lengthy lines of people waiting, hoping to be selected for entry.

Once the car stopped, the chauffeur was there, helping her from the car, and then Fitz took her arm and led her to the front doors, where a burly man nodded to Fitz and escorted them inside the famous nightclub.

As Fitz led her across the room, the massive crowd of people overwhelmed Viola. She fought to absorb everything at once: the throngs of dancers in all manner of attire—one man wore only a shower curtain. Two women were kissing, their breasts nearly falling from their plunging necklines. Everywhere she looked, Viola saw big hair and big jewelry. Velvet jumpsuits and satin dresses and body suits and short shorts. Lots of fur on naked chests, feathery boas, and glittery sequins.

They reached a huge stairwell and ascended it up to the balcony level. Fitz waved over a man wearing a Tarzan sheath. The man led them to a booth with a prime view of the dance floor beneath them. "Champagne or bourbon?" he asked her.

"Bourbon," she said.

He ordered both, and as they watched the crowd ebb and flow, he pointed out to her Liza Minnelli and Bianca Jagger and Andy Warhol. A woman floated past their table, wearing a zoot suit. Across from them, six people had squeezed into a booth to share fat lines of cocaine using rolled up fifty-dollar bills.

A young man wearing only a thong and white roller skates placed their drinks on the table. Fitz and Viola toasted each other, and Viola asked, "So, where's the client you're entertaining?"

"He'll be along. Truthfully, he's not a client at all."

Viola's eyebrows shot up. "I thought you said?"

"It is a meeting, but slightly different from what I told you."

Viola moved to get up, to leave, but Fitz's hand planted itself firmly on her arm. "Wait," he implored. "I promise that this is all on the up-and-up. I swore there would be no funny business and there won't be. Just let me explain."

She glared at him.

He leaned across the table. Softly, he said, "I asked you here tonight because I want to offer you an opportunity to make some serious money."

"If you think I'm going to sell my body..."

"Of course not!"

"Then start explaining."

Fitz poured himself another glass of champagne. "A business opportunity has presented itself which I believe could benefit both of us quite handsomely. A colleague will be here shortly and we'll explain the nuances of this opportunity, and hopefully, you'll be amenable to it. If not, there will be no hard feelings, no remorse, no second-guessing each other. My only request is for you to keep this conversation strictly confidential. Can I trust you to do this?"

Viola was intrigued, but not completely sold on his sincerity. Then Fitz smiled, his face aglow as if he had just spotted an angel sitting on her shoulder. He crooked his finger to invite someone closer.

A man appeared, wearing a poorly styled wig and dark sunglasses. He wore blue latex gloves on his hands, the type worn in hospitals.

"Viola Cordova, meet Jonathan Silver."

They shook hands, and the odd-looking man scooted into the booth beside Fitz. He waved to the roller-skating waiter.

"Two more of everything," he said, his voice rich, smooth, as if he were accustomed to asking people to bring him things. Viola detected a very slight accent—Scottish or Australian, perhaps?

Fitz said, "We promise to keep this as simple as possible, Viola. The opportunity I mentioned involves initial public offerings. In the financial world they are known as IPOs. Stock offerings. Take Coca Cola for instance—a company that began with private equity and which is therefore privately owned. If the owner of the company decides to sell shares of the company, it is known as 'going public.' Shares are offered to the public, with the company receiving a huge boost in revenue to expand the company or to hire more employees or to purchase better equipment. With me so far?"

"Yes," Viola said.

"The owner of the company also stands to profit from going public, especially if it is a company with a promising future."

"Okay," Viola said slowly. "What does this have to do with me?"

Lowering his voice further, he said, "There are instances when Jonathan gets early word of a company preparing to go public. Information which would be known to him, and to us, before the public is made aware of it. This type of information is priceless."

"Why?" she asked.

Jonathan Silver took a sip of champagne followed by a gulp of bourbon. Scratched his cheek and said, "If a person or persons—even other companies—were privy to this type of information, it might influence them to buy large quantities of the stock on the very day the company went public. Then, as public investors jumped on board, the potential for the stock to trade higher becomes significant. Hefty profits can be attained. Get the picture?"

"I certainly do," Viola said evenly. "It's still a gamble though, isn't it? I mean, it's not much different than choosing red or black on a roulette wheel. The value of the stock can go up or it can go down or simply remain stagnant. A pure gamble, right? Again, what does this have to do with me?"

She glanced at Fitz; his smile beamed at her.

He's proud of me.

Fitz jumped back into the conversation. "Here's how we see it: with access to privileged information before it becomes public knowledge, it does beg the question—why allow the information to die on the vine? That's where you enter the picture."

Fitz stopped speaking for a moment, retrieved a gold cigarette case from a pocket. Plucked out a cigarette, offered the case to them. The conversation lulled as all three lit their cigarettes.

He continued, "We would create a holding company, a fake company. Hire a firm to set things up for us. Everything would flow through them. Our hands would be clean. Our privacy level would be 100 percent. Your role, Viola, would be to purchase IPO shares of companies we deem to be viably profitable investments."

Viola's brain twisted and turned, contemplated the implications, the risks involved.

"What's in it for me?" she blurted.

"Sixteen percent of the profits," Jonathan Silver murmured. "Very good compensation for very little work."

Fitz interrupted, "This would require extreme confidentiality, Viola. Not a word, not a peep to anyone. Not to your best friend or your lover. Are we on the same page with this?"

My lover? she thought sarcastically. Aloud she said, "Can I have a day to think about it?"

They both nodded. Then, Jonathan Silver smiled for the first time since he had sat with them.

"I do honestly hope you will join us," he said. "I believe we will make a splendid team."

He reached out his gloved hand as if to shake Viola's but instead, he lifted her hand to his lips—a proprietary gesture, as if it were his right, his privilege to do so—and kissed it.

A moment later he slipped from the booth, became invisible, swallowed by the mass of people. Slowly, Viola turned, saw Fitz's eyes boring into her own.

"Why didn't you tell me this was the real reason you wanted me here tonight?" she hissed. "Why did you lie to me?"

"I couldn't tell you," he said calmly. "I couldn't risk you saying something or having someone at McNulty's overhear. I am sorry about this, and you have my word, there will be no further lies."

Viola dumped the last of the champagne into her empty glass, downed it in one long gulp.

"Who is this Jonathan Silver? And why was he disguised?"

Fitz drummed his fingers against the tabletop. "Unfortunately," he said, "that's the one thing I cannot reveal. A level of anonymity and discreetness is involved, and without Jonathan Silver, there is no game; there is no fortune to be made. It's nonnegotiable, Viola, so either you're in all the way or you're not in at all. It's your call."

She breathed deeply, looked over the banister to the floor below. A slight ruckus had ensued, and Viola saw that Cher and Diana Ross had arrived. Everyone down there was going gaga.

"How much risk is involved?" she asked absently.

"Minimal, as long as everyone maintains strict protocol. Keep our mouths shut and our money well hidden."

"How much money are we talking?"

"Hundreds of thousands, if not millions."

Viola thought about it. It would take her ten lifetimes of working at McNulty's to earn that kind of money. She thought of all the years she had worn hand-me-down dresses and scuffed shoes that were either too big or too small for her feet, depending on the year.

"Okay," she said. "I'm in."

DISGUISED?

October 29, 1977

FITZ

Hangovers were as much a staple of Fitz's life as was Kellogg's Corn Flakes with bananas and strawberries. On that day, however, his hangover could easily have been categorized as a post-climatic blowup.

When he woke, it was obvious that the morning had come and gone, and midday had conveniently squeezed itself into its place. His body felt abnormally stiff, as if he had helped to push a semi-trailer uphill on a steep climb.

Thank God I'm alone, he thought miserably. Dealing with someone else while he felt so sick and vulnerable would have been unbearable.

Naked and shivering, he hovered outside the shower, then plunged head-first into the icy water. Cold needles stung like bees as he forced the knob to a warmer setting. With the sprinkle of hot water to calm him, he tried to piece together segments from the previous night.

His immediate recollection: the limo that had driven him to Viola's apartment. Her waiting outside, looking like a fire siren just waiting to be set off. Their entrance into Studio 54 and the immense sense of importance he had felt as they waltzed past the enviable velvet ropes.

He soaped a handful of shampoo into his hair. He had not expected the weird get-up Damon had worn last night. The wig was a bit off; the sunglasses were smart. But the blue latex gloves? What the hell was that about? If he hadn't wanted to stand out or to be remembered in any way, why wear gloves so identifiable?

As he scrubbed glitter and stardust from his hair, he wondered if Viola had seen through Damon's "Jonathan Silver" cover. Oh fuck, of course she had; she was smarter than them both. "Keep it low key," he had urged Damon. "Simple. Easy. Nothing to get her riled up about, nothing to make her suspicious."

How well had that worked, my friend?

Fitz toweled off, brushed his teeth, combed his hair. Knew he would have to right the ship and set things straight. Truth was—there wasn't room for mistakes in this game. Not by Fitz, not by Viola, and most certainly not by Damon.

GOODBYES

November 15, 1977

For most of my adult life, I had not believed in omens. What were they, really? Just fancy words for wishful thinking. My opinion of omens had since changed.

On the morning of my visit to the cemetery, it became incredibly clear to me that it was time to move on with my life. Time to leave Atlanta. To leave behind the person whom I had regrettably become.

After the kid and I returned from the cemetery, he rushed off to do an errand. Alone in my quiet bungalow, I opened my dresser drawer, lifted out the little yellow envelope Savannah had given me. The envelope with a key to a safe deposit box.

Her words echoed in the room as if she were standing right there, pleading with me, "If anything happens to me, I want you to take whatever is in the box for yourself."

Shaking, I unclasped the envelope and tipped out the small key. A tiny slip of paper fell out with the key. It appeared to have been torn from a newspaper or magazine. It read,

"Life begins at the end of your comfort zone," by Neale Donald Walsch.

It made me realize that I was stuck in a life that was destined to go nowhere but downhill.

For a moment, I reeled. When she had given me the envelope, had Savannah somehow known that one day I would need her encouragement, her little push to head me in a direction toward which I sorely needed to be headed?

I walked the key and the slip of paper into the kitchen, taped the paper message to the door of the refrigerator, and knew that every time I read it, it would propel me to take the steps necessary to finally move on.

That was my first omen.

The second one had no connection to the first.

But it was an action that inevitably led to my reaction.

That morning, long after Pink Floyd's music wafted through my windows, the kid showed up at my bungalow with freshly baked blueberry muffins, muffins which his mother had popped from the oven just minutes earlier.

I poured us coffee, set out paper plates and napkins. We sat at the small bistro table in the kitchenette.

The kid appeared aloof, skittish, as he avoided my eyes. What was jack-knifing through his brain?

"So, how was your visit with your dad last week?" I asked as I took a mouthful of the warm muffin. Delicious, my mouth and brain agreed.

The kid shrugged his shoulders. "Okay, I guess."

"You guess?"

The kid's shoulders folded in on themselves. His face blanched as if he had just tasted something awfully foul.

"We're leaving Atlanta," he blurted.

"Leaving? Where are you going?"

"Chicago," he grunted.

I took a deep breath. "Wow. Why?"

The kid shuffled his legs beneath the small table. "Mom's been seeing someone. A basketball coach who's been transferred to Northwestern

University. Says if we join him there, he can guarantee my acceptance to the school next semester."

My eyebrows tilted toward the ceiling.

"They've got the best journalism program in the country," he said defensively.

I remained quiet because it felt like a curveball coming at me at a hundred miles an hour. *How will I survive without the kid? How will I be able to say goodbye to him?* Instead, I cleared my throat and asked, "When will you leave?"

"Day after tomorrow," he croaked, trying to hold back a torrent of tears. "They sprang it on me yesterday, but it's been planned for a while."

I reached across the table, touched his hand as he had done to mine so many times in the past. "Sounds like this will be a good move for you."

Angrily, he shook his head. "No! I don't want to leave you. You're the only real friend I have."

As I smiled weakly, my own tears threatened. "You too. But this is bigger than both of us. School is important, Daniel."

He looked as if he were ready to melt onto the cracked linoleum floor.

"Listen to me," I said sternly. "Apply yourself to your studies. Do not wait for someone else to create your path. Do it for yourself. Allow yourself to be in control of your future. You can and will do important things. I know you will."

We hugged fiercely before he walked from the bungalow, walked out of my life forever.

"I'll write," he promised over his shoulder.

"Okay!" I yelled back.

I watched his long frame retreat across the thin patch of grass that separated our bungalows, watched him hoist himself up and over his tiny wooden back porch.

Heard the creak of his back door for the very last time.

My tears did not cease until the following morning.

My exit plan hatched two days later.

Thinking back on it, I believe it evolved when I said goodbye to Savannah at the cemetery that day.

The writing was already on the wall.

But I knew my plan could not be a half-baked scheme, not when the most serious decision of my life would change the course of my life forever.

No matter how crippling the fear, I had to discover what was in Savannah's safety box—provided there was anything at all remaining in it. If the contents of the box held anything worthwhile to help propel the crux of my plan, I would be grateful. An empty box would mean an irrelevant and unattainable escape plan.

It took another three more weeks and five failed attempts before I was finally able to take the literal first step toward reinventing my life.

ARRESTED

November 17, 1977

FITZ

They say it is always darkest before the dawn. But who are *they*? And why are they always correct?

At a time of night when most people had been asleep for hours, Fitz was permitted his one phone call after having been arrested, cuffed, and placed into a holding cell in the one-twelfth precinct in Forest Hills.

Weary and confused, he could not determine where the stink of his cellmates began or where it ended. Impossible to conclude when they had last bathed or eaten or changed their underwear.

Time was not a luxury in prison.

When allowed his one phone call, Fitz's foggy mind reminded him, *I can't call Dad. Not in the shape I'm in.*

Instead, he dialed Damon's phone, his hands shaking, legs quivering. Damon would know how to fix this.

But even as he dialed Damon's phone number, his brain wobbled, and he feared he might pee himself right there at the officer's desk. The sergeant seated there was obese, with an egg-shaped bald head and a gut that pressed heavily onto the top of the desk.

How many Big Macs are swimming in that gut? Fitz wondered.

He wished he were sober, if only to explain how difficult it had been to avoid the young girl. What was her name? Jeannie? JoJo?

Usually, it was an easy task to talk himself out of a jam, but that night, and under those circumstances, he had known he was doomed. Damon's phone rang four times before Fitz heard his friend's mumbled voice. "It's me, Damon," Fitz said haltingly. "I'm at the one-twelfth precinct in Forest Hills. I need you to come and get me. I'll explain later."

"What the hell are you talking about?" his friend croaked. "Do you realize what time it is?"

"Yeah, but we can discuss it later. Right now, I need you to come and get me."

The sky was bloated with heavy clouds when Damon Ross escorted Fitz from the precinct steps and into a waiting yellow cab. Fitz looked awful: eyes bloodshot, hair disheveled, laces missing from his shoes. In his hand, he clutched his expensive leather belt, his mouth caked with white residue from the two Tums that Damon had offered him to stanch a backlash of vomit and acid reflux.

Fitz stumbled into the back seat. His trousers slipped low, exposed his blue-checkered boxer shorts. Damon was utterly disgusted and looked as if he wanted to slap Fitz's face.

Inside the car, Damon asked the driver to increase the volume of the radio. Then he looked at Fitz, said, "What the fuck were you thinking? Do you realize what you've done?"

Fitz dropped his head, ambivalent to the question. Damon shook him. "Fitz! Answer me, dammit!"

Fitz's head lolled on his shoulder. Though he was in a fog of his own making, he sensed Damon's fury, knew he had crossed an invisible line. *I am so stupid. Why do I keep doing this to myself?*

The yellow cab stopped at Yellowstone Boulevard in Forest Hills. Damon hauled Fitz from the taxi and into the building's lobby. They rode the elevator to the fourth floor. Damon searched Fitz's pockets, found his key ring, and unlocked the door.

Two big cats welcomed them with loud meows. Damon dragged Fitz into the bedroom, removed his shoes and socks, pulled down his trousers, settled him into the bed. In the kitchen he poured dry cat food into dishes and refreshed the water bowls. Finished, he locked the door behind him, trotted down the four flights of stairs, and exited the building.

"You idiot," Damon mumbled under his breath. "If you've screwed things up for us, I'll kill you. I swear, I will fucking kill you."

Fitz slept for six hours. A haze of pain throbbed from his head to his spine when he heard the cackle of his apartment buzzer followed by a heavy rap of knuckles pounding the door.

He opened the door, saw his friend Damon standing there, a big, muscular tyrant of a man, and for a moment, Fitz felt cowed. He stepped back, held the door ajar, allowed his friend inside, closed the door behind him. In the small, galley-sized kitchen, Fitz pulled two glasses from a shelf. A whiskey bottle followed. Then the crunch of ice cubes hitting glass.

"What the hell are you doing?" Damon asked.

"Swallowing the hair of the dog," Fitz grumbled.

"You look like shit."

"No kidding," Fitz replied. He shrugged past Damon and into the living room. He sat on the sofa and lit a cigarette. "Are you here to berate me?"

"No. You can berate yourself, you goddamn idiot."

Fitz looked down at his boxer shorts, picked at invisible lint. "I'm sorry, Damon. Things just got a little out of control last night."

"No excuse, man," Damon said.

"Why? You've never made a mistake?"

"Not like this!" his friend roared. "Not when everything is stacking up big for us. Do you realize what a mistake like this could cost us? We can't afford to be under a microscope!"

Fitz ground out his cigarette. Looked out of the windows toward the Manhattan skyline beyond. "I am so sorry, Damon," he said softly. "I know I screwed up. It won't happen again."

"Fuck, yeah. Because if it happens again, we're totally screwed."

Fitz nodded, his stomach roiling as if he were on a bobsled speeding down an icy mountain trail.

Damon whispered, "I told you when we first discussed this opportunity that I would not go to jail. Not for you, not for anyone. Either you play by the rules, or you forfeit your interests. There is no middle ground here."

Fitz slumped forward, head in his hands, sobbing.

"I'll pay off the uniform who arrested you, make sure he loses the paperwork," Damon said. "Then you're going to find a therapist to help with your problem."

Fitz hung his head.

"Look, man, you like young girls. I get it," Damon said. "But you're going to have to jump off that train wreck today because you're not fooling anyone. You have a problem, and you need to address it. Quickly."

Fitz felt his face turn red; he was embarrassed, emasculated. Damon softened his tone. "Can you imagine the damage you could have inflicted if a rookie beat cop had wanted to fully pursue this incident? Or if a cub reporter itching for a by-line kept digging into you and Viola and eventually into me?"

He pinched the bridge of his nose as if trying to stave off a migraine.

"You need to change things, Fitz. It's the only way to protect yourself, your reputation, and our financial partnership."

Fitz nodded aggressively.

"There are plenty of real women out there for you, even with all of this damned women's lib crap going on."

Fitz sniffled, wiped at his nose with his hand.

Damon stood, swallowed the last gulp of his whiskey. Walked the few steps to Fitz, grabbed him in a great bear hug.

"I love you, man," he said. "And I've let you in on an incredible money-making scheme. But unless you get your shit together, our partnership is over. I can't allow my reputation to be sullied by your reckless behavior. I hope you understand what I'm saying."

The rest of Fitz's day passed in a blur of rain-streaked windows and howling wind and the slow, steady drip of water that plunked from the ceiling and into the bathroom sink.

Cigarettes were smoked and torched. A bland cheese sandwich was half eaten, and a gallon of vomit was expelled.

But Fitz knew that Damon was spot on. Without a wife to steady him, to give him credence, his reputation could be erased as easily as chalk on a chalkboard.

POPEYE

November 16, 1977

VIOLA

The seventies seemed like a rebirth. The gloves were off. Vietnam had become a short memory. Women craved equality.

And life—as it had done for eons—continued its trek forward.

Viola Cordova stretched out on her bed, comfortably warm beneath a layer of blankets. She had woken earlier than usual, decided it was due purely to excitement and expectation of the days ahead.

During Fitz's last visit, he had asked, "Did you meet with Popeye?"

Smiling wickedly, she had said, "Yes. Everything is in place to pull the plug."

Popeye was their code name for William Calhoun, the stockbroker who would be transacting their IPO stock purchases. He owned Barbary Investments, a small firm in Connecticut. He worked independently and seemed like an up-and-up type of guy who was interested in making wads of money.

Legal documents for their holding company—now with the legitimate name of NYC Holdings—had been processed by a business services company in Delaware, and Viola had forwarded copies of the documents to William Calhoun.

She had also signed and delivered a bank signature card to Chase Manhattan Bank, which was followed by a delivery to her home of blank checks, deposit slips, and a checking account ledger for NYC Holdings. She was now authorized to legally sign checks, make deposits.

Fitz had been happy with the news, reminded her, "Every transaction with Popeye must be done in person. No telephone calls. Ever. Too easy to trace."

"What if something goes wrong and I need to reach you? Or Jonathan?"

"Nothing will go wrong if you follow instructions. But should you need to communicate with us, here's a number you can call." He deftly slid her a small, nondescript business card.

"Dial the number from a payphone, preferably one that isn't anywhere near McNulty's or your apartment. Let it ring three times, then hang up. One of us will contact you."

Then he had quietly asked for a refill of his drink. "Are we clear on all points?"

"Yes," Viola had crisply replied.

Viola's belly fluttered along with her pulse. It was really happening. She was staring into the face of her future.

"Are you nervous?" Fitz asked. "Do you want to back out?"

"No. No, of course not," she quickly responded. She was not about to turn away from a potential windfall into her bank account. Already, she had decided that if she made a decent score from the venture, she would buy a big house, move from Uncle Sammy's rent-controlled shoebox where she currently lived. She would buy something spacious and grand with plenty of windows and bathrooms.

"Jonathan is one smart dude," Fitz said. "And if we both play our cards right, he's going to make us very, very rich."

"I sure hope so," she said with a huge smile.

Viola threw off the blankets, scurried to the bathroom.

She had no idea of the trap she had been caught in.

ANOTHER OMEN?

November 17, 1977

On the morning of the kid's departure, on a day shrouded in dark clouds and heavy rain, and soon after their moving van had puffed its way down the street, I allowed myself a final cry. Then I showered, dressed in my best black pantsuit, and drove downtown to the First Bank of Georgia.

Sheets of rain assaulted my poor old Volvo faster than the windshield wiper blades could sluice it away. I struggled to see through the dreary windows and was grateful for the slow crawl of traffic. For the first time in five months, I had left my home unaccompanied.

I shook in my shoes.

The First Bank of Georgia was a short drive from the highway, and I soon steered the Volvo into the bank's small parking lot. For several long minutes I sat there, the car running, the radio silent, my breath fogging the interior windows.

I feared that if I stalled for even another moment, I would surely lose my nerve. I grabbed my handbag and a big black umbrella from the passenger seat and hurried out of the car. Huge puddles of water swamped my shoes as a damp chill snaked its way down my neck and past my shoulder blades. My thin suit jacket was no match for the day's weather.

Tentatively, I entered the near-empty bank, left a trail of water in my wake. "I would like to access my safe deposit box," I asked meekly of the bank employee who greeted me.

The man smiled, escorted me down a circular stairway. We stopped at the desk of a dowdy woman with a hairstyle that was three decades too old. A woman who looked like she should have retired years earlier. Behind her thick glasses were eyes as big and round as an owl's.

"I'd like to access my safe deposit box," I repeated politely. I felt uncomfortable, downright awful pretending to be someone who was smarter, more self-assured than me. But surely this dowdy old woman would not see through my emotional unease.

"Of course, dear. Do you have your key?"

I nodded, handed her the little yellow envelope. Watched as the woman pushed a wide ledger in my direction. "Just sign here, dear."

My heart galloped wildly. I panicked. I had not given this possibility a thought. What should I do?

Then, quickly and decisively, I scribbled a combination of both my name and Savannah's. An illegible signature difficult to decipher. But I need not have worried as the bank lady did not give the ledger or my signature a second glance.

Instead, she said warmly, "This way."

I followed her dingy brown skirt and sensible shoes along a narrow hallway, where we stopped at a wide vaulted room.

"Let's see," the bank lady said. "Box 428. Yes, right here."

She pointed to a box at the third-tier level. I removed the key from the envelope, inserted it into the box, and turned it half a rotation. Nothing happened.

"Remove your key, dear. I need to insert my key now."

I watched the bank lady insert her key and with another half rotation, the little gray door swung open, and she removed a long, narrow box. Reverently, she handed it to me.

"Follow me," the bank lady cooed. A few steps later I was ushered into a small cubicle, windowless and tight. A straight-backed chair and a thick shelf masquerading as a desk filled most of the space.

"Just give a yell when you're done," she said sweetly. Gently, she pulled closed the door behind her.

Nervously I stared at the box, as if expecting a snake or a jack-in-the-box to pop up and scare the living lights out of me. It was one thing to fantasize of what might be in the box, but another thing entirely to face the reality of it.

Slowly, I opened the lid, peered inside.

And my eyeballs nearly popped from their sockets.

I faced row upon row of neatly bundled stacks of one-hundred-dollar bills. Crisp and smelling of fresh ink. *What did you do, Savannah? Were you embezzling money from your family's business as your brother suggested?*

For a half moment, I railed against the thought of removing the money. Then I quickly removed every bundled stack and transferred them all to my big, bulky handbag. Curiously, I reached further into the depths of the box, my fingers halting against a large, creased envelope.

Immediately, I upended its contents.

Sat back and caught my breath.

Staring up at me was a small pile of documents—half a dozen driver's licenses from a variety of states—each with a different name, a different photograph. There were three passports and those, too, revealed different names, different photographs.

As I looked closer, it became clear that the picture on each document resembled Savannah's pretty face, her hair color, her age.

At the bottom of the pile, I unfolded a Certificate of Birth Registration and with it, a Social Security card and a simple paper driver's license. All new, without smudges or dirty fingerprints.

It was too much for me to decipher—I needed to be in the safety of my own home to figure things out, so I pressed all the documents back into the envelope and squashed it atop the stacks of money in my purse. *What the hell is this, Savannah? Were you planning your own escape? Did your daddy find out what you were doing? Did he threaten to kill you?*

I shuddered at the thought of big Johnston Cranston, with his affinity for gallon-sized cowboy hats and antique pistols. Shook at the thought of him intimidating Savannah with one of his pearl-handled guns. *Is that why you did it yourself, Savannah?*

For a moment, it felt as if the walls of the cubicle were closing in on me. I was afraid I might scream. I jumped up, the legs of the chair scraping along the cement floor. My heartbeat pulsed maniacally in my neck. I could count the fast beats as they matriculated, one-two-three, one-two-three, again and again.

For God's sake, Margaret, pull yourself together!

After a ten count, my legs steadied and the queasiness that had vaulted from my stomach to my throat quelled. Weakly, I yelled out, "I'm done in here!"

When the bank lady returned, we retraced our steps back to the vault, repeated the sequence with the keys. I thanked her for her help and hurried up the circular stairs to the bank's lobby.

In a daze, I walked outside and into the sweet smell of rain, my umbrella forgotten inside the small cubicle.

Two hours after I left the bank, and an hour after I soaked in a hot bubble bath, and fifteen minutes after a first glass of wine, I dumped the contents of my handbag onto the coffee table in the living room. Earlier, I had pulled shut every window shade, had yanked closed every curtain.

First, I carefully counted the money: seven thousand, eight hundred dollars. More money than I had ever held in my hands at one time. But it had to be hidden until I needed it. As I pondered a safe hiding place, my eyes strayed to the ugly upholstered green chair that sat near the stereo. The chair the kid always favored.

Swiftly I jumped up, walked to the chair, turned it upside down. As I had guessed, the seat bottom was sewn with a silky material.

I grabbed scissors from the kitchen, slit an opening from top to bottom. I removed yellowed, stringy foam, replaced it with most of the money, then re-sewed it.

After righting the chair, I sat down on it. Nothing tore. Hundred-dollar bills did not pour from the sewn slit.

Pleased, I shoved the chair back to its normal position.

Again, I busied myself with the documents. Each of the driver's licenses had already expired renewal dates, but the passports had several years remaining until expiration.

I reexamined the Certificate of Birth. It certainly looked authentic, printed on glossy paper—bold white words on a flat black background:

Issued by the Bureau of Records, County of Jasper
Date of Birth: 1950 June 26, AM 9:52
Certificate Number: F147-893
Place of Birth: State of Indiana, St. John's Hospital
Mother: Roberta Marz
Father: Unknown

I blanched, nearly fell to the floor.

June 26 was the date of the accident.

And, ironically, 1950 was my actual birth year.

Was this another omen?

A LAME THANKSGIVING

November 24, 1977

JEFFREY

In myriad ways, Thanksgiving Day was a holy mess for Jeffrey Kaye. Enduring the holiday meal with his mother's church lady friends topped the list. They were a tight-knit group of old biddies who reeked horribly of cheap perfume and mothballs.

He managed through forty-four anxiety ridden minutes alone with them while his mother added the finishing touches to the bird and the mashed potatoes and the dinner rolls. He was forced to chat, to answer mindless questions regarding his future: Did he have a special girlfriend? Would he return to work at the DMV? How terrible was the fire in Athens? Had the girl he had been in bed with died?

The phony story he and his mother had concocted to stave off questions about his scars and his limp—and specifically to avoid suspicion that he might indeed be the sole survivor of the Olympian Airways crash—was a good, credible story that passed muster with anyone they shared it with.

It began with a partial truth—he had been in Athens on vacation. And, oh, what a magical first night it had been as he sat at the rooftop bar of the Intercontinental Hotel, his breath whisked away by the nighttime view of the Parthenon glowing brightly from across the way. But it was there that the truth abruptly ended. For certainly, he had not been in bed with a dark-haired beauty when her second-story apartment had caught fire, and no, they had not scurried from her bedroom and up to the roof one floor above, nor had they jumped from the rooftop, and no, the nonexistent dark-haired beauty had not died.

Jeffrey wished he were a cockroach, able to skitter away beneath the baseboards, far from the stale breath of Mrs. Mackenzie, who sat to his left. His eyes flitted and darted about the small sitting room. And, as if for the first time, he was acutely aware of the worn linoleum that puckered up in the corners of the room, the wall paint, which had dulled to a sickly yellow. Even the draperies hung like useless legs on a crippled soldier.

Thankfully, once the meal had ended and dessert was served, Jeffrey feigned exhaustion to escape to his room. He managed to sneak a can of beer with him, cleverly avoiding his mother's eagle eye, for she monitored him like a convict on parole.

Dutifully, he had visited therapists, endured psych evaluations—had easily overacted his symptoms of intense anxiety and acute panic attacks—simply for the drugs they dispensed to him with comforting regularity.

Doses of Xanax and Sertraline and another pill for chronic insomnia. There was also his ready stash of marijuana, which helped him more than any prescribed drug.

An hour later, after the leftovers had been stored and the dishes were washed, Jeffrey Kaye slipped from the apartment. Outside, the air was chilly and invigorating, and he felt the dull stench of the day begin to evaporate.

Nearby, he watched as building superintendents hauled banged up metal trash cans to the gutter for the next day's sanitation pickup. Across the street, Mr. Padding, who owned a small newspaper kiosk, vigorously cursed a group of young guys trying to sell nickel and dime bags of pot to other rough-looking young guys.

Jeffrey walked—it was a stutter step with the use of his cane—and noticed the light foot traffic as he eclipsed the two-block walk toward the bodega on the next corner. Thirsty and desperate for a smoke, he entered the cramped store, searched out a quart-sized bottle of Budweiser beer, carried it to the cashier's counter.

"Box of Marlboro, please," he asked the bored kid at the register. He paid, turned, and nearly bumped face-first into the pretty woman who lived in old man Carrano's apartment.

"Sorry," he whispered to her. She smiled, nodded at him, and began to walk away. She stopped, turned to him, said, "You're my neighbor in 4D, aren't you?"

He nodded dumbly.

"I'm heading home. Are you?" she asked.

"Yup," he replied as he ripped the cellophane from the cigarette pack.

"I'm Viola. Can I walk back with you?"

"Okay. Though it may be slow going." He lifted his cane to eye level. "I'm Jeffrey."

He lit a cigarette and thought, *My God, she is so beautiful and so out of my league.*

"How was your Thanksgiving?" she asked as they began their trek home.

"Pretty lame. Yours?"

"Same."

They chatted as they walked, mostly about how they hated the forced holiday cheeriness, the ridiculous traditions. When they reached their building, she spurted, "Would you like to pop in and have a drink?"

"Uh, sure. Okay."

At the stairwell, he looked at her sheepishly. "Maybe you should go up first. It will take me a little time to get there."

"Don't be silly. I'm in no rush."

As Jeffrey mounted the stairs, he wondered how long it would take for his mother to realize he was not in his room. Wondered if she would be shocked to learn that he was about to share a drink with Sammy Carrano's gorgeous niece.

Once inside her apartment, Viola tossed off her shoes, asked if scotch was okay with him.

"Fine," he replied.

He sat in the closest armchair, glanced around the room. The walls were a soothing minty green color and filled with artwork and African masks, a huge tapestry. Vases of all shapes and colors held pretty flowers.

Viola returned, handed him a fat glass filled with scotch and ice cubes before settling onto the sofa, her legs tucked beneath her.

"So," Jeffrey said after a long swallow. "You must be Sammy Carrano's niece, right? He was always going on about you coming to New York to live with him. Nice guy. Sorry to hear he passed."

He noticed a glitch in her expression—surprise, bewilderment? It was gone in a moment and again, she smiled. "Yes. Sammy Carrano is... was...my uncle. And yes, he was a genuinely nice guy."

Feeling awkward, Jeffrey unconsciously tapped his cane on the floor—a staccato tap, tap, tap, which often drove his mother crazy. He took another sip of his drink. "This is excellent scotch. Very smooth."

"Yeah, expensive too. The manager at McNulty's lets me take home a bottle every now and then."

"Oh, you work at McNulty's. I've been there once or twice. Before my accident."

"Yes. I tend bar there. It's an okay job. Plenty of nice customers. A couple of jerks," she said, shrugging her shoulders. She placed her finger into her glass, swirled the ice cubes round and round.

Without looking at him, she said, "If you ever need to talk to someone about what happened to you . . . I mean about the fire in Athens. . . Sorry-

-your mother told me what happened to you during your vacation . . . sorry, I'm rambling."

Instantly, Jeffrey wanted to cry. Felt his chin quiver and his eyes water as he forced back his tears. Then, as if in a fluffy dream, Viola rose, walked near to him. She placed her hands on his shoulders, leaned in close.

"You're a survivor, Jeffrey," she whispered. "You should be immensely proud of that. Because surviving anything in our crazy lives is a major accomplishment."

She sat back on the sofa, lifted her glass, said, "I personally know that to be true."

WORST PARTY EVER

December 16, 1977

FITZ

For a month, Fitz remained conveniently absent from the tempting after-hour party scene. His arrest prior to Thanksgiving had soundly frightened him. It was like walking a tightrope without a safety net. He knew damn well he had slipped under the radar thanks to his good friend Damon. Never again did he want to see the inside of a prison cell.

But nine days before Christmas, his willpower petered out.

An invitation to a party at a huge industrial warehouse on Seventh Avenue lured him. A party which catered to wealthy men with a penchant for young girls.

Fitz's invitation came via Gregory Maison, a wealthy financier he had befriended while vacationing in Acapulco a few years earlier.

The "special parties" could easily pass as private chamber of commerce events, as they brought together a conflux of influential people: bankers, attorneys, politicians, financial gurus, surgeons, business owners. Fitz had made a handful of important business contacts at the parties. People like William Calhoun, and Andy Trumbolt, Chief Financial Officer of Raintree Products.

Fitz was not sure if Damon knew that his Raintree contact was a frequent attendee at these parties, but Fitz was not about to unveil that truth to his friend.

Interacting with the guests at these parties helped them to form a common bond, a camaraderie of intimacy, each aware that they were privy to the other's private secrets. It allowed Fitz to glean an abundance of useful information in a nonthreatening atmosphere.

When Fitz arrived at the given address, he turned the corner onto Thirty-Second Street to search for a narrow side door into the warehouse—a door which, to the naked eye, was barely visible, as it blended directly into the dark night. He entered a code on the door panel, a code unique to each party. Without the proper party's code, admittance would not be allowed, regardless of how many previous parties one might have attended. This was the strictest of the rules.

A huge metal elevator, normally used to transport racks of women's clothing, lifted Fitz to a hard landing onto the second floor of the warehouse. He walked from the elevator and into a door marked FIORELLI DESIGNS. There, he came face to face with Big Pauly, who sat behind a desk, monitoring an impressive array of security cameras. During his younger days, Pauly had been a boxing phenom. No one dared to mess with him, and no one gave him lip. Not if they wished to leave the party with their extremities intact.

Fitz handed Pauly five hundred dollars, fully aware that a portion of the money would go to the girls who entertained the guests and that a portion would take care of liquor, food, drugs, and security.

Pauly's eyes barely glanced from the security cameras as he pressed a button to activate a fake wall that swished open. Fitz quickly stepped through the door and heard it close behind him.

Inside, the party was in full swing. Velvet sofas and divans were crowded with men and girls; topless women served drinks. A huge buffet was available, and a shoulder-high shelf offered lines of cocaine. A small group of people laughed as they shared a bong. There were doorways, which led to private rooms, and, in one area of the huge space, a disc jockey spun music as a group of girls danced together.

Fitz accepted a glass of wine, strolled among the guests. He nodded and smiled at familiar faces but did not recognize any of the young girls. He wandered to the bar, spent a chunk of time chatting baseball stats with the mayor's assistant.

He excused himself to use the restroom, opted for a stall rather than the urinals. As he urinated, he heard an echo of shouts from beyond the restroom, followed by a loud commotion. Abruptly, the music ceased. Screams echoed, along with the sounds of shattering glass and heavy thumps. A succession of eight or nine bangs reverberated loudly.

Fitz quickly zipped up, lowered the toilet lid, and lifted himself to squat atop it. He heard pitiful cries, pleas for help and mercy. His heart pounded in triple time; his sweaty palms on the stall's walls shook as they tried to keep him balanced. He repeated a learned childhood prayer as a mantra to calm himself.

He might have stood on that toilet for six or seven minutes, but to Fitz it seemed like hours.

And then, silence.

Except for the far-off sound of sirens careening their way toward the warehouse.

Fitz knew he had to escape the restroom, flee the warehouse. He could not, must not be identified in the sweep to come.

He counted off ten seconds, then slowly lowered himself to the floor of the stall. Gently he unlatched the lock then tiptoed past the urinals and the sinks to the door. He waited there another ten seconds, heard only the sounds of tepid cries and tentative footsteps. He creaked the door open, peeked outside, then wished he had not looked.

There were bodies and blood everywhere. The buffet and coke shelf had been upended. Smashed liquor bottles leaked alcohol, and a small fire had begun behind a divan where three people were slumped dead in their seats.

Fitz eased himself from the lavatory, walked gingerly past the bodies sprawled on the main floor. Squeezed his eyes closed at the puddles of blood pooling everywhere. From outside, the blare of the sirens grew louder and nearer, and he realized he had to leave immediately.

In plain sight on the southeast wall, he found the button to engage the electronic door. Fitz pressed it, stepped through, and found Big Pauly slumped over the security cameras, a long knife protruding from his left eye.

There was not time to think or to assist in any way—nor would Fitz have tried to assist. Removing himself from the premises was his only priority. He slammed his finger into the elevator button, jiggled on his tiptoes as he waited for the monstrosity of metal to reach his floor. As soon as it did, he dashed inside, repeatedly pounded the button for the first level. When the doors finally pried apart, he darted out, pushed open the nearly invisible side door, just as the police sirens screeched to the corner of Seventh Avenue.

Quickly he sprinted away—jogged half a dozen blocks—until he stopped in front of a tired storefront at a corner building. He pressed himself against the glass windows, willed his heart to calm, his breathing to steady. Sweat poured from his face, his neck, his underarms. His expensive shirt was soiled with perspiration.

At Thirty-Second Street he flailed his arms for a taxi and luckily, one appeared instantly.

“I’m going to Forest Hills,” he gasped as he crawled inside the cab.

Swallowing hard, he looked from the taxi’s windows, watched as streetlamps and garbage cans and empty streets whizzed past.

He could not obliterate the memory of the blood he had seen smeared everywhere—a massacre.

He wanted to wish away the bodies of the people slumped atop the sofas, on the floors. He wondered if those using the private rooms had been spared the onslaught.

Poor Pauly, he thought.

And poor Andy Trumbolt, with his face nearly blown off. What was the poor guy's family going to think?

As Fitz began to calm, he wondered how and why the massacre had happened.

Pauly had been there as the ultimate protection.

And the parties were strictly by invitation, accessed only with the particular party's code.

Was it a robbery?

Maybe.

Was it a drug dealer stiffed on a payment?

Yes, a definite possibility.

Or it was something more sinister.

Maybe the daddy of one of the party girls had gotten mightily pissed off.

TELL-TALE SIGNS

December 18, 1977

VIOLA

Viola Cordova stood behind the bar at McNulty's. She stared absently out of the big plate-glass windows that faced the sidewalks, watched as large, fat snowflakes blanketed the city. Residents had been warned of the blizzard to come, but Chubs had adamantly proclaimed, "Weathermen are always wrong. We're staying open."

Some of their regulars had braved the weather to down a few beers, but the restaurant side of the tavern remained empty.

The clock above the door showed 6:32 p.m. The snow had begun to fall shortly after five o'clock and already, Viola saw how swiftly the snowfall had accumulated. She watched silhouettes of bodies glide past. Women with scarves and kerchiefs wrapped about their heads, men in bomber jackets and long coats, their cheeks ruddy from the cold. Teenagers who slipped and slid by in their woefully inadequate high-top PF Flyers.

As she turned away, her peripheral vision spotted a familiar shape walking with its stop-and-go gait. The cane slipped with every step. It was Jeffrey, his hair windswept as he brushed snow from his eyelids. Why the hell was he out in this weather?

Viola knew that secretly, he wanted her. She read it in his eyes, in the tug of his mouth. Hell, most men wanted her. But this was Jeffrey, and she did not want to hurt his fragile ego, did not want to derail any progress he might be making in his rehabilitation—both emotionally and physically—but she refused to lead him into believing he would ever have a romantic chance with her.

A moment later, she saw Jeffrey enter the tavern, watched him hop awkwardly onto a barstool at her section of the bar. When he spotted her, he smiled broadly, handed her his cane to place behind the bar for safekeeping.

"What are you doing out in this storm?" she asked him.

"Oh, it's just a few snowflakes," he joked.

She poured him a pint of beer, watched him light his first of several cigarettes to come.

"How's your mother?" she asked.

"She's visiting her sister in Jersey, thank God. I've got the place to myself until next Monday."

Viola swore she saw a twinkle in his eye. "You're welcome to keep me company if you like," he said softly.

She smiled, leaned across the bar. "I'm sorry, sweetie, but my heart is already taken."

"Lucky fellow," he said weakly.

At that moment, another brave person rushed through the door, anxious to be out of the storm. The man approached the bar, pulled off his bulky parka, and whipped off his cap. Viola caught her surprised gasp when she saw it was Fitz.

She nodded at him. Weeks earlier, they had decided to remain discreet if either Fitz or Jonathan Silver visited McNulty's. No longer would they visit to knock back a pint of beer, visits were strictly to transfer information regarding their partnership's business.

"Gin and tonic, please," Fitz mumbled quietly.

As she mixed the drink, she noticed Jeffrey watching her, saw him stare at her as she placed the drink in front of Fitz.

She kept her voice low and steady as she asked, "What's up?"

He took a long sip of the drink. Looked down at the bar top as he said, "Raintree may be held up for a bit."

Viola swiped at invisible spills on the bar. "Why?"

"A top guy there was murdered. The CEO prefers the details of his murder to blow over before making the leap."

Viola stopped wiping, stared hard at Fitz. "So, we're on hold for the first transaction?"

"Yeah. As of now."

Viola's attention was diverted as she heard Jeffrey's voice from the other end of the bar. "Hi, need a refill down here."

Viola frowned, gave a barely discernible nod in Fitz's direction. Before slipping to the other end of the bar, she watched Fitz gulp the rest of his drink and shrug back into his parka. He turned abruptly and exited the bar.

Viola watched Jeffrey as his eyes tracked Fitz's movements. It frightened her. Reminded her of Leroy Stills.

It was not a pleasant memory.

She refilled Jeffrey's glass, smiled at him.

Then she walked around the bar and out of Jeffrey's sight. She slipped into the kitchen and retrieved her coat. "I'm not feeling well, Chubs," she mumbled. "I've got to leave."

Then she retreated from the back door and into an alleyway that stunk of cat piss and rotted fruit.

When she arrived home, she bolted her door and slid a chair underneath the doorknob for extra security.

A NEW PERSON EMERGES

December 20, 1977

When the dreaded call finally came, I remained as unprepared for it as I had been for the past six months. Some might have regarded the call as an early Christmas present, but I did not.

Hearing the voice of Aurora Robb from the Federal Aviation Administration nearly knocked me off my feet. I was embarrassed to be quivering and shaking like an old lady about to be mugged.

"How are you doing, Margaret?" she asked. I heard the stress, the fundamental weariness in her voice.

"As well as might be expected," I responded.

An uncomfortable pause followed, then Aurora's stern voice said, "I am making this call to you as a courtesy, Margaret. The FAA and NTSB have issued strictly preliminary conclusions regarding the June 26th collisions, but I wanted to share them with you before the press gets wind of it. Again, these are not definitive conclusions, and the investigations will continue."

"Thank you," I managed to whisper.

"The prelims are very generic, Margaret. These are the excerpts, and I quote: 'Contributing to the accident was a ground radar system that tracks taxiing aircraft, which was clearly in default, and the controller's view of runways may have been obscured by heavy fog. Controller's toxicology results confirm negative for all controlled substances. Preliminary conclusion: runway incursion related to human error coupled with failed mechanism in ground radar system.'"

Aurora Robb cleared her throat. "End quote."

Human error. Those words nosedived to the bottom of my belly.

Human error translated to my error, for I was the one at the controls that day. How might I forgive myself for snatching those lives and leaving behind gaping holes in the hearts of their friends and loved ones?

Clearly, the moment those preliminary reports were released to the mainstream press, I would once again become a media pariah—despised and hated for the rest of my worthless life.

When I ended the call with Aurora Robb, I felt as old as the earth itself.

Twenty-six hours later, I stared into the small bathroom mirror.

The woman who looked back at me was not the woman I believed her to be. This forgery of myself had forgotten how to smile, how to feel alive.

I lit a Virginia Slims cigarette. Took a sip of wine. With the money and passports from Savannah's safe deposit box, it would be easy to run away. The call from Aurora Robb had simply ignited me to action.

The Nice 'N Easy hair dye had been purchased. Midnight Black, the darkest shade they offered. Following the instructions, I applied the nasty-smelling product onto the long strands of my hair. Allowed the appropriate amount of time to lapse before shampooing it out.

After a quick towel dry, I began the arduous task of snipping away the curls, the strands, the length of my hair until all that remained was a jet black, super-short pixie cut, which made me look so much younger than my old, ratty hairstyle.

Next, I fiddled with contact lenses prescribed to me by a doctor three towns away. Using colored contact lenses, a person could easily change their eye color from brown to blue to green or to any color they desired.

My own eyes were a dull grayish brown—a murky swamp-water color—but when I slipped in the new smoky gray contact lenses, my transformation was full-on incredible. Against the blackness of my hair, my gray eyes looked like a sky hell-bent on causing trouble. Satisfied with the outcome, I tossed my old tortoise shell eyeglasses into the garbage.

Already, I felt the power of transformation taking control of me. I was determined, as if I had just tossed a gargantuan monkey from my back. The clock showed 10:59 p.m. I glanced at the front door, where two black nondescript suitcases and an oversized duffel bag waited patiently for their traveler. They were the same dull pieces of luggage used by millions of travelers every day. The type that would hardly raise an eyebrow.

One suitcase held clothing: jeans, tops, underwear, two of my best business suits. The second was jammed with shoes, a pair of hiking boots, and a bulky jacket. For an oddly sentimental reason, I tossed in a few personal keepsakes: birthday cards from Mom and Savannah, several childish drawings created by the twins.

But my real treasures were inside the large duffel bag: six thousand dollars tightly wrapped inside an assortment of heavy white cotton socks. The phony IDs and passports I had safely tucked inside a large clasped envelope.

Folded on top of everything was an easy-to-get-to change of clothing, a sleep shirt, and my wallet, which held five hundred dollars in cash and my new identity.

After a second glass of wine, I destroyed my Georgia State driver's license, my birth certificate, social security card—and most importantly, my Hewitt-Jackson employee badge—cut them all into tiny bits and burned them in the kitchen sink.

At noon on December 23, I left my bungalow for the final time. Engaged the timer that would set the lamps to turn on and off, to make it seem that someone still lived in the small bungalow. Newspaper delivery had been canceled, and the mailbox emptied.

I locked the door behind me, left the key underneath the mat. My old Volvo took me to the local train station, where I parked it on the lonely dead-end street that abutted the station. Quickly, I removed the license plates and placed them into the duffel bag. The insurance and registration papers I shoved deep into my jean pockets, eventually to be shredded and discarded into rubbish bins and toilets at various rest stops along the train route.

The local train would take exactly fourteen minutes to bring me to the Peachtree main station in Atlanta, where I would purchase, in cash, a one-way Amtrack ticket—with a sleeping compartment—to New York City. The trip should last eighteen hours and eleven minutes.

I believed I had thought of everything, including having secured temporary housing at a women's hotel on 63rd Street. Once settled, finding employment would become my priority.

I boarded the train along with dozens of other travelers. Took an aisle seat next to a teenage girl with smudges beneath her eyes and dirty fingernails. Maybe she was running away from a difficult home life. Maybe she was running from the police. Or someone had broken her heart.

My duffel bag sat nestled on my lap, my Atlanta Braves baseball cap pulled low onto my forehead. No one seemed to be paying any attention to me at all, but still, I was nervous.

The last passenger boarded our compartment, a tall man who grabbed the last aisle seat one row in front and to the left of me. When he turned to speak to his seat companion, I nearly gasped aloud.

His resemblance to my father was uncanny, and for that split second in time, I wanted to run to him, throw my arms around him, tell him how desperately I missed him. But that was impossible because my father had died when I was nine years old. My sweet father, who had Dean Martin–type good looks and the same penchant for gin.

The story went that Daddy had driven into Mineral Bluff for an after-work drink at Kelly's Tavern. Mr. Kelly claimed that Daddy and a lady friend were at a small table near the tavern's big plate-glass window when a Chevy Impala jumped the curb and plowed right into them.

The woman who had died with Daddy was a mystery, certainly not a woman of Fannin County. The fact that Daddy was with this mystery woman had foisted a great deal of unwanted gossip and angst upon my poor mother.

I jumped as I heard the train's whistle hiss loudly, and then the train jolted and slowly inched forward. The man resembling Daddy was back in his seat, his face hidden by a newspaper. The teenage girl seated next to me had not moved or said a word.

Surprisingly, when the train arrived in New York City, I had a momentary twinge of sadness as I departed the train and waved a final farewell to Margaret Lido.

Lily Marz had just been reborn.

CHRISTMAS FOR ALL

December 25, 1977

10:25 a.m.

Surely, Christmas morning's snow-covered streets and trees and fire escapes must have delighted every waking child that day. At midmorning, Jeffrey Kaye stumbled from his bed and into the living room to find a small mountain of gifts beneath their tree. "Are these all for me?" he asked.

"Of course they are," his mother answered. She remained in her ratty terrycloth robe, pink curlers in her hair, her face incredibly pale without her usual makeup coverings. In her hands she nestled a cup of coffee.

"Go on. Open them," she nudged.

He felt a stab of guilt as he had only one gift for his mother—a wool scarf with matching gloves.

Pathetic.

His mother's gifts to him were a treasure trove of items: jeans and sweaters, a new leather wallet, a large bottle of Aramis Men's cologne, two books by Stephen King.

That afternoon, while his mother attended church services, Jeffrey clicked on the television, watched the old Alistair Cooke version of *Scrooge*. Twice, he walked out to the hallway to smoke a cigarette. Standing near the stairwell, he wondered if Viola was at home.

It was odd the way she had left McNulty's the night of the blizzard. So suddenly and without even a good night to him.

After stubbing out his second cigarette, he stopped at Viola's door.

He knocked gently, then pressed the doorbell.

He heard nothing, shrugged his shoulders, and walked back to his apartment.

2:02 p.m.

Viola Cordova was not at home when Jeffrey Kaye knocked on her apartment door for she was in Brooklyn with Alex Calder, a regular patron at McNulty's—a big guy, muscular and fit, with large workingman's hands and a short crewcut.

After Chubs had shouted "last call" at eight o'clock on Christmas Eve, Alex had asked, "I know a great Chinese restaurant in Brooklyn that never closes. Not even on Christmas Eve. Would you like to join me?"

She had nodded yes.

After stuffing themselves on Peking duck and plum wine, she had agreed to go home with him.

When she woke on Christmas morning, Alex had already prepared for them cheese omelets, crispy bacon strips, and hot cocoa. It was the sweetest thing any man had ever done for her.

Together they watched all the old black and white Christmas movies, munched popcorn, and sipped mulled wine. She teased him about his holiday decoration—a three-inch-tall ceramic tree with built-in red lights—then admitted to him that she was not a huge fan of holidays.

After another round of lovemaking, she finally headed home.

With any luck, she would not bump into Jeffrey Kaye in the hallway.

5:11 p.m.

As Viola rode the subway home from Alex Calder's apartment in Park Slope, Fitz drove to his parents' home in Roslyn for their annual Christmas dinner. He did not anticipate a festive evening, as it usually turned into an obscene shouting match between his mother and father. But the drive to their home was pleasant—with plenty of houses decorated with blinking red and green lights and with big air-blown Santas on front lawns. It made him smile and helped to staunch his uneasiness.

He pulled into his parents' circular driveway, parked behind a vehicle he did not recognize. He opened his trunk, removed an armload of gifts, carried them inside. The eight-foot Christmas tree was the first thing he saw, beautifully decorated with crystal ornaments and red velvet ribbons. He heard voices float from the living room, followed the sounds.

His mother spotted him first, waved wildly to him as if he were a movie star and she a star-struck fan. Then he spotted the old man seated near his father, and he nearly toppled the gifts.

His grandfather was there. *Why isn't he in Sicily?* Fitz thought sickly.

The old man was shorter than Fitz remembered, yet still with a full head of hair, now cottony white. His eyes were small and beady like the eyes of a raven. Not a person one wished to have as an enemy.

His grandfather hugged him tightly, cupped his cheeks. "It's good to see you, Junior," he said. His grandfather had never approved of using Fitz's nickname.

"Good to see you, too," Fitz said. "I didn't know you were coming."

"Yeah, well, I wanted to surprise everyone." His voice was surprisingly soft, almost melodic.

They chatted until Fitz's mother called them in to dinner, a feast, actually: burrata mozzarella with prosciutto and melon, honey-glazed ham, string beans, sweet potato souffle, freshly baked dinner rolls. She also brought out the expensive wines Fitz's father collected.

After dinner, they opened presents, enjoyed cannoli and Italian cookies.

"Come on, Junior," his grandfather said as he stood up. "Let us have an anisette and a smoke. We can catch up."

Fitz followed his grandfather into his father's den. As the anisette was poured, he felt uneasy. A cigar was handed to him, and although Fitz did not care to smoke, he lit one, not wanting to disrespect the old man.

They sat in matching leather chairs, puffed their cigars, exhaled billows of smoke toward the ceiling.

"So, Junior," his grandfather said. "You look well. The girls must be knocking down your door, no?"

Fitz laughed. "I'm not with anyone right now."

His grandfather squinted at him, said, "Funny, whenever I ask your mother if there's a special girl in your life, she says no."

Fitz smiled. "Just haven't met the right one yet."

His grandfather took a long pull on the cigar, stared at a painting directly behind Fitz's head. "Are you a homo?" he asked.

"What? No! Of course not," Fitz said belligerently.

"Okay, okay. Just asking."

A protracted silence followed.

Finally, his grandfather leaned forward, spoke softly. "Junior, I know about your arrest for soliciting an underaged girl, and I know you were present at that warehouse massacre."

Fitz's chest heaved. "How did you find out?" he mumbled.

The old man smiled, the creases in his face stretching wide. "Junior, I know everything that goes on with my family. I have eyes everywhere. You should know that by now."

Fitz looked down at his feet, at the tassel loafers he had purchased a week earlier for two hundred dollars.

"Have you told them?" he asked, pointing his chin toward the living room.

"No."

"Are you going to tell them?"

"Well, that will depend on you."

Fitz raised his eyebrows.

"Junior, I own a hefty stake in Fitzgerald Alloy Corporation." He waved his hands in the air as if this was meaningless information. "Yeah, yeah, don't look so surprised. I made a substantial investment into your father's shaky business when he married your mother. I wanted him to keep her comfortable, to make sure she had a generous allowance. So, for the sake of the business and for the family's good name, you need to make some changes to your lifestyle."

The old man crushed out his cigar. "People respect me; they respect my choices. Things happen on my say-so. But if our clients were to learn that my grandson is playing footsies with little girls, well, that is sure to be a big problem for me. And if it's a problem for me, it's a problem for you too."

Fitz felt his face flame.

"Find a real woman, Junior. It will keep the gossips at bay. I strongly suggest you take this advice to heart."

His grandfather rose, patted Fitz's cheek, and walked back to the living room.

FLY, FLY AWAY

March 7, 1978

New York City was the elixir that helped to restore my life, the rebirth of my life as Lily Marz. At first, my heart felt as if it had been hollowed out like a juicy pumpkin ready for carving. There I was, such a tiny bit of a person scrunched deep within the big, blustering city. A place where apples and cherries were purchased at curbside bodegas and not alongside country roads. A place where people fled to underground transportation to move them to aboveground destinations. Where noisy buses and speeding yellow taxis, and fast-pedaling bicycle messengers all juggled road space with hot dog carts and pedestrians.

But almost immediately, the city felt like a second heartbeat inside my chest. The sights, the sounds, the fast-paced atmosphere—all of it a one-hundred-eighty-degree turn from every place I had previously lived.

I had chosen well for a city residence: the Barbizon Hotel for Women on 63rd and Lexington. A perfect location for women with a limited budget and twenty-four-hour security for its all-female residents. There was a laundry room and several color TVs on the eighteenth floor lounge, but rooms did not have private baths or air conditioning. The hotel boasted shops, a beauty parlor, and restaurants. Room service was not an option.

My room was #617, a comfortable space with a twin-sized bed, a dresser, one chair, and a sink. The walls were a pretty shade of pink with a flowered bedcover and matching curtains.

During my first few weeks in New York, I explored the city, inhaled everything it had to offer. I dallied between the lovely Christmas windows at Macy's and the ice skaters at Rockefeller Center. I traipsed to the Empire State Building, rode the ferry to the Statue of Liberty, visited museums and art galleries and Greenwich Village.

I stayed up late reading *Mommy Dearest* and *Chesapeake*, splurged on a Broadway ticket to *A Chorus Line*, ate hot dogs and pretzels and roasted chestnuts from street vendors. The wonder of the city tickled my eyes, my ears, my feet. How I desperately wished New York were my rightful birthplace. My life would have turned out very differently.

When I inquired of a reputable dentist, the Barbizon concierge suggested to me his own dentist, a nice man who capped my front teeth so that the gap between them disappeared. The difference it made in my appearance was astounding, and for the first time in my life, I felt attractive.

Of course, day by day, I fought to chip away at the dreadful pile of memories from my past life. To help myself cope, I pretended that my mother and Savannah had never existed, therefore, they could not be dead. My stepfather and the twins—simply figments of my imagination. I fought to squash their memories the moment they began to linger, for I must never slip up and jeopardize my new identity.

By mid-January, I spent long days reading the job classifieds, but the trick was to find a position for which I might suitably qualify. My typing skills were of the hunt-and-peck type, and I simply could not see myself as a secretary or bank clerk—certainly not after the frenetic pace of my previous job.

Nor would I attempt to waitress, for I was a major klutz. I longed for an opportunity to utilize some of the FAA skills I possessed but feared those very skills might raise too many questions.

Sometimes I wanted to pinch myself, to prove that my life in New York was real, not a dream, not a fantasy. A few times, I allowed myself to wonder if the old Volvo had been towed away, if its license plates had been discovered in a trash bin at one of the train stops, if my landlord had re-rented the bungalow.

The kid frequented my thoughts too. I wondered if he had been accepted at Northwestern. Had his mother married the basketball coach? Was he happy? Did he miss me?

One Wednesday afternoon, as I sat in the lounge searching the *Daily News'* want ads, a beautiful woman with nutmeg-colored skin joined me in the room. She carried a can of TAB and introduced herself to me as Lena Robinson.

"Nice to meet you, Lena," I replied with a big smile.

"How long have you been staying at the Barbizon?" she asked.

"Oh, since the end of December."

Lena was stunning—big brown eyes set within a diamond-shaped face. Her body was long and lean, strong—as if she were a runner or a swimmer. She said, "I'm on the third floor, number 303. I've been here for four months now. What do you do?"

I laughed aloud. "Well, not very much of anything right now. And you?"

Lena laughed too. "I'm an actress-to-be. Hoping to land a role on Broadway. Well, me and a hundred other girls."

We bonded immediately and that night we dined together at the Minstrel, an affordable restaurant in the downstairs lobby. We sat at a table near the windows that looked out onto Lexington Avenue.

Lena ordered us a bottle of champagne and we chatted amiably, found we were both fond of politics, poets, must-see movies, and must-read books. She was great fun. Smart, witty, confident. She reminded me of Savannah, with her no-holds barred tongue and her flippant attitude.

But when she asked me where I was from and what I was searching for in New York, I nearly clammed up.

"I'm from a rural town in Indiana," I said, partly hidden behind my champagne flute. This was the first half lie I had said aloud to anyone but myself. "My parents were farmers, but Dad died suddenly, and Mom remarried." *Stay as close to the truth as possible,* I warned myself. *It will be easier to remember my lies if they mimic the truth.*

"Do you have siblings?" Lena asked as she drained her champagne glass.

"No," I responded quickly.

Thankfully, the conversation turned to Lena and her hopes for a starring role on Broadway or a TV sitcom, or God willing, a blockbuster movie.

"I'd even settle for a TV ad," she joked.

Blaming it on the champagne, I blurted to Lena how important it was for me to find a job and quickly.

"Honey," she drawled. She was on her third glass of champagne. "Why didn't you say so? I know lots of people who might be able to help. What can you do?"

I sat back against my chair and wondered just how much information I dared to share.

"Well," I said. "My dad's brother was an expert map charter. He taught me how to read and study maps since I was a kid." My second lie of the day.

"And I've always been interested in science; you know, cloud formations and how cyclones originate. I'm organized—perhaps to a fault—conscientious. I take pride in my work." *Oh my God, do I sound like a moronic fool?*

Lena smiled. Leaned on her elbows and looked deeply into my eyes. "Lily Marz, we are going to become great friends."

The next afternoon, Lena knocked on my door. She wore a tangerine-colored dress and shoes with heels that seemed to reach to her knees. "Hi," she said as she waved a sheet of paper at me. "You have an appointment with these people tomorrow at three. Wear your best sensible outfit. They know I recommended you. Good luck! I'm off to an audition."

After closing the door behind Lena, I glanced at the paper in my hand. In block handwriting, it read: THREE O'CLOCK WITH MYRON LEVINE. JET KING ENTERPRISES, 666 MADISON AVE. SUITE 604.

At promptly three o'clock the next day, I arrived at the address. I wore a neat, just-above-the-knee black and white checkered suit, white blouse, black pumps. I had gone easy on the makeup—just a bit of lipstick and a swipe of blush. I had never been much of a makeup girl, so why start now?

Suite 604 was located directly across from the elevator. JET KING ENTERPRISES was stenciled in bold lettering on its glass doors.

Inside, a young woman in a tight red miniskirt welcomed me. She took my name, asked me to wait. The reception area was elegant: fine artwork, expensive furniture, soft carpeting. A few minutes later she escorted me along a plush hallway. As we walked, I glanced at the photographs that lined the walls: President Reagan shaking hands with a middle-aged man, another of the same man hugging Billy Jean King, a host of pictures of airplanes and jets.

Ushered into a large office, I shook hands with a man who introduced himself as Myron Levine. I immediately recognized him as the man in the photographs. He was exceptionally tall and wore a tailored dark gray suit. Underneath the suit was a white shirt, crisp and clean, his tie a toned-down gray and white stripe. We went through the same give-and-take of information as happened during most job interviews.

"So, Miss Marz, as I understand it, you're new to the city." He said this as a statement, not a question, as if it was a most interesting bit of information.

"Yes. I am."

"Do you know anything about Jet King?"

"I'm afraid not, Mr. Levine." *Have I screwed things up already?*

Slowly, he opened a drawer, pulled out an almost crushed pack of cigarettes. Held the pack out to me. I declined, aware it might seem rude to accept a smoke during a job interview. He settled into his big, cushioned chair. Began to sway in half loops.

"Here's what we do here, Lily. We are a corporate business jet company. We own small to mid-sized aircraft, and we transport company executives to meetings, events, conventions, and vacation spots in Europe. We charter out by the hour or by a flat fixed fee or as a select block of time. A great perk for company executives and a legitimate business expense. At times we transport government officials and highly recognizable religious figures. Movie stars and moguls."

I nodded because I did not know what else to do.

"Our scheduling manager is pregnant, six or seven months into it," Mr. Levine said. He crushed his cigarette into an ashtray, which looked to have been molded by a child.

"We need an immediate replacement," he said. "Someone sharp, with a good eye for detail and with sound, logical judgment. A person willing to give more than 100 percent of themselves; someone willing to commit to the company as if it were their own company."

Again, I nodded.

"Think you have what it takes?" he asked. "Think you have the ability to drop anything you're doing at any moment if necessary?"

I looked steadily into Mr. Levine's eyes. "Sir, I am the perfect candidate for your organization. The person you need." Twelve minutes later I was told to begin work on the following Monday.

FAVORS

March 7, 1978

JEFFREY

Until the telephone call came requesting that Jeffrey Kaye return to work at the Department of Motor Vehicles, his life had spiraled into a vacuum of utter boredom.

His shrink had urged him to return to work. "You've got to get back into the real world, Jeffrey. You must try to assimilate, get yourself into a routine. It will do you good to be out of the house. Away from your mother for a few hours."

That morning, Jeffrey stared from his bedroom window at the icy sidewalks and stalled traffic on the street below. He chewed his lip as he watched Mrs. Bingari walk her nasty little poodle along the avenue.

His thoughts were of Viola Cordova—weren't they always centered on her? Like a deranged lover, her presence stalked him into the supermarket and lurked at him from the subway station. She was there at the newspaper kiosk or seated two rows in front of him on the bus.

Of course, she was never physically there.

It drove him mad and when these bouts occurred, he would dry swallow two, sometimes three of his anxiety pills to quell the paranoia.

He wondered if he might be in love with her. But what was the purpose of being alive if the love you felt was not returned in kind?

Since the night of the blizzard, she appeared spooked whenever they bumped into each other in the building lobby or the elevator or when he stopped for a beer at McNulty's.

Chain smoking had become a deadly habit for him. He would walk out to the hallway, stop near the stairway, pull out a Marlboro, flick his Bic lighter, and stand there, smoking and waiting, wishing Viola would appear. Wished he could watch her lithe body rushing up the steps two at a time, eager to be inside her apartment.

Sure, some mornings he had seen that big guy leave her place. Noticed that she did not always return home on weekends. And why had she stayed on in her uncle Sammy's place after he died? Why hadn't she returned home to Florida? Who was she, really?

The call from the DMV was from Jeffrey's previous manager. Marvin Paradiso was a soft-spoken older man who offered Jeffrey a terrific opportunity—an easy spot taking license photos at the West 31st Street location. No specific skills were required for the position: just snap the photo, review, call the next person in line.

Marvin Paradiso had arranged the position for Jeffrey's benefit—not because of any altruistic duty or any sense of loyalty to Jeffrey, but because someone important had required this of him.

Jeffrey had eagerly accepted the position, hoped it might alleviate his boredom and help to ease his anxieties. But he would never learn that his mother had begged her church lady friend, Alicia Paradiso, to request this favor of her husband, Marvin.

READY TO TRADE

March 10, 1978

FITZ

Mistakes usually do not rear their heads until after the damage has been done. Numbers remain inverted on a tax form; a purchased car is either too big or too small. The wrong paint colors are chosen.

Fitz's biggest mistake would not dawn on him until the very last day of his life.

On a freezing Friday afternoon, with the sun begging to push through the clouds, he drove across the state line from Delaware into New Jersey, his personal business completed with the same firm that had helped them to create their shell company, NYC Holdings.

A redhead with startling green eyes and a sweet smile had assisted him in opening an offshore account bearing the name of a private shell company owned solely by Fitz and steeped with multiple layers of protection to keep his ownership anonymous.

He knew that once they began pulling in money from their IPO scheme, he would need a place to stash his cash. Somewhere safe, where assets could be hidden, taxes avoided. A country that did not extradite Americans for tax evasion.

A Swiss bank in Zurich, Switzerland, easily fit the bill.

Fitz lit a cigarette, cracked the car window, settled his speed to an easy-going sixty miles per hour. The Bee Gees were on the radio, and Fitz sang along with the catchy tune.

As he approached the George Washington Bridge, he thought again of his sound reasoning for having created this new personal offshore account.

Quite simply, as much as he trusted his friend Damon and Viola, there was always that little niggling speck of unease. *Face it,* he thought, *when it comes to money, people can get crazy, do inane things we might never expect. The only one you can really trust is yourself.*

He had hurried this process along because Damon revealed to him that the Raintree IPO was finally set to go on March 15. Fitz felt a pang of regret as he remembered their mole from Raintree, last seen slumped against a wall with half of his face blown off.

Shuddering, Fitz shook off the memory. He had not been to an after-hours party since the robbery. Mostly because the party hosts were lying low, just waiting for the hoopla from the Seventh Avenue massacre to smooth over.

He needed to be patient.

Fitz arrived back in Manhattan at quarter to six. McNulty's would be in full swing for happy hour. He parked in a public garage, cursed the obscene prices charged. He pulled his coat collar tight and lowered his head against the wind. Turned the corner and walked into the crush of people inside the tavern.

PAYDAY

March 15, 1978

VIOLA

It was her regularly scheduled day off. The day was clear, perfect for a drive. She drove a mid-sized sedan, previously rented from Avis Rent-A-Car. Viola found the trip to be leisurely, right up until she reached the Cross Bronx Expressway. There, the highway was clogged with a slew of vehicles—cars, trucks, taxis, heavy equipment vehicles—and up ahead a car had jumped a divider and landed on the opposite side of the highway.

She inched forward behind an ugly green Ford Pinto.

On Friday night, Fitz had shown up at McNulty's. The bar was packed with a bunch of drunken rowdies and twice, Chubs had to escort someone out the front door for lewdness. It was unclear how long Viola had been waiting to catch Fitz's eye because people stood four and five deep waiting to order drinks.

When their eyes finally locked, he asked for a beer and shuffled to another part of the bar. Two hours later, when the crowd had thinned, she found him chatting up a woman—young, sexy. Viola remembered her, had double-checked her ID once when she had just turned twenty-one.

A shiver of jealousy crept along her spine. Her eyes lowered to his left hand. The wedding ring was missing. Had he taken it off to lure the pretty girl?

Just then, Fitz glanced Viola's way, smiled, and hopped off the barstool. He whispered something into the girl's ear, and she turned halfway to look at Viola.

Fitz walked to the end of the bar. Motioned for Viola to meet him near the kitchen. They met near the swinging doors, far enough from the bar to avoid suspicion.

"Who's the girl?" Viola asked petulantly.

Fitz smiled. "Just a girl. No one special."

"Do you often talk to young women when your wife's not around?"

"Well, I talk to you, don't I?"

Viola pouted. Hated herself for doing so.

Fitz reached out and placed a ten-dollar bill in the pocket of her white shirt.

She froze as his hand brushed against her breast.

"There's a slip of paper wrapped around the money," he whispered. "The Raintree IPO is a go for Wednesday the fifteenth. Just follow the directions on the note."

He smiled his best smile at her. Said, "This is the first one, Viola. There will be plenty more to come." Then he gently kissed her cheek and returned to his seat at the bar.

In her bed that night, Viola felt uncomfortable about their exchange. As if she was a schoolgirl with a crush. Her behavior was embarrassing, and she vowed never to allow him to make her feel that way again.

Her first meeting with Mr. Calhoun of Barbary Investments—code name Popeye for NYC Holdings—had taken place at a diner in New Jersey. He was a jovial, overweight man in his mid-fifties with a smattering of blond hair and a purple-colored birthmark on his left cheek. She had given him the necessary paperwork to prepare a trading account for NYC Holdings. For their first, and for all future trades, she would meet him at his offices.

When the go signal was given for the Raintree IPO, Viola had driven to Calhoun's offices in Connecticut. Tucked midway into a strip mall, she found Barbary Investments cramped between a dry cleaner and a sandwich shop. She had been expecting an elaborate office complex with dozens of employees buzzing about.

When she entered the double doors, she was pleasantly surprised to see a large, clean reception area, blue shag rug, nicely upholstered chairs, framed movie posters on the walls.

Greeted by an exquisite-looking black woman with a large Afro and a huge smile, Viola was led into Mr. Calhoun's office. Immediately, she noticed the absent sounds of typewriters clacking, phones ringing, voices chatting.

He entered the room a moment later, smiled at her, and shook her hand. On his desk was a bank of six telephones and a Quotron machine. She later learned the Quotron machine was used to monitor up-to-the-minute stock prices.

After a few minutes of small talk, she relayed to Mr. Calhoun that NYC Holdings wanted to purchase shares of the IPO of Raintree Cosmetics. They discussed quantities and pricing while he studied the Quotron machine, jotted notes, then stood.

"I'll be right back," he said.

While she waited, she glanced about his office: a diploma on the wall, a crowded shelf filled with books and ledgers, a colorful Rubik's cube. A small side table held a sad-looking potted plant and a photograph of a girl—Viola guessed her to be fifteen or sixteen—wearing a short party dress that was too seductive for a teenager.

When Mr. Calhoun returned, he caught her looking at the photo.

"She's something, isn't she?" he asked.

Viola nodded. "Your daughter?"

"No, my niece."

Mr. Calhoun cleared his throat and handed her a receipt for the purchased Raintree Cosmetics shares; in exchange, Viola wrote him a check from the NYC Holding's account.

They quickly finished the rest of their business, and Viola was back in her car less than forty minutes since arriving.

As soon as Viola returned home, she changed from her skirt and blouse into a pair of baggy jeans and an old pale blue sweatshirt, the type of old sweatshirt you knew you should toss into the trash, but which is so comfortable, you just cannot bear to part with it.

She puttered around the apartment for an hour. Then she grabbed her jacket and scarf and headed outside. The wind had died down and the moon was full, big and white like a gigantic snowball. She opted for a long walk to a telephone booth that stood on a street corner seven blocks between her apartment and McNulty's.

She squeezed into the booth, plunked coins into the slots, slowly dialed the phone number she had memorized. She heard it ring three times, then hung up as directed. Either Fitz or Jonathan Silver would reach out to her. She looked up at the cloudless sky and continued walking toward McNulty's. *Nothing like being at the place where you work when you're not working,* she mused.

The bar was semi-crowded; the restaurant was full. It was noisy, filled with laughter and conversation and the sounds of plates and glasses clattering. She took a seat at the bar, the same seat Fitz usually took when he visited. The seat next to hers was empty, but a pack of cigarettes and a freshly poured beer remained.

Viola acknowledged Dorothy, the shift's bartender—a tall, thin woman with a plain face who seemed clearly uncomfortable behind the bar. But she was related to Chubs, and that summed up her reason for being there. "I'll take a beer, please," Viola said.

As she reached into her pocket for money, she felt movement beside her. Turning, she saw it was Jeffrey Kaye.

He smiled, jokingly said, "Wouldn't have expected to see you sitting on this end of the bar."

"Yeah, I know. But my fridge is empty and I'm thirsty, so this seemed as good a place as any," she joked back.

Jeffrey seemed happy, not at all upset that she was romantically unavailable to him. Obviously, she had overreacted the night of the blizzard. How would he have been able to follow Fitz with his limp and his cane and the snow on the ground? No, that was something Leroy Stills might do. *Guess it was just my imagination in overdrive, that's all.*

As they drank their beers and talked, Viola wound up learning a great deal about Jeffrey. His likes and dislikes, his hopes for the future. He talked at length of his love-hate relationship with his mother, but when she asked about his father, he chuckled.

"My mother has been married and divorced three times. Never got pregnant. She met up with a Tire World mechanic, and bang, here I am."

Stupidly, Viola blurted, "But your mother is so religious!"

"Yeah, she found God right after the Tire World guy. She's always been overprotective, and I've allowed it. Easier than fighting her."

"So, why continue to live with her?"

Jeffrey lit a cigarette, offered one to Viola. "My mother says it isn't right for a son to abandon his mother. Not after all she's done for me."

"You know that's not fair to you," Viola said gently.

"I know. My shrink tells me that all the time."

Involuntarily, Viola shuddered. His shrink?

Just then she spotted Fitz in the doorway, his eyes scanning the room looking for her. She gently tipped her head toward the bathroom, told Jeffrey she needed to use the restroom.

She met Fitz near the bathroom, then quickly pushed him into the kitchen. Chef Manny glanced up at them, went back to grilling a large piece of fish.

Viola led Fitz into the pantry, closed the door behind her.

"How did it go today?" Fitz whispered. "You met with Popeye?"

"I did," she said coyly. "It went without a hitch."

"How many shares?"

"Twenty-two hundred."

"Price?"

"Twelve dollars, thirty-two cents. I gave him a check for $27,104 dollars."

Fitz slipped a thin calculator from his pocket. Tapped out a quick calculation. He looked up at her, smiled his gorgeous smile.

"You did very well, Viola. The stock closed the day at slightly over eighteen dollars a share. I wouldn't be surprised if we see it jump to thirty or more in the next week or two."

He pecked her cheek and swiftly exited the pantry, then the kitchen. Viola waited by the kitchen door, slowly counted out sixty seconds, then followed him out.

When she returned to the bar, Jeffrey Kaye was putting on his coat.

"Hey," he said. "It was nice talking with you. I have to head home. Ma's making pot roast."

Viola said good night and watched him limp out the door.

CALL IT A HAPPY DAY

April 11, 1978

It was the type of day when you just knew that everything would go right. There would be a bounce to your step. A feeling of light airiness as if a fairy had sprinkled happy dust on you while you slept.

My train was on time, two minutes early, in fact. And Marco, the good-looking kid behind the deli counter, had my bagel buttered, my coffee steaming. Everyone on the streets of Madison Avenue seemed in a jolly mood, smiling, full of good jives.

So far, things had fallen into place for me, and I felt truly fortunate, considering the brief time I had been in New York.

My job as a flight scheduler at Jet King was exciting. I juggled flights for clients in Hong Kong, Tokyo, Singapore, and London, as well as a dozen domestic flights. I assisted extravagantly rich wives who wished to vacation or party in Malibu, Puerto Rico, Acapulco. It amazed me, the number of CEOs and government officials and wealthy travelers who were willing to part with big chunks of their money simply for the ease and anonymity of traveling in great comfort via Jet King.

We were five schedulers in all—three women, two men. The rest of the company included managers, secretaries, human resources, and the accounting office.

The only thorn in my side was the one person I had to deal with on a regular basis—Bunny Dupree—a bitter woman who managed the accounting office. She was nearing retirement age and obviously resented it. Her hair was a bird's nest of curls, her pancake makeup a throwback from another generation. Having Bunny in charge of accounting was like having an alcoholic supervise a liquor store. For whatever odd reason, Bunny and I clashed heads every step of the way.

But that day was different; even Bunny smiled at me. Every flight I had scheduled was on time and everyone I spoke with was happy, deliriously so.

At 4:55, I looked up to see Mr. Levine at my desk, a thick envelope in his hand.

"This package needs to be delivered to an important client traveling on an incoming flight. It needs to be handed to him directly. Would you mind delivering it?" he asked.

"Of course," I replied.

He handed me the envelope; a quick glance showed it was addressed to Larry Fitzgerald. I hurried onto the Special Services transport van that waited outside for me. I was the only passenger aboard as we headed to Teterboro Airport in New Jersey—with me delivering a package deemed far too important to entrust to our regular messenger service.

We arrived at Teterboro at 6:11 p.m. I was directed to arrival hangar #5. The setup there was unique: space for several aircraft, designated rooms for food and beverage storage, and a parts and supply room for mechanical engineering. Peripherally, I noticed prefabricated office cubicles with plexiglass see-through windows. The furniture looked dated, as if it had been transferred from a prison. There were side doors leading to God knows where and mechanics wearing blue Jet King jumpsuits.

Private pilots and in-flight personnel mingled among the mechanics. Jet engines roared and groaned as a continuum of planes arrived and departed. My head spun as a rush of adrenaline coursed through me. The frenetic activity had me salivating and tossed me backward into the life I had once lived and breathed every single day.

Our arriving flight had taken off from Pasadena, California, and was due to arrive at 6:47 p.m. Two passengers aboard. I watched as the aircraft glided onto the runway, watched as the flight stairs lowered and two men descended. The first had silver hair and wore a dark suit. Behind him followed a younger man, a near replica of the older one but with dark hair. Very handsome, very masculine.

My eyes trailed them as they entered the hangar. The younger of the two looked in my direction. I barely breathed as they approached me.

Professionally, I asked, "Mr. Larry Fitzgerald?"

The older man smiled—an honest and happy smile—as I held out to him the envelope I had been clutching.

"Thank you," he said. His voice was velvety, a voice I imagined would belong to a beloved uncle or grandparent.

Then the younger man smiled, his eyes devilishly alive, as if waiting for something exciting to happen. He reached out his hand to shake mine.

"Hello," he said. "I'm Larry Fitzgerald Junior. My friends call me Fitz."

His hand clasped mine. "Nice to meet you. I'm Lily Marz. I work for Jet King at the corporate offices."

"Well, in that case, I hope to see a lot more of you."

I nodded, handed him my business card. A moment later, a sleek black limousine pulled up to the hangar and the two Fitzgerald men waved goodbye to me as they slid inside the vehicle and were whisked away.

My insides liquified like clarified butter smothering popcorn. Other than Vern Taylor, I had not met another man who could shake me to my core. This man was a dreamboat.

PILLOW TALK

April 15, 1978

JEFFREY

It was Jeffrey Kaye's fifth Saturday free from work since returning to the DMV. Shortly after nine, he woke, wondering why he did not hear the clatter of pots and pans as his mother scrambled eggs or mixed pancake batter. The house was awfully quiet.

Then he remembered: his mother had left the previous morning to attend a three-day prayer retreat in Pennsylvania. Starving, he pulled on a pair of jeans and a turtleneck T-shirt. Laced up his Nike high tops.

He took his cane and walked the two blocks to Feingold's Deli. Sat at a table near the window so he might people watch as he ate. He wolfed down a bacon and egg hoagie and three cups of coffee. Sat back in his chair, lit a cigarette, watched the pretty girls as they passed by the window. Jeffrey knew he did not have much to offer a woman—especially a woman like Viola. He was stuck with a go-nowhere future because his mother had strictly counseled him against racking up life-crushing student loan debt.

He crushed out his cigarette, paid his bill, and walked home. The scent of spring was in the air, sweet and comforting. He remembered the last conversation he'd had with his mother the night before her trip.

"Jeffrey, isn't it time you started dating again? Lucy Monroe's daughter DeeDee is still single," she said.

He winced, remembered meeting DeeDee while in the grocer's with his mother. She was okay looking, had a nice body. But she was no Viola. And he had felt awkward and embarrassed by the cane and the scars that peeked from his shirt collar. DeeDee's eyes had immediately zeroed in on both.

Back in the apartment, Jeffrey was restless. He plopped onto the ugly brown sofa and flicked through an assortment of music videos on MTV, then smoked half a joint. When he tired of the videos, he went into his bedroom and from his closet retrieved a legal-sized blue envelope stamped DEPARTMENT OF MOTOR VEHICLES.

Returning to the kitchen, he sat at the table, upended the envelope, and watched as tiny photographs spilled out to create a small anthill-sized mound.

His job at the DMV was simple. Snap the picture of the licensee, save the photo to the system, call the next person in line.

Jeffrey recalled his first few days of training to use the DMV's new digital camera, remembered the day he discovered his coworker Charlie Hughes sneaking New York State DMV digital photographs into his satchel.

Charlie was as skinny as a sketching pencil, with a huge mustache and droopy hound dog eyes. He grinned as Jeffrey stared at him, not the least bit concerned that he was removing private property from a state facility.

"Hey man, no big deal," Charlie said. "These are just pics which didn't come out right." He pointed at a blur that circled a blonde woman's eye. "See here? Can't use this one. DMV wants them just so. They got to be right, man."

"What do you do with them?" Jeffrey asked.

"I look at 'em," he laughed, "But I only take the pretty ones." Then, abruptly, Charlie had shut down his clown face and said, "You're not going to say anything, are you, buddy?"

"No. Of course not."

After the encounter with Charlie, Jeffrey had begun to pluck throwaway photos that reminded him of people he knew: the superintendent of their building, an old high school teacher, the kid with the black ponytail who worked at Ace Hardware. There were others, too, ones which resembled him and his mother.

Jeffrey enjoyed mulling over the photos. Enjoyed knowing he had in his possession a little snatch of other people's lives. And, as Charlie Hughes had said, "Man, you never know if one of these little clips will come in handy one day."

The next night, Jeffrey took a taxi to McNulty's. Inside the bar, it was immediately clear that Viola was not there. It was odd, as Saturday night was usually her busiest shift.

When a big, heavily muscled guy vacated a seat, Jeffrey slunk into it. To his immediate right was a girl. Cute, not pretty. Overweight, but not fat. Her hair was shiny and dark, worn Farrah Fawcett style. A thin white blouse showed ample breasts.

Jeffrey continued to monitor the front door, hoping Viola might stroll through at any moment. When he finally diverted his attention to the beer in front of him, he realized the girl beside him was staring at him. *She can't be staring at the scars on my neck,* he thought. *Not while I'm wearing this ridiculous turtleneck in the middle of April.*

He snapped his head toward her, saw she was smiling at him. She introduced herself as Pamela and within a span of minutes he learned all there was to know about her. She was twenty-two, recently transplanted from New Jersey, worked as a secretary in a bank, and two days earlier, had been dumped unceremoniously by her cheating boyfriend.

The girl chatted on and on and after a second beer, she made it perfectly clear that she wanted company for the night.

Bedroom company.

Her bluntness startled Jeffrey. He did not know where to look or what to think. He hesitated. Of course, he wanted to have sex. It had been a year since he had any type of intimacy. *But the scars! I'm not ready for this!* his brain screamed. *Not prepared for it.*

Finally, he offered up a big fat lie.

"I'm sorry," he said, "but I can't. I've got to pick up my girlfriend from work."

Pamela's face turned stony; her lips twisted into a nasty frown. She jumped from the chair.

"You're such an asshole," she sneered loudly. She yanked her handbag from the back of the chair and stomped out of the bar.

Momentarily, Jeffrey was embarrassed. Then he thanked God that Viola was not there to witness his humiliation. He quickly paid his tab and though his extremities ached miserably, he made the lonely walk home.

Inside his apartment, he stripped down to his boxers, retrieved the envelope of DMV photographs.

He removed the photos which most closely resembled Viola and placed them on the bedroom pillow beside him.

POSSIBILITIES

April 18, 1978

FITZ

Her name was Kelly. She looked like a farmer's daughter. Young, ripe, curly Shirley Temple hair, and big inquisitive blue eyes. She was sweet and delightful and sensually talented. The hefty tip he had given to her had been well earned.

It was Fitz's first party event at the private club in Howard Beach, and he was thrilled to have a membership.

The club was the size of a mansion and sat on a dead-end street that also housed a huge wedding event center. A small canal ran behind the club, and guests often enjoyed drinks and appetizers on the back deck facing the calm water.

The first party had everyone jittery. The possibility of a bust always had guests on alert—until the booze kicked in and everyone finally kicked back. Overall, and with the fiasco on Seventh Avenue behind them, the party was wildly successful.

After leaving Kelly behind in the private room, Fitz enjoyed a drink at the bar and chatted with a political candidate who would next year attempt a run for city council. *Couldn't hurt to have a politician as an ally,* Fitz thought happily.

But there was a strange moment of discomfort when Fitz turned away from the bar and noticed a man of about forty glancing at him. Fitz's heart leaped when he realized it was Ron Platt of R&P Aeronautics, one of his father's largest accounts.

Fitz quickly ducked his head and turned, pretending not to have seen Ron. At the same time, a young woman with a long braid linked arms with Ron and together, they walked away.

Fitz left his drink on an empty table and quietly left the club.

As he drove home, he wondered if Ron Platt had recognized him. *He's Dad's client, and I've only met him once for a quick handshake.* Then he thought, *But even if he did recognize me, he would be a fool to reveal having been at the same club with me.*

Still, his unease drove all the way home with him.

As he lay in bed that night, he understood how close a call it had been to spot someone familiar at the club. He knew he should heed his grandfather's advice and search for a life partner to divert attention from his special needs. At the very least, it would stop gossip in its tracks and protect him and his family from embarrassment.

He sat upright, remembered the woman from Jet King, the one who had waited to deliver a package to his father at Teterboro Airport. The woman with the intriguing gray eyes and the jet-black hair. She was petite like a kewpie doll, with narrow hips and small breasts.

Not voluptuous like Viola, who had too much woman packed into one body.

No, Viola would be too much woman for him to handle.

But the gal from Jet King had a physicality that appealed to Fitz. *If we're compatible, she could fit the bill as someone to comfortably escort to gallery openings and special events. Someone I could float in front of important clients without raising eyebrows.*

He smiled to himself.

She just might be his perfect foil.

MONEY TREE

April 25, 1978

VIOLA

The money in Viola's bank account had multiplied faster than bunny rabbits in springtime. It had Viola's face glowing with a sweet pink hue that settled into the hollows of her cheeks. She was reaping the benefits of the IPO profits she and Fitz and Jonathan Silver had shared. Never had she had so much money at her fingertips.

Their first IPO purchase of Raintree Cosmetics had netted her three thousand, four hundred and fifty-two dollars.

Euro-Medical Supplies, purchased only two days ago, had already skyrocketed eight, nine, ten dollars above purchase price.

Thinking about the money made her swoon.

Still, she had a job to do for NYC Holdings. She posted their transactions—income and expenses—into a large ledger. For her percentage of the profits, she wrote herself a check, posted it to the ledger, deposited the money into her savings account.

Jonathan Silver, however, insisted she write his proportional check payable to JS Corp, which she assumed was another of Jonathan's myriad business holdings. As directed, she posted the transactions as "consultation services."

Fitz requested his checks be made payable to a company called Zig Zag, LLC. When she inquired about the company, he said simply, "It's a company I owe a debt to."

She had not questioned it further.

On the first of each month, Viola sent a copy of her ledger to their business accountant—a man she had never met, but whom Fitz assured her was a steely eyed business cohort.

Already, Viola had happily pocketed eight thousand four hundred and eighty-five dollars.

Often, she wondered what her foster parents would think if they knew of how much money she had accumulated in such a short span of time.

But, sticking to their plan, she had spoken to no one about their business arrangement; not a word of it to Alex or to Jeffrey Kaye. Even Chubs was in the dark about what they were doing.

For the first time in her life, she was fully and capably responsible for every decision she made. She did not need a man telling her what to do or how to do it. She was financially independent now. It was liberating.

Still, with a niggle of guilt, she thought about her foster brothers and sisters.

Wondered how their lives had turned out.

Wondered if her foster parents were still alive. Or dead.

And was grateful for having escaped a life which most assuredly would have mimicked their own sorry lives.

FIRST DATE

April 29, 1978

It never crossed my mind that Larry "Fitz" Fitzgerald might phone me. Honestly, ours had been a brief encounter, a matter of moments at the Jet King hangar at Teterboro. Six seconds for our eyes to cling together like survivors to a life raft. A nanosecond of time for my skin to heat, followed by a tick-tock of time as my hand brushed his when I passed him my business card. Two more breaths until he said, "Well, in that case, I hope to see a lot more of you."

At the time, I thought they were meaningless words, a polite statement to say to someone he had just met.

Yet, there I was in my room at the Barbizon Hotel for Women, caught up in the moment and scurrying for something appropriate to wear for our date—my first date in New York City as the woman known as Lily Marz.

It was difficult choosing something appropriate: sexy yet simple, fashionable but understated. Finally, I slipped into sleek dark slacks and a low-cut flaming red silk top. A pair of red heels complemented my shirt. When I took a final glance in the mirror, I liked what I saw.

Fitz had offered to send a car for me, and it arrived punctually at seven o'clock. The driver was adept at maneuvering around the Saturday night traffic, but I was perplexed when we stopped at the entrance to the Metropolitan Museum of New York on Fifth and Thirty-Seventh.

Until I spotted Fitz waiting there, hands in his trouser pockets, looking sharp in navy slacks and a light-blue open-collared shirt. The shirt looked as if it had cost more than my monthly salary.

As I exited the car, he reached to assist me. I smiled at him and asked, "Why are we here? The museum is closed."

"Not for us," he chuckled. Surprised, I followed him around the corner to a door held open by a dark-skinned man with intense blue eyes. He welcomed us inside.

"Lily," Fitz said, "this is the museum's curator, Gregory Maison. Gregory, this is Lily Marz."

Gregory escorted us on a tour of the museum, which was currently hosting a new, provocative series of paintings and sculptures by up-and-coming New York artists. When the tour was complete, he led us to another room, larger, but with fewer artistic displays. Center stage in the middle of the room was a small table decorated with lovely red flowers and small votive candles.

Gregory pulled out a chair for me, placed a cloth napkin onto my lap, and from a nearby bucket, pulled out a bottle of champagne. He smiled as he filled our glasses, his eyes crinkling into a sweet blanket of warmth.

"Please enjoy the champagne," he said. "Dinner will be served shortly."

With an exaggerated wink at Fitz, he left the room.

The moment he was gone, I stared at Fitz and sputtered, "How did you manage all of this?"

"Gregory and I are good friends," he said warmly. "We go back a long way."

"Ahh," I said. I sipped the champagne, which tasted smoother than ice cream.

Fitz smiled at me. "I didn't want our first dinner together to be in a crowded, noisy restaurant, so Gregory helped me out."

I fingered my glass as my eyes scoured the room—such an intimate setting, back lit with serene lighting and the intoxicating smell of fresh flowers. Fitz and I discussed our careers, his on an upward trajectory, mine taking tiny baby steps.

"I hear a tinge of a southern accent," Fitz said. "Where are you from?"

"Georgia, most recently. Born in Indiana."

"How long have you been in New York?"

"Since late last year."

"Do you like it here?"

"Oh yes," I chuckled. "There's a pulse to this city. You can hear it on every street, feel it sweeping through the buildings."

"So, what made you leave Georgia?"

I glanced down at my empty glass. "A bad breakup, you could say."

"Those are tough," he agreed. Gently, he changed the subject, spoke of the success of his father's business, how his having joined the company had helped with the company's growth.

"And Jet King. Do you enjoy your work there?" he asked.

"Yes, I do. But it's hard to imagine how incredibly wealthy some people are. Just yesterday, I scheduled a private jet to fly six young women from Beverly Hills to San Juan for a bachelorette party. Can you imagine? Jetting off to a bachelorette party!"

We chuckled as a woman in a white dinner jacket and a chef's hat wheeled a cart alongside our table. Ruby-red plates with silver trim were set before us. I peeked down to see a grilled lobster, already removed from its shell. It was accompanied beautifully with parslied fingerling potatoes and a delicate arrangement of grilled tomato and asparagus.

A crisp white wine was poured, and truly, it was the most sumptuous meal I had ever enjoyed.

After we finished dinner, the woman returned, cleared away the empty plates. Both Fitz and I sat back from the table, our bellies full. I was happy, contented. Interacting with Fitz was easy and comfortable.

It was such a far cry from the sad, bereft woman I had been in Atlanta.

Gregory Maison returned to us. “After dinner cocktail? Dessert?”

Fitz ordered a brandy; I asked for bourbon, rocks.

“I wouldn’t have pegged you for a bourbon gal,” Fitz said.

“My best friend taught me to enjoy it. And how to chug it like a man.”

The chef brought us our drinks and an elaborate dessert that resembled a small mountain.

We both laughed aloud and then Fitz rolled up his shirtsleeves in mock preparation for attacking the dessert. As he did so, I glimpsed a tattoo on his inside forearm—a rose and a name I could not easily read.

“Old girlfriend?” I asked with a smile.

He shook his head solemnly. “My sister. She was a nurse killed in Vietnam.”

“Oh my God,” I whispered. “I am so sorry, Fitz.”

He nodded, took a deep swallow of his drink, and I did the same.

“So, what about you?” he asked. “Any family here or back in Georgia?”

“No,” I said. “My parents and grandparents are gone, and I was an only child.” I was careful to leave no strings, no threads, nothing he could dig up to reveal who I had been.

“That’s too bad,” he said.

I simply nodded.

Afterward, we thanked Gregory for his gracious kindness and left the museum. We strolled along Fifth Avenue, chatting, laughing, relishing the sweet night air. Nearing midnight, Fitz hailed us a cab.

It idled at the curb of the Barbizon Hotel as Fitz walked me to the entry doors. “Sorry,” I said, “but men are not allowed. . .”

"Sshh," he whispered. His arms circled my waist as he leaned in to kiss me gently and sweetly. Just his soft, full lips parting mine and fueling a desire I had long buried.

When we finally pulled apart, he asked, "Can I see you again?"

I nodded. Of course, when Fitz stepped back into the taxi, I would not know that he had left his mark on my lips, to then skip away into the deep darkness in search of the lips of a different type of woman.

An incredibly young one.

Of course, I did not know.

SCREAMS IN THE NIGHT

May 16, 1978

JEFFREY

When nightmares crawl like pesky fleas ready to burrow deep beneath your skin, it is nearly impossible to forget the nasty tendrils of fear they leave behind.

Jeffrey Kaye understood the feeling well.

His dreams were nocturnal bouts of torture that woke him in a state of intense agitation, with his tangled bedsheets nearly strangling him and with his voice booming—booming so loudly he would wake his mother and their neighbor, Mrs. Rossi.

His mother would rush in to comfort him, to soothe him. "It's okay, Jeffrey. Everything will be okay," she would murmur.

But Jeffrey knew differently.

That night's cloudy nightmare started as many of the others had: Jeffrey walking through a haze of fog, the smell of urine impossibly strong. In the dream he was blind, could only feel his way with his hands. He fell against someone. There were cries in the darkness, then incredible pain as he tumbled through the sky to the bottom of...he did not know where.

When he mentioned the nightmares to his psychiatrist, he was told, "Victims of accidents can suffer from flashbacks, and these are a normal reaction to trauma. Usually, flashbacks of the event will fade over time. However, recollection of the accident may help to ease your panic attacks. Don't fight your memories, Jeffrey, even if they are difficult."

After that last disturbing dream, Jeffrey was not sure if he wanted to remember anything at all about the accident.

A YEAR LATER

July 1, 1979

My year-long romance with Fitz had been nothing short of spectacular, and I often pinched myself to be sure it was really happening. I was so happy, yet worried that I was not worthy of the happiness. Sometimes the past had a way of spiraling me into reverse. I fought against it because I loved my current life, loved that Fitz had become the perfect half to complete my whole.

After our second date, our eyes had lingered, and then, like dancers in a ballet, we glided into each other's arms.

More than a year later, we were hopelessly in love—at least it was true on my part. We spent every weekend at Fitz's apartment in Forest Hills, while during the week I maintained my room at the Barbizon Hotel.

Fitz insisted it was a good arrangement. "During the week I'm so busy entertaining clients and traveling. If we lived together, it would be a shame to leave you alone so often."

I agreed, but only half-heartedly.

Sunday morning dawned beautifully. It was early, and I heard birds chirping gleefully as they applauded the sun's arrival. Fitz and I were snuggled close, with empty champagne flutes lying horizontally on his night table. The turquoise blouse I had worn the previous night remained on the floor, like a floozy's tossed-away garment.

Fitz's arm was heavy across my chest. I gently extricated myself, pulled a faded Yankees T-shirt over my head. I padded into his kitchen, quietly brewed coffee, then shuffled to the living room, lifting window blinds along the way.

Sunlight poured in as the aroma of freshly roasted coffee wafted into the room. Back in the kitchen, I poured myself a cup, added cream and sugar, carried it into the living room. Fitz's apartment was small but comfortable and clearly had been decorated with a man's touch.

Bulky club chairs and a wall unit brimming with books and albums and a stereo dominated the room. The walls were bare of artwork, photographs; his bedroom littered with discarded clothing that had conveniently missed the laundry basket.

As I sat in one of the chairs, I stared out of the living room windows, sipped coffee, and allowed myself to sink into the memory of the past night's passion.

Making love with Fitz was comparable to tasting ridiculously expensive French wine and finding it was worthy of its exorbitant cost. With Fitz, every touch, every kiss, every gasp of breath, was pure magic.

Truth: I was addicted to him. His scent had become my perfume. His voice, my seducer. I became lost in the very fabric of him.

"Hey you," I heard, and nearly upended my coffee cup. I swiveled to see Fitz behind me, naked, hair rumpled, a huge grin on his handsome face.

"Come back to bed," he said softly.

I could not jump up fast enough.

ALL ABOUT *LILY*

July 11, 1979

FITZ

Fitz nursed a beer while he waited for Viola to show up for her 6:00 p.m. shift. It was a Wednesday night, and McNulty's was surprisingly empty. *Good,* he thought. *Easier to talk to her without interruption.*Viola breezed through the doors just as Fitz finished his thought. She looked happy, her hair pulled up into a bun; a black tank top showed off her tawny skin. She looked as if she had just come from a boat ride or an afternoon at the beach.

He smiled at her.

For a short hiccup of time, his confidence in Viola had waned, and he wondered if he had misread her. But his reservations had disappeared the moment their first trade had proved wildly profitable. She had performed to perfection, and Fitz was now convinced that Viola Cordova was the best thing to ever cross his and Damon's path.

Fitz never wondered how Damon and Viola spent their share of the IPO profits. All he knew was that money was rushing in like a tidal wave, and he was happy to be riding the wave. That month, he had been on a giddy shopping spree: a 14 karat gold rope chain, a Rolex watch, season tickets for the NY Giants games, wads of money to spend.

And, of course, there was his secret account in Zurich.

So much to be grateful for.

He watched as Viola slipped behind the bar, tossed her handbag under a counter, and swiveled to face Fitz. Once again, he remained awed by her beauty.

Quietly, she whispered, "Well hello, stranger. Where have you been hiding?"

He could not tell her how busy he had been entertaining Lily. How easy it was to have her beside him at family and business functions. He could not tell Viola how smart and energetic and fun it was to be with Lily. How she made it ridiculously easy for him to continue his visits to the private parties, without her ever being the wiser.

"Been so busy with work," he told Viola. Then he leaned in closer and whispered, "Jonathan has a selection for us."

He watched her smile fill her face, seeping into every crevice, every little line that had sprouted around her eyes.

Slyly, she looked to see who might overhear.

Fitz whispered, "We're buying twenty-seven thousand shares of Calypso Entertainment. It's poised to tick up four dollars and change within a week. When it happens, it will be an immediate sell. Got it?"

"Of course," she said.

IF THEY COULD SEE ME NOW

July 17, 1979

VIOLA

Viola Cordova climbed from the bed of her latest boyfriend, Philip LeClair—an older man who knew how to properly please a woman. For reasons that remained a mystery to her, she tired of boyfriends after only a few weeks. Somehow their little idiosyncrasies quickly sprouted and managed to grate on her nerves.

But there were always plenty of men ready to step into the shoes of those she had discarded. Her foster mother would have called her a tramp.

While Philip remained in bed snoring loudly, Viola slipped into the bathroom and ran the shower. She stood beneath a stream of hot water, thought of the many men she had used strictly for pleasure and had then tossed aside like old slippers that had outlasted their usefulness.

She was not sorry about it. Did not feel a need to apologize for her actions. Hadn't men been doing the same thing for centuries?

For Viola, there would always be a man in her life.

As she shampooed her hair, she thought of the money she had deposited into her personal bank account yesterday. Twelve thousand dollars—a tremendous windfall—all of it just sitting there, earning interest every day, building her nest egg for the future.

How she wished that Leroy and Bobby Lee could know of her financial success. Wished she could stick it in their craws for how poorly they had treated her. Wouldn't they be sorry now?

And then she thought of Lucy, her friend at Scooters who had made it possible for Viola to pretend to be Uncle Sammy's niece so that Viola could live in his low-rent apartment. If not for Lucy, she might have been saddled with Leroy for the rest of her sorry existence.

It would have been satisfying to be able to repay Lucy's generosity, but her friend had long since departed Scooters.

Once dressed, she checked again on Philip, who was still on his back and snoring. Quietly, she tiptoed from the bedroom to the front door and gently stepped outside.

It was a beautiful morning, the birds and the bees humming among the flowers in Philip's window planter. The streets were quiet, just a person here and there walking to the subway or the bus stop, coming or going, same as her.

As she neared her apartment, she stopped at the Korean market on the corner, where the fruits and vegetables were the freshest. Once home, she brewed a pot of coffee and glanced at her new mobile telephone, which sat on a side table next to the sofa.

Jonathan Silver and Fitz had agreed that it had become a drain on Viola to travel back and forth to William Calhoun's office in Connecticut—often on short notice—to conduct their transactions. The mobile phone line was strictly for communications with William Calhoun.

At 10:22, the mobile line rang, just as Viola carried a third cup of coffee into the living room. The sound startled her; she jostled the cup as the coffee sloshed over its rim, warming her wrist where it settled. She yanked the massive thing to her ear. "Yes?" she said breathlessly.

"The trade went through without a hitch," she heard William Calhoun say. "We sold twenty-seven thousand shares of Calypso Entertainment at twenty-one dollars and eighteen cents per share. Quite a tidy profit, my dear. You're a natural at this."

He laughed heartily, and Viola visualized his big Jell-O belly jiggling. When she hung up the phone, she chugged down the remaining coffee as if it were a shot of tequila.

Finally, she could see her future seated squarely in the palms of her hands.

If only Fitz were a part of her life, she would be fully contented.

LIFE DECISIONS

July 31, 1979

JEFFREY

The person reflected in the huge gym mirror could not be Jeffrey Kaye. That man was hefting heavy weights. Left arm, right arm, repeat.

But it was Jeffrey Kaye. Arms pumped up with definition, legs muscular, neck and shoulders broad, though still scarred with puckered white clumps of flesh. But Jeffrey no longer cared if anyone gaped or inquired about the scars. His false story of having been in a house fire in Athens was so well rehearsed, he had begun to believe it.

He dropped the weights onto the matted floor, swiped at sweat on his brow. During the two years since the crash, he had regained his health and much improved use of his leg and hip. The cane was no longer an accessory to his wardrobe. He had regrown his thin beard and mustache, and his hair was shorter than most of the men his age.

He smiled at himself in the mirror. A week earlier, his lawyer had advised him that a settlement from the accident was imminent.

"The discovery portion of your claim has been completed," Shannon Laura O'Reilly had told him. "We've alerted the defendants of their liability exposure. We have a solid case of human error coupled with the malfunction of the ground radar equipment. It's reasonable to believe they will likely lose in court and may be willing to work out a fair settlement."

"A settlement?" he asked. "So, I won't need to appear in court?"

"Not if we can avoid it, Jeffrey. Litigation can be very lengthy, sometimes up to five years. In your case, our investigators have identified that an important piece of mechanical equipment meant to help keep track of taxiing planes was faulty. This allows us the opportunity to settle out of court—with an earlier settlement date and/or a significantly higher settlement amount."

"How much of a settlement?" Jeffrey asked, his heart thrashing wildly.

"All considered, our ask is four point three million. From which you will pay my fees and expenses."

Jeffrey's knees buckled as he heard the amount.

"We'll need to respond to the preliminary offer to negotiate in a timely manner. May I give them the okay to move forward?" his lawyer asked.

Jeffrey's mind marched to its own tune. *It's a bundle of money. I can quit my job. Ship Mom to Florida. Finally clear her out of my hair.*

"Jeffrey?" his lawyer nudged. "Do I have your permission to accept the preliminary offer to negotiate?"

"Yes," he said, finally. "Yes, of course."

"Very good. I will schedule a meeting with the appropriate parties and will be in touch with you once a settlement has been negotiated."

Jeffrey realized he was about to become rich. Far wealthier than his pitiful salary at the DMV would ever provide.

He would purchase a home of his own and finally be free of his mother and their crappy apartment. He was anxious to be rid of his cramped childhood room, the faded pre-war linoleum floors, the outdated mirrors, the nasty ring around the bathtub, which could not be scrubbed away, no matter how much Ajax was used.

In advance of the settlement, he enlisted the services of a top-rated Queens realtor, a woman who understood his timeline and would scout suitable residences for him.

It saddened him, though, to know he would be leaving Manhattan behind for Queens. That he would be leaving behind McNulty's and the few friends he had made there.

Somehow, Viola had become a peripheral friend. An invisible gash had left a cavity in their friendship. Whatever the instigating trigger, it was not as organic as a disagreement or a foul argument. It had been a slow meandering of expanding distance, much like two cars pulling away from each other on a busy highway.

But it had happened, and their relationship eventually fizzled into an awkward, "How are you?" at the mailbox.

He had tired of wooing her a long time ago. She was already taken. DeeDee Monroe was his girl now, had been for a year. She loved him—was never disgusted or repulsed by his scars—but his feelings for her did not run as deeply. But she might just be the best for which he could hope.

BIRTHDAY WISHES

August 6, 1979

My day had been just a wee bit short of insane. A morning container of coffee sat untouched near my phone, and lunch remained a fantasy. Our newest client, Calypso Entertainment, was a beast of an account. Constantly, I had to reschedule and reroute Jet King's domestic fleet to accommodate Calypso's last-minute demands.

August sixth was my real birthday—Margaret Lido's birthday, not Lily's. There would be no celebration, no cards, no birthday cake.

That had all happened on June 26—my fake birthday and the recurring anniversary of the Atlanta plane crashes. For that birthday, Fitz had arranged a special dinner party, but it was difficult to pretend to be happy and excited, knowing full well I was the one responsible for the irreparable damage caused on that day.

For everyone's sake, I smiled, hugged an endless stream of people, laughed with friends. Lena Robinson, my best friend from The Barbizon, had recently landed a small role in a wildly popular sitcom, and we spent endless minutes chuckling over the good fortune that had finally come her way.

I cheek kissed Fitz's parents and my friends from Jet King. Listened to toasts to me, which were flattering but grossly undeserved. There were gifts and good wishes and a huge vanilla cake with more candles than I wished to count.

On that morning of August sixth, I turned twenty-nine. Not a soul in New York was aware of it—except for the ghosts of Savannah and my mother. And, my stepfather, Howard Ford—who once had a knack of reminding me that I was born on the date of the first atomic bomb being dropped on Hiroshima. A pleasant thought that he offered to me at the start of every one of my birthdays.

Startled, I heard Margie shout to me, "Pick up line two! Fitz is on the phone." I smiled at her, lifted the receiver. "Hi, Fitz," I said.

"Hi, honey. Listen, I'm in between meetings, but you asked me to remind you that today you need to exchange your old driver's license for a New York State one. It expired back in June and if you don't get it done, you'll have to retake the driver's road test."

Oh crap, I forgot all about it. "Thanks for the reminder."

"Okay. I have to run. Call you later."

I hung up the phone, checked my watch. It was almost three o'clock. If I left the office immediately, I could be at the DMV by three thirty. Quickly, I hoisted my purse from my desk, told Margie I had to leave early.

It was so foolish of me to wait so long to exchange Lily's driver's license.

I did not have the luxury of being foolish when it came to my identity.

CATCHING A GLIMPSE

August 6, 1979

JEFFREY

The Thirty-First Street location of the DMV was busier than usual on that sweltering August afternoon. Overhead fans rotated and spun out occasional faint breezes but did little to comfort the twin lines of agitated individuals who waited their turn in line. Lone people and people with bored and rowdy children all shuffled slowly to the intake windows to await approval of their paperwork.

Jeffrey Kaye's day had been a nonstop revolving door of people. He snapped license photos then moved the person down the line to Hector, who then printed the licenses and handed them out.

Briefly, Jeffrey lifted his eyes from the equipment.

And that was when he spotted her—the sexy woman with short, dark black hair, dressed in a somber business suit, reading a Stephen King book to pass the monotony of being at the DMV. His eyes lingered on her as she stood rooted between an angry-looking matron and an old, hunched man, both who nearly dwarfed her with their height and girth.

When finally, she reached Jeffrey's counter, he sank into her eyes as she handed him her paperwork. They were incredible: stormy gray eyes, wide, expressive, and lit up like a firecracker.

He could not pull his eyes away from hers.

"Is something wrong?" she asked.

"No. No. Sorry. Just step back and do not smile," he emphasized as he smiled directly at her.

The picture was snapped.

"Thank you," he called as she hurried toward Hector then burrowed through the throngs of people toward the exit doors. The rest of the afternoon remained a blur.

When the last person was photographed and Jeffrey was about to shut down his equipment, he wished he had thought to ruin one of the snapshots of the gray-eyed woman. He would have been able to retrieve the blurred photo and include it in his collection.

Glancing at Hector as he tidied his area, Jeffrey quickly flipped through the shots he had taken within the past two hours. Flipped through until he found hers.

Her name was Lily Marz. He printed her picture and shoved it inside his trouser pocket.

He would spend the night with it on his pillow.

DISCOVERED

August 25, 1979

FITZ

He heard a buzzing sound, like a bee hovering. He swiped at his ear. The buzzing sound grew louder. Fitz lifted his head from the pillow. Looked at Lily, who slept next to him. A glance at the clock showed six in the morning.

He threw his bedsheets aside, climbed from the bed. Gently closed the door behind him then plodded down the hallway naked except for his white boxer shorts. At the front door he peered through the little peephole. *Jesus,* he thought, *What the hell is he doing here?*

He opened the door; his father pushed past him.

"Dad, what are you doing here? It's six o'clock on Sunday morning."

His father pivoted toward him, waved a sheet of paper in the air. "How could you do this to me?" he demanded loudly.

"Sshh," Fitz cautioned. "Lily's asleep in the next room. And what the hell are you talking about?"

His father lifted the paper close to Fitz, pointed at an entry. "Audrey discovered this ten-thousand-dollar charge to your business credit card."

"Our Audrey?" Fitz asked. "The bookkeeper?" He had been funneling expenses through the business for a long time without anyone the wiser. Besides, he thought, Audrey was as dumb as an empty shoe.

"Yes, goddammit! A ten-thousand-dollar charge to a company called YG, Inc. A business with an unlisted phone number and a post office box in Queens as its address."

Shaking his head, Fitz said, "I don't know anything about it, Dad."

His father pushed him hard against the closed door. "Don't lie to me, Fitz," he growled. "I know all about this place. I had someone check it out."

Fitz pushed his father away.

His heart hammered painfully. He started to open his mouth to speak, but his father cut him off.

"Don't even think of offering me some bullshit story. YG stands for Young Girls. And you paid a membership fee to a faceless company so that you could screw young girls. It's despicable. Deplorable. And it's a fucking crime, Fitz."

His father was livid, red-faced, his hands bunched into fists at his side. "If this gets out and ruins our business, your grandfather will have two sets of balls as trophies." Fitz slumped over, covered his face with his hands. "I'm so sorry, Dad," he croaked.

"Sorry won't do, Fitz."

Just then, the bedroom door creaked open, and Fitz saw Lily's small head peek through. "Is everything okay, Fitz?" she asked.

"Yeah, baby. It's Dad. We have a business problem to sort out."

She nodded sleepily and closed the door.

Fitz looked at his father. "What can I do?" he pleaded. "The damage is already done."

His father paced from the small entryway into the living room. Fitz followed him and with shaking hands, shook a cigarette from its pack, lit it.

After a long pause, his father said, "No, the damage is not done. Not yet. Not if you marry Lily. She's a sweet woman, and she is obviously in love with you. We can make a big splash of the wedding. Keep every tongue from wagging."

Fitz shook his head in disbelief. "But I don't love her," he whispered.

"Well, you'll learn to love her, you idiot. You think that every man who gets married is in love?"

Fitz looked like a sailor going down with his ship.

His father posed in front of the living room window, arms folded across his chest, voice thick and heavy and laced with emotion. "I don't see another way, Fitz. Either you end this obsession with young girls and marry Lily, or I will disown you. I'll force you to leave the company in disgrace, and I will cut you off from every single privilege you've been so lucky to enjoy."

He turned, raised his hand in a stop motion as Fitz attempted to interject. "Think hard, Fitz. Do you really want to risk it all? Do you want to risk your grandfather's wrath? Because, even from Sicily, he is still a powerful and dangerous man. I'm certain this is the route he'd want you to take."

Fitz's heart deflated. If he married Lily, his life would be dictated by a matrimonial bond.

And if he did not, his life would be finished.

WEDDING BELLS

October 7, 1979

VIOLA

She stretched like a lioness, warm and cozy in her bed next to Philip LeClair. After a while she shimmied from the bed, sprinted into the bathroom, brushed her teeth, then pulled on sweatpants and a hooded sweatshirt.

It was a quiet Sunday morning as Viola ran to the corner deli to buy containers of coffee, bagels, and cheese Danish. In her arms she cradled copies of the *Daily News* and the *Post* and the *New York Times*. Sunday was her day to devour newspapers.

Shivering, she hurried back to the apartment, the morning cooler than she had anticipated. Philip remained asleep, so she emptied one container of coffee into a mug and read the entire *Daily News*.

Finally, Philip appeared as a mirage in the kitchen doorway. With tousled hair and his bathrobe indecently exposing him, she laughed, said, "Good morning, sleepyhead."

He kissed her, sat at the other seat at the table. A long gulp of coffee was followed by a bite of a Danish, that nearly halved it. Playfully, she slapped at his wrist.

Philip pored over the *Times*, as Viola dug into the *Post*. Philip would never read "the rags," as he called them. The *Times*, however, was too cumbersome for her, though she would inhale the business section as soon as Philip left her apartment for his own. She was anxious to monitor NYC's IPO stock picks, but was careful not to allow Philip seeing her do so. Later that afternoon, after he had left her apartment, she gathered the crumpled newspapers to toss down the garbage chute. But as she lifted the folded sheets of the *Times*, her eye caught a caption that nearly felled her.

LARRY "*FITZ*" *FITZ*GERALD TO WED *LILY* MARZ

The words swayed before Viola's eyes. *But he's already married,* she thought wildly. She studied the grainy picture of Fitz and the woman. He stood tall next to her in a tuxedo, she in a dark dress, their arms draped about each other.

Heavily, she slumped onto the sofa. *Why did he lie to me about already being married? Why, during all this time, has he not been honest with me? What was he afraid of?*

Her throat felt clogged with vomit. She rushed into the bathroom and heaved up the coffee and the Danish she had enjoyed earlier. Looking at herself in the mirror, she wondered how she could have been so stupid, so easily misled. *I am smarter than him,* she chastised herself. *How did I allow him to fool me?*

She stared again at the announcement.

Lily Marz, 29, of New York City is engaged to marry Larry "Fitz" Fitzgerald Jr., 29, also of New York City.

Mr. Fitzgerald is an executive with Fitzgerald Alloy Corp. Ms. Marz is a flight scheduler at Jet King Enterprises.

"Fitz" is the son of Mr. & Mrs. Larry Fitzgerald Sr. Lily Marz has no immediate family in New York.

The wedding will commence on February 14, 1980, at St. Mary's Catholic Church in Great Neck. Reception to follow at the Carlyle Country Club in Roslyn.

Viola blanched.

It was crystal clear.

The son of a bitch was a liar.

What else had he lied to her about?

CHRISTMAS EVE

December 24, 1979

Christmas Eve was the first real holiday I shared with Fitz's family since our engagement. His parents' home in Roslyn was a magnificent two-story Tudor, gaily lit with holiday lights and with a great big nativity resting on their front lawn. I forgot how Catholic Fitz's mother was. Have I mentioned the Christmas tree? It was huge—at least ten times the size of the scrawny tree my stepdad brought home year after year.

I was nervous that night, of course I was. To me, it felt like a test to see if I was worthy of the Fitzgerald name. His mother, Theresa Anne, treated me sweetly, but I sensed a tentative hesitancy when it came to connecting with me on a more familiar footing. Fitz's father, however, was delightful. He hugged me warmly, pecked my cheek, offered me a cognac along with his seat near the blazing fireplace.

Fitz's marriage proposal had come as a complete shock and as unexpected as a meteor skyrocketing toward earth. We were at a swanky restaurant on a double-date with Fitz's friend Damon and Damon's girlfriend Gigi—a clueless girl far more interested in her reflection in her compact mirror than anything that was happening around her.

Drinks and dinner had been served. Champagne had miraculously appeared. Fitz was suddenly on one knee, flashing a diamond ring as big as an apple as he asked me to marry him.

That was two months ago.

But on that Christmas Eve of 1979, as I sat near the fire sipping my cognac and staring at the huge diamond on my left hand, I sensed a cosmic shift that was about to change my life forever.

I was chatting with Theresa Anne when she jumped up and shouted, "Dad! You made it!"

"Of course, I made it, sweetheart. Wouldn't miss a Christmas Eve with you," said the old man. He was ancient, pushing ninety-three, as Fitz would later tell me. He had pure white hair, thinning, but still covering his full head. His eyes were inky and sharp, not milky as was usual for people of his age. He walked without assistance, a huge smile on his narrow face.

After much hugging and kissing and back slapping, Fitz introduced me to the old man.

"Lily Marz, my grandfather, Arturo Domenici. Gramps, this is Lily, my fiancée."

He gently took my hand, stared into my eyes, then kissed both of my cheeks, European style. "You are lovely," he said softly. "How did my grandson manage to find a woman so lovely?"

Fitz and I laughed and hugged each other. Theresa Anne brought her father a glass of red wine and settled him into a Barco Lounger near to me. We all chatted comfortably, warmed by the fire and the alcohol.

When Fitz's mother called us to dinner—a seafood meal she claimed to have "thrown together"—the aromas assaulted me. There were clams, oysters, shrimp scampi, lightly crusted lemon sole, and lobster claws drenched with drawn butter. There was a medley of rice and vegetables and a platter of assorted cheeses and bottles of wine.

When Theresa Anne began to clear the dirty plates, I jumped up to help.

"No, no, no," Grandpa Arturo said. "Sit with me. I want to get to know you."

I shot a questioning look at Theresa Anne, but she nodded, insisting I sit with her father.

"Tell me about yourself," Fitz's grandfather asked.

"Well, I live at the Barbizon Hotel for Women, and I work as a flight scheduler at Jet King Enterprises."

Fitz's grandfather nodded pleasantly. "You are from Manhattan?"

"No. I'm from rural Indiana originally."

"Ahh. A farm girl?"

I laughed. "Not quite, though I did help my father feed the chickens."

"I see. And your family? Are they here, too?"

I shook my head. "No. Unfortunately, my family is gone. I was an only child."

"Oh, sweetheart, I'm sorry about that. Family is the most important thing in one's life." I lifted my wineglass, nodded. Felt my heartbeat accelerate. How much more lying would I need to do tonight?

"C'mon, Grandpa," Fitz said jovially, "She's not on trial here. Give her a break."

We all chuckled, left the dining room to return to the living room.

As we walked there, I turned to Fitz's grandfather and asked, "And you? Do you live in the city?"

"No. Not for a long, long time. I live in Sicily. So beautiful. You will come to visit, yes?"

Fitz interjected. "Of course, we will, Gramps. We'll honeymoon there, right, Lily?"

As surprised as I was, I agreed.

Black coffee and cheesecake and two-inch-high rainbow-colored cookies followed. Holiday presents were distributed.

My gift to Fitz was a Tiffany tie clip and key ring; his to me was a sapphire bracelet. I had carefully chosen a pale yellow cashmere scarf for Fitz's mother and tan kid leather gloves for his father.

It was a magical Christmas Eve. More than I could have hoped for and one I would remember for a long time.

But there was much I was unaware of that night. Words so carefully left unsaid; secrets unspoken.

So much that was yet to flit past me like ghosts in the night.

GULLIBLE

December 28, 1979

FITZ

It was Damon's thirtieth birthday, and they celebrated at a fun piano bar called Marie's in the Village. The piano player, Marie, was well into her late eighties, but she still played a mean piano. Patrons sang along with her, eating food tastier than any served at a higher-priced restaurant in the city. Alcohol flowed, people clapped madly, and there was no doubt that if a person graced Marie's piano bar, it was unlikely they could have a better time anywhere else.

Fitz and Lily had joined Damon and his girlfriend Gigi for the celebration at Marie's.

That night, Gigi appeared looking older than Damon, heavily made up and overly hair sprayed. Her relationship with her compact mirror remained intact. As a celebratory group, however, they were having fun.

When the two women rose to use the restroom, Damon switched seats to sit closer to Fitz.

"We've got a buy," Damon said. "I know it's been quiet, but that's the IPO market for you at this time of year. But this, Fitz. This is big."

"I'm listening," Fitz said.

"The drug company, Tricon Pharmaceuticals? They're soon to release a new drug. Liedopetitin, a strong painkiller. Doctors will use it to treat everything from sports injuries to post-operative pain."

"Okay. Why is it on our radar?"

Damon craned his neck to see if anyone could overhear, but with the tinkling music and the loud singing and hand clapping, it was impossible.

"I have a guy on the inside at the FDA," Damon whispered close to Fitz's ear. "He claims the drug will be approved in January. Tricon is currently trading at $24, $25 a share, give or take a few pennies. But when the news breaks that Lidopetitin will be approved by the FDA? Share prices are going to go through the roof."

Fitz grinned, swallowed a huge gulp of his martini.

"But we have to move quickly," Damon urged. "We've got to get in before the FDA releases the news."

"I agree."

"Good. Because we've got to get to Viola tonight. Make sure that she gets our trade done first thing Monday morning. Before the market opens."

Fitz felt his stomach drop to his ankles. He had not seen Viola in weeks, had purposely avoided her since his wedding announcement had appeared in the Sunday *New York Times*.

He wondered if Viola had seen the announcement, and if she had, it was sure to be a huge embarrassment for Fitz.

He had lied to her. Told her he was already married. What would she think now?

He looked down at his left hand. The wedding band he usually wore when he went to McNulty's was at home, tucked beneath his socks. Besides, how could he show up at McNulty's with Lily?

Fitz stumbled as he said, "Damon, we can't bring the girls to McNulty's. Viola might recognize you."

Damon's eyebrows lifted. "She won't recognize me, Fitz. I think you're more concerned about Viola seeing you with Lily."

"Well..."

Damon sat up straighter. "We're not letting this opportunity slip through our fingers. We are going to McNulty's tonight, my friend. I'll occupy the girls while you give the information to Viola. Emphasize to her how important it is to get the trade done on Monday morning. No excuses."

When the two women returned to their table, Damon signaled for the bill and said, "Hey, we're heading over to McNulty's for a nightcap. I'll get the bill. Fitz, you grab us a cab."

As their taxi approached McNulty's, Lily innocently whispered, "Fitz, why are we here?"

"Just having a nightcap to top off Damon's birthday celebration," he said quietly.

They exited the taxi, and Fitz ushered the women through McNulty's doors and toward the north side of the entrance—away from Viola's station. Still, Fitz froze as he saw Viola's eyes nail him in place, two orbs of red-hot lava as they lasered into Fitz's.

Securing seats at the bar, Fitz gently kissed Lily and said, "I need to run to the restroom. Be right back." To Damon, he whispered, "Order a round of drinks while I take care of business."

Fitz skirted the bar, caught Viola's eye as he chin pointed toward the kitchen.

Both arrived one step short of the other. Viola grimaced as they plowed through the swinging pass-through doors and into the pantry closet.

"Viola, I owe you an explanation," Fitz stuttered immediately.

"You owe me nothing but respect," Viola hissed. "Why did you lie to me?"

"I didn't mean to. Honestly."

Fitz lied as easily as if he were a jailhouse snitch. “My dad thought it was a safe play to pretend I was married. Women who worked for our clients were all over me all the time. I wasn’t interested, but I also didn’t want to jeopardize our business relationships. So, I pretended to be married. It was easier. My dad wanted to protect his business, and I stupidly went along with it.”

“That doesn’t explain why you lied to me.”

Fitz hunched his shoulders. “I don’t know, Viola. I really don’t know.”

“So,” she asked. “Which one is your fiancée? The dark-haired one? Or the bimbo?”

“The dark-haired one.”

“Lucky her,” Viola snickered.

Fitz ignored her sarcasm, pulled her deeper into the pantry. “Listen,” he urged. “We have a big purchase to make. One that might make it the haul of our lifetimes.”

Viola pretended indifference. “Okay,” she said. “Who and how much?”

Fitz inhaled deeply. Took two steps closer to Viola.

“Tricon Pharmaceuticals. Purchase eighty-two thousand shares. Opening price is no factor. But Vi, it’s crucial that it’s done before the opening bell on Monday morning.”

Viola glared at Fitz. “And the ‘why’ behind this purchase?”

“Tricon will be releasing a breakthrough drug that has enormous potential. That’s all you need to know.” He winked at her. “Get it done. Okay?”

He watched Viola nod, then he headed back to the other end of the bar. Women were so gullible.

BUY AND SELL

December 28, 1979

VIOLA

She counted off a full minute before she left the kitchen. Walked slowly to her station. From across the bar, she studied Fitz and his little entourage.

Viola grimaced. She hated the way Fitz protectively draped his arm around the dark-haired woman. Hated the way he laughed and joked with her.

She fumed, knowing that they could buy and sell her in a matter of minutes. For too long a moment, she was the poor foster child again. It was an awful feeling and difficult to shake off.

Thankfully, they did not remain at McNulty's for long. When they finally left, Viola thought she saw Fitz's fiancée take a misstep, watched him take her arm to hold her upright. The bimbo with them was a mess; her head lolled on her shoulder, and she could barely walk without her boyfriend's support. Mascara ringed her bloodshot eyes, and bright red lipstick grossly smeared her upper lip.

When Viola's shift ended and she had counted her tips and washed the crust and stickiness from the bar and pulled her peacoat over her dirty white blouse, she did not hurry to the subway, nor did she wait for a bus.

Instead, she walked through the blistering cold to clear her mind. The wind bit at her like an untrained puppy, the sky clear and brilliant and offering a neat slice of a quarter moon's shine.

Her thoughts were frayed and erratic. Why had Fitz proposed a business partnership with her so early in their friendship? What had made him trust her so?

And, the awkward meeting with the strange man at Studio 54?

What had she missed in all of this?

When she finally reached her apartment building, her face was chapped and raw from the arrogant weather. It was almost 3:00 a.m., but she could not feign exhaustion. No, she was wide awake, her brain and body working double-time to understand the arrangement she had agreed to with Fitz and Jonathan Silver.

Inside her apartment it was warm and cozy. She tossed her peacoat onto the couch, turned on the TV, prepared a cup of tea.

For more than an hour she mulled over the financial arrangement she had agreed to with the two men.

"What's in it for me?" she had asked pointedly.

"Sixteen percent," Jonathan Silver had quickly responded. "Very fair compensation for very little work."

As she sipped the warm tea, she thought about it. Realized it was not adequate compensation.

She tallied the numbers in her head.

Yes, she did receive 16 percent of the profits. Which meant that Fitz and Jonathan were reeling in 84 percent of the profits. And if one were to add up the profits from all their transactions to date....

Viola bolted upright.

They had played her!

Cut her in for such a small piece of the pie. "It's not fair," she said aloud. "I'm doing all the leg work for this team and reaping the smallest reward."

She stood up, paced the small living area.

Why shouldn't I grab a piece of the action, too? If this new Tricon Pharmaceutical buy is so important, why shouldn't I buy into it separately?

Fitz and Jonathan won't know about it. This is an opportunity for me to cash in as lucratively as they will.

But making the purchase via Calhoun would be too dangerous. She would need to find a broker without a connection to either of them.

She rushed into the kitchen, pulled open a cupboard, and from an unsteady shelf pulled out the Manhattan Yellow Pages. She flipped through the big book until she found the bold caption for FINANCIAL BROKERAGE.

Stunned by the sheer number of advertisements, she finally settled on American Brokerage Associates, a reputable name in the financial industry.

On Monday, she would empty her bank account.

She would buy as many shares of Tricon Pharmaceuticals as she could afford.

She would show those two boys a thing or two.

MORNING AFTER

December 29, 1979

Waking that morning was downright awful. My head pounded, my mouth as foul as a dirty kitty litter box. Lifting my head was a mistake as a carousel of dizziness joined the revolt in my stomach.

You're familiar with the sensation, aren't you? The one cocktail too many that pushes you over the edge? Your body's downward spiral from which you wake in the morning, wishing you had died during the night? Yeah. That was the feeling I experienced that morning.

Carefully, I glanced at the spot next to me on Fitz's bed.

Empty.

How? He had drunk way more than I had.

Delicately, I lifted myself into a seated position, sat perfectly still until I was certain I could slip from the bed without fainting right there on the beautifully crafted wood flooring.

Thankfully, the bathroom was just beyond the bedroom. I peed, splashed my face with icy water, and crept down the hallway to the kitchen. Each time my feet lifted and touched the floor, I heard cymbals clang together in my ears, reverberating until I feared my brain might pulse right out of my skull.

It was eerily quiet in the apartment. Not even the hiss of the Mr. Coffee machine to welcome me. I glanced at the kitchen clock: 12:55. In the afternoon!

Near the refrigerator, I spotted a note—scrawled in Fitz's uneven handwriting: *Called into the office. Big problem to deal with. Take it easy today. You deserve it. Love, F.*

I brewed a pot of coffee but was too nauseous to drink it. I spilled the entire potful into the sink and slunk back into bed after swallowing three aspirin. Thank God it was not a weekday.

Bleary-eyed, I turned on the TV, watched Channel Two News. Connie Chung. I respected her. She always spoke with sincerity.

As my eyes drooped, I faintly heard Connie say that a settlement had been reached in the 1977 collision of an Olympian Airways flight with an Air Com jumbo jet.

My eyes flew open, and I vomited onto Fitz's beautifully crafted wood flooring.

A SETTLEMENT AT LAST

December 29, 1979

JEFFREY

When the broadcast aired, Jeffrey Kaye was with his girlfriend DeeDee Monroe in a ridiculously cheap motel room near LaGuardia Airport. Tangled in the sheets with her, he was not witness to the breaking news.

Not until he arrived home—his mother waiting anxiously in their kitchen, a meat stew simmering on the stove—did he learn of the settlement.

"Your lawyer called earlier," his mother gushed. Her cheeks were as pink as the nail polish she wore. "There's a settlement, Jeffrey! You need to call Shannon Laura O'Reilly right away!"

Jeffrey's fingers splayed on the telephone pad; his heart jumped about like a kangaroo. It was Saturday. Would his lawyer be in her office? Sweating, he counted off the rings until she answered: three, four, five . . .

"Shannon Laura O'Reilly here," her voice boomed through the receiver.

"It's me, Jeffrey," he gasped.

"Right. Good," she responded. "We've a settlement, Jeffrey. Not the original number I had hoped for, but a good solid number, nonetheless. Very fair."

Jeffrey nodded vigorously, like one of those hula dolls on car dashboards.

"The award figure is three point one million," she said easily. "Most aircraft disaster survivors wind up with a settlement of one or two million. I pushed for a higher sum due to the extent of your injuries, loss of income, medical needs, extreme emotional distress." She waited a beat. "Acceptable?" she asked.

He nodded as if she could see him through the thick telephone wires. "Yes," he croaked.

"Excellent. After deducting my fee and reimbursable expenses—which you should review prior to agreeing to the settlement—you will receive a check for two million, twenty-two thousand dollars."

Jeffrey inhaled sharply. *Oh my God,* he thought. *I'm a millionaire. A multimillionaire.*

It was over. Done with.

Finally, finally, it was over.

NEW YEAR, NEW CLUB

February 2, 1980

FITZ

The new private club that Fitz joined was Candy Land, conveniently located across the street from the elegant Garden City Hotel in Nassau County. The owner of Candy Land was a tough street punk, wildly rich from selling cocaine and meth to people who could ill afford it. The club would soon become a useful money laundering operation for his drug business.

Fitz's pal Gregory Maison had introduced Fitz to the club when Fitz confessed to him that he could no longer patronize YG, mostly due to his father's discovery of Fitz's activities.

The new club's location worked perfectly for Fitz as he often entertained clients at the Garden City Hotel. There in Nassau County he felt sheltered from the prying eyes in Queens County. It would be a stretch for anyone—his father, Lily, his grandfather—to find him out there, away from the city, away from Queens and Brooklyn, where his family's arm had a very wide reach.

It was a frigid Saturday night as Fitz drove to Nassau County. He had lied to Lily, told her he was headed to his own bachelor party in the Village, that he might crash at Gregory's place if they became too wasted. Luckily, she had bought the whole story.

When he arrived at the club, the parties were in full swing: disco music blared, girls danced, booze flowed, coke was sniffed. Fitz went to the bar, ordered a single-malt scotch. Watched as an extremely popular, effeminate newscaster chatted up a boyishly attired girl. Seated not far from him, Fitz recognized a golf pro ogling a pretty little thing. Then he spotted Marnie.

Greg Maison had come through big time for Fitz, as the girl usually was booked weeks in advance at YG, Inc. *Guess the money was enticing enough to have her follow me here,* he thought.

Marnie was nearing her seventeenth birthday, but she always managed to look and dress as if she were much younger. She sauntered close to Fitz, smiled, and reached up to stroke his cheek.

"Ready?" she asked as she grabbed his belt buckle and pulled him toward her.

He grinned and followed her to one of the empty party rooms.

WEDDING NERVES

February 10, 1980

In four short days, I would be getting married. On Valentine's Day. A Thursday. Fitz's father had insisted on the date, and since he was paying for everything, how could I refuse?

Of course, Fitz's mother, Theresa Anne, had managed to hijack all the wedding plans. I was not particularly unhappy about it because Jet King had just added two additional destinations to our schedules, and I was too busy to concentrate on much else.

Truthfully, even if I did have the time to plan and coordinate the event, Theresa Anne would have continued to take charge. I had little input in anything—not the venue, nor the food, not the seating arrangements or the music.

But when it came to deciding on the floral pieces, I refused to budge. Calla lilies, I insisted upon. Fitz's mother presumed it was vanity on my part—because of my name—but that just proved how little she knew about me.

Calla lilies were my mother's favorite flower.

I did, however, select my own dress. A bejeweled, body-hugging gown, cut low enough in the bodice to tease, but not too risque as to offend Fitz's Catholic parents.

Lena Robinson was to be my maid of honor, and Fitz chose Damon as his best man. Domingo Martinez, a Jet King pilot who had become a dear friend, agreed to walk me down the aisle.

And though I was crazily in love with Fitz, I hoped I was not making a huge mistake.

Because it was not only Fitz I was marrying. His family was part of the deal too.

STRUGGLES

February 11, 1980

The wedding was not the only issue with which I struggled.

I feared I might be pregnant. All the symptoms were there: nausea, fatigue, irritability. A two-week-late missed period.

When I shared my fears with Lena, she exclaimed, "Honey, you're just stressed out about work and the wedding. Do yourself a favor and get a home pregnancy test."

Which I did. And which, thankfully, proved I was not pregnant. I was just stressed out as Lena had predicted.

But what Lena did not know was that I was also struggling with the recent revelation of a settlement being reached with a survivor of the 1977 air disaster, which I remained partially responsible for having caused.

The old me, Margaret Lido.

Daily, I scoured newspapers for any snippet of information I could uncover about the survivor. Yet not a mention, not a blurb anywhere. Not a name, or an age, or a resident city.

I seriously began to wonder if someone had truly survived the crash.

It was difficult to imagine how one person—of all those passengers booked on both fully filled flights—had managed to survive.

How, with noxious gases and flames and sheared metal and crushed seats as obstacles?

It was unnerving to think that the survivor—maimed or crippled or horribly burned—was out there waiting, biding their time to find me, to make me pay for what I had done.

Was it a man or a woman? Young or old?

Was the survivor an American? The Olympian Airways flight had arrived from Athens, Greece. The Canadian flight was returning to Montreal.

The survivor could be anyone. Anyone at all.

WEDDING BELLS

February 14, 1980

VIOLA

People often swear that everything that happens in life happens for a reason. Either through divine intervention or because the universe has taken control of things.

Perhaps it was so.

Viola Cordova had benefited from that benevolent reasoning. She was not simply happy, she was giddy, teetering on the edge of hysteria. And rightfully so.

It was Valentine's Day, the 14th of February, and with the noon tick of the clock she had transferred twenty-one thousand four hundred and ninety-five dollars directly from her personal American Brokerage account and into her Chase Manhattan Bank account.

After exiting the Sixth Avenue branch of the bank, she had mentally counted her profits without aid of calculator or adding machine. A few weeks prior—armed with the salient information which her business partners had provided—she had purchased a solid bank of shares of Tricon Pharmaceuticals for her personal brokerage account.

Sure, NYC Holdings had scored a home run of a profit on the Tricon deal.

But so had she. And neither Fitz nor Jonathan Silver were aware of her personal investment. The two men were already rolling in money, and it was time for her to do the same.

As clouds meandered across the sky, brief shafts of sunlight played along the sidewalks and skirted the dark, dirty mounds of snow that buttressed the street corners. Viola shuffled along Sixth Avenue, oblivious to the street noises and the shrill barks of sidewalk vendors hawking their goods. She roped her way through throngs of people as they scurried past, then hailed a taxi to take her to St. Mary's Catholic Church in Great Neck, New York.

She glanced at her watch: 1:17 p.m. She would be there in time. As the taxi weaved through traffic, she felt her earlier euphoria ebb into despair.

Upon arrival at the church, she pleaded with the driver to wait for her; offered him double the fare on the meter.

Viola shivered as she walked along the uneven path that led to the church—a huge monstrosity of a structure that appeared to lurk right through the naked tree branches. Opening the ornate wooden doors, she slipped inside. Immediately, she heard the incantations of a priest reciting prayers that echoed through the cavernous space. She sank into an empty rear pew.

Indignantly, she watched as Lily Marz pledged her vows to the man for whom Viola longed, the man who had lied to her about already being married. Why had he found it necessary to make such a fool of her?

She watched icily as Fitz kissed his new bride.

Then, quietly, and undetected, Viola slipped away before the bride and groom could walk past her along the red-carpeted aisle.

MOVING ON

February 14, 1980

JEFFREY

Valentine's Day held little romance for Jeffrey Kaye. After a yearlong relationship with DeeDee Monroe, she was no longer a part of his life. It had been prudent to let her go—she was as belligerent as a gator being wrestled—leaving him no other reasonable choice. She had handcuffed him with her manipulative and overbearing nature—a carbon copy of his mother—and he refused to live the next thirty or forty years of his life in the same cuckolded manner. As far as he was concerned, DeeDee had been a blip of a diversion, an interruption in an already difficult stretch of his life.

Besides, he did not want her hands in his pockets when he became rich. Someone like DeeDee Monroe would squander his money in short order.

Luckily, their relationship ended the first week of January, for on that Valentine's Day, Jeffrey's monetary windfall arrived via Federal Express delivery. As he held the check in his unsteady hands, he pictured his lawyer—her hair frizzy and full, the size of a small pineapple, wearing a nicely tailored green suit and squat, sensible shoes—as she professionally and confidently signed his two million, twenty-two-thousand-dollar check.

He had beaten the odds for survival and wondered if the Tire World mechanic had passed along his own survival genes to Jeffrey. But he did not dwell on that thought for long. He had far more important things to think about.

Jeffrey immediately phoned the realtor he had contacted the previous year. Once he explained to her that he was prepared to make the move from Manhattan to Queens, she set to work. It took them only two trips—both to a place called Colgate, just minutes from the bridge and within a recently developed community called Arlington Estates.

"This is ideal for you," his realtor gushed. She was a fifty-something year-old woman who looked like an aging hippy, worn out by too many years of drugs and alcohol, but she was revered as an extraordinary realtor. The house she had pushed him to consider was in a cul-de-sac, the last house at the end of the street. It offered plenty of living space and boasted window views of the bay.

"A water view," the realtor gushed. "But it won't stay on the market for long. Two of the four homes on the street have already been sold." Jeffrey offered to purchase the property for cash, with a guarantee for the title to close quickly.

As soon as his new house was in escrow, he called a Floridian realtor to secure a townhome for his mother in the same lovely retirement community where her two sisters already resided. A check for one hundred thousand dollars would help to furnish her new home and to complement her monthly pension.

Once the real estate properties were secured—which happened quickly because cash was king—Jeffrey met with a financial planner who invested a good portion of his settlement monies into annuities and mutual funds. The advisor strongly warned, "Don't blow off your job. It would be the biggest mistake you could make at your age."

With his financial future safely secured, he purchased a new car—a 1980 sparkling blue Range Rover. When he walked out of the dealership, his legs shook as if a small earthquake had just rocked him.

He was finally ready to move on, to start a new chapter of his life.

And to start it without the aid of his mother or DeeDee Monroe nipping at his heels.

SURPRISES

March 1, 1980

Stretched out like a languid lioness, I stared out of the window, past the olive groves that surrounded our villa in Taormina, Sicily. The beauty and tranquility of the land took my breath away.

Our honeymoon had been exquisite, and I was sorry that we were returning to New York that afternoon.

Fitz's grandfather had gifted us the honeymoon in Sicily: a villa staffed with a cook and housekeeper, and I was stunned when I heard Fitz converse with them in a perfect Italian dialect. I was unaware that he spoke the language so easily. Why had he never mentioned it? Funny how you can marry a man you are madly in love with, yet be in the dark regarding the tiny, yet infinitely important tidbits of his life.

Taormina was a place I could not—on my best day—have imagined. On the east coast of Italy, it sat near Mount Etna, an active volcano, which, I cannot lie, frightened me a bit. The village's main stretch hosted charming shops and cafes, and one could see the Corvaja Palace while dining. We visited the ancient Greco-Roman Theatre and the Duomo, a historic Catholic Church. In the Piazza we drank Campari and soda and watched a small group of nuns as they sipped espresso coffee and munched biscotti. We swam in coves and lounged on sandy beaches. We ate with abandon, drank local regional wines, and sipped freshly made limoncello. And of course, there was passionate lovemaking, which woke me each morning and lulled me to sleep at night.

Several times during our stay, we visited with Fitz's grandfather, whose villa was even larger than ours. A live-in nurse resided with him for his elevated age had begun to physically hinder him. But although his body refused to cooperate, his mind remained alert and sharp.

On that final afternoon of our honeymoon, we dined with Fitz's grandfather on his outdoor patio, sampled ripe tomatoes sliced onto freshly baked bread and drizzled with olive oil and basil. There was sharp parmigiana cheese and olives and figs. We sipped a delightful Pinot Grigio as we ate, stuffed ourselves on wedges of delicate ricotta cheesecake.

When Fitz rose to use the restroom, his grandfather leaned in toward me, cupped his hand atop mine. "I'm glad my grandson chose to marry a lovely woman like you," he said. "You're the right type of woman to keep him in line."

Then he winked at me. *To keep Fitz in line. What did that mean?*

When Fitz popped back to the table, the old man discreetly removed his hand from mine. The nurse reminded Fitz's grandfather that it was time for his afternoon pills and a nap. We kissed him goodbye, and I wondered if it would be the last time we saw him.

That afternoon, we flew first class on a Pan American jet to New York. I was still skittish about air travel ever since the accident I had helped to cause. As we sipped champagne, I looked down at my diamond engagement ring, surrounded by its sister wedding band.

I guess it had not yet settled in.

Now, I was Lily Fitzgerald. A married woman. So far removed from my early life in Georgia, where I had been a young, benign, clueless girl. The type of girl surely not destined for a life in New York City or a wealthy husband like Fitz.

My mother and Savannah would have fainted had they attended our lavish country club wedding reception, where more than one hundred and twenty-five guests joined in the celebration. Eighteen of the guests were on my list. You get the picture, I'm sure.

Endless streams of expensive wines were poured, as if they flowed from water bottles; tuxedoed waiters wore white gloves and served appetizers with Italian names too difficult to pronounce.

The opulence and expense of the celebration was daunting to me, but I forced myself to revel in the glow of the evening. Fitz and I danced and kissed and kissed some more. There were speeches and good luck toasts.

As the party wound down, guest after guest approached us with their hearty good wishes and double cheek kisses—as if we were in Paris—followed by a demure handing over to Fitz of white envelopes.

As I looked at him quizzically, he whispered into my ear, "They're wedding gifts. Cash, checks."

I was confused: wedding gifts were usually new toasters and blenders, satin bedsheets or wine decanters. But money?

I must have dozed for a bit for I was startled when Fitz gently touched my shoulder. "Hey, wife," he whispered slyly. "We're beginning our descent. Almost home."

My watch said 10:30 p.m. But the sky outside was not dark. Then I realized we had gained back the six-hour time difference from Italy. In New York it was only four thirty in the afternoon.

My neck felt stiff, and I was exhausted.

"Oh," Fitz said as he peered out the tiny window. "My father is picking us up at the airport."

"Why?" I asked, more tartly than I should have said.

"Don't know. He left a message at the villa. Said he had a big surprise for us."

But I was not in the mood for a big surprise. I was in the mood for a hot shower and our bed. I looked sideways at Fitz, but he seemed unfazed.

"He left a message this morning," I repeated. "Why didn't you tell me?"

He shrugged his shoulders. "Didn't seem important." Then he smiled and squeezed my knee. "Hey, a surprise following a honeymoon is usually a good thing."

He leaned over and gently touched his lips to mine. But why hadn't he told me? Was he already aware of the surprise? Or was I being paranoid?

As we waited for our luggage I glanced about, spotted a skinny man with pock-marked skin and oily hair holding a printed sign: Mr. & Mrs. Fitzgerald. I poked Fitz with my elbow, pointed to the man.

"Oh yeah," he said. "One of Dad's regular drivers. The car is probably out front waiting for us."

Tiredly, I sighed, watched as our luggage rolled to a stop before us. Fitz hauled the heavy bags as if they were weightless bolts of material.

The driver waved to us, took possession of our bags, and walked us to a big shiny car that idled at the curb. We climbed inside, and Fitz's father turned from the front seat to shake Fitz's hand.

"Good trip?" he asked.

"You bet," Fitz responded.

"Did you enjoy yourself, Lily?" he asked me.

"Oh yes, Larry. Very much."

"We're family now, Lily," Larry Senior chuckled. "Just call me Dad."

I remained silent as Larry Senior and Fitz discussed business. My eyes were dry and tired, and the road signs we passed were not familiar.

"Where are we going?" I asked. "Seems we're headed in the wrong direction."

"Nope, we're headed in the right direction," Larry Senior's voice boomed. "We're headed to Colgate, just about ten minutes from the Colgate bridge."

"Okay," I murmured. "But why?"

"You'll find out soon enough, dear girl."

His "dear girl" words made my stomach churl. Such an outdated, ridiculous salutation. It was 1980 for God's sake!

Soon we approached the Queens border and I spotted a glimpse of water as it shimmied in the waning daylight. Moments later, the car turned onto a long driveway. Ahead, a sign welcomed us to Arlington Estates. We halted at a small guard booth. The driver spoke to the guard and instantly, two huge iron gates parted to allow us entry.

We drove a quarter mile to Bayview Terrace Road. We passed a golf course and a country club, turned right, and stopped before a two-story brick and stone house with a big gabled roof. I gawked at the three-car garage, the immense lawn. A quaint lamppost stood as a sentry along the lawn's edge. There were tall Italian cypress trees that appeared to reach to the heavens. Squinting my eyes, I saw we were within a cul-de-sac—with only four homes widely spaced on the semi-arc of land.

The house loomed huge before my eyes.

"Welcome home!" Fitz's father roared.

WE'RE FAMILY NOW

March 1, 1980

FITZ

With a frigid wind blowing at his back, Fitz watched Lily gape at the new house his father had gifted them for their wedding. How nerve-racking it was for him to watch her features convert from utter surprise to uneasy apprehension.

As he stared straight ahead at the looming two-story house, Fitz cringed as he heard her say, "A house? You bought us a house as a wedding present?" Her voice dripped with incredulity. "Who does that?"

"The Fitzgeralds do that, honey," Larry Senior quipped. "You'll love it. Let's go inside so you two lovebirds can eyeball the place."

Fitz's stomach cramped; he knew that Lily was shocked by his father's assumptive generosity.

As they walked through the front door, Lily whispered to Fitz, "Did you know about this?"

He was not sure how to respond, so he simply shrugged.

They stepped into a large foyer, which spanned outward into an even larger living area. A wall of windows overlooked the bay and the bridge beyond, where lights twinkled alongside the gently lapping water.

The view is breathtaking, Fitz thought. *How can she not love it? How can she not be over the moon with joy? It isn't every day that people are handed the keys to a magnificent home in an upscale neighborhood.*

Yet, Lily's posture was stiff as a starched shirt.

She should be happy, he thought gruffly. He would not tolerate conflict between Lily and the family. Conflict would ruin the very reason he had married her.

"Okay, kids, walk this way. I'll give you a tour," Larry Senior said.

Fitz stared up at the fifteen-foot ceilings, which made him feel as if they were in a museum with walls large enough to hold massive works of art. They traipsed through a chef's kitchen, a formal dining room, and a large office with built-in bookshelves. Upstairs, they viewed four bedrooms, and Fitz counted five bathrooms and a powder room. Outside, a two-story wooden deck offered incredible views of the Bay and the Colgate Bridge.

The entire house seemed to have flown off the pages of *House & Garden* magazine. *It's insane,* Fitz thought. *My Forest Hills apartment can fit inside this place at least five times, with room to spare.*

His father practically gushed as he showed them the three-car garage. "Check this out," he said. "I had a self-locking steel door installed between the garage and the laundry room."

He gently tossed his arm around Lily's shoulder. "Just wanted my new daughter-in-law to feel safe and secure in her new home."

"I appreciate the effort...Dad," Lily said quietly. "It's just, I thought that one day Fitz and I would choose a home together."

"You don't like the place?" he said.

Fitz caught Lily's eye, silently begged her to say the right thing.

"No, no, I love it," she said quickly. "Sorry. I did not mean to seem unappreciative. We're just exhausted from the wedding and the honeymoon and the long plane ride home."

She stood on her tippy toes and kissed her father-in-law's cheek. "Thank you for your generosity," she said, a big smile on her face.

Larry Senior hugged her close. "You're family now, Lily. And we take care of family, don't we, son?"

Fitz clapped his father's back. "We sure do, Dad."

OPPORTUNITY

May 11, 1980

VIOLA

There was a comforting rhythm to monotony. Everything orderly and precise. No unexpected surprises.

For three months, Viola had welcomed the monotony of her life, but deep down she knew she was fooling herself. Her days and nights were a mere pretense of a life being lived, the steady crossing off of hours and days from a calendar. Of work shifts to come and of bills to be paid.

Since Fitz's wedding, Viola had struggled to snap out of her funk. Gin had not worked. Neither had the men she bedded.

And though she did not see Fitz quite as often—he popped into McNulty's only to deliver IPO purchase instructions—whenever she did see him, it fueled her infatuation anew.

And she hated him for it.

Following one of his infrequent visits to McNulty's, she found herself crying into her pillow that night, angry with herself for carrying on about him as if she were a young girl and he a pop idol.

She sorely missed the feisty teen she had been, the girl who peeked around every corner in search of excitement and adventure. She missed the strong, stoic woman she had been when she left Leroy at the rest stop in Florida.

She missed herself.

Aimlessly, she paced the already worn linoleum that led from living room to foyer to bedroom.

Six weeks earlier, she had taken up with a banker—a forty-something stuffy type who wore suspenders beneath his Brooks Brothers suits and smoked Cuban cigars, and who threw money around as if it were confetti.

He whisked her off to Miami and the Hamptons for long weekends, bought her expensive gifts, and was a surprisingly competent and athletic lover.

Six weeks later, their affair had run its course.

He wanted love and commitment.

She did not.

She wanted Fitz. And only Fitz.

And if he had not lied to her about already being married, she would not have squandered her opportunity to nab him.

She pulled a cigarette from its box, lit it, and continued her back and forth trek of the apartment.

I've done everything possible to replace Fitz's hold on me, she thought wearily.

It had not been too difficult. She was sexy and smart. Not textbook smart, mind you, but street smart, and men seemed to find that attribute terribly exciting.

It had excited the beefy construction guy.

And Philip LeClair. And the recently dumped banker.

As she glanced from the bedroom window, she counted off all the others she had dragged along on her quest: Jesse the mechanic and Pedro the schoolteacher. Ben the insurance auditor, and Jorge the professional volleyball player.

So, there she was, thirty-one years old, with her feet firmly cemented to McNulty's and to Uncle Sammy's deteriorating, rent-controlled apartment.

"Even Jeffrey Kaye and his mother have flown the coop," she said aloud as she angrily flipped the butt of her cigarette into the toilet bowl.

Jeffrey Kaye, who had lived two quick steps across the hall and who had wanted her as badly as she wanted Fitz. She had treated Jeffrey poorly, like an annoying gnat. His obvious desire for her was intense and had at times frightened her.

Mid-stride, she stopped. *Is that how Fitz thought of me?* she worried. *An annoying gnat? Was it the reason he lied to me about being married?*

"No!" she yelled to the deaf walls. She was not that person. She was not pathetic and needy.

Viola flung herself onto the sofa, screamed into a pillow. She lay there for an hour or two.

When she finally sat up, she twisted her neck left, then right. Shrugged her shoulders to loosen the cramped tightness that had settled there. *I should move from here.* The thought came to her unexpectedly, as if she had abruptly decided to book a trip to Taipei.

Why not? she chastised herself. *Not a move from New York, no, no. I love this city. A change to a new neighborhood? Something more...upscale? I can easily abandon this apartment. I don't rightfully belong here. I am not Sammy Carrano's niece.*

Lack of money was no longer an obstacle.

And money was power, she reminded herself. She remembered her foster mother's words to her: "Always squirrel something away for a rainy day."

But what if that rainy day never came? Viola wondered.

Might she believe differently if she were sharing her life with Fitz? Might she be willing to take more chances, to roll the dice on life, love, and commitment?

She would never know for certain, just as she would never know if a future with Philip or the banker or Jorge the volleyball player might have provided her with a perfectly happy and satisfied life. But they were men who had not made her heart hammer in her chest. Men who had not made her shake with desire.

Why had Fitz chosen that little mouse Lily Marz instead of her?

SURPRISE NEIGHBOR

May 13, 1980

JEFFREY

A stranger might have described Jeffrey Kaye as a bull in a china shop. Or a detonator on a bomb ready to explode.

His footsteps echoed through the quiet rooms of his new home, his thoughts as disjointed as chess pieces on a lopsided board. The big house, which he had longed for since grade school, was only a sad, empty space. Without his mother to putter in the kitchen, and without her nonstop chatter, he was terribly lonely. It was maddening to admit how much he missed her. Wondered how that was even possible when, gleefully, he had counted the days to her departure to Florida. He had imagined a glorious sense of relief once she was gone.

But the relief was short-lived and proved to be an emotionally challenging time for Jeffrey. Like a ghost, he trolled the house, tried to make sense of his present situation. Wondered how he had manipulated the hows and the whys of his arrival to this precise stage in his life.

The settlement money from the accident should have put that sorry travel day behind him. But it had not because his nightmares—though not as frequent—remained. It dismayed him that he could not remember anything of that day other than boarding the plane and gulping a beer.

That window of time between Jeffrey's last drop of Bud and waking from his coma was completely lost to him.

When he tried to force his brain to recall that lost time, it caused his anxiety level to crawl along his belly like a crab scuttling back to the ocean. He knew it would be prudent to swallow one or two of his prescribed Xanax pills—a simple solution to quickly calm him. But he fought the urge. His dependency on the pills had become an unwelcome crutch, and he refused to walk about in a stupor for the rest of his life.

Surprisingly, too, he missed Viola—her smile, her airy, arrogant, confident persona. It had been a long time since he had gone to McNulty's Tavern. It had been an uncomplicated way for him to exorcise her from his fantasies. Clearly, she was unattainable to him. A friend, yes—but a distant one at that.

His only real friend was Charlie Hughes—who, during Jeffrey's early days of snapping license photos at the DMV, had shown him the ropes—and who had recently moved on to a higher-paying position at the US Passport Office. The two often shared a beer on Friday nights, and Charlie had insisted to him, "Buddy, if you ever need anything, I'm here for you, man."

Charlie's new position had stunned Jeffrey. Charlie at the US Passport Office? Charlie, who was stoned every single day of his life? Had they not vetted him? Sure, he was a Vietnam vet, but honestly, who in their right mind would allow someone like Charlie to maintain a position of authority anywhere? Jeffrey mulled the thought as he walked to his outside deck. The sky was a soft blue; the bay water ebbing and flowing to the shore. He spotted a mama bird feeding tiny worms to her hatchlings.

Back in the city he had made a few friends at McNulty's. Acquaintances, really. All of them losers just like him, all of them passing time and hoping that someone would walk through the doors and inject a scintilla of excitement into their dull lives.

He thought of DeeDee Monroe and of how she might have been one of those someones. But that was early on, before the real DeeDee had unveiled herself. The selfish, shallow DeeDee that lived and breathed beneath her skin. But during that morning, even she would have been a welcome relief from the loneliness.

Back in the living room, he turned on the TV, anxious to hear voices other than the ones in his head. Watched a silly game show, then finally, he gave in to his anxiety and swallowed a Xanax. Only one.

Shortly after, he began to unwind. *Or unravel,* he thought mirthlessly. According to Charlie Hughes, "Sometimes life deals you a pair of aces, and sometimes you wind up with a pair of deuces. You just have to make the best of either."

His new home was a pair of aces—and fit for a king, he thought. *If only I had a queen to share it with.*

Later that day, as Jeffrey drove his new Land Rover through the Arlington Estates main gate and had ridden the quarter mile to Bayview Terrace Road, he slowed the car to nudge past an All Borough moving van, which idled in front of the second house on his cul-de-sac.

He hovered a few yards away, watched as burly men unloaded furniture and television consoles and heavy crates and hauled it all into the stately home. As Jeffrey pulled further away from the moving van, he glimpsed a white Lincoln Continental as it drove onto the home's wide driveway. Following on its heels, a sharp-looking forest green Chevy Camaro pulled into the second driveway alongside the Lincoln.

The person inside the Lincoln did not exit, but the woman in the Camaro quickly jumped out, as if stung by a bee.

Jeffrey stared at the woman. His pulse quickened as his brain registered what his eyes had already captured. It was the black-haired woman with the unforgettable smoky-gray eyes. The woman he had photographed at the DMV months earlier.

The woman whose picture he slept with every night.

MOVING DAY

May 13, 1980

It was difficult to remain upset with Fitz's father.

Can you blame me?

The man had purchased for us a baby mansion. A house we could not have afforded for the next ten or fifteen years. And if the real estate market should boom in price? Great, but still...how arrogant is it of a person to purchase a home for two people without a wee notion of what they might appreciate in a new home?

Neither Fitz nor I had broached the subject of purchasing a home, let alone moving from the vibrancy of the city we both loved and craved. We had agreed that I would give up my room at the Barbizon Hotel and move into Fitz's Forest Hills apartment. True, it would be a tight squeeze until we decided on a more appropriate living arrangement, but that should have been our decision.

Not Larry Fitzgerald Senior's decision.

Fitz's mother, on the other hand, was as docile as a kitty when broached with the subject.

"Sweetheart," she had cooed to Fitz. "You know your father. He's only looking out for your best interests."

So there we were on that beautiful spring day, a day that Fitz and I should have been strolling arm in arm through Central Park, feeding the squirrels, and eating doughy, salted pretzels. Instead, we waited for the All Borough moving men to finish escorting our furniture and boxes into the moving van, which was parked outside of Fitz's apartment building.

My room at the Barbizon Hotel had been emptied weeks earlier. With tears in my eyes, I had hugged goodbye Mrs. Carlson, the receptionist. Had tightly squeezed Tony, the handsome Lobby Bar's bartender. Parker, the elevator operator, tipped his hat to me, and Clark, the front entrance security man, winked and wished me well for the future.

I was a nervous wreck all day, wondering what I had stumbled into by marrying Fitz and the rest of his family. My biggest concern about relocating to Colgate was the obstacle of commuting to Jet King's Corporate offices in Manhattan.

But Fitz's father had an answer for that too. "Lily," he had said, spreading his arms wide. "Honey, that's why you're both getting new cars."

Fitz and I were equally dumbfounded.

Larry Senior grinned, dangled two sets of keys from his fingers. "Kiddo," he said to Fitz, "these are yours. I know how much you like big cars, so the Lincoln is for you." He gently tossed me a key ring. "Lily, these are yours. You seem to like to move quickly, so . . ."

The key ring with the small flat emblem that said CHEVY CAMARO grabbed my breath in a bear hug. Deep down, I wanted to toss the keys right back into his smug face.

But . . . a Camaro? My dream car?

This entire restructuring of our lives—new home, new cars, new community—well, it was disarming. I did not want or need anyone to control my life. I had had enough of that playbook back in Georgia, after the disaster.

I could almost feel Savannah's sweet hands as they stroked mine to calm me. Could almost hear my mother's voice whispering, "Don't worry, sweetie. It will all work out. It always does."

On the day of our move, something strange happened.

The mailbox in the Forest Hills lobby remained full of dull white envelopes. Yes, I had forwarded our new address to the post office, but I had wanted to retrieve any errant mail that might have been stuffed into the mailbox that morning.

There was the usual junk mail: life insurance offers, an entry into the Publisher's Clearinghouse Sweepstakes, grocery store advertisements. But sitting atop all the junk mail was a blue envelope with a return address that read, DINER'S CLUB INTERNATIONAL.

Without a second thought, I flipped the seal of the envelope, predicting it to be another advertisement. Instead, I faced a credit card bill for twelve thousand twenty-five dollars.

With a double take, I saw that it was Fitz's name on the billing line. The hefty charge was from a company called Candy Land, USA.

I hurried back up to the apartment. The moving men were gone, and the rooms were empty. I felt a small pang of regret at having to leave behind the cozy apartment.

Fitz stood in the living room, hands in his pockets as he gazed out at the street below.

"Fitz?" I asked hesitantly. I held out the bill to him. "What is this?"

He did not turn around. "Fitz?"

"Yeah? Sorry, I was lost in thought." He turned, offered me a weak smile. I nodded, understood how bereft he felt about leaving his nest.

"This bill just came. It's for more than twelve thousand dollars. A charge from a place called Candy Land, USA. Do you know what this is for?"

He hesitated a moment too long, allowed his stunned eyes to give him away, darting from my face to the floor, to the buildings beyond the window. His body posture leaned slightly forward, and I could sense the wheels in his brain working to form some reasonable explanation.

Then, as if by magic, he straightened, smiled, took his hands out of his pockets.

"Geez," he said. "The account managers had this brilliant idea to send gift baskets to all of our clients to welcome in spring. A marketing ploy."

He chuckled. "We were so busy that day, I guess I forgot to use my business account. I'll have the bookkeeper take care of it right away."

It sounded reasonable. And I wanted to believe my husband.

Yet, a little niggling doubt persisted. I tried to shake it off. Assumed that my overactive imagination was, once again, going to town.

Later, when we finally arrived at Arlington Estates, the big All Boroughs moving van was waiting in front of our new home.

Larry remained in his car, just sitting there, staring at the garage doors. With my heart fluttering, I jumped from the Camaro, ran up to the front door, and used our new house keys to allow the moving men entry.

Peripherally, I noticed a blue Range Rover idling a few yards away. Then, abruptly, the car inched its way down the street and onto the driveway of the last house on the cul-de-sac. *Just a nosey neighbor*, I thought absently.

Quickly, I lit a cigarette and wished I had a vodka tonic to go along with it. As I sidestepped behind our house, I strolled along the path that led to the water's edge. A thin strip of sandy beach welcomed me as the sun began to set, and I hoped with everything I had in me that this house, this marriage would become all for which I had hoped. That the life I had left behind would remain a blot of faint memories. And just maybe, God had forgiven me my sins.

It was impossible to tell how long I stood there, rooted in place, staring at the sunset. Fifteen or twenty minutes had passed; the sun was already half hidden beneath the horizon. Slowly, I turned and walked back toward the front of the house.

Fitz remained in his car. He was talking on his newest toy—a wireless Motorola phone, which Fitzgerald Alloy Corp had purchased for him. It was the size of a brick and about as heavy.

If I was expected to be excited about our new home, then surely my new husband should be just as excited.

I rapped on the driver side window, smiled, and cocked my head toward our front door. Watched as Fitz hastily ended his call and exited the car.

"Let's go, baby," he gushed. "We've got a new home to break in!"

DUPLEX

May 13, 1980

VIOLA

McNulty's was noticeably quiet when Viola arrived for her shift on Tuesday. She busied herself taking inventory, restocked bottles that were soon to be empty, rewashed already cleaned glasses.

The loud ring of the phone startled her. She lifted the receiver. "McNulty's Bar and Grill. Viola speaking."

"Hi there. This is Cooper Harrington from Harrington and Associates."

"Cooper who?"

"Cooper Harrington. Viola? We met at McNulty's a few weeks ago?"

Viola's mind was blank.

"Do you remember me, Viola?" he pressed. "I gave you my business card?"

Why did his every sentence sound like a question?

But then she did remember. Cooper Harrington was a preppy-looking guy with a flat nose and a golden stick shoved way up his ass.

"If you've got a moment," he said, "I think I've found a place for you?"

Clarity finally dawned. Now, she remembered having mentioned to him that she might be interested in relocating to a larger apartment in a nicer neighborhood.

"Okay," she said warily.

"Something's come up, Viola. There's a couple who own a duplex on Central Park South. A very hip couple. They're about to leave on a yearlong sabbatical throughout Europe and Asia. They're looking for a responsible person or persons to sublet the unit while they're gone."

Viola's ears perked. This was interesting.

"When are they leaving on this sabbatical?"

"The first of next month. If you are interested—genuinely interested—we need to move very quickly. At least three other realtors are in on this one."

Viola grabbed a pencil and a piece of scrap paper from a counter drawer. She wrote down the address, discussed the sublet fee, and agreed to look at the duplex the following day.

A SWISS ACCOUNT

May 15, 1980

FITZ

For Fitz, the predawn morning crackled with energy. He felt it in his bones, felt its velocity spin wildly inside his brain. His body hummed with an untapped urgency that had his legs quivering like a newborn pony.

He had left the house in Colgate at 5:17 a.m. It was 11:17 a.m. in Switzerland.

Shadows of light barely breached the horizon. He sailed along the bridge's wide lanes, with hardly another vehicle in sight. Through the toll booth, then a race toward the Belt Parkway and into Brooklyn.

Lily had barely stirred when Fitz left their bed. He had thrown a Gap T-shirt over his head, tucked it into his jeans. A brief note was left on the kitchen island. "Problem at the factory. Call you later."

She would believe it. So gullible. Just like his mother.

When he arrived at the factory, he had a burst of uneasiness. He had never been to the factory so early in the morning, not without his father or the line workers already there, certainly not without the lights blazing and the machines humming.

But the factory floor was desolate and dark. His footsteps echoed throughout the empty aisles; the huge machines, like extinct dinosaurs, loomed far above his head. There was a momentary flux of fear, and he quickly shuffled along the factory floor. He took the stairs two at a time to the upper levels.

A creaking sound stopped him mid-stride.

No, he thought warily. *It's just me being paranoid.* He was one of only three people within the organization to possess the keys to the factory and the relevant alarm code sequences.

As the sun blazed through the windows, he scurried into his office, huffing and puffing as he locked the door, sat at his desk, and made a long-distance phone call to the International Bank of Switzerland.

Speaking to a somber-sounding man, he recited the US country code followed by his SWIFT code and then his nineteen-digit account number. Even to his own ears, all of it sounded extremely weird. Still, the international money wire transfer was processed successfully, and Fitz found himself breathing a hell of a lot easier.

As Fitz waited for the codes to travel along the cable lines, he recalled the first time he had moved money to his secret Swiss bank account. That time, he had carried the money on his person, with two nylon pouches strapped to his body—one on his hairy chest, the second strapped right above the waistband of his trousers. Another bundle of money had been carried on board in a ratty gym bag.

That first time, he had moved nearly two-hundred thousand dollars from a New York–based bank and into a private bank in the city of Bern, Switzerland. A place where transparency was an iron-clad curtain.

That time had been different. His responsibilities had been different. Run of the mill responsibilities: be a good son, a good cog in the wheel of his father's business.

But now, married to Lily, he found himself caught up in an additional tangle of responsibilities: a wife to take care of. Children to produce and raise.

His freedoms had been confiscated; marriage would no longer allow him the pleasure of coming, going, and traveling as he pleased, or whenever he pleased. International money wire transfers helped him to circumvent the problem.

His friend and business partner Damon Ross—known only to Viola as Jonathan Silver—had shared a gold mine of privileged information with them, useful information, which had converted itself into a virtual golden goose laying the proverbial golden eggs.

Fitz thought about the arrangement they had made with Viola: a minor cut of the profits, a pittance compared to what the two friends received.

Fitz was smart; he always thought one step ahead of everyone. With a collection of safety deposit boxes scattered throughout a handful of banks around the city, he knew he was safe. Everything he did, every move he made, was a secure investment in his future. He had safely hidden wads of cash from his wife and his parents and the IRS.

Sure, he had been extravagant in some of his spending sprees: butter-soft Italian leather jackets, matching Louis Vuitton luggage for him and Lily. A ridiculously expensive interior designer—nothing was too good or too expensive for Fitz.

Secrecy, however, well, that was hard to buy.

Should his marriage with Lily turn sour and end in divorce, she and her legal team would be in the dark regarding Fitz's Swiss accounts. A divorced wife would receive nothing from an account that—for all intent and purposes—did not exist.

Unfortunately, it had been necessary for him to jot on paper his Swiss bank account number and the SWIFT code—numbers too damned long and impossible to commit to memory—and he had hidden it, tucked it up inside the toe of an old shoe. A place Lily would never have reason to look.

By 8:00 a.m. the factory floor hummed with activity. Machines lurched to life, voices filled the cavernous spaces, telephones rang with urgency.

Fitz slipped from the back door, found his car, and rushed toward the Belt Parkway. He drove recklessly. Crossed from lane to lane, sped up, slowed down, sped up again. Often, he waited until the last possible moment to hit the brakes.

When he arrived back at Colgate and opened their garage doors, he saw that Lily's car was already gone. He sighed heavily. Another problem averted.

He hurried from the Lincoln, inserted his key into the interior steel door's lock. Went inside and heard the satisfying clunk of the metal door as it closed behind him.

The doorbell rang at 12:38, and Fitz rushed to open the door.

He found a skinny man with a Van Dyke beard shuffling his lean body on the front steps.

"Mr. Fitzgerald?" the man asked.

"Yup. That's me."

"I got a work order here to jackhammer into a cement floor in a closet?"

"Yes. Come on in."

Fitz led the man into the room he had allocated as his personal office space. Fitz thought the guy might be stoned. Could be a good thing. Could be a bad thing, he thought all at once.

Fitz showed the contractor into the room. Opened the closet door. The bearded man looked at the racks of clothing, looked at the built-in island with half a dozen deep drawers, the tall shelving unit that could easily hold two dozen pairs of shoes.

"So," the bearded man drawled. "What are you looking to accomplish?"

Fitz pointed to a corner of the closet. "I want you to dig out a spot right there," he said. "Two feet by two feet by five feet deep."

"Okay."

"And I want the rug to snug back into place just as it does now."

The bearded man chuckled. "Guess you're looking to hide something there?" he asked.

Fitz frowned. "Buddy, I'll pay you an extra hundred bucks if you stop asking questions."

A NAME ON A MAILBOX

June 22, 1980

VIOLA

It was late afternoon, yet McNulty's still hummed with brunch patrons who slurped Bloody Marys and mimosas—safe Sunday cocktails before heading back to a fresh week of work.

Viola glanced at the big Budweiser clock. Another fifty-five minutes until she would be on her way home.

On her way to her new home, the duplex on Central Park South. The fancy apartment building that boasted a concierge and an elevator that opened directly into her living room.

The rental agent had sealed the deal for her, and on the first of June, she had packed her clothes and personal items, had tucked them into boxes along with some of the pillows, curtains, and plants she had purchased to help convert Uncle Sammy's apartment into a warmer, friendlier, more lived-in space.

She paid the superintendent's son twenty-five bucks to load her stuff into his van and transport it to the duplex.

Three weeks later, she was as comfortable there as if she had lived in the space her entire life. And she was not sure how she would be able to leave it when the year's lease was up.

The sublet fee was exorbitant but doable because of their latest IPO investment. It had been a quick in-and-out transaction that allowed NYC Holdings, and Viola's personal account, to garner a tidy profit of 212 percent.

The return on that transaction had allowed her to pay the entire year's sublet fee up-front. For Viola, it felt as if she were living in New York for free.

So, why were her emotions seesawing as they were? *One day it's as if I'm on top of the world and the next day, I'm sputtering at the bottom of the ocean.*

A therapist would have helped her to realize her "ups" happened as she added money to her bank account and the "downs" happened when she wished she were going home to Fitz.

When Viola's shift ended, she decided to stay and have a beer before heading home. Chubs had set up a small grouping of round tables and chairs on the sidewalk so that patrons could enjoy a meal or a cocktail as they people watched.

She grabbed a Bud and her purse and settled at the last available outdoor table. It was early evening with a warm breeze blowing. If she closed her eyes, she could pretend she was at an outdoor bistro in Paris or Venice.

"Hey, Viola," a voice said.

She need not open her eyes to know who had spoken. The smooth voice was unmistakable.

"Hello, Fitz," she said. She opened her eyes and smiled at him. "How's married life treating you?"

"Not too badly. Mind if I sit for a minute?"

"Of course."

Fitz placed an elegant leather briefcase beside his chair. He looked like a high-priced lawyer, or a banker or the CEO of a major corporation.

"Heard you moved to a new place," he said.

"News travels fast."

"Yeah, it does." He lowered his voice. "It's very possible that Jonathan will not have another IPO for a while. He believes he's being closely watched at work. Which means things will cool down for a bit."

"Okay. I understand."

"Also," he whispered, "I'm not living nearby anymore, which will make it difficult for me to pass information to you here at McNulty's... when things do start to roll again."

She nodded wordlessly.

Deftly, Fitz lifted the briefcase to his knees, pulled out a business card. "I have a wireless phone now, too. A business phone. It will be easier for us to communicate when we start up again."

She looked down at the card. Saw Fitz's name, the wireless phone number. Sadness swept through her. Now, she would rarely, if ever, see Fitz.

"Vi?" he nudged her. "You okay?"

"Yeah," she chuckled. "Sorry, I was in la la land for a minute."

"Just remember that this number is for your eyes only." He handed her another card, turned it to the blank side. "I'll need your number too."

She quickly jotted her number in a neat, precise style. "For your eyes only?" she quipped.

"Of course."

Viola asked if he wanted a beer, but he said no, he had to get home. She took a sip of the Bud, her tongue gently wiping away a line of foam from her bottom lip. Normally, a move like that would have sent the boys into a frenzy.

But not Fitz. It hardly fazed him.

As he rose to leave, he kissed her cheek. She waited a few minutes, finished her beer, then hailed a taxi. It was a miserable ride to Central Park South. The taxi's stop-and-go motion made the beer slosh in her stomach. She hoped she would not throw up.

Finally, she got out of the vehicle and walked through her building's front door. She waved to Marco, the concierge, and although he smiled warmly, she could sense his hungry eyes devouring her.

At the mailboxes, she rummaged her purse for her keys, accidentally dropped them. She bent to retrieve them and when she straightened, she was staring at a name on a mailbox just three boxes from her own.

She squinted at the name: *FITZ*GERALD.

She shook her head in denial. No, no, no. Fitz and his wife could not be living in this building.

A first name was not listed. Not even a first initial. It could be anyone. If she opened a yellow pages directory, how many Fitzgerald listings might she find? Thirty? Fifty? Two hundred?

Viola took a deep breath, opened her own mailbox, pulled out a few envelopes, locked the box. Standing tall, she walked toward the concierge's desk.

Marco smiled as she approached. He was handsome, olive-skinned, and way too young for her. Those days were over.

"Good evening, Ms. Cordova," he said.

"Hello, Marco. May I ask you a question?"

"Yes, of course. How can I help you?"

She pointed toward the row of mailboxes. "There's a box there for someone named Fitzgerald. Do you know who it is?"

"No idea," Marco said as he shook his head. "A woman comes once a week to retrieve the mail. An older, fuddy-duddy-looking lady. But no deliveries for a Fitzgerald. Never had a guest ask to be buzzed upstairs. At least, not during my shift."

Viola stared into Marco's creamy brown eyes. "Can you tell me what apartment Fitzgerald is in?"

Marco grimaced. "I'm sorry, Ms. Cordova, but we have strict privacy policies, and I cannot give out that type of information."

"Oh, I'm so sorry. I don't know what I was thinking," she said as she waved goodbye to him. Once inside the elevator, she realized how ridiculous she must have sounded.

Of course, Fitz doesn't live here, she scolded herself.

CHANCE MEETING

June 26, 1980

JEFFREY

Every living thing in the world seemed to have awakened at the very same moment in time. Tulips and daffodils, chrysanthemums and roses, and the bright green sod of front lawns. A squirrel munched a mouthful of peanuts. A woman trotted along wearing a sleek running outfit as she pushed a child's stroller, the slap, slap of her feet against the sidewalk in perfect cadence with the rolling wheels of the stroller.

Seated in his Range Rover at the Park & Ride, Jeffrey enjoyed the sequence of it all. He patiently awaited the 7:55 Express bus that would take him to his job at the DMV. *Such a beautiful day,* he thought. It was also the third anniversary of his having survived the plane crash.

But three years changes a man. He had grown not only physically but mentally and emotionally. And for the first time in his life, he felt a renewed energy, a measure of confidence that had previously eluded him. He was certain that his visits to the Arlington Estates fitness center had aided his improvement. His body felt stronger, more capable. The weakness in his leg and hip had greatly improved, and his need for the anxiety medication was reduced.

He had forged a few friendships at the gym, other guys who spotted him when he bench-pressed. Guys he sometimes joined for a beer or a Yankees game.

And, if anyone asked about his scars, he answered as he always did: "A house fire in Greece. A jump from a second-story window."

But there was a guy who frequented the gym, a guy with pretty-boy looks and an attitude to match. A guy that was sometimes snarky with his fitness trainer. A guy that left Jeffrey with a bad, stinking feeling.

Startled, Jeffrey heard the rumble of the express bus approach. *Right on time,* he thought, as he hauled his backpack over his shoulder, exited his truck, and jogged to join the short line that had already formed to board the bus.

He walked halfway down the aisle, plopped down into a window seat. Shrugged off his backpack and placed it on the seat next to him. He pulled out *The Stand*, a Stephen King paperback, but did not open it.

Absently, he stared out of the smudged window. Last weekend, he had spent three days visiting his mother in Florida and had barely recognized her when she retrieved him from the airport.

"Mom," he had gushed. "Look at you! You look great!" His mother had lost more than twenty-five pounds and boasted a Floridian tan and a smartly styled haircut. She had joined a women's golf club, played canasta and pinocle and bingo, and frequented the early bird dinner specials with his two aunts.

This was what she needed all along, he thought somberly. *Something other than me to occupy her life.*

During one of those early bird dinner jaunts, his mother had asked, "What about you, Jeffrey? Have you been dating?"

He could not tell her about the woman whose picture he slept with at night. Instead, he lied.

"Yeah, Ma, I'm seeing someone. Nothing serious."

"She's not a gold digger, is she?"

He laughed. "No, Ma, she's not."

Jeffrey looked up as the bus driver announced, "7:55 Nonstop Express to New York City leaving in three minutes."

It was then that Jeffrey spotted the forest-green Chevy Camaro as it screeched into the Park & Ride lot. Watched as the car was haphazardly parked and as the black-haired woman with the smoky-gray eyes lurched from the car and ran to the waiting bus.

His eyes followed her onto the bus, followed her eyes as she searched out a seat on the full 7:55 Express. He saw her spot his backpack on the empty seat next to him and quickly hauled the pack to the floor.

Gratefully, she slumped into the seat next to him. "Thank you," she whispered breathlessly.

He nodded, afraid his voice might come out as a squeak instead of a real sound. He quickly flipped open the paperback. From the corner of his eye, he watched her run her fingers through her hair as if combing it. Watched as she took a very deep breath and sagged loosely into the seat.

Finally, he turned to her and smiled. "Guess you just made it," he said.

NONSTOP EXPRESS TO NYC

June 26, 1980

It was my fake birthday again, a day which notched up my age one rung higher on life's shaky step ladder. It was also the third anniversary of the accident. Each year was a rerun of that day, a jumble of miserable memories that slashed my heart in half. All night I had slept in fits and starts—hugged the bedsheets, then tossed them off. My body clung to Fitz's, then shrugged away to the farthest end of the bed.

When the alarm clock shattered my eyelids open, I looked awful. Scruffy, weary-eyed, clearly exhausted. The shower barely helped. Fitz had left a birthday card and a dozen peach-colored roses on the counter propped close to a note: *At the gym, then straight to work. See you tonight at La Vie En Rose. Happy Birthday.*

Terribly late, I grabbed my purse and keys and headed to the garage. As I rushed through the steel door, I heard its vibrating clunk as it closed behind me, and I was grateful that Fitz's father had thought to include it as an upgrade to our home. Having to fumble with keys while in a hurry would have simply added to my stress.

I drove to the Park & Ride, two quick miles away. Nestor, the gate guard, had informed me of the express bus service to the city, and I found the commute to be a much easier and less stressful trip. I could sit back, read a book or a newspaper, or simply nap.

But that morning, the clock ticked wickedly fast, and I knew I could not miss the 7:55 bus into Manhattan. A late arrival to a Jet King staff meeting would not be tolerated by my manager. My foot was heavy on the pedal, and I was so focused on getting to the bus on time that I could not appreciate the warm spring breeze, the sweet scent of freshly mowed lawns.

I literally could not stop to smell the roses.

The express bus idled at the curb as I careened into the lot and frantically slid into the first parking spot I saw. I locked the car and ran—cursed my high-heeled shoes—just as the driver began to close its doors.

“WAIT! WAIT! I shouted.

The bus halted, the doors jerked open, and I wobbled up the steep stairs. Paid my fare and swooped my eyes along the narrow aisle in search of an empty seat. Midway along, I watched as a man yanked a ratty backpack from the seat beside him.

Wearily, I slumped down into the seat. “Thank you,” I said breathlessly.

He nodded, opened his book as I combed my fingers through my hair, my purse snug in my lap.

I was about to close my eyes, hoping to grab an hour’s worth of a nap, just as my seat companion turned to me and smiled. “Guess you just made it,” he said.

“Yes,” I replied. “And in the nick of time.”

He tilted his head, scrunched his eyes. “You look awfully familiar,” he said.

“Just one of those faces, I guess.”

“No. Your face is anything but ‘one of those faces.’”

“That’s nice of you to say.” He turned his body toward me, reached out his hand, and said, “I’m Jeffrey. Jeffrey Kaye.”

I was desperate to close my eyes, but instead, I shook his hand and said, “I’m Lily.” Rarely did I offer my last name to strangers.

We were silent for a few moments. Until he said, "I know I've seen you somewhere recently. Hmm . . . I live at Arlington Estates. Maybe I've seen you at the supermarket or the post office?"

Surprised, I blurted, "I live at Arlington Estates too."

"Really? I live on the cul-de-sac on Bayview Terrace Road."

I stared at him, my mouth opening in a big O. "I live on Bayview Terrace too."

Now, it was his turn to stare. "Wow, that is a coincidence. I'm the last house at the end of the block."

So, he was the nosey neighbor I had spotted on the day our moving truck was being unloaded.

"We're in the second house," I offered. "My husband and me." It suddenly felt important to mention that I was married.

"Well, neighbor," he said genially, "I guess I'll see you around the neighborhood."

I nodded as he opened his paperback and I pretended to look out the window alongside him. *He's not bad looking. Nicely cropped beard, hair combed neatly to his collar. Clean shirt, but he could use a new backpack. A year or two younger than me...*

...I stopped mid-thought as the awful truth dawned: *Oh my God. On my real birthday, I will be thirty!*

My random thoughts were tangled, as if in a kaleidoscope of distorted colors. *Why am I thinking like this? I'm too focused on my age, my job, Fitz. Tonight's fake birthday dinner with Damon and his new girlfriend. God, Damon goes through women the way I go through cookies—way too fast.*

Before I knew it, we had reached Manhattan and the driver was calling out the first stop. Jeffrey said, "That's me," as he grabbed his backpack and threw it over his shoulder. I moved my legs so he could slip past me. "See you next time," I said.

As he slid past, I saw the strap of his backpack catch a bit of his collar and expose a layer of puffy pink skin along his neckline. A cluster of welts or scars? Tattoos?

I watched him exit the bus, saw him limp slightly as he walked toward Bleecker Street. Then the bus pulled away, and my thoughts shifted headlong to our office staff meeting and the balloons and birthday cake that surely awaited me.

That evening, a private car service drove me to the Garden City Hotel. Fitz waited for me at the entrance to La Vie En Rose, a ridiculously expensive French restaurant. As we entered, a tall man with shoe-polish black hair and a pencil-thin mustache—a caricature of a Parisian—rushed to greet us.

"Monsieur Fitzgerald," he exclaimed. "So nice to see you again. We have your preferred table ready. Madame, this way, please."

As I turned to follow the gentleman, I caught Fitz's grimace. We were led to a round table near a bank of tall windows. Lace napkins and crystal wine glasses adorned the table, along with a small vase of white tea roses.

After the man excused himself, I asked Fitz, "Why does he know you by name?"

Fitz's eyes danced around the room before he answered, "I entertain a lot of clients here, Lily." Then, his eyes shifted to the entrance doors. "Damon and his new girl have arrived," he said.

As Damon and his date approached us, I tabled our conversation. Damon reached down to kiss my cheek, handed me a small gift-wrapped box, and wished me a happy birthday.

"Lily," he said softly, "this is my girlfriend, Brenda."

Smiling, I shook her hand. "Nice to meet you, Brenda." *She's a big girl, taller than Damon. Plenty of curves, pretty face. I wonder how long this one will last.*

The box in my hand was from Tiffany's. I lifted the lid and inside found a lovely bracelet engraved with my name. "This is beautiful," I said. "Thank you so much."

Despite my fatigue, we enjoyed a lovely evening, and I found Brenda to be much sweeter and brighter than I had given her proper credit for being. Lavishly, we drank and dined and promised each other that we would do it again soon. My fake birthday dinner had turned out quite well.

Unexpectedly, Fitz's grandfather died the next day.

SOMETHING'S WRONG

September 30, 1980

Two hundred and twenty-nine days. That was how long I had been married to Fitz.

Ninety-five days since his grandfather had passed away.

Eighty days since I realized how abruptly Fitz's behavior had changed.

He was not mean or physically abusive, but flippancy substituted for charm, and arrogance had switched places with kindness. Marital decency had been left blowing in the wind. And none of it was a good look for Fitz.

It just happened—like a curtain lowering on the final act of a play.

At the time, I did not put two and two together. It started when Fitz insisted that he represent the family at his grandfather's funeral service in Sicily. Fitz's father was adamant that the business could not survive the upcoming quarterly crunch without him. A trip to Sicily to pay his respects to the old man was out of the question.

The situation did not fare well for Fitz's mother either—she was deathly afraid to fly, and not even her father's funeral could sway her to make the trip.

When Fitz volunteered, I was so proud of him. "I'll go with you," I offered eagerly.

"No, no, no. I am going to do this on my own. For my family. I want to be certain that the funeral and burial are done the right way." He took my hands in his, looked into my eyes. "Thank you, Lily, but I've got to do this on my own."

I did not argue, did not want to further upset Fitz. With my friend Domingo's help, we secured a seat for him on a Jet King private plane headed to Milan, with the pilot agreeing to make a second stop in Sicily.

Without Fitz in the house, I felt isolated and lonely. And I must admit, I was a little bit afraid. The vastness of the house with only me in it felt wrong. But after the first three nights alone, I began to unwind, placed my fears on a temporary hold.

I expected to hear from Fitz within a day or two, anxious to know if he was emotionally okay, but his phone call to me did not happen until five days later. Relieved to finally hear his voice, it helped to temper my annoyance with him.

"The funeral was very well attended," he told me sleepily. "My grandfather had a lot of friends."

"That's good to hear. How are you doing?"

He yawned in my ear. "I'm fine, Lily. But I'll need to stay in Sicily a little longer. To settle my grandfather's estate." I was surprised by the news. This had not been part of the plan.

Sicily and funeral: yes.

Extended stay: no.

Fitz did not sound sad or bereaved and had not asked about me or his parents, or how anyone else was coping with his grandfather's death.

"Can't your mother settle the estate via telephone?" I asked.

"No, she cannot. Her incompetence would screw up everything." Again, he yawned loudly, and I realized it was three in the morning in Sicily.

As I kept my temper in check, I asked, "When will you be back?"

He hesitated. "Twelfth of July. I'm booked on Pan Am into LaGuardia. I get in about four in the afternoon. Dad will send a car for me."

So, he had spoken with his father before speaking to me—his goddamn wife! Was it really going to take him another ten days to settle the estate? Hadn't there been a final will that spelled it all out?

Hopefully, my steely voice reflected my fury. "You should have let me book you on Jet King."

"Huh? Oh, I didn't want to bother you, babe. I got to go, okay? I'll call you in a few days. Love you." Abruptly, the call disconnected.

I stared at the phone in my hand, shook my head sadly. *Sometimes we want more than a person can give.* It was after Fitz's return home from Sicily that our life together began to fully unravel.

Fitz was cocky and self-absorbed and seemed to have removed himself from our marriage. Nights were spent at meetings, dinners, and charity events lasting longer than his days at home with me.

When I asked him why he did not include me in some of his business events, he smiled his charming smile and said, "Lily, you would be bored to tears. Trust me, listening to me talk about nuts and bolts and metal plates, well, I wouldn't wish that on my worst enemy."

Sex became an occasional robotic routine. All the sizzle that had made our lovemaking so passionate was gone. Fizzled out like a lit cigarette tossed into water. It was strikingly clear that during those infrequent intimate moments, Fitz was not in the bed with me at all—his body was simply going through the motions.

It was hard to admit, but our relationship was on the rocks.

And, I felt a fool for having bought into all the lies he had told me.

Every story. Every deceitful comment. And, if Fitz was smart, he should be worried of my reaction to his dishonesty.

ARROGANCE

October 31, 1980

FITZ

Halloween arrived as cold and damp as a grave. The sky was in a dark mood. Trees stood naked, their fallen leaves crushed beneath a squadron of sneakers and boots. Everyone appeared gloomy and sullen.

Everyone but Fitz.

He glowed with anticipation and happiness.

Since his grandfather's death, he had been reborn into a bigger, braver version of himself. No longer cowed by the old man's powers and threats, he was finally free of the travesty of being Don Arturo Domenici's grandson.

And now, all he wanted was to be free of his wife, for Lily was like a mama wolf—her claws always pointed and ready. She was a demon standing in the way of Fitz's pleasures.

The funeral had gone well, with plenty of old ladies crying quietly into their lace hankies. It made Fitz wonder if, in earlier years, the women had been his grandfather's bedtime companions. The three-day viewing—followed by a lengthy church service and a day-long reception—all of it was a huge, cumbersome bore.

Fitz thought it only reasonable that he reach out to his buddy Gregory Maison back in New York to arrange a visit to one of Sicily's special clubs.

His pal had come through, and Fitz was permitted into Piccolo's—a well-regarded exclusive club—and he was rewarded with a beautiful young Italian girl. A girl who knew her way around a man's body, a girl who understood the pleasures he sought.

The next afternoon, Fitz met with his grandfather's attorney in Calabria—a quick ferry ride from Taormina.

His grandfather's will was read by a ramrod, straight-backed attorney who wore a poor excuse for a wig and said aloud, "...And, to my grandson, Larry Fitzgerald Junior, I leave the monetary sum of three hundred thousand dollars."

Fitz swooned, thought he had heard wrong. He had not expected a bequeath from his grandfather's estate. But he couldn't very well reject the money, now, could he? He should thank Lily for this unexpected outcome—for his grandfather had fawned over her. But Fitz would not whisper a word of his grandfather's bequeath. He would keep the little nugget a secret.

In time, his parents would learn of his inheritance, but that was down the road and who knew what might happen by then.

As expected, his mother was to receive his grandfather's entire estate. Everything—including 57 percent of Fitzgerald Alloy Corp. Fitz knew this would irk his father until his dying day.

The following morning, he instructed his grandfather's attorney to wire his inheritance to his numbered Swiss bank account. Then he returned to Piccolo's and did not depart there until the day he was to return to New York.

STARTING OVER

November 5, 1980

FITZ

Five days after returning home from Sicily, Fitz met with Damon Ross at a seedy restaurant in Chinatown. Between bites of egg foo young, pork dumplings, and egg roll, they chatted amicably, caught up on events of the past few months.

Damon swallowed a gulp of tea, swiped a napkin across his lips. Wiped his hands, then looked at Fitz.

"You know," he said sheepishly. "I think I may have been a bit paranoid thinking that someone in my office was keeping a close eye on me. It's been months now and there are no red flags being waved."

"You're in the clear then?" Fitz asked.

"I think so. The brass has not called me to the top floor, and no one thinks there are shenanigans going on. My desk is intact, and I've just been handed two new major accounts."

Fitz smiled at his friend. "Does that mean we're back in business?"

"Hell, yeah," Damon replied. "There are two ripe companies—one is a big recognizable name that's ready to go public within the next few days. The other is a live start-up in the flavored iced tea market—this one, too, is ready to fire."

"That's great news. Let's get it done."

Damon slid a manila envelope across the table to his friend. Fitz opened it, read the two company names, and whistled softly.

To Fitz, the world looked brighter than a glowing star. Soon he would be drowning in money. Money that Lily would never be able to get her hands on.

After leaving the restaurant, Fitz phoned Lily.

"Hi," he said sweetly. "Sorry, but I have a late afternoon conference call with an Asian client and then dinner with the people from McBride."

"So, I shouldn't expect you until later tonight?"

"Yeah. I didn't want you to wait up."

"Okay. Thanks for letting me know."

"Right. Bye."

Fitz heard the weariness in Lily's voice. He felt a bit awful for causing this anxiety to her, knew she did not deserve it, but he was desperate to extricate himself from their marriage, from their faux life together. Stringing her along was cruel; he knew it. But he could no longer pretend to give a damn about her or their relationship.

Now, it was only a matter of time until he told Lily that he wanted a divorce.

Later that night, as every clock in New York ticked toward midnight, Fitz drove the company Cadillac from Candy Land in Garden City to McNulty's. He double-parked the car in front of a busted-up Volkswagen.

"I'll be right back," he said to his companion.

He strolled into McNulty's, eyes dancing back and forth between the tavern and the restaurant. He spied Viola. She was leaning across the bar, chatting up a good-looking guy—movie star good-looking.

He caught her eye and tilted his head toward the restrooms. He hurried to the back of the pub, waited for Viola to meet him in the hallway near the bathrooms.

"Well, look what the cat dragged in," she said.

"And hello to you too," Fitz replied with a wide grin.

"Do you have something for me?"

"I do." He slipped her the envelope. "Two big ones, Vi. Follow the directions and get it done, okay?"

"Of course, Fitz."

Abruptly, he about-faced and walked back through the pub and out of the front door.

A SIGHTING

November 5, 1980

VIOLA

Viola stared at Fitz's back as he strutted from McNulty's. Watched him circle to the driver's side of a big black Cadillac. Watched him slip into the car, lean over, and kiss someone in the passenger seat.

It was difficult to tell who was in the seat, for the lamplight above Fitz's car blurred the occupants. His wife, she mused. Abruptly, she turned away from the window.

She glanced at the big Budweiser clock behind her; another hour until her shift ended. She glanced at the envelope she had tucked underneath the bar, next to her purse. With two new IPO purchases in the works, she was relieved to know that her bank account would soon be replenished. There had been a drought since their last purchase, especially as she had continued to spend money as if she were the Shah of Iran. Expensive wines, name-brand jeans and tops, jewelry, and pricey perfumes.

But her gut was constantly twisted, all twirled up at the sight of Fitz. He had walked into McNulty's—so handsome in a white turtleneck beneath a black suit. Bitterly, she wondered if he and Lily were returing from a movie gala or the ballet or a ritzy nightclub.

She knew she should not be resentful. She had met a wonderful man, Josh Arlington, an architectural genius with a strong face, a perpetually happy smile, and merry green eyes. A real sweetheart. Someone her adoptive parents would have been happy for her to marry.

"Last call," echoed through the pub. Patrons began to settle tabs, gather pocketbooks and briefcases. Cheeks were kissed, hands were pumped, and the pub settled into quiet retreat.

Viola wiped the bar. Hand washed glasses and emptied the remaining lemons and limes and olives from their trays. Dumped garbage and removed it to the back alley.

Exhausted, she left the pub, hailed a cab to her duplex. She avoided small talk with the cabbie, wanting only a long soak in her deep tub. When she arrived at the apartment building, she paid the driver, said a quick hello to the night doorman, and walked through the entrance doors.

At the mailbox, she stopped to collect her mail. Said a brief good night to the evening concierge and waited for the elevator to take her up to her penthouse rental. An elegant looking woman, stylishly coiffed and dressed, entered the elevator with her. Each smiled at the other in a neighborly way.

The woman pressed the button for the tenth floor, and Viola counted the minutes until she would be out of her clothes and soaking in a lilac-scented bubble bath.

The elevator slowed to a stop at the tenth floor. The doors swished open as the woman turned and bid Viola a good night. From behind the woman's retreating body, Viola saw Fitz standing in front of the apartment door directly across from the elevator.

Shocked, she watched as he placed a key into the apartment door's lock.

A girl—young, fifteen, sixteen—stood beside him, her hand making circular motions on his ass. They were oblivious to the hovering elevator.

Viola blanched, her thoughts as jumbled as pieces to a difficult puzzle.

Finally, the elevator doors swished together, and Fitz and the girl disappeared.

Viola hurried into her apartment as the elevator doors closed silently behind her. She slumped to the floor, her back against the cool closed doors. A hollow, buzzing sound blared in her ears. Had she really seen what she thought she had seen? Was she jumping to conclusions? Was the girl his niece or a cousin?

No way, she scolded herself. The girl's hand caressing Fitz's ass was very real and very sensual.

She chewed her lower lip. *So, I wasn't overreacting when I saw the mailbox stenciled with the Fitzgerald name. Surely, Fitz and his wife do not live in the building. Fitz would have to be nuts to bring that young girl into his marital home.*

Viola rose from the floor, lit a cigarette. She walked a tight circle in the large living room.

Did Fitz's wife know about the girl?

Did she know about the apartment?

Was Fitz still married?

The following morning dawned as dimly as a fading lightbulb. Viola was groggy from lack of sleep. She chugged two cups of strong black coffee, showered and dressed. At exactly 10:01 a.m., she telephoned William Calhoun from the wireless phone, instructed him in the purchase of the first of their two new IPO deals.

Once the transaction was complete, Viola took her raincoat from a hall closet and rushed outside. The doorman whistled her a cab, and Viola hurried inside the bright yellow car just as the skies dumped buckets of rain onto the Manhattan streets.

Thirty-seven minutes later, she smiled like a cat that had just swallowed a fat mouse. At that very moment, she personally owned two exceptionally large stakes in the same IPO which William Calhoun had just purchased for NYC Holdings.

Stepping from the American Brokerage Associates building and back onto the rain-sloshed streets, she could not stop wondering, *was Fitz still married?*

A FRIENDSHIP BLOOMS

November 8, 1980

If it had not been for my burgeoning friendship with Jeffrey Kaye, I believe I would have been—for the second time in my life—the loneliest woman in America. Those days, Fitz was gone all the time. That week there had been a trade conference in Minneapolis, the week before, a two-night's stay at the corporate apartment in the city.

It was useless to argue with him about his extended absence from our relationship. Sadly, ours was not the marriage I had signed on for. I missed him, and, as ridiculous as it sounded, I still relished the infrequent moments of tenderness that Fitz threw my way. I was like a hungry dog with a gnawed-through bone.

You are wondering why I would put up with such nonsense. Why I had not flown the coop, as people say. I guess being alone and abandoned frightened me more than the disrespect shown to me by Fitz.

Do not for a moment think I was not ashamed of myself. What would Savannah think of the person I had become? What would my mother think? It was hard to answer those questions with my entire family missing in action.

My world felt safer with Fitz in it. He had become my substitute family, and if I left him, wouldn't I be abandoning the only family that remained in my life? I would have preferred not to be the one dangled out on high; I did not want to be the person whose emotions were juggled like sharp knives in a circus act.

Those types of cuts might be deadly.

Things would have played out differently if Lena Robinson was not in California shooting a pilot for a new TV series. Or, if Domingo had not become a first-time father. With my two closest friends busy with their own lives, I floundered. Though I socialized with a handful of coworkers, they were merely acquaintances, not anyone who might substitute for Lena or Domingo.

Certain friends were irreplaceable.

And so it was that Jeffrey Kaye comfortably filled my empty niche.

Every weekday morning since our first meeting on the 7:55 Express bus into the city, I boarded the crowded, bloated bus. And Jeffrey was always there, seated near a foggy window, his ratty backpack securing the seat next to him, saving it for me.

Initially, I could not have imagined we would have so much in common: both of us huge Stephen King fans, both addicted to baseball and action movies and silly game shows. In short order, we began to plan outings, activities that platonic friends might enjoy together. While Fitz spent long hours entertaining business clients, Jeffrey helped me to rearrange the furniture in our family room. In return, I taught him how to play chess.

Together we selected paint colors for my bathrooms and guest room; I helped him to balance his checkbook. During warm summer evenings when Fitz was on extended business trips to California or North Dakota or Massachusetts, I joined Jeffrey on his outdoor deck, sipping bourbon mixed with lemonade while we played game after game of gin rummy.

No, a romance did not brew between us. He never tried to kiss me, never got handsy. He was always polite and pleasant and incredibly easy to spend time with. We were just two people taking up space in each other's space.

So, it was on a warm summer Sunday that we attended a local arts and crafts show, followed by brunch at a lovely outdoor café in Port Washington. We sat on blue-striped chairs on a deck overlooking Manhasset Bay. Lazily, we watched as boats drifted past, chuckled at seagulls squabbling over scraps, and enjoyed oversized umbrella drinks.

It was likely that the warmth on my shoulders and the ease of the day allowed me to finally broach the subject of the marks on his neck.

"Those scars. How did you get them?" I asked softly, pointing to the exposed skin on his neck.

Jeffrey sighed, his eyes lingering on the glistening water. "It was a house fire in Greece."

My hands rose to my lips. "Oh my God, Jeffrey, how awful."

He shook his head. "Yeah. It was."

"What happened? I mean, how did you survive?"

He looked down at his hands. "I had the winning raffle ticket for a trip to the Greek Islands. Met a woman in Santorini and wound up extending my visit. We were in her house when the fire started. We jumped from a second-story window, but not before the flames had fireballed up the stairwell and into the bedroom."

Gently, I placed my hand over his.

"If I hadn't extended the trip," he whispered. "I might not have been in that fire in the first place."

With tender eyes, he looked at me. "I had a lot of injuries, Lily. Severe burns. A collapsed lung, broken hip, and pelvis. A piece of my earlobe melted. It took a long time to recover." He smiled, bravely said, "Now, I feel as good as new."

"I'm happy for you, Jeffrey. You were very brave." I sipped my drink, asked, "When did this happen?"

"Seventy-seven. End of June."

My heart crescendoed.

Jeffrey's accident had occurred about the same time as the accident in Atlanta. What if he had not extended his stay in Santorini? Would he have been on the ill-fated flight from Athens to Atlanta?

My head spun dizzily. Why was I riding such a ridiculous train of thought? Obviously, Jeffrey had not been on that Athens to Atlanta flight. He was here with me, at this lovely café, enjoying a pleasant afternoon.

He waved to our waiter, signaled for another round of drinks.

"What about you?" he asked, forcing me from my reverie. "You haven't spoken much about your life. Or your husband. Actually, I don't think I've ever seen him." Then he grinned wickedly. "He does exist, doesn't he?"

Playfully, I slapped at his arm. "Of course, he exists, silly. He just works a lot."

"Uh-huh. And what does he work at?"

"He's a marketing guru for his father's company, Fitzgerald Alloy Corp. They have contracts all over the country—the world in fact—so it keeps him pretty busy." Now it was my turn to avoid his gaze. "He travels an awful lot," I said sadly.

Jeffrey nodded. Offered me a tiny, knowing smile.

Soon after, we headed back to Arlington Estates—Jeffrey to his house, me to mine. Fitz did not return home until five days later.

Which was when the fireworks really began.

DANGEROUS CURVES AHEAD

November 10, 1980

FITZ

He had been too careless, too loose with his lips. Clearly he was at a major disadvantage because once he began drinking, he could not stop. It was for this very reason he allowed himself to take risky chances—chances that might easily put him behind bars for a long, long time.

In the light of day, Fitz knew he should not have taken the girl to the company's corporate apartment. Anyone could have seen them—a neighbor, a visiting guest, his father making an unexpected appearance. Thankfully, when they arrived at the building, the night concierge was in the restroom and the elevator stood there, empty and waiting. The girl, Lori—with the long blonde bangs that hung just above her sparkling blue eyes and those lips that gave incredible pleasure—had stumbled with him into the apartment.

If he had been seen with her, eyebrows would have been raised and questions would have been asked. The police might have been notified. And what position would that have put him in? He could never ask Damon to bail him out of a mess like this again.

Why had he allowed his sane self to lose an argument with his irresponsible self? He should not have coaxed her from Candy Land—

it was too risky. He had pushed his luck, and surely it would be only a matter of time before his luck ran out.

But the girl was so sweet, so young and gentle, her body as soft as a baby's blanket. This one was different.

Lethal. Addictive. He ached just thinking about her.

The following morning, as he shaved, Fitz had a jarring memory. A niggling, intrusive thought that made his razor slip from his hand and into the basin of soapy water.

He and Lori had been ridiculously drunk. Sloppy drunk—their words slurred; voices too loud, too abrasive—obnoxious enough for the cabbie to ask them to "shut up already!"

Fitz groggily recalled speaking of his secret Swiss bank account and the private investment opportunities, which were allowing him to become ridiculously wealthy.

He could barely look at himself in the bathroom mirror. Had Lori remembered his braggadocio words? Had the cabbie? And what if they had heard?

He berated himself for having dropped his guard in a moment of weakness. Now, he was forced to juggle counter-offensive measures to protect himself.

I need to have a stash of money at hand in case something ugly goes down, in case I need to run quickly. And my passport—I need that too. Taking chances is out of the question.

Fitz breathed deeply. Once, twice, three times. Finally, his heart slowed from the jack-rabbit rhythm clamoring in his chest. He allowed himself an uncompromised moment of thought, a chance to think things through slowly and carefully.

Obviously, a go-to, immediate escape plan was necessary—one that did not include Lily or anyone else. His goal was freedom and a place where he would be just another guy, off to a vacation getaway.

Slowly, his razor was lifted from the basin, cleansed under a stream of warm water. He dressed quickly, rushed from the master bedroom, and skipped down the stairway to the lower level. A quick glance revealed that Lily had already left the house.

He was grateful for her absence, grateful to keep his agitation close to his chest.

With his foot heavy on the gas pedal, he drove to Forest Hills, wound through a maze of streets until he found the Chase Manhattan Bank tucked mid-street on Yellowstone Boulevard. He found a metered parking spot, walked a short distance to the entrance.

Within minutes, Fitz was tucked inside a secluded room with a double-sized safe deposit box sitting unopened on the scarred desk. He waited two full minutes before reaching into the big box then quickly emptied its contents into a large duffel bag opened on his lap.

When he exited the bank, he clutched the bulging bag beneath his arm as if carrying a women's purse. He hurried to his car, drove back home to Colgate. His watch showed 3:52. Lily would not be home until after six. *Plenty of time for me to get this done,* he acknowledged.

When he arrived at Arlington Estates, he waved to Nestor as he passed through the big iron gates. He drove directly into their garage, cut the engine, and hoisted the heavy bag into the house. He hesitated one small step beyond the doorway, listened for the heavy clank of the steel door closing behind him.

Upstairs in his makeshift office, he removed his coat, draped it across the desk. He slid open the closet door, stepped into the huge walk-in closet. He shuffled past a neat row of his suits, another tidy row of white and blue shirts, a collection of ties. There were shelves filled with polo and golf shirts, at least a dozen pair of shoes.

At the back of the closet a thick overhead shelf held their matching his and her Louis Vuitton luggage. Beneath the shelf was a long pole filled with Lily's fancy dresses and his tuxedos. He pushed them all aside, squatted, and peered into the dark crevice as his hand searched out a tiny square of brown rug.

Gently, he tugged the loose remnant upwards and toward him. Crawling in closer, he stared into the deep hole that the contractor had dug there. He tried to shove the duffel bag into the hole, but the bag's width was too big and would not fit.

"Damn," he muttered aloud. He crawled out from the space, looked up, and saw their matching luggage pieces. He pulled down one of the smaller carry-on bags. It was not as wide as the duffel, but it was longer, sleeker. He unpacked the duffel, transferred the stacks of money into the carry-on luggage.

Back underneath he went, sweating as he maneuvered the luggage down into the hole. It fit perfectly. He tucked the loose piece of rug back into place and crawled out. He brushed dust from the knees of his trousers, closed the interior closet light, and hurried to take a shower.

Not that night, but soon enough, he would tell Lily he wanted a divorce.

SHOE PAPER

November 30, 1980

The discovery of a little slip of paper tucked inside one of Fitz's tasseled loafers was purely accidental. I had not been snooping through his closet, though Fitz would have you believe otherwise.

If I were to have snooped, it certainly would not have been to peek inside one of his rarely worn shoes. No, if I were that type of wife, I would have rummaged through his jacket and trouser pockets.

Wives did do that, didn't they?

If they were jealous types? Or had doubts of a spouse's fidelity?

But back to the shoe paper discovery:

The morning after Fitz arrived home from Minneapolis, we received an invitation from the Arlington Estates developer to attend a black-tie Christmas gala at the country club. I was eager to attend the event, eager to meet other community families.

My one black-tie event dress was in Fitz's closet alongside his tuxedo. I swung open the doors, spotted my emerald-green silk dress—the backless one, the one I would wear if I were ever to walk a red-carpet event. I draped it over my arm, slipped Fitz's tuxedo off its hanger. Both would be dropped at the dry cleaner that morning, a quick stop on my way to the Park & Ride.

As I turned with the clothing in hand, I noticed that a piece of our matching luggage was missing from its spot on the upper shelf. At first, I thought Fitz might have used it for his recent trip and had forgotten to return it to its spot.

"But, no," I said aloud. "He returned home with his big black duffel bag. I watched as he unpacked it."

I stepped backward, leaned up on my tippy toes to see if the luggage had been pushed further back on the shelf. As I craned my head back and stood up on my toes, my heeled shoe slipped, and I began to stumble backward. I grabbed at the shoe shelf in front of me. Shoes tumbled onto me, cluttered the floor around me, but the shelf had saved my fall.

I gathered the fallen shoes, put them back in place. As I lifted the last tasseled loafer, a tiny folded note slipped to the floor.

Curiously, I unfolded the spot of paper, read: *US 405 3172 8905 00426 1935 00*

What the hell was this? I turned the note over and saw another lengthy list of numbers scrawled: *CH 77-00741 010347853032*

At Fitz's desk, I searched for pen and paper. Copied the letters and numbers exactly as they appeared. I tucked the original paper back into the loafer, returned the shoe to its shelf. I grabbed my dress and the tuxedo and hurried out of the closet.

At Sky King, and only a few minutes past lunch, I was asked to accompany two dozen cartons of God-knew-what to Teterboro Airport. The shuttle ride allowed me time to mull over the slip of paper I found in Fitz's shoe earlier that morning. What did all those numbers mean? And why were they hidden in Fitz's shoe?

When we arrived at Teterboro, a dock worker unloaded the cartons, and the shuttle driver went to use the restroom. I walked into the employee break room, saw my friend Domingo Martinez sitting alone at a table, munching a sandwich.

"Hey there," I said as I plopped down next to him.

"Hi, Lily! Long time no see. How are you?"

"Good, good. How's the little guy doing?"

His face glowed. "He's simply perfect, Lily. And he's getting so big, so fast."

Domingo was such a good friend, a great pilot, and a devoted father.

We chatted a little longer, then I pulled my copy of Fitz's shoe paper from my pocket, handed it to him. "Domingo, do you have any idea what this jumble of numbers might mean?"

He tilted his head toward me. "Sure, they're numbers for an international wire transfer."

I stuttered, "...not sure I understand."

"Well, sometimes it's necessary to transfer money between countries. I have had to do it several times myself. Especially if I'm booked on a last-minute overseas run and I'm out of cash."

He spread the paper out onto the tabletop. Used his fingers to point to the numbers. "Okay, the two letters here, they represent our country code. Every country has its own code."

I nodded. He continued, "The first three numbers are a check number. The following eight numbers are the bank identifier number, and the last eleven numbers are a bank account number."

"And what about these?" I asked, turning over the slip of paper.

Aloud, I read: "CH 77-00762 011623852957."

Domingo looked me square in the eye. "Well, CH is the country code for Switzerland; the two numbers following are a check digit number, and the next five numbers are the bank identifier numbers. The remaining numbers are for a numbered Swiss bank account."

Numbly, I looked at him. "What is a numbered bank account?"

“Well,” he said quietly, “numbered accounts are not attached to the name of an individual or entity but to a number. The number replaces a name and appears wherever a name would usually appear in transaction records. And numbered accounts are expensive.”

“So,” I said shakily, “if I were to string all of this together, it might appear that Fitz wired money from an unknown New York bank account directly into a numbered account in Switzerland. Am I on the right track?”

Domingo sighed. “Yes, you are.”

Heavily, I sat back into the rigid plastic chair. Fitz was hiding money from me. But why? I had never asked him for anything. I regularly contributed to the running of our household. Why did this seem so shady?

The shuttle driver shouted from the hangar—the shuttle bus was returning to our corporate offices. I stood, pecked Domingo’s cheek, and whispered, “Thank you.”

Fitz sauntered home shortly before 8:00 p.m. I sat on the sofa, watched the lovely Vanna White flip letters on the big white board of Wheel of Fortune. I heard Fitz as he dropped his briefcase in the hallway, heard the heavy thump it made as it hit our maple wood floors.

I refused to look up as he went into the kitchen. Paid him no heed as he filled a glass with ice and poured two glugs of whiskey into it. He came into the living room and plopped heavily beside me.

“Vanna White, huh?” he asked.

I barely nodded, unable to look at him. During the turn of the next board letter, and as I stared directly at the television screen, I silently handed him my copy of his shoe paper note.

Immediately, he jumped up, spilled whiskey on his trousers and the sofa.

“Where the hell did you get this?” he roared.

“It fell out of a shoe in your closet,” I huffed.

He tensed beside me. "What the hell were you doing snooping in my closet?"

"I wasn't snooping, Fitz, I nearly fell and grabbed the shoe shelf to steady myself. The note fluttered out of a shoe."

He glared at me, and for a frightening moment, I feared he might strike me.

"You expect me to believe that?" he yelled. "Come on, Lily! You can do better than that!"

It was my turn to glare at him. "It's the truth," I said slowly. "I have no reason to lie."

He paced the room, ran his fingers through his hair.

"Okay," he growled. "If you must know, those are my father's personal international bank accounts. He does business around the globe, and it's easier for him to deposit funds into international accounts rather than to bring overseas currency into the States."

It was a reasonable answer. One I should have been able to believe.

And how I wanted to believe him.

But, I simply could not.

HOLIDAY MAGIC

December 13, 1980

On the second Saturday of December, Fitz insisted his assistance was needed at the office to help settle a client's overdue invoice. I believed his story as much as I believed in the tooth fairy.

With Fitz supposedly stuck in Brooklyn, I invited Jeffrey to accompany me on a Christmas shopping trip to Manhasset—a small hamlet on Long Island where those with money could easily squander it at very expensive luxury shops.

Strolling along the streets, we were thrust into full holiday mode, my arm tucked harmlessly into Jeffrey's. We smelled Christmas in the air, tasted the bite of frigid air in our mouths, our throats. Old-fashioned gas lamplights were decorated with red and green loops of garland, and shop windows were draped with snowy decorations. The tinkling sounds of holiday music accompanied us everywhere.

In one lovely shop, a woman as thin as Twiggy helped me to select a pair of gold cufflinks for Fitz. At another boutique, a Gucci leather handbag was chosen for Fitz's mother, and I settled on a handsome blue silk tie for my father-in-law.

For a few minutes, Jeffrey and I separated, which allowed me to search out a soft leather trifold wallet as his Christmas gift. This package I stowed in my large purse. We walked along the pretty town, window-shopped shoes and handbags and sweaters, admired fine art in a small gallery. A quaint pub enticed us inside where the smell of mulled wine and cinnamon permeated the air.

We settled into a wide booth. I ordered white wine; Jeffrey asked for a dark beer.

"So," I said. "Are you going to the holiday gala at the country club?"

"Yup. Are you?"

"Wouldn't miss it," I replied, without mentioning how unhappy Fitz was about attending the party.

"Why not?" I had argued. "We hardly go anywhere together. I want to attend, and I want you to attend with me. That's not too much to ask, is it?"

Fitz was afraid to say no to me, which immediately settled the matter.

As I stared into the yellowy liquid in my glass, I watched as Jeffrey's hand waved in front of my face. "Earth to Lily," he quipped.

I looked up and smiled. Tentatively I asked, "Will you be bringing someone to the party?"

"Yeah, I am," he sighed. "A girl from work. I hate going to these things alone."

I nodded, knew the feeling well. But deep down, I was jealous, an unusual twinge of envy circling me like a pack of hungry wolves. *I am a married woman,* I chastised myself. *I haven't a reason to feel this way.*

"Is she nice?" I asked, the question sounding ridiculous to my own ears.

He shrugged. "She's okay, I guess."

My mouth opened before my brain had a chance to digest his response. "So, have you been in a relationship before? Something serious?" My gaze was steady on his face.

Jeffrey fidgeted. "I was kind of a loner before the fire. Awkward. A bit of a mama's boy." He laughed self-consciously. "Never met my father, so I didn't have a man around to help me figure out the ropes of being a guy."

He took a long gulp of his beer. "After the accident and during recovery, I had an awful lot of time to think. And I realized that I had allowed my life to slip through my fingers. Not living your life is like already being dead."

His words hit a chord with me. They frightened me, sent chills up my arms. I nodded, not sure how to respond. It seemed eerily incredible that my life after the airline crash had so closely mirrored his life before the house fire.

My eyes locked onto his.

I tempered the urge to clutch his face in my hands, to flutter-kiss his eyelids and to settle my lips full on his mouth.

Luckily, the waitress arrived to take our lunch orders, and I quickly returned to being Jeffrey Kaye's friend.

A MOLE IDENTIFIED

December 16, 1980

With Christmas slightly more than a week away, the New York City Regional Office of the Securities and Exchange Commission was eerily quiet. Only a handful of scattered employees remained at their desks during the lull of the financial markets at that time of year.

Senior Examiner T. Howard Jenkins of the Division of Enforcement flipped through a thick folder of documents. He had memorized every sheet of paper inside the folder.

Jenkins was a big man, beefy. A man one might imagine should be wearing boxing trunks rather than his dark blue pinstriped suit. He was a follow-the-rules man, deplored cheating and scheming of any type. Not at school. Not at work. Certainly not on a mate.

His office mirrored every other bureaucratic office ever designed: windowless with ugly green walls and more filing cabinets than chairs. On the desk was a picture of his dog and a coffee mug painted I LOVE MY GOLDEN RETRIEVER.

His intercom buzzed; his secretary said, "Ms. Wilcox is here."

"Good. Please send her in."

The office door creaked open; a head popped around the door. "Come in," he said. "Have a seat."

A woman walked into the office shouldering a large tote and clutching a black and white composition notebook—the type kids in grammar school used to practice their penmanship skills. She sat in a chair opposite her boss.

"How are you, Brenda?" T. Howard Jenkins asked.

"Very good, sir."

"I'm anxious to hear your report."

Jenkins had placed Brenda Wilcox on assignment at Dawson-Brown specifically to identify the person or persons leaking inside information to outside individuals for personal gain.

Brenda smiled, folded her hands in her lap. "Sir, I am happy to tell you that our plan has produced some interesting and merited activity. Damon Ross believes I have a romantic interest in him, and he also believes that I am CEO Karl Brown's executive secretary. He also believes that I am privy to everything that goes down at Dawson-Brown."

It was Jenkins' turn to smile. "Go on."

"On one afternoon during lunch, I innocently mentioned specific information about the upcoming Euro-Medical Supplies IPO. Sure enough, there was an exceedingly large purchase of their IPO at the opening bell. On our second date, I let it slip about Calypso Entertainment, and sure enough—same scenario—exceedingly large purchase of that IPO at the opening bell."

"By whom?"

Brenda flipped through her notebook. "A company based in Delaware. NYC Holdings, LLC." She looked up at T. Howard Jenkins. "As you know sir, these Delaware corporations are usually formed as dummy companies to move or launder money and escape the tax man. Filing through a Delaware registered agent affords the highest level of confidentiality as they do not obtain or store information regarding members and managers. So, a bit of a dead end there."

"Okay. Anything else?"

"Yes. We dined with his best friend Fitz. A last name was not revealed to me. I also met his wife, Lily."

"Do we know where this Fitz is employed?"

"It's very vague, sir. From the conversation, I gathered that he is a marketing executive for a nuts and bolts company. The wife, however, mentioned a job at Sky King, a private executive travel firm."

Brenda Wilcox scanned her finger further down the page. "A call to the company revealed her to be Lily Marz. With a little digging I learned that she was married but, had not yet legally changed her name. The personnel manager was tight-lipped. Sorry, I couldn't dig up any more without a subpoena."

"Good work, Brenda," Jenkins said. "Now, does the name Viola Cordova ring a bell?"

Brenda shook her head. "Haven't heard it before."

"Would you be surprised to know that Viola Cordova has also made high-volume trades in the very same IPOs that were made by NYC Holdings?"

"Well, that is surprising."

T. Howard Jenkins sat back in his chair, folded his hands behind his head, and smiled. He already knew that Viola Cordova and others were involved in her nefarious trading scheme. Her activities had come to his attention from the blue sheets—internal reports of high-volume trades prior to the tendering of certain initial public offerings. Highly suspicious trades related to corporate takeovers that manipulated market prices.

"Here's a little coincidence to chew on," Jenkins said. "NYC Holdings does indeed have a Delaware registered agent. And although we cannot trace the members and managers of the company, the registered agent is required to maintain the firm's contact person's information."

He leaned forward in his seat. Gave Brenda Wilcox a big, wide, happy smile. "Viola Cordova is the contact person for NYC Holdings, LLC."

"Wow," Brenda whispered. "So, this woman is making high-volume trades for both the Delaware company and for herself personally. Which means that with Dawson-Brown as the banking firm of record for the suspect IPOs, it's clear that someone on the inside is feeding the information to Cordova."

"That's right," Jenkins said. "If Damon Ross is the mole sharing the information with Cordova, it is highly possible that both have benefited to the tune of hundreds of thousands—perhaps millions—of dollars."

"We'll need subpoenas," Brenda said as she scribbled into her notebook. "One for the broker for NYC Holdings and one for Viola Cordova's personal broker. We'll need trading records, monthly account statements, broker documents, order tickets."

"Banking records too," Jenkins replied.

He did not tell Brenda Wilcox that the folks at Dawson-Brown had had their suspicions about Damon Ross for quite some time and that they had already supplied him with Damon's telephone and calendar records and his Rolodex.

It was only a matter of time now until they formally identified the mole.

Senior Examiner T. Howard Jenkins could not wait to see both Damon Ross and Viola Cordova in handcuffs.

CHRISTMAS GALA

December 23, 1980

If you had been a fly on the wall during the night of the Christmas gala, you would have seen firsthand how the evening played out.

Was I gorgeous in my backless silk green dress that hugged all the right places? You bet.

Was my hair as dark as the night and my eyes as opaque as a plume of cigarette smoke? Absolutely.

And Fitz? Well, he looked like he belonged on the cover of *GQ* magazine. As I helped him to straighten his bowtie, he caught my reflection in the vanity mirror. "I invited Damon and Brenda as our guests tonight."

Surprised, I responded, "Why would you do that, Fitz? This is a party for the homeowners, not strangers to our community."

"Oh please, Lily," he snickered. "Tonight will be one long, boring, drawn-out affair. At least Damon and Brenda will help to liven it up."

I could have commented, could have replied with a snarky remark. But why ruin the night before it began?

It was a quick four-minute ride to the country club, where red-vested valets scurried to open doors and park cars.

It was three short steps up to the double doors that looked as if they might be the entranceway to a Scottish castle. Inside the club's lobby, I was wowed by the white and black Italian marble floors that led us into the grand ballroom. Paneled walls of deep red mahogany helped to softly cushion the room and above us, elegant chandeliers cast a perfect glow.

People were already on the dance floor as a deejay spun a lively disco tune. Russian vodka flowed from an ice sculpture carved into a model of the Arlington Estates entry gates. The room was filled with guests that ranged from the wealthy to the very, very wealthy.

It felt as if we were floating through the room. We moved among the many people, unsure if their merry laughter and big smiles were real or phony. We spotted an empty high-top table midway between the dance floor and the dinner tables. It was difficult not to notice how appreciatively Fitz was being eyed.

Silently, I watched as Damon and Brenda walked toward us, Brenda looking oddly uncomfortable. She wore a basic black knee-length dress and a string of pearls. All very conservative looking and nothing like the woman who had partied with us on other occasions. A white-gloved attendant approached and offered us flutes of champagne.

We accepted and spent several minutes chatting about the weather and if we would be lucky to have a white Christmas that year.

A gentle tap on my shoulder made me turn to see Jeffrey standing behind me, all smiles and looking boyishly handsome in his tuxedo. His date, Sally, was a mousy little thing, and I was sure that she would have been more comfortable driving a tractor on a farm somewhere in the Great Plains, rather than here in the elegant ballroom.

Introductions were made. Fitz squinted at Jeffrey and asked bluntly, "Do I know you from somewhere?"

Jeffrey smiled. "I don't think so. Nice to meet you."

To Fitz, I said, "Jeffrey lives at the end of our cul-de-sac. Maybe you've seen him in the neighborhood?"

Fitz shrugged his shoulders and turned to speak to Damon, leaving me feeling appalled and embarrassed by his blatant rudeness.

It was then that the night took a very bizarre turn.

Mid-sentence, Fitz halted his conversation with Damon. His eyes lasered onto someone across the room. Following his gaze, I landed on a woman, blonde, wrapped in an icy blue dress that sashayed with her like a second skin. Diamonds—on her ears and wrapped about her neck—sparkled brighter than the chandeliers. Dozens of pairs of eyes were distracted by her entrance. She hung onto the arm of a man with a rash of red hair styled in a nearly forgotten fifties pompadour.

I nudged Fitz. "You're staring at her. Do you know her?"

He gulped the last of his champagne, smiled. "Yeah, she's a bartender at a pub I once frequented."

"She's a knockout," I murmured.

"Yeah, if you go for that type."

Fitz poked Damon's arm, said, "Come on, let's get some martinis for the girls." I hated when he referred to us as "girls." *Why was he acting like such an ass tonight?*

"Be back in a minute," he said to me.

Brenda, still looking uncomfortable, excused herself to make a phone call. A moment later, Jeffrey's date whispered to him that she needed to use the restroom.

Jeffrey's eyes were leveled on the woman in the icy blue dress. "Do you know her, too?" I asked sarcastically.

"Actually, yes. She lived across the hall from me for a year or two."

In disbelief, I quickly swiveled my head toward the bar, where I watched as Fitz and Damon approached the woman; watched as Fitz took her elbow and steered her away from the crowded bar. The woman smiled at her red-haired escort, mouthed something to him, then disappeared behind a wall with both Fitz and Damon. *Where were they going? And why?*

My eyes lingered on the empty spot where they had been a second ago. When I turned back to our high-top, I saw that a man—someone neither Jeffrey nor I knew—had joined us. His tuxedo screamed "off the rack from Sears."

Rocking on his feet, he slurred, "Hello. I'm Victor Des Moines. Just like the city." He was a compact man with a graying goatee and John Lennon specs.

"Hello," Jeffrey and I murmured.

Happily, he said, "Randolph Arlington developed this project. Did you know that his son Josh was the architect?"

Before we could reply, he continued, "And River Source Construction built it." He burped loudly, letting loose a stench of stale tobacco and whiskey. Then, he thumped his chest and said, "I was the assistant foreman on the project."

"Well, it certainly is a beautiful development," I said politely. *Where the hell were Fitz and Damon?*

Victor Des Moines nodded his head vigorously, spun to grab two flutes of champagne from a passing waiter. He swallowed one glassful quickly, placed the empty flute in front of me like a gift.

"Yup," he slurred, "real pretty." He downed the second glass of champagne. "What section do you folks live at?" he asked as he swayed on his feet.

"Tranquility Bay," I responded.

"Ohhhh," he said, drawing out the word. "That was the last section we completed."

He laughed loudly, removed his Lennon specs. "Yeah, we had a little problem with that section," he drawled. "But we got it done in time."

His bloodshot eyes were at half-mast as Jeffrey nudged him. "What do you mean, a little problem?"

Des Moines' eyes somersaulted into a faraway look as his feet shifted left to right and left to right, repeatedly. It was nerve racking.

"Yeah," he said as he fumbled a cigarette from his trousers. "By the time we got to Tranquility Bay, we were way behind schedule. So, we had to rush the process."

He leaned in closer, the stench of his foul breath reaching all the way across the table. He whispered, "The way I understand it, the project manager paid off some of the building inspectors to be sure that every home passed inspection. There was a foundation problem. Too much sand. Not properly reinforced. Something like that."

He hiccupped, scrunched his face. "Well, wait a minute. That may have been another project. One out in Staten Island. But I'm sure you folks are safe in your homes."

And then, Victor Des Moines departed our table as if he were not in the middle of a one-way conversation. Stunned, I looked at Jeffrey. "Do you think we should be worried?"

"No way. I wouldn't pay much attention to a guy as drunk as he is."

Fitz and Damon returned to our table, their hands empty of the purported martinis they were in search of. Brenda and Sally soon followed. I gave Fitz one of my looks—the one that clearly said, "Where the hell have you been, and what have you been doing?"

He ignored me, just as the deejay's voice implored everyone to find their dinner seats. I struggled to remain calm, but anger pulsed under my skin like a bad rock song. I wanted to strangle Fitz and to seriously pummel Victor Des Moines for having left me with such an uneasy feeling.

We sat for dinner, Fitz to my left and Jeffrey to my right.

There was caviar and chilled lobster claws, silky French cheeses folded into miniature pastry puffs, topped with dollops of fig jam; platters filled with petite filet mignons, crab-stuffed sole and orange-glazed duck legs.

I barely ate a bite.

Neither did the woman in the icy blue dress who stared at me from the opposite table.

PARTY FAVORS

December 23, 1980

Viola Cordova had sailed into the holiday gala as if she were royalty, and the moment Fitz spotted her, he felt an accelerated thump in his chest. It was not caused by how stunning she looked—draped in an icy blue dress that left little to the imagination and a choker of diamonds twinkling brighter than the North Star.

No. It was the surprise of seeing her at the Arlington Estates Country Club. Had Damon spotted her too?

Of course, Damon had seen her. "What the hell is she doing here?" he whispered to Fitz.

"No idea. But it's not good for any of us."

Fitz eyed Viola's escort and knew he had to get to her before she opened her mouth and revealed inappropriate information about their relationship. She might easily allow words and sentences to leave a trail of suspicion pointed squarely at them.

Aloud he said, "Come on, Damon. Let's get these girls some martinis."

Fitz knew Lily's eyes would follow him like a laser beam. He didn't care. All that mattered was the surety that Viola would keep her cool and pretend they were all simply acquaintances and nothing more.

Damon reached her first, said hello, and shook her date's hand. Fitz followed on his heels and asked if they could have a word with her privately. "We just want to share news about a mutual acquaintance," he said to her escort.

Fitz took her elbow and gently steered her toward a back room, which Nestor, the gate guard, had recently shown him.

Viola allowed Fitz to steer her away, his scent as intense as the fire burning within her. They entered a small room used to store excess dinner plates, crystal stemware, and elegant silverware. At one point in her life, Viola may have been tempted to hide a few of the pieces in her purse or under her blouse.

"How are you Fitz?" she asked. "And you, Jonathan? It's been a while, fellas." With a slight tremble in her hand, she reached into her clutch for a cigarette, lit it with a slim gold lighter embossed with her initials.

"What are you doing here, Viola?" Fitz asked.

"I'm attending a party. Same as you."

"This is a private event. How did you know we'd be here?"

"Oh please," she sighed. "You think I'm here to spy on you?"

"Only reason we can think of," Damon said. *Thank God she still thinks I'm Jonathan Silver.*

"You two are morons," she laughed. "Josh Arlington is the architect of this ridiculously expensive property, and he invited me along. That's the whole story."

She took a long pull of her cigarette, exhaled loudly. "Why are you two acting like you're spooked?"

Fitz glanced around, set his eyes on hers. "Just making sure you don't leak our special relationship to anyone here tonight. Especially to your boyfriend."

Viola stubbed the cigarette out beneath her silver pumps. "Do you really think I'm that stupid? If you do, then you have a bigger problem than you assumed."

Brenda Wilcox watched as Damon and Fitz guided the woman in the icy blue dress away from the bar crowd. They were all acquainted, for the woman willingly followed them from the room. If so, was this the break she had been waiting for?

Earlier, when she had entered the ballroom and plucked her dinner placard from a table—monitored by two women who looked to have been alive since the Civil War—Brenda was momentarily stunned to see the name ***VIOLA* CORDOVA** neatly printed on a table card.

It was the name her boss had tossed out to her during their last meeting.

Was it possible the woman in the icy blue dress was Viola Cordova and that she and Damon Ross were in cahoots together? Was this proof that Damon was the mole? It seemed more than a reasonable possibility. And if he was the mole, how did Damon's friend Fitz and his wife fit into the picture?

Seated beside Lily, Jeffrey gulped back two shots of Russian vodka. The night had turned into a fiasco instead of a party. First, Viola had shown up—and seeing her had felt like an electrical shock sprinting up his body.

Having kept his distance from Viola had proven to be a helpful solution to exorcise her from his fantasies. Jeffrey knew Viola should have been off his radar screen, but he had learned that the hard way. The way a heart breaks and moans in despair if the real thing does not wind up in your arms at night.

Second, his date, Sally, was clearly miserable. From the start, she was uncomfortable. A headache had been feigned, a brief apology offered, and an abrupt disappearance followed.

I should have known better, he thought. *Was I trying to make Lily jealous?*

He hated himself for thinking that way. Lily was a married woman—an unhappily married woman—and he was a single guy who had no business hoping that their friendship might bud into romance.

He slugged another shot of vodka. If he really wanted to be honest with himself, he would say it aloud: “I think I’m in love with Lily.”

He pinched himself hard, swiveled his head. *I did not say that out loud, did I?*

Thank God he had not.

Across the dinner table, Jeffrey watched as the guy—whatever his name was—tried to nuzzle his date’s neck, and he nearly laughed aloud as she deftly nudged him away. Next to him, Lily was poised at her husband’s ear. Her body language said it all: she was furious with him.

After another swig of vodka, Jeffrey remembered the guy who had shimmied up to their table—uninvited, no less—and had implied there might be a problem with their homes. Too much sand. Not properly reinforced.

Couldn’t be, Jeffrey thought drunkenly. He and his realtor had done their homework before purchasing the house on the cul-de-sac. Solid architect, five-star real estate developer. Top-notch construction firm.

“You just can’t trust a guy that drunk,” he reminded himself.

AFTER-PARTY REGRETS

December 24, 1980

Lies and dishonesty hovered everywhere, buried deep in the souls of the deceitful, and wavering among those still too ignorant to comprehend the writing on the wall.

As we left the country club, snow fell and left behind a white trail that glowed beneath the inky sky. My anger did not allow me to appreciate the sight.

Once home, I promptly stomped up the stairs to our bedroom—a room the size of a fancy hotel suite. My green dress was peeled off. Stockings and shoes quickly followed.

"I don't understand why you're so upset," Fitz said as he entered the room. He undid his tie, tossed it onto a chair.

"Then let me explain it for you," I huffed. "You were rude. Belligerent. You were offensive. Does that spell it out for you?"

Fitz pulled off his jacket, pulled down his trousers, stood there in his starched tuxedo shirt and his boxers.

"Once again, you're overreacting, Lily."

"Oh, and was I overreacting when you and Damon lured that woman out of the ballroom? Who the hell is she anyway?"

"It's really none of your business, Lily," Fitz huffed.

"I'm your goddamn wife! It is my business!"

He dropped into the chair on which the tie lay, smothered it beneath him. Ran his hands through his hair as his face crumpled into itself. "If you must know, she's been in love with me for years."

My mouth hung open. "In love with you?"

Fitz jumped up, upset the perfume tray on my dresser. Bottles fell and clattered; a strong scent of alcohol and flowers filled the room, the stench nauseating.

"Yes!" he yelled loudly. "Her name's Viola, and she's a bartender at a pub in the city. A place that Damon and I regularly frequented. We haven't been there in a long time, specifically to avoid her. She refused to back off, though I told her numerous times I was not interested in her that way. That I was already in love with someone else."

He walked to one of the long bedroom windows. Pushed the huge curtain back. Snowflakes fell heavier and began to create small white mountains on the streets below.

I stared at Fitz as he hunched beside the window.

"Why did you and Damon walk her out of the ballroom tonight?" I insisted. "I have a right to know."

When Fitz finally turned, his beautiful face gazed at me. Softly he said, "We wanted to warn her not to create a scene tonight. That she was to keep her distance. To stay away from me and you. To stay away from everyone at our table. That's why, Lily."

Slowly, the tension in my shoulders began to relax.

"Any other surprises I should be prepared for?" I mumbled.

"No," he said as he took me in his arms and kissed my cheeks, my eyes, my neck.

I guess I wasn't the only one good at keeping secrets.

REIGNITED

February 21, 1981

As the long gray days of winter kept us all captive, I felt certain my marriage to Fitz was on far stabler ground than it had been before Christmas. Due to an abundance of inclement weather and oft-canceled airline flights, his business trips were severely restricted.

An unexpected and harsh winter storm had dumped more than two feet of snow on New York's suburbs. Plows did not come through to clear the streets; the transit system was out of commission, and the 7:55 express bus from Colgate to Manhattan was temporarily halted.

Have I mentioned how bitterly cold it was? I knew then how the Norwegians felt during their long drawn-out winters. It seemed like forever before we heard a bird sing or a sprout of green to push up through the frozen ground.

But for me, the storm felt like a lifesaver, having unexpectedly occurred on our first-year wedding anniversary. Confined together in our home, it seemed the crack in our marriage was beginning to seal.

We spent the better part of a week sipping wine and munching cheese; one evening Fitz prepared an elegant roast. I was on breakfast duty: pancakes, waffles, decadent French toast dripping with thick, sweet strawberry sauce. It was a wonder we did not gain ten pounds during that week.

Love had found its way home to us again.

Or so I thought.

TRYST AND SHOUT

June 6, 1981

I never realized how quickly time evaporates.

So it was that in 1981, a brutally harsh winter dissolved into a lovely spring, which then somersaulted closer to summer. It was a lovely June day; purple crocuses dotted our front lawn, trees flaunted shiny new leaves, the air was exquisitely warm as it caressed my exposed skin.

Fitz was away, had left for Cincinnati on Thursday afternoon—a terribly important meeting with a potential client with a war chest full of cash. The trip would be short, he informed me. "I'll be back Monday night. Dad will be on the trip, too, so it has to remain brief, or my mother will have a hemorrhage."

At the time, I felt perfectly contented with my new life, my job, the reconnection with Fitz, and my friendship with Jeffrey. It was due to this incredibly good frame of mind that I invited Jeffrey Kaye to lunch with me at La Vie En Rose at the Garden City Hotel.

Together, we rode there in his boxy Range Rover; arrived too early for our reservation. The maître-d' suggested we wait in the hotel's lobby, and he would gladly retrieve us when our table was available.

I sat on an uncomfortable green sofa bordered with equally uncomfortable pillows. Jeffrey sat across from me on the only seat remaining and began a conversation with the man seated next to him.

Everything was fine—until the door to the restaurant swung open. I thought it might be the maitre-d' coming to retrieve us.

Instead, what I saw had my throat locking, my face flushing and all of the saliva in my mouth evaporating.

There was Fitz, walking from the restaurant's open door. Graciously, he held the door open for a much younger woman who followed him out.

No! Not a young woman. A girl! A young girl! With blonde hair and long bangs. How can he be here if he's in Cincinnati? I wondered stupidly.

Paralyzed, I watched as he and the girl walked a few brisk steps toward the hotel's elevator bank.

Watched them smile tenderly to each other, two lovebirds entering the lobby elevator.

It seemed impossible not to scream as the doors slowly slid together and Fitz turned to the girl, placed his hands on her neck, and pulled her close for a full, sensuous kiss.

Obviously, Jeffrey and I did not enjoy a leisurely lunch at La Vie En Rose that day.

Instead, we drove back to Arlington Estates. I sobbed and wondered aloud what I had done to deserve this.

"Hey," Jeffrey said softly. "Don't go there, Lily. You are not the cause of his actions."

We remained silent until we arrived at my house, and without asking, Jeffrey accompanied me inside. We sat on the sofa, kept our distance. Stunned, I was unable to speak. Somewhere in the house, a clock ticked. From an open window, birds sang to each other.

"My life as I know it is over," I mumbled.

"Maybe not," Jeffrey kindly offered.

"It's over! I will never forgive him for this." I felt dead inside. Useless, unwanted. Discarded, as if with a wave of a hand, I had been left with only the lingering memory of my husband's mouth on another's lips.

Several quiet minutes followed, until Jeffrey softly asked, "What will you do?"

My nose dripped, but I didn't care. All I could think of was Fitz kissing that girl. *The bastard had lied to me! Cincinnati was a joke, and the laugh was at my expense. Had he been with that girl since Thursday? Was he coming home to me on Monday to tell me how much he missed me?*

"Lily, are you okay?" Jeffrey asked, stretching to touch my hand.

Tears fell to my lap as I shook my head. "I don't think I'll ever be okay again." *How could I be okay after Fitz had just snapped me in half?*

"I'll ask for a divorce. He wouldn't dare to object."

"Whatever your decision, I'll be here for you," Jeffrey said.

He rose, retrieved his keys from a side table. "If you need me, or if you just want to talk, call me. Or come over. Whatever you want."

After Jeffrey left, I remained on the couch, the house silent as a cemetery save for the ticking clock. Dusk settled, ebbed into night. When my stomach rumbled loudly, I made a slice of toast, turned on the television.

I carried the toast and a glass of ginger ale into the living room. Channel Two News was airing—the eleven o'clock newscaster was a very pretty, earnest, green-eyed beauty with dimples and a mass of red hair.

At first, I hardly digested her words. Chaos in the White House. A multi-state rally against gun violence. And then, abruptly, her tone changed.

"We've just received breaking news from the National Weather Bureau, indicating that a tropical storm—now in the center of the Atlantic Ocean—is quickly gaining momentum and is headed directly toward the East Coast."

She touched the headpiece secured in her ear. "We've been told this is a fast-moving front that may unleash hurricane-like winds and heavier than usual rainfall. Coastal flooding may occur, causing beach erosion and property damage."

The pretty newscaster looked up from her notes and offered a shy, intimate smile. "Please stay tuned to Channel Two News Live at 6:00 a.m. with Mark Connor for weather updates regarding this potentially dangerous storm."

CONFRONTATION

June 8, 1981

Monday morning at Jet King was a nightmare. Flights were added and canceled, schedules were in turmoil, important files had been misplaced. It was obvious to everyone that I was a mess: eyes shrunken to the size of peas, my nose as clogged as if cotton balls had been stuffed up each nostril.

Yet, I managed to make it through the day. Seems I always found a way to make it through the day, regardless of how terrible the experience.

And I had had plenty of practice with terrible experiences.

Wound too tightly to eat, I skipped dinner, waited for Fitz to return home from his "trip to Cincinnati." I was utterly deflated and exhausted, and upon hearing his key in the front door, my stomach notched itself into one gigantic knot. *Stay strong,* I warned myself. *Do not give in to his excuses or his promises. I'm the one in charge now.*

Casually, Fitz walked into the living room. My eyes remained steady on the television screen.

"Hi, babe," he said as he walked toward me.

Don't even think of putting those lips on mine. As he reached the arm of my chair, I held up my hand in a STOP signal. Without glancing at him, I handed him a sheet of yellow paper.

"What's this?" he asked.

"Read it."

"Okay," he said jovially. "It says: I want a divorce."

He lowered the paper. "Is this a joke, Lily?"

Slowly, I turned to him, my face blank. "It's not a joke, Fitz. You should know that by now."

Shocked, he plopped into the chair beside me. "I don't understand. Why?"

"How many reasons do you need? Because I have plenty."

He blinked rapidly then shrugged his shoulders in an "I-don't-know-what-you-mean" action.

Angrily, I spat, "Don't you dare play me for a fool. You lied to me about the trip to Cincinnati! On Saturday I saw you at the Garden City Hotel. You were with a young girl. I watched you kiss her in the elevator, you bastard! Kissed her as if she were a grown woman, for God's sake! Whatever you did with her is criminal, and you're lucky I haven't yet reported you. How many other lies have you told me?"

"It's not what you think," he stuttered.

"Yes, it's exactly what I think!" I yelled at him. I jumped from the chair and with shaking hands, lit a cigarette. *Keep it under control,* I reminded myself.

Fitz's face dissolved like Alka Seltzer in water; his color changed from a healthy pink to an awful shade of white. "You're right, Lily," he said softly. "I haven't been the best of husbands. But I can change," he implored. "I just need a chance to get myself under control. I need help, Lily. Professional help."

"Yes, you do need help, Fitz. And the sooner, the better."

I bit back all the words I wanted to fling at him, words to crush him as gravely as he had crushed me. "I'll be filing for divorce in the morning. Let's not allow this to become ugly, okay?"

Fitz stared at me, his eyes misty. He was playing on my heart strings, but the song fell flat.

"What about my father?" he asked helplessly. "I can't tell him why you're leaving. What will he think?"

"That's not my problem. You'll have to fix that one yourself."

I walked to the TV, shut it off.

Without looking at Fitz, I said, "You can sleep in the spare room until everything is settled. Anything you need to say to me can be said through my attorney. I've left his contact information on the kitchen island."

Stoically, I stepped past him, walked to the stairway that led up to the bedroom. Climbed three stairs, stopped, and looked back at Fitz.

Seeing his beautiful face wracked with disbelief almost made me smile.

IPO NIGHTMARE

June 9, 1981

William Calhoun had perspired right through his expensive Tom Ford custom-made shirt as fear and helplessness fought for his attention.

He thought he would have been in the clear. The dummy company Viola had set up to purchase IPOs should have been extremely safe. It was a Delaware company. Managers and partners were not included on registered documents. But Viola's name had been included as the contact person for the dummy corporation.

Senior Examiner T. Howard Jenkins of the Securities and Exchange Division had twice visited him, clearly digging for information. "Can't give you anything without a subpoena, Mr. Jenkins," Calhoun had told him.

When he thought about the transactional purchases he had made for her dummy company, he wanted to kick himself for being so cavalier. Every purchase she had instructed him to make involved excessive volumes of stock IPOs—the type of companies she could not have known a damn thing about. And each purchase had netted her company astronomical profits.

They're closing in on Viola. No way she could have done this on her own, Calhoun mused. *Someone fed her the information. And now, I will be under their scrutiny, too.*

When the SEC personnel finally came with their subpoena, everything was fair game: account records, transactional recordings, invoices, his goddamn phone records.

It was the phone records that frightened him most.

He had made plenty of calls from his office to Candy Land to secure escort dates. To RSVP to private parties. And if they subpoenaed his business tax records, he would be in a world of trouble. He had used his business credit card to fudge personal expenses: Candy Land's membership dues, expensive bar tabs, "special services."

William Calhoun knew he would be ruined if any of it leaked to the public. His brokerage license would be suspended; he would be banned forever from selling stocks and options. Ridicule and embarrassment would haunt him for the rest of his career. If he had a career left to worry about.

On a whim, he phoned Viola on her mobile, pointedly asked her if she had ever personally purchased any of the same IPOs that he had purchased for NYC Holdings.

"Why would you want to know that?" she asked suspiciously.

"Viola, the SEC has subpoenaed all of my records regarding NYC Holdings."

"Why? For what purpose?"

Clearing his throat, Calhoun said, "Your excessive volume purchases of non-tendered IPOs has raised a red flag at the SEC."

"Shouldn't you have known that?" Viola snapped.

"I did not advise you on the stocks to purchase, nor did I suggest an amount to purchase. You dictated both."

A long pause followed.

"Viola, I am trying to give you a head's up here. If you have privately purchased the same IPOs which I purchased for you through NYC Holdings, you are in a mess of trouble."

"What should I do?" her voice wavered.

"If I were you, I'd leave the country."

SURPRISE, SURPRISE

June 9, 1981

FITZ

Fitz sat in his office, unshaven, raw defeat etched on his face. Dully, he stared out of the window that faced the ugly warehouse at the rear of the factory. Sleep had evaded him. Lily's discovery of him with Lori at the Garden City Hotel had come as the biggest surprise of his life.

And now she wanted a divorce. There would be no fighting it. Her attorney would file papers citing spousal infidelity. Their marriage had been an intentional sham all along. He did not love her, had never loved her. Had cared nothing about their relationship. This was all his dead fucking grandfather's fault. The old man and his father had forced him to marry Lily, and he had done so with a gun pointed at his head. It was his father he was worried about. What plausible excuse would he believe?

His secretary interrupted his thoughts. "Fitz, you've got a call on line five. William Calhoun. Says it's urgent."

Fitz grabbed the phone to his ear. "William, hi. My girl said it was urgent."

"It is, Fitz. You referred me to Viola Cordova. She wanted to purchase stocks through her NYC Holdings company. Do you remember her?"

Fitz hesitated. "Yeah, I remember her. Why?"

"The SEC is gunning for her. Excessive volume trades on non-tendered IPOs. Raised a red flag for them. But that's not all. She also made similar purchases into a personal brokerage account."

"What!" Fitz roared. He jumped from his seat, the desk lamp crashing to the floor.

"Listen, Fitz. If you are involved with her in any way, you may be headed for trouble with the SEC yourself. This gal is going to sing like a diva if it means cutting herself a deal. And anyone who may have fed her inside information has trouble brewing for themselves, too."

Fitz felt faint. Sweat popped on his forehead, above his lip. Panicked, his heart slammed inside his chest. He could barely respond to his friend.

Finally, he mumbled, "Thanks for the head's up, William."

In slow motion, Fitz hung up the phone. *I need to run,* he thought. *And fast.*

HELP!

June 9, 1981

VIOLA

After the call from William Calhoun, Viola was frantic. She envisioned a dozen sccnarios—none of which were pleasant. Furiously, she heaved the cumbersome wireless phone against the kitchen wall, then rummaged through a drawer, found a hammer, and pulverized what remained of the phone until it was nothing more than a mess of plastic, wires, and batteries.

Breathing heavily, she stepped back from the mess, pushed away a clump of hair from her damp forehead. Trembling, she stumbled into the living room of the vast duplex, stared out at Central Park. Her eyes jealously followed a slew of arm-in-arm strollers, dog-walkers, people who hadn't the serious problems that she was being forced to deal with.

This life—well, it had not advanced as she had hoped it might. By now she should have met a life partner, a person with whom to share her future, her hopes and dreams. She had thought—prematurely, of course—that Fitz might be the one to fill that empty void.

But his wedding to that limp dishrag Lily had squashed any hope of her ever being with Fitz. And now she had to deal with William Calhoun's phone call. Hadn't she happily agreed to Fitz and Jonathan Silver's business proposition because it provided her complete anonymity from legal scrutiny?

Yet, here was Calhoun suggesting to her that she leave the country. And how the hell would she do that without a passport? Viola was boxed into a space with little breathing room.

Fitz must help me out of this mess. I'm not going down for it alone, that's for sure.

Now, she wished she were back home with her foster parents. She had been safe there, cared for and worried about.

Why had she wanted to run as far as possible from them? The world she had imagined to be so much bigger and livelier was far scarier than she could have predicted.

Viola sat staring at the park until the blackness of night eviscerated it from her sight.

Josh Arlington answered her call on the second ring. His voice was sleepy when he answered.

"Josh? It's me. Viola."

Josh propped himself up against his pillow. "Everything okay, Vi?" He glanced at his clock radio. It was 3:32 in the morning.

"Yeah. Everything is fine. I need a small favor, though."

Josh snuffed, "It couldn't wait until morning?"

"It is morning, you fool."

Josh was not amused. "What do you need?"

"An address for Larry Fitzgerald Jr. He lives at Arlington Estates. It's really important, Josh."

"Yeah. Okay. Call my office in the morning. Tess will help you."

The line disconnected before Viola could say thank you.

A SNOOP

June 9, 1981

Damon's luggage had been packed and ready for fifty-two minutes. His gut had warned him that someone was breathing down his neck at Dawson-Brown, and his gut had been correct.

That Tuesday morning, he was to be on the fourth floor for the Ralston meeting. He had grabbed a folder, walked out of his office. Stopped at his secretary's desk—a temp from Manpower to replace his regular girl who had just started her maternity leave.

"I'll be at the Ralston meeting," he told her. "Shouldn't take longer than an hour, hour and a half."

But the meeting had breezed along quickly and ended twenty-five minutes sooner than expected. He rode back up to the eighth floor, walked along the hallway toward his office. When the temp at the secretary's desk saw him, she visibly paled.

He walked past her desk, saw that his office door was halfway shut. Rarely did he close his door, so rather than entering the office, he slipped slowly past it. Peeked in and saw Brenda—her back to him—sorting through files on his desk.

He continued walking, turned at the next hallway, and found the emergency exit stairwell. He hurried down the ten flights and once outside, jumped into the first cab he saw.

He fumed at himself. *Fucking Brenda. I should have known. She was better at asking questions than she was in bed. Who the hell was onto him? The Feds? The SEC? Did it matter? It was big trouble either way.*

He sighed heavily, wished the cabbie would lower the radio.

The good news was that his name did not appear on any documents or banking records related to NYC Holdings. The bad news was Viola. She wouldn't hesitate to give up him or Fitz to save her own ass. And, if Brenda had been planted at his office to spy on him, he must be high on the chain of suspicion.

The taxi hit a major traffic jam on the West Side Highway. Cars were halted in every direction; two ambulances and a fire truck could be seen several blocks away. *Great,* he thought, *just what I needed.*

The music on the radio was interrupted: THIS IS AN EMERGENCY WEATHER NOTIFICATION FROM THE NATIONAL HURRICANE CENTER. TROPICAL STORM MONA HAS BEEN UPGRADED TO A GRADE TWO HURRICANE. RADAR IMAGERY SHOWS THE STORM IS MOVING QUICKLY TOWARD THE EASTERN COAST OF NEW YORK AND IS EXPECTED TO MAKE LANDFALL ON BROOKLYN AND QUEENS ON THURSDAY. PLEASE CHECK YOUR LOCAL LISTING FOR UPDATES.

When Damon finally arrived home, he immediately packed two large pieces of luggage and left a cryptic message on Fitz's answering machine. "Hey, pal. I'm out of the country beginning tonight, conference in Japan. Won't be back for at least two weeks. My parents have decided to meet me in Okinawa, so I may stay on a bit longer."

TROUBLE FOR TWO

June 10, 1981

FITZ

Fitz had not slept since receiving Calhoun's call. It floored him to know that the SEC had subpoenaed NYC Holdings' records and that Viola had purchased the same IPOs for her personal accounts. He felt deceived and as tightly squeezed as a fat orange.

Should I flip on Viola? he wondered. *Would it help my situation?*

Damon had already checked out of the picture. Had gotten himself as far from America as he could—Japan of all places—and it was doubtful that he would reappear anytime soon.

But for Fitz, there was not much time—they would be lucky if they had even a day to run. Adding to his stress was the approaching hurricane. The weather reports were dire; food and water had been hoarded—the markets and bodegas had been stripped of all but the least necessary items.

THINK! he screamed at himself. He paced the living room floor, watched as the sun made a pathetic attempt to show itself. Whatever plan he concocted, it had to take place tomorrow. One day later, and they would all be in handcuffs. He shook Lily awake. "Get up, Lily. We have a major problem. There's fresh coffee. Meet me in the kitchen."

Moments later, Lily appeared downstairs wearing a Beatles T-shirt and running shorts.

"What's going on Fitz?" she asked crossly. She poured a mugful of coffee, took a tentative sip.

"Hear me out, Lily," he said shakily.

"What have you done?"

"Uh, I don't know where to begin, but here it is."

Sheepishly, he told her the story—the whole story. Damon feeding them insider information; Viola making the purchases for their dummy company and then getting way too greedy and purchasing the same IPOs for her personal accounts. How the SEC was now on to them.

Lily's face paled. "Those are criminal activities, Fitz! You could go to jail."

Very softly, Fitz responded, "Not just me, Lily. You're still my wife. They're going to assume you were in on the fix."

Lily's mug crashed to the floor. "You can't be serious?"

"I'm very serious. Judge me all you want. Blame me for everything. But we must figure out a plan, or we will both wind up in jail for a long, long time."

He watched as Lily slumped to the floor.

A MEETING OF MINDS

June 10, 1981

5:40 a.m.

I was speechless after Fitz's confession, barely felt the warm coffee drenching my jeans. As innocent as I was of their insider trading scheme, Fitz was right—as his spouse, a finger would certainly be pointed at me as an accomplice.

Whether Fitz knew—or cared—he had unwittingly thrust me into a compromised situation. Immediately, all of my old guilts and fears and regrets gathered like a devil wind in my mind.

I had narrowly escaped my old life. Would I be able to do it again?

Like a robot I rose, wiped the spilled coffee from the floor, searched for my cigarettes. As I smoked, my brain chugged into gear.

It was imperative that we put an escape plan into place, but as far as I was concerned, neither Fitz nor Viola could be trusted. I needed an exit strategy of my own, one that didn't involve them.

And I needed a new passport.

Because I had never legally changed my name to Lily Fitzgerald, federal agents might not know that Fitz and I were married. To them, I would be Lily Marz as shown on my documents. But, fingerprints do not lie. They would prove that I had shed air traffic controller Margaret Lido's skin to become someone who was a complete fraud. How would that possibly help my situation?

But, of course, our situation changed minute by minute.

The doorbell rang, zapping air from my lungs.

Was this it? The police already here to arrest us? The clanging of the bell was insistent, angry. Fitz went to the front door. I watched him peek through the frosted glass window, heard him moan, "What are you doing here?"

As I scrambled toward the door, Fitz opened it, and a brief flash of blonde hair skipped right past me.

It was Viola, dressed in tight black leather pants and a matching leather jacket. She looked sexy and angry and belligerent.

"You TRAITOR!" she shouted at Fitz. "You insisted that NYC's privacy would be 100 percent! That we would have the highest level of confidentiality! Now I'm the one holding the bag for everyone!"

"Calm down, Viola!" Fitz yelled. "You are not holding the bag. Except for the one that's filled with your own money."

As if in a daze, we stalked into the living room. Fitz might have pretended to be furious, but the look on his pained face assured me he was terribly frightened. He stared at Viola, a look riddled with disbelief. His voice caught as he said, "If you hadn't been so greedy, they never would have connected the dots. You fucked up, Viola. Not me. Not Jonathan."

Perplexed, I asked, "Who is Jonathan?"

"Not important," he mumbled, his eyes still glued to Viola's.

Finally, he said, "Okay. There's only one way out for all of us. We must get to Switzerland. They don't extradite for tax and securities fraud."

Viola raised her hands in surrender. "Whoa, I don't have a passport."

"How can you not have a passport?" Fitz said.

"I just don't!" Viola screamed at him.

"Okay, okay!" I shouted. "We'll figure this out."

"Yeah, right," Viola screeched. "Just like you figured out that your husband likes little girls, huh?"

Viola might have shocked Fitz with her accusation, but I barely acknowledged it. Instead, I said, "That is not up for discussion. If you want a way out of this predicament, then shut up."

Fitz's cigarettes were on the coffee table. I snatched one from its pack. Inhaled deeply as I reevaluated our situation.

"Fitz, put on the local news," I said. "We need to understand the hurricane's velocity and speed."

Then, I abruptly walked upstairs and into the big closet in our master bedroom. Pulled down the box I had hidden on the top shelf. A box I had not looked at since arriving in New York.

I lifted the lid, found a newspaper clipping about the accident at Hewitt-Jackson and an almost faded picture of Savannah and me seated on the porch of her daddy's big house.

"Oh, Savannah," I murmured. "What should I do?"

When I returned to the living room, Fitz was focused on the television. "The news keeps getting worse," he groaned.

I tossed several US passports onto the coffee table. "You need a passport, Viola. I may know someone who can help."

Fitz looked at me as if I had grown a third eye. "Where in God's name did you get those?"

I ignored him. "If we want to leave New York quickly, we need to act quickly."

It was 6:19 and outside, daylight struggled to break through the clouds. Jeffrey would be awake, sipping his coffee and readying to drive to the Park & Ride.

I grabbed the passports and my keys and hurried to the front door. Shouted to Fitz, "Don't do anything rash! I'll be back as soon as I can."

As I sprinted down the street, my eyes were trained on Jeffrey's house at the end of the cul-de-sac. At his front door, I pounded as hard as

I could. He opened the door, saw my face, and grabbed my elbow. "Get in here," he said.

After I repeated a synopsis of the situation, I showed Jeffrey the three passports, which I had taken from Savannah's safety box back in Georgia. Thankfully, he did not question how or why the passports had come into my possession.

He studied them carefully, said, "The photos don't come close to matching either of your faces."

"What can we do, Jefferey?" I asked desperately.

"There's a chance, a slim chance, but it might work," he said solemnly. "I have a friend at the Department of State. He owes me a favor and wouldn't turn away from an envelope of cash, either. If I can reprint your photo from your DMV record, he may be able to recreate the passport using your picture with the passport owner's name and birth date."

He searched my eyes. "It would mean an entirely new identity for you, Lily. Do you think you can live with that?"

If only you knew, I thought.

"Can it be done quickly?" I implored. "There's a monster of a storm coming."

"I hope so."

"And for Viola?" I asked. "Can we use one of the other passports for her? Does she have a driver's license photo that you can use?"

"I'll check. But Lily, you are my priority, okay?"

"Okay," I responded.

His eyes locked with mine, and I saw a profound depth of emotion linger there, something I had never seen in my husband's eyes.

It was love. Pure and simple.

For the past year he had telegraphed his feelings for me. Feelings that surpassed friendship. The same feelings that had stirred in me, but which I was too afraid to admit aloud. Too afraid to admit because I was still a married woman.

"Lily, I will get you a passport with a new identity, regardless of what I have to do," he said. "Now, how do we get you out of the country during a hurricane?"

I smiled sadly. "I work for Jet King. There are ways."

PASSPORT SHUFFLE

June 10, 1981

7:42 a.m.

Because I feared the telephone at our house might be wire tapped, I remained at Jeffrey's house to call my friend—and pilot—Domingo Martinez. Though I offered very few details of my sticky situation, he promised to help.

"Jet King has a private flight scheduled to Zurich tomorrow at 1800 hours. I'm sure it will be canceled within the next hour or so due to the weather."

"Then we're stuck, aren't we?" I moaned.

"No," he said, then lowered his voice. "The manifest for that flight contains a government diplomat, so the flight will have a priority clearance once the storm passes. I can make sure your names are on the manifest. And Lily, I don't live far from Teterboro. You and your friends are welcome to stay with us until the flight is rescheduled."

My eyes welled with tears. "You're a lifesaver, Domingo. I promise, I will find a way to repay you for this."

1:30 p.m.

Jeffrey phoned, asked me to meet him at the Park & Ride. I made it there in record time, parked my Camaro in the last available spot. Jeffrey jogged to my car, got in quickly. "Here," he said, handing me a bakery bag and a Styrofoam cup filled with coffee.

"Thank you," I whispered gratefully. I flipped the lid from the coffee, inhaled its rich aroma, tasted its warmth in every part of my mouth. Inside the bag was a big blueberry muffin. As I took a bite, Jeffrey placed the three passports onto the bench seat between us.

"This one," he said, lifting the passport close to my eyes, "is yours. The age is a close match, and your DMV photo worked perfectly."

I stared at my real picture and my new fake name: Kelly Collins. "Wow," was all I could manage to say.

He lifted the second passport. "This one's for Viola. Her DMV photo is a bit blurred, but it should do."

The name on the passport read Zoe Zimmer.

"We used the third passport for you as well...a just-in-case-of-emergency passport. Not as good as the Kelly Collins, but in a pinch..."

I looked up at Jeffrey. "What about Fitz's passport?"

He shrugged his shoulders. "The three passports you gave me were for females. I'm sorry, Lily. He'll need to use his own."

My thoughts railed. *If Fitz can't get to Switzerland safely, well, too damn bad for him. Same for Viola. And if she loves him, she can have him.* I had married a man who was a liar and a cheat. A man who preferred little girls to real women. It turned my stomach to think I had not recognized these traits before we were married. But I had seen them; deep down I had had a very good idea of the person Fitz was. And I had accepted it, which made me as much to blame for our farce of a marriage as it did him. Once again, it was time for me to look out for myself.

2:48 p.m.

News regarding the hurricane became horrifically worse. Seventy-plus mile per hour winds would certainly close highways and bridges. Downed electrical power lines and fallen trees could impede roadways and cause blockages and severe damage.

The sky had already turned a motley gray, and the usually calm bay waters had become choppy, angry. Even birds were burrowing in for safety. If we were able to beat this storm, we would be incredibly lucky.

Fitz paced nervously as Viola stared at the Channel Two news meteorologist. I approached her, tossed her a passport. "You're now Zoe Zimmer," I said. "Fitz, you'll need to use your real passport. I didn't have one for a man."

"And that's supposed to make me happy?" he snorted.

"I no longer care what makes you happy. This is your mess, remember?"

He pretended to ignore me. "So, what's your big plan?"

My eyes danced back and forth between Fitz and Viola. This was clearly a chess match with Viola as a pawn. Fitz was the king, but as the queen, I had infinitely more power.

"I've made arrangements for us," I said. "A flight to Zurich tomorrow. One suitcase each. No exceptions." Warily, I glanced at Viola. "I have some jeans and shirts to get you through the next few days."

Viola scowled.

"If you prefer," I quipped, "you can risk returning home to pack, but tonight, you may find yourself sleeping on a cot in a prison cell. Your choice."

The room became as quiet as an empty church.

"Our names will be added to the manifest for the Zurich flight," I continued. "We'll leave here before dawn. Before the storm closes in and we're left stranded."

"How the hell are we supposed to get to Switzerland during a hurricane?" Fitz asked.

"We won't," I responded. "A coworker lives a short distance from Teterboro. He's offered us to stay with him and his family until the flight is rescheduled."

My face remained blank as I added, "It's the best we can hope for under these conditions."

PREPS

June 10, 1981

4:06 p.m.

It seemed to me as if the day could not get any longer. A glance at the kitchen clock showed it was late afternoon. I wished it were midnight. The three of us looked like ghosts—pale, waning, just waiting for something to happen.

Or not to happen.

As I trudged up the stairs to Fitz's office, my legs felt as tired as if I had danced the night away. In the closet I tugged down a rolling suitcase and my Louis Vuitton carry-on bag from the upper shelf. From the floor, I scooped up Fitz's black duffel bag.

Then, like a cartoon lightbulb going off above my head, I remembered the slip of paper hidden inside one of Fitz's loafers. I found the shoe, slipped my hand inside. It was empty. Of course, Fitz had removed it! But it was irrelevant, as my copy of the numbers was tucked safely inside my wallet.

I dragged the luggage to the master bedroom. Into the rolling bag I crammed a heavy parka, boots, several hooded sweatshirts, two pair of shoes.

On my bed, I left a tiny pile of clothing: jeans, a sweater, underwear, bras. My fancy green dress. Necessary toiletries.

Into the black duffel bag to be used by Viola, I placed a handful of my old baggy jeans and tops that I had outgrown. My smaller Louis Vuitton carry-on bag also remained empty on my bed. I unfastened the luggage ID tags from each of the bags, put them aside.

I carried the duffel bag and the rolling suitcase downstairs and left them in the laundry room near the steel door leading to the garage. Back upstairs, I passed by the spare room, which Fitz had been using. Next to the bed, I spotted the second Louis Vuitton carry-on bag that had been missing for some time. Fitz had wasted no time packing.

7:35 p.m.

To keep busy I prepared a platter of cheeses: brie, provolone, mozzerella. Added some black and green olives, purple onion, some sweet butter lettuce. Emptying the shelves of the refrigerator, I added thin strips of red peppers, dill pickles, and bright red cherries to the mix.

The pantry did not have much to offer, but I did find a box of Ronzoni pasta. I boiled the pasta, mixed it with left-over red sauce I had prepared just two days earlier.

From the liquor cabinet I grabbed bottles of expensive wines: dry Chardonnays, a few bold Cabernets, several aperitifs. We would not be returning, so it made sense to enjoy whatever we had.

It was a veritable feast.

Or a last meal.

By nine o'clock we were tired and nervous. Our eyes glazed with exhaustion, yet each of us was afraid to close our eyes to the other's. Ridiculous, of course, but . . .

10:33 p.m.

Fitz snored loudly, jarred me awake. But it was not Fitz snoring.

It was me. I had woken myself.

To my left, Viola was stretched out on the chaise, her blonde head resting on her shoulder. She had removed the leather jacket, lay there in a sheer black camisole. She was a classic beauty, and I found it hard to pull my eyes away. I would have understood if Fitz had been in love with her.

Bleary-eyed, Fitz stared at the television screen. "Go up to bed, Fitz," I said. "We have a long day in front of us tomorrow."

He nodded his head in agreement, silently walked upstairs.

I was upset with myself for having fallen asleep. It was incredibly important that I remain awake and sharp, so I loaded the dishwasher with dirty dishes and wine glasses. Discarded the trash. Tightly pulled closed the draperies.

Alarm clocks were set for 4:00 a.m. Everyone was to sleep in their clothes. Identifying jewelry—rings, watches, lockets—had to be left behind. We would meet at the steel door that led to the garage at exactly 4:20 a.m.

As midnight approached, I unplugged the telephone wires then went upstairs to my room.

1:35 a.m.

In my bed, I lay awake. Glanced at the alarm clock then slipped from the bed and into my slippers; quietly peeked in at Fitz asleep in the guest room. Snoring loudly, he was sprawled atop the bedcovers where he had plopped earlier, still dressed in his jeans and T-shirt and Nike footwear.

Of course, he was.

Earlier, I had crushed three sleeping pills into each of his and Viola's pasta dishes; had masked the bitternes of the pills with plenty of garlic and oregano and parsley. Several tall glasses of wine accompanied the meal. They would sleep the sleep of the dead for another four hours, then they would wake as groggy as winos sleeping it off in a prison holding cell.

Fitz's Louis Vuitton carry-on bag remained at his bedside. Quietly, I picked it up, carried it back to my room. Shut and locked the door behind me.

Quickly, I unzipped the bag. Stared down at Fitz's passport resting atop a pale blue shirt. I lifted the shirt and saw stacks and stacks of money, all of it tightly bundled with bright red rubber bands.

I had guessed correctly: if Fitz had hidden money from me in a secret numbered account, of course he would have ready cash hidden at home, as well. And he would not flee without it.

From his bag, I removed Fitz's blue shirt and his passport; removed the luggage tag and replaced it with my own luggage tag. I moved my green silk dress and a fresh change of clothing, placed them atop the money in the switched Louis Vuitton carry-on bag. Ran the bag downstairs. Hid it behind a huge potted plant in the entry foyer.

Back upstairs, I crammed my own Louis Vuitton carry-on bag with nightshirts, baseball jerseys, tennis shoes, several heavy hardcover books. Fitz's blue shirt was the last thing I replaced in the bag, with his passport atop the shirt. I snapped his luggage tag onto the bag, hefted it to be certain it felt as heavy as the money bag had felt.

Silently, I walked the bag back into the guest room, placed it near the bed. If Fitz should happen to open the bag, he would immediately see his passport and blue shirt, and if he checked the luggage tag, he would read his name on it.

Finally locked inside my private bathroom, I completed my final task. I burned the newspaper clippings of the accident and the twins' childish drawings, my mother's and Savannah's birthday cards.

But I could not destroy the faded photograph of Savannah and me seated on the porch of her daddy's big house.

AUF WIEDERSEHN

June 11, 1981

4:00 a.m.

Simultaneously, all three alarm clocks shrieked. I jumped up, splashed icy water on my face, scrubbed my teeth as hard as if I were trying to remove rust from a dented car's fender. For a moment, I thought I heard the windows rattle. I ran back into the bedroom, lifted the blinds.

Rain drenched everything; trees were bowed as if in prayer. A gauzy mist obscured a view of the bay. All I could see was the dark marble of night.

My heart lurched painfully. *This cannot be happening to me. Not again.*

As I trembled behind the window, the bay roared as water angrily slapped at the shoreline. Already, a rush of water had reached all the way to our rear patio. The storm had gotten a head-start on us!

"Move it, guys!" I shouted down the stairs and across the upstairs foyer. "The storm has already made land!"

Fitz appeared, groggy and disoriented, hair sticking up in all directions. His hand tightly clutched the carry-on bag.

Downstairs, Viola, too, was partially awake—face pale, hair matted, eyes frightened. Her mouth was a single gash across her face. "Where is my bag?" she whispered.

"It's packed and ready to go," I responded briskly. "Fitz, put the luggage in the car. Hurry."

He followed my instructions. I heard him grunt as he heaved the luggage into the trunk of his car.

I hurried to the laundry room. Viola stood with her back holding open the heavy steel door. "Let's go," I said to her. We hurried to Fitz's car, heard the heavy clunk of the steel door as it closed behind us.

Viola slipped into the back seat. I leaned into the front seat to get in. Abruptly, I stopped, screamed, "My passport! I forgot my passport, Fitz! Give me the keys!"

Fitz pulled the keys from the ignition, handed them to me. He still looked half asleep.

I ran back to the door, managed to get the key into the lock, forcefully pushed open the door.

I ran along the hallway toward the front entry. Stopped dead in my tracks to listen for the sound of the steel door clicking shut. Without his keys to open the door or to drive his car, Fitz and Viola would be stuck for at least two, three minutes.

Two minutes for me to grab the Louis Vuitton carry-on bag I had hidden behind the potted plant in the foyer, then to jump into Jeffrey's Land Rover and speed away.

Two and a half minutes until they realized I would not return.

Three minutes until Fitz would jump from the car, tug the emergency release cord, and open the garage doors.

I smiled. Without his car keys, he could not drive the car out of the garage.

Which had been my plan all along.

But like most things in life, it did not happen that way...

TRUTH OR CONSEQUENCE?

June 11, 1981

4:20 a.m.

In the foyer, I yanked the Louis Vuitton bag filled with money from behind the potted plant. Opened the front door and stepped into a flood of water. In seconds my sweatshirt was soaked through, my hair plastered to my head. Rain blurred my vision, but there, idled in front of my house, was Jeffrey's big blue Land Rover.

I trudged through the water, held the money bag tightly with both hands. Jeffrey leaned across the passenger seat, pushed open the door. I jumped inside the car and yelled, "Go, go, go!"

The Land Rover fishtailed from the street, the wiper blades unable to keep up with the deluge of rain. I turned in my seat to look out the rear-view window—hoping that Fitz had not yet managed a way out of the garage.

At least not yet.

Instead, what I saw made me scream.

In horror, I watched as our front lawn and driveway, the garage, and the front façade of our home were swallowed into an enormous sinkhole. Like a domino effect, the other three homes on the cul-de-sac followed. I gasped, realized that if I had taken five seconds longer to leave the house

I, too, would have been buried with them. And if Jeffrey were not with me, his house would have been plunged into the hole, too.

Hysterically, I looked at Jeffrey. His face was as white as cottage cheese.

"This is not what I intended to happen!" I cried.

He reached for my hand, held it tightly. "Of course, it wasn't."

It was true—I had never intended to take Fitz and Viola with me to Zurich. Their names had not been given to Domingo for inclusion on the flight manifest. I was so angry with Fitz for his disloyaties; for all the times he had fooled me into believing he loved me. For the loneliness that had swamped our marriage.

Mostly, I was furious about the trouble Fitz had embroiled me in.

As for Viola, she meant nothing to me.

But Jeffrey—he meant a great deal to me.

When we met at the Park & Ride so I could retrieve the new passports, his eyes had misted as he confessed, "I can't bear the thought of living the rest of my life without you. I love you, Lily."

And I loved him too. I trusted him, had faith in his sincerity. Trusted the look of absolute love in his eyes as they lingered on me. "Come with me, Jeffrey," I had whispered.

The plan to escape together was put into motion. We had only a tiny window of opportunity to slip away—to buy ourselves a few precious minutes to run before a groggy Fitz remembered the spare key that we kept hidden in the garage closet.

We drove in silence as Jeffrey maneuvered the Land Rover through a river of water that rushed the roads, overflowed onto sidewalks, and seeped into homes and shops. Cars were stalled in torrents of water; I watched as a pink Volkswagen Beetle floated past us. We witnessed drivers climbing through side windows to scurry up to the hoods of their cars for fear of drowning. Watched as helicopters were thrust left and right, tumbling through the sky as rescue workers tried valiantly to save those struggling in the heavy torrents of water.

The trip was grueling, unnerving. Fallen tree limbs and electrical power lines lay everywhere. Huge pine trees had been felled as easily as if they were saplings. A sailboat teetered upon a rooftop.

Seven exceptionally long hours later, we safely arrived at Domingo's home near Teterboro. The private flight to Zurich did not depart until two days later.

There were news accounts of the devastation that Hurricane Mona had left in its wake: fifty-six people dead.

Listed among the deceased were Larry Fitzgerald Jr. of Colgate, New York, and Viola Cordova of Manhattan.

FINALE

March 29, 2043

Age, as they say, does have a way of creeping up on us. Growing older meant withered skin, knobby knuckles, buckling veins. None of it very pretty. All of it evidentiary. Through the years, I had never given a moment's thought to the ways in which my body might defy me, the ways it might deny me the ability to do the things I longed to do, but was unable to do.

Life did not always make sense, did it?

My scattered thoughts are interrupted by Aggie, Jeffrey's home hospice nurse. "Mrs. Kaye, it's getting close to the time."

I nodded, rose from the armchair. Slowly, I shuffled to our bedroom, which was converted into a hospital room. A place where Jeffrey lay, thin as a scarecrow, monitors humming, an IV bag slowly dripping a powerful combination of lidopetitin and morphine into his scrawny arm.

Years earlier—after we escaped the hurricane that had killed so many—we made it safely to Switzerland and fell in love with Zurich. Seven months later we married in a quaint, one-hundred-year-old church. Jeffrey's mother, Nancy, attended our wedding, but sadly, it would be the last time we saw her. After a ten-year residency, we became permanent Swiss citizens.

We learned to ski and hike, made life long friends, enjoyed parties and celebrations. Later in our life together, we were lucky to have a daughter. Tessa was our masterpiece, with just a wee bit of me mixed in with an abundance of Jeffrey. Proportioned so perfectly, for I need not have passed along a generous portion of my spotty genes to an unsuspecting child.

The cash I had stolen from Fitz on the day we disappeared helped us to establish ourselves in Zurich. We purchased a sweet chalet high atop a mountain and on clear nights we could see the whole of Switzerland from our perch. After a visit to the Swiss bank in Bern, I transferred all of Fitz's hidden money into a different numbered account. This allowed Jeffrey and me to be financially set for life.

Our marriage lasted fifty-two years.

And for all of those wonderful years, I continued my life as Kelly Collins-Kaye, though when Jeffrey and I were alone, he would teasingly call me Lily.

I believed I had played my cards correctly. That is, until Jeffrey was on his deathbed. Now, looking down at him, dwarfed by the big bed and the humming machines and the pill bottles lined up like little soldiers on the bedside table, my heart ached.

Lowering myself into a chair next to the bed, I took his hand, cradled it in my own; ran my fingers along what he joked were his old man veins. In that instant, his hand weakly tugged mine.

Slowly, his eyes opened, milky and opaque, and I wished I could peer into his sweet, clear blue eyes once again. To see his love reflected there.

Weakly, he whispered, "I know who you were, Margaret Lido. And I will love you through eternity."

His eyes fluttered, then closed forever. The humming machine stuttered for a few seconds until it became a flat, single belligerent sound. If my eyes blinked, I could not recall it. If my lungs inhaled even a whiff of a breath, it was lost on me. If I never again uttered a sound or remained paralyzed with grief, surely I deserved it.

But, Jeffrey did not deserve to die this way.

Aggie rushed into the room, and I heard myself wail, a fragile, broken sound as she gently removed the IV needle from Jeffrey's arm, clicked off the machine. She stood next to me and said, "I'm terribly sorry for your loss, Mrs. Kaye. I'll make the necessary notifications."

She closed the door behind her as she left the room.

Shaking, I leaned in closer to Jeffrey. Gently, I moved a tiny lock of his white hair away from his forehead. Kissed his lips, his cheek—still warm and fighting death's grip. I rested my head on his chest. "How did you uncover my secret, Jeffrey? How did you learn I was Margaret Lido? Of course I know the answer, silly man! With Aurora Internet, secrets are impossible to remain concealed. Unlocking buried secrets has become as easy as tying one's shoe."

Tears streaked my cheeks and dampened Jeffrey's pajama top.

"But, I discovered your secret too, Jeffrey. You were never in a house fire in Athens, were you sweatheart? You couldn't have been because you were on the Olympian Air flight that day—the day I caused that horrible crash. You were the sole survivor of my destruction, but you never let on about it."

I lifted my head from his chest, found a tissue, blew my nose. I leaned my elbows onto the bed, gently stroked his cheek. "But you still managed to love me, and for that, I am grateful."

His body was still warm and for a moment, I allowed myself to believe that he was simply taking a nap; that soon we would walk downstairs and enjoy a cognac in front of the fire.

My knobby hand gently touched his chin, felt along the thin scruff of white stubble, then traveled down to his sunken chest. Tears poured, but my voice remained low and husky as I whispered, "But Jeffrey, you would not have liked the Margaret Lido I was back then. She was not a good person. And it's important to me that you know why."

I wiggled myself onto the bed—all bony arms and legs—and rested myself close to him.

Whispering quietly, as if someone might overhear, I said, "I killed my mother, Jeffrey. Pushed her hard down the stairs as she carried a heavy load of laundry. Her neck snapped; she died instantly. Why did I do it? Well, you didn't know her, Jeffrey; she was a very weak woman. No backbone at all. She didn't fight for me when my stepfather refused to allow Vern Taylor into our home because he was a Black boy. You see, before you stepped into my life, Vern and I were terribly in love. We were going to marry at the end of the school year. We'd both be eighteen and wouldn't need anyone's permission."

I took a deep breath before continuing. "My stepfather was an out-and-out bigot. He drove Vern away with his disgusting rhetoric. And, with the snap of a finger, the two of us were over, just like that. I was heartbroken and livid with grief. One morning, I decided that if I had to lose the man I loved, then Howard deserved to lose the woman he pretended to love. An eye for an eye."

Gently, I rubbed my hands along Jeffrey's brittle arms. "It's important that you know this Jeffrey: I made Howard Ford's life a living hell. After the accident, I did everything imaginable to force Sheriff Maynard to suspect Howard of my mother's death. Instead, the sheriff waved the death certificate in my face. 'No foul play here, Margaret,' he drawled. 'Try to let it go and get on with your life.' That document proved I was off the hook for her death, but so, too, was Howard off the hook. And that wouldn't do, Jeffrey. That wouldn't do at all."

My head throbbed, but I was anxious to continue. "For the ten days after my mother's death, I followed my stepfather like a hawk, harrassed him at work and at home. I left dreadful messages for all to hear. 'I know you killed my mother, Howard! I know you did it. And you're going to pay for it.'"

I took a deep breath, rubbed Jeffrey's belly as if he were a child with a tummy ache. "On a dozen occasions, I showed up at his office, loudly insisted that he turn himself in to Sheriff Maynard. But what I really wanted, Jeffrey, was for Howard to disappear, because I knew he believed I had killed my mother. And that scared him. As it should have. His silence would guarantee my freedom. So, finally he ran. Sold the family home in record time, took the twins, and left Georgia behind. Never to be heard from again."

I sighed into Jeffrey's chest. Snuggled closer to him. Glanced at the sparkling diamond tennis bracelet on my wrist.

My mother's bracelet. The gift to her from my father. My real father. Oh, it was so special to her.

But she did not deserve to have it as much as I deserved it.

My father had loved me, loved me much more than he had ever loved her. Wasn't it obvious? He had died with his lover by his side. Not with my dowdy, boring mother, with her drab, dishwater hair and her hips as wide as the refrigerator. No, eventually he would have abandoned us; he was too smart to revolve in the orbit of her meaningless, dull world. Who could blame him?

Gently, I rubbed Jeffrey's shoulder, willed him to open his eyes, to wake up and kiss me. "Don't leave me here alone, Jeffrey," I whispered. I could not imagine my life without him, without his sweet smile and his gentle touch. How would I face another morning, another night without him?

Every sinew of muscle, every limb and nerve right down to my fingertips was icy cold. I worried this was the punishment I rightly deserved, the punishment Margaret Lido deserved.

The door to the room squeaked open, and Aggie peeked her head around the door's frame. "Mrs. Kaye?" she asked. "The undertaker will be here shortly. Do you need a bit more time?"

"I do, Aggie. Thank you."

Again, the door swished closed quietly behind her.

I unraveled myself from Jeffrey's body. From the small side table, I found a cigarette, a lighter. Hesitated as I glanced at Jeffrey and slowly replaced them back into the drawer.

"You were not happy that I wouldn't stop smoking, were you sweetheart? I'm sorry for that."

I paced the room, but every few seconds I stopped to stare at Jeffrey. To stare at my dead husband who was growing colder by the minute.

"No, you wouldn't have liked the old Margaret Lido," I murmured as casually as if we were sipping a bold Cabernet at our favorite restaurant. "She was a vengeful person. And Savannah became the object of that vengefulness."

I peeked through the venetian blinds that separated us from the outside world. The night sky had swirled into an ice cream sundae replica of strawberry reds and white marshmallow cream and Milky Way browns.

Fresh tears erupted, and my stomach ached. The wall clock ticked time, a slow reminder that I would not have Jeffrey to myself for much longer. I returned to the bed, sat, and gently stroked his cheek. "Savannah did not kill herself, Jeffrey. No, she had help. My help."

Sniffling, I continued. "It was during the week of my recess from the FAA's training center. I was home from Oklahoma, met up with Savannah at Carousel's. We had drinks, chatted, and oh, it was like old times again. But when Savannah so casually suggested that I 'dip my toe into someone else's pool,' I nearly raged."

Breathing deeply, I calmed myself. I certainly did not want to have another heart attack here in the room where my husband lay dead.

"You cannot imagine what it was like, Jeffrey. I was back home in Georgia, with the ache of missing Vern Taylor far more real to me than the moon in the sky. Savannah had snatched my little world and crushed it like a walnut. Eviscerated it into tiny little pieces."

I sighed, stared at the periwinkle blue ceiling. "Sweetheart, two days before I was to meet Savannah at Carousel's, I spotted her and Vern

Taylor, snuggled together like two birds in a nest. My Vern Taylor! They were at the Blue Martini, lost in each other's eyes, kissing with the same passion that Vern had once kissed me. The look of love on their faces registered an intimacy so profound, it hurt me to watch."

I swiped at tears that caked my mascara into ugly rivers of mud. "It was so obvious, Jeffrey. They were in love. Desperately in love."

The side drawer containing the cigarette and lighter tried to snatch my resolve, but I refused. "I couldn't allow it to continue, Jeffrey. You understand that, don't you? They had utterly disrespected me."

I wanted to scream, to yell and beat my fists against the bedroom's walls. But I would not. Soon they would be coming for Jeffrey, and I feared Aggie might hear me, might rush in and ruin my confession.

"I had to end their relationship," I implored Jeffrey. "Vern belonged to me! I needed Savannah out of the picture. But how? It happened so innocently, so easily, that I couldn't have planned it better."

My brain was so tired. My bones as old as a museum's relic. The past floated before me like a rerun of an old black and white movie...

Me and Savannah at Carousel's. Drinks. Lots and lots of drinks.

And each time Savannah coasted into the restroom, I added a bit more barbiturate to her shots of tequila. She didn't realize it, not with the tequila and the lick of salt and the bitterness of the lime that followed. Four, five of those and Savannah was buzzing like a bumble bee.

She was too drugged to drive. Mitch, the bouncer, helped me maneuver her into my old Volvo. "We'll leave her car here and pick it up tomorrow," I told Mitch. "I'll drive her home."

"You're a good friend, Margaret. She's lucky to have you."

If only you had seen my best friend, slouched in her seat—hair tangled and matted, her eyes not even half-moons in her head. Her short dress scrunched up to her waist and her underpants exposed. Loudly, she belched up a wicked scent of booze and nicotine and taco chips. Disgusting.

Vern would have been appalled.

I drove us to her house, a mansion tucked into the landscape of old Georgia—with horse ranches and farms and plenty of land—a huge home she continued to share with her parents and brother.

Her father's Rolls Royce was not in the driveway and neither was her brother's BMW. I remembered Savannah saying they were all at a two-day business convention in Augusta.

Savannah barely moved. I hefted her from the passenger seat, looped her arms around my neck and practically dragged her up to the massive front door. Her head lolled onto my shoulder, and more than once, I had to move it aside so she would not drool down my neck.

Inside her satchel, I found her keys. After closing the door behind us, I stopped, listened. Not an echo of a sound inside the house. Savannah's room was on the main level, and I tugged her like a rag doll, until finally, we made it into her room.

Huffing, I settled her onto a small divan. Her bedroom was the size of an arena. Quickly, I pulled closed the draperies. A pale gray shag rug covered the floors; the walls glowed a soft shade of pink.

When I looked back at Savannah, she was snoring loudly. "Savannah!" I yelled. "Are you awake?"

Of course, she wasn't. I knew it was safe.

At her big armoire, I opened the doors, stared at the top shelf. Took a very deep breath and reached for the shoebox marked SCHOOL PHOTOS. Gently, I removed it from the shelf. Opened its lid. Moved about the tissue paper until I found the small pearl-handled pistol that I knew Savannah kept hidden there.

I checked the chamber. Sure enough, six bullets scowled back at me. From my own handbag, I removed a pair of winter gloves I kept nestled at the bottom of the bag. Laziness, I guess.

After I put them on, I stood behind the divan, behind Savannah, and again called her name. No response.

Pulling her right hand upward, I eased the gun into her hand. Placed it directly at her right temple. I shifted and together, we pulled the trigger, and I was surprised at how quiet the pop of the gun was.

"I'm sorry, Savannah," I choked, "but you and Vern together? I couldn't allow it."

In the distance I heard the blare of a siren. An ambulance was roaring up the mountainside. Only a few precious minutes remained.

I turned, hugged Jeffrey. "Oh, if only you knew the irony of it all. I had not known—not for certain—not until I rummaged through Savannah's safe deposit box. Yes, I found the money, had expected to find it, especially after her brother's call telling me of her suicide and possible embezzlement of family funds. But the three passports? And all with photos so closely resembling Savannah's face? It was disarming. And it was then that I knew for certain, Jeffrey."

I whispered in his ear. "Savannah was planning to run away with Vern. Running from Atlanta and her father and from me, Jeffrey! From me! It was unacceptable."

Gasping, I heard the ambulance's tires crunch on our driveway. I kissed Jeffrey. Kissed him repeatedly, two, three, four times. I did not want to let him go.

"I hope you can forgive me, Jeffrey, but everyone I have ever loved, except for you, of course, had betrayed me. I never dreamed I might be capable of such appalling acts. But don't we all have a little bit of cruelty within us? A depravity mixed in with all the goodness?"

Sobbing, I said, "I never meant to hurt you, Jeffrey. The plane crash was an accident. An accident waiting to happen."

And then, in an eruption of activity, Jeffrey was whisked from the room.

All that remained was the bare essence of him, like the wisps from a campfire smothered too soon.

My hands caressed the blankets that had covered him.

How easy it was to bury our sins like old keepsakes.

To be opened only upon one's death.

But for those who unearth our secrets, our little lies . . . Surprises lurk.

So, there we have it. I leave it for you to decide.

Fact or fiction?

Right from wrong?

ACKNOWLEDGEMENTS

Books do not get written without the help and knowledge of people who sometimes know you better than you know yourself.

To my dear friend Ellie Nicholas, who has been in my life for fifty years, I am grateful and thankful for the countless hours you devoted to help bring this book to its conclusion. Your talent and wisdom are gift wrapped presents which I am lucky to unwrap again and again. A toast to our future collaboration.

To my friend Mona Schwartz, who has read my stories for thirty-plus years; even the work that has been terrible. I respect your opinions and keen eye, and sincerely thank you for your honesty. And you are a great travel buddy!

To Ellen, this book would never have been written without you. Thank you for everything. Especially my writing room!

To all my Las Vegas gal pals: Adrienne, Sarah, Mary, Joan, Fran, Jacque, Jean, thank you for your friendship, love, and support.

And finally, to my wonderful family, thank you for always listening, for always caring and for always loving me.

A special thank you to Gatekeeper Press, especially Jennifer Clark. It has been an absolute pleasure to work with you—you never let me down. Cheers and here's to working together on the next project.

AUTHOR'S NOTE

To all of the air traffic controllers who remain anonymous and unseen and, who help to move us from one destination to another, Thank You.

Made in United States
North Haven, CT
10 August 2022